"WONDERFULLY INVENTIVE!"

Mel Gilden, author of *Surfing Samurai Robots*

A greenish vapor rose from the backwater near the bank. It climbed silently toward where Sebastian had fallen. For a moment, he felt his mind invaded. Then everything shifted. He was again in the halls of Château d'Oignon, pursuing the sounds of a child crying.

Slowly Sebastian became aware of Corwyn pulling him away from the edge of the drawbridge. He sat up, holding his head.

"I feel awful. What happened?"

Corwyn checked him for broken bones. "You took quite a spill."

"I've never fallen like that before. There was a terror to it, and something else. And when I tried to talk, the words that came to my tongue were foreign."

"Foreign?"

"Oui."

"The best kind of fantasy—
a novel with heart and soul and a funny bone"

Nancy V. Berberick, author of *Stormblade*

Worlds of Fantasy from Avon Books

THE PENDRAGON CYCLE
by Stephen R. Lawhead

TALIESIN
MERLIN
ARTHUR

THE DRAGON WAITING
by John M. Ford

THE GRYPHON KING
by Tom Deitz

THE SHINING FALCON
by Josepha Sherman

THE WHITE RAVEN
by Diana L. Paxson

Alchemy Unlimited

DOUGLAS W. CLARK

AVON BOOKS ⬟ NEW YORK

ALCHEMY UNLIMITED is an original publication of Avon Books.
This work has never before appeared in book form. This work is a novel.
Any similarity to actual persons or events is purely coincidental.

AVON BOOKS
A division of
The Hearst Corporation
105 Madison Avenue
New York, New York 10016

Copyright © 1990 by Douglas W. Clark
Cover illustration by Dean Morrissey
Library of Congress Catalog Card Number: 89-92500
ISBN: 0-380-75726-5

First Avon Books Printing: August 1990

AVON TRADEMARK REG. U.S. PAT. OFF. AND IN OTHER COUNTRIES, MARCA
REGISTRADA, HECHO EN CANADA.

Printed in Canada

UNV 10 9 8 7 6 5 4 3 2

This book is dedicated to my two fellow Adobe Writers,
Bob Julyan and Neal Singer.
They were there from the beginning, and without them
I wouldn't have had the audacity to try writing a novel.

ACKNOWLEDGMENTS

Over the years, many individuals have contributed to the development of this book, and their support is gratefully acknowledged: My wife, Sharon, who finally convinced me the writing itself should be its own reward; Nancy V. Berberick, who has been a great friend as well as a colleague; Chris Miller, an editor with skill and sensitivity who encouraged this project long before it was ready to be published; Maria Carvainis, my agent, who has relieved me of many of the details that go with this business; Jan Carley, who first showed me what my characters looked like; Mary Rosenblum, Diane de Avalle-Arce, April Matthews and T. Jackson King, who critiqued various "final" drafts; and finally, the members of both the Science Fiction & Fantasy Workshop and the Southwest Writers Workshop. Doubtless there are others I have overlooked, and for their omission I apologize.

Prologue

"Your first day, *señor*?"

The novitiate nodded and smoothed his new robe, the coarse, black cloth as yet unacquainted with dust and sweat. "*Si*. How did you know?"

The older man wrinkled his nose, pointing to the garlic the younger man wore around his neck.

"They advised me to wear it," the novitiate responded. "For the sake of my soul, they said. Don't you wear one?"

"If the demons come for you, *señor*, they come." The older man shrugged, then turned back to his barrel. "Garlic won't stop them when it's your time. Just keep your wits about you. And the lids on tight."

The novitiate scowled, fingering the garlic clove. Then he tucked the clove on its cord inside his robe where it couldn't be seen. The garlic's hardness on his chest was a comfort against his fear.

"I am Carlos Ramon Francisco Vasquez de Diego con Queso," he said. He assumed a bearing he hoped his grandmother would think worthy of his name. "And you?"

"They call me *Tortuga*, the turtle," the older man said in a low class drawl from the coast near Barcelona. He laughed. "I

1

am slow, but only because I'm careful. I don't want a spill."

Tortuga hammered a plug in the bunghole of the barrel and rolled it aside. As he wrestled another barrel toward the vat in the center of the room, Carlos watched in awkward silence. Although ostensibly in charge, Carlos knew little of what he and Tortuga were supposed to do.

He did know the barrels were sent to this station by officers of the Holy Inquisition from all over Spain. And he understood all too well what the barrels contained—demons. But what happened to the demons in this room that enabled the barrels to be shipped safely out of Spain?

Tortuga paused in his work, interrupting Carlos's thoughts. "I had a friend here once. He saw another man about to be . . . stricken, so he hurled himself in the way before it could happen."

"Was your friend taken instead?" Carlos asked, eyes wide.

"Of course."

Carlos crossed himself. "He was very brave."

"No," Tortuga said. "He was only a thief who stole another man's possession. *Comprende, señor*? Another man's possession?" He guffawed heartily.

Carlos tittered nervously, uncertain whether the story was true or merely a misplaced attempt at humor. Either way, it lent support to the rumors Carlos had already heard.

Carlos and his fellow novitiates had been sent from Zaragoza only two days earlier to fill shortages in the station's work force. The Dominican priests piously assured them that the growing need for men reflected only the success of the Holy Inquisition.

They should know, Carlos thought. During the two hundred years since the order was founded in 1215, the Dominicans had been entrusted by the popes with conducting the Inquisition throughout Europe on behalf of the Church of Rome. The importance of both Inquisition and Dominicans had increased in that time. Now Carlos and his fellow novitiates looked forward eagerly to a time, perhaps within their own lives, when the Inquisition in Spain would achieve even greater glory, cleansing the faith of the entire Spanish peninsula.

But if Carlos ever hoped to contribute to that future goal, he had to survive his first assignment. For he had heard tales, spoken in whispers, of the work force at this station being relentlessly decimated as the workers themselves fell in need of exorcism by the Inquisition.

Apparently, those who worked in this place often fell prey to the very malady they sought to eradicate from the soul of the land.

"Are you ever afraid, having to do such terrible work in this place?" Carlos asked.

The older man wiped sweat from his forehead with the back of a beefy hand, then waved the hand at the room around them. "Why should I fear, when the priests tell me both my work and this place are sacred and under God's protection?" Tortuga gave Carlos a sly glance. "Of course, until those priests also come to work at my side, I am cautious. But my spirits, *señor*, are good." He laughed uproariously. "*Comprende*? My spirits are good?"

Carlos grinned weakly, secretly offended by the man's sense of humor.

Exorcising demons made up only a small part of the Inquisition. But the exorcisms were among the most dangerous of the Inquisition's efforts. Once the demons were driven from their victims—a hazardous activity in itself—the spirits had to be safely contained until they could be shipped out of Spain.

It did no good to free one man of possession only to expose his neighbors to a similar fate.

So the demons were sent to this station to be mixed with vats of water and temporarily stripped of their strength by the addition of sacred substances. Thus incapacitated, the demons could be transported in reasonable safety out of the country, where they would eventually emerge to affect only the unworthy citizens of foreign lands.

At least, that was the theory advanced by the theologians.

Naturally, Spain's shipments of exorcised demons into other lands had to be made in secret lest the people in these receiving countries complain. But individuals could be found willing to accept the risks of such a task, provided the rewards were sufficient.

Tortuga poured the contents of the new barrel into the vat and quickly added a few drops of liquid from a small glass vial. Then he sealed the lid on the vat and connected the empty barrel to a spigot at the vat's base.

"What's that?" Carlos asked, pointing to the vial.

"Holy water."

Mechanically Carlos crossed himself again. "But why so little of it? Surely that's not enough for so large a barrel or so treacherous a journey."

"We're a long way from Rome," Tortuga replied. He began

turning a crank in the side of the vat. Carlos heard water splash inside as wooden paddles churned the contents. "Often the holy water shipments are late," Tortuga went on. "Until they arrive, we are sometimes forced to use water blessed by former popes. Or even the waters passed from the loins of a virgin, when one can be found."

Carlos was young and vastly curious about the loins of virgins, but felt too self-conscious to ask. "Is holy water still effective once the blessed fathers have departed from their terms on earth?" he asked instead.

Tortuga shrugged again, the slow surge of his shoulders reminding Carlos of the movements of a giant tortoise. Then he grinned. "Just pray the water is still sacred enough to last from here to the other side of the mountains. After that, it's not our worry."

The novitiate peered nervously at the cavernous stone crypt around them, remembering rumors of a trail of poor bedeviled fools leading from this remote station all the way into the Pyrenees and over to the plains of Gaul.

"What do we do if there is a leak?" he asked at last.

"Oh, *señor*," Tortuga said, suddenly serious, "don't even speak of such a thing. To mention the possibility is to invite the devil in."

"Oh," Carlos said, watching the floor. Then, "But what do we do when there is one?"

At last, Tortuga glanced to where the novitiate was staring. He stopped turning the crank.

"*Dios*," he moaned as yellow-green slime spilled from a hole in the vat where the spigot had been only moments earlier. The viscous ooze pooled on the floor, giving off the sickening stench of a clutch of *huevos* left to spoil in the sun.

Carlos knew he should run, but perverse fascination held him. He watched as a greasy mist rose from the ooze, a vile presence with roughly human form. It turned lazily on the air to stare at him, and when the empty sockets of its eyes fixed in his direction, Carlos felt their gaze penetrate his soul, violating him and tearing his innermost secrets from his grasp.

The being seemed to laugh. Then, as Carlos watched with growing horror, its countenance changed. Slowly, its face became that of his grandmother, imperious matriarch of his family and self-appointed defender of the faith for as far as she could make her influence reach. Carlos was more terrified of his hawk-nosed and dark-eyed grandmother than of any Inquisitor or demon. In Carlos's village, it was said that even God trembled before this woman.

"Carlos!" she cried, wrinkling her nose as if he were responsible for the loathsome smell in the vault. Her voice made no sound in the stone room, yet it reverberated inside Carlos's head. "Carlos Ramon Francisco Vasquez de Diego con Queso, don't think you can escape me just by joining the Dominicans and getting yourself sent halfway across Spain. I know all about the sins you've committed, and I've come to punish you for them myself in case God in His infinite wisdom doesn't get around to it." She raised a bony arm, draped with the black shawl of mourning that had been the mainstay of her life for the three decades since her husband's death. Her finger stabbed at the air inches from Carlos's face.

"When you were six, you put tadpoles in the holy water font of the church," she proclaimed. And Carlos, knowing it had been an unforgivable act, cringed at being discovered at last. "At seven, you charged money to let older boys spy on your sister while she dressed. At eight, you made up sins for confession to impress your friends with the penances you were given by the priests. Then at nine—"

But whatever transgressions Carlos committed at nine were saved from disclosure as Tortuga gave Carlos a shove. *"Sangre de cristo,"* the older man gasped, "don't just stand there waiting for it to get you."

Carlos blinked, startled to find the demon specter again before him. "Huh? Where'd my grandmother go?"

"Grandmother?" Tortuga snorted. "For me, it was my wife!"

Carlos stared at the advancing demon, unable to comprehend why his grandmother would marry a low-class laborer named Tortuga or how she had kept the fact hidden from her family for so many years.

Tortuga pushed again, his movements sluggish from the demon's paralyzing influence. "Hurry," he cried. "Whatever you saw, it wasn't really there. That was just the demon. Now get out. For the sanctity of your soul, *señor*, run!"

The vision of his grandmother had already led Carlos to doubt the sanctity of his soul, but even a tainted soul was preferable to the fate which crept silently through the air toward him. Carlos shuddered at the prospect of spending eternity locked in that vision's grasp.

Without a backward glance, he stumbled from the chamber and down the long corridor outside. His shrieks of warning echoed through the stone halls of the building, distorted into a garble that sent workers fleeing from room after room along the corridor. By the time Carlos reached the safety of the outside world, with its bright sunshine and refreshing breezes through nearby olive groves, he had been joined by most of the others who worked at the station.

Only then did Carlos realize that Tortuga was not among them.

It was several hours later before officers of the Inquisition could enter the chamber where Tortuga was. Carlos trailed behind them. They found the older man thrashing aimlessly on the floor in the slime, his body seeming to act out the torments of some inner hell while his eyes glittered with the evil consciousness that had overtaken him. His mouth wore a slack, idiotic grin and his tongue lolled out, drooling.

Carlos's fingers crept once again to the garlic under his robe at the sight. Then he turned away, aware for the first time of his own mortality and ashamed at the relief he felt that the man on the floor was not he.

The exorcist, wearing the purple stole and surplice of his office, stepped forward. He shook his head sadly and crossed himself in a businesslike manner.

"Ye unclean spirits, depart!" he intoned, reading from his book the formal rite of decontamination.

Even as the exorcist began, his colleagues gripped Tortuga firmly by the arms to prevent any violence and hustled him off to an awaiting cell for safekeeping.

CHAPTER 1

The Reluctant Apprentice

SEBASTIAN WHISTLED A MINSTREL'S TUNE AS HE WALKED ALONG
the dusty, rutted road that was the main French thoroughfare
from the Abbaye de Sainte-Tomate in Justienne to the town of
Pomme de Terre. Around him, the fifteenth century glowed with
promise, full of rumored changes spreading even here from Italy.
So infectious was the mood of the world on this spring morning
that even Sebastian's spirits lifted.

Perhaps from his new position in Pomme de Terre, he thought,
he would finally be able to regain his rightful place among the
nobility. Certainly there was little else about his upcoming em-
ployment from which to take any consolation.

Apprenticed to an alchemist, indeed!

He pulled his shoulders back and held himself straighter. After
all, he was noble born and should carry himself in a manner
befitting his true station, regardless of his present, temporarily
reduced social rank.

At noon he sat on a low, jumbled rock wall marking the edge
of a peasant's field to eat the meat and onion pie he had brought
from the abbey. He turned sideways on the wall so he could
watch the peasant and his wife tilling their field. They tramped
the muddy, upturned soil with bare feet, their clothes rolled up

to keep them from the dark earth which streaked their legs to the knees. As they worked, they shot Sebastian furtive, sideways glances, eyeing him with suspicion. Across the field by a cottage, their children paused in the midst of chores to stare back at Sebastian with open-eyed curiosity.

When he finished his pie, Sebastian carefully licked the flecks of crust and gravy from his fingers, savoring these final remnants of a life willingly left behind. He washed the food down with wine from a small flagon and stood up to dust the crumbs from his lap, then turned to the field.

"Hey, you there, *villein*," he called. "How far is it to Pomme de Terre?"

The peasant, after confirming with gestures that he was indeed the object of the question, trudged as close to Sebastian as he dared. There he stopped and shrugged broadly.

"I said, how far to Pomme de Terre?" Sebastian asked, speaking louder.

The peasant, looking pained and puzzled at the same time, only bowed obsequiously, motioning to his family behind his back as he bobbed toward Sebastian from the field. The peasant's wife set her mouth grimly as she backed toward the cottage and hustled her children inside.

"How far?" Sebastian called again, yelling now. "Pomme de Terre?" He pointed up the road.

The peasant's face broke into a grin, exposing a mouth of blackened or missing teeth. He gestured at the road, first in one direction and then the other, then at Sebastian, and finally at himself and his cottage. All the while, the man spoke in thick, heavily accented syllables that Sebastian struggled to understand, his frustration rising as it always did when faced with the vagaries of the French tongue.

"Bah!" Sebastian finally said in disgust, realizing the man wasn't speaking French at all. "Stupid peasant. What did I expect?" He dismissed the man with a wave of his hand and started up the road once again.

The man was probably a Basque from the disputed lands of Gascony and Aquitaine to the west, Sebastian figured. Like other refugees, the Basque and his family had undoubtedly slipped into the independent fiefdom of Gardenia to eke out a better living safely removed from the decades-long conflict between England and France which had ravaged much of Gaul.

Sensitivity toward the plight of a peasant was foreign to Sebastian. Yet some of the arrogance he had felt since morning evaporated as he considered the similarities between his and the peasants' plights.

During the early afternoon, a light, cooling breeze drifted down from the mountains. Later, the breeze stopped and the heat built up, sucking the recent moisture from the ground and lying upon the land like a suffocating blanket. By the time Sebastian reached a stone footbridge across the River Ale a few miles below Pomme de Terre, he was sweaty and tired.

He paused on the bridge, leaning over the low wall to gaze at the water below. It flowed cool and clear beneath him, inviting him to slide down the bank and into its refreshing current. For a moment, Sebastian considered the possibility. But the banks were steep and the hour late. As it was, he would be pressed to reach Pomme de Terre and locate his new master by nightfall. What with the brigand companies that roamed the countryside at night, preying upon lonely travelers, he had no wish to be locked outside the town gates after dark.

He contented himself with resting on the bridge for a while, flicking bits of sand from the wall and watching them tumble to the stream below. He breathed deeply of the humid air, which lay perfectly still upon the land, and dreamed idly of days gone by when his family had been one of property and influence.

So wrapped up was he in his thoughts that he failed to notice a gradual change in the quality of the air until it had already begun to work its effect on him. Finally he became aware of a faint, nauseous smell that reminded him of the midden heap behind the abbey after a hot summer day. As the odor grew, his muscles sagged, no longer responsive to his wishes. His vision blurred. Instead of the idyllic, gurgling stream he had watched moments earlier, the water now seemed dark and roiling with alien menace.

A thin tendril of greenish mist coiled up from the dark waters, rising toward his face. Sebastian gripped the stones of the bridge until his knuckles turned white. He tried to force his eyes away, but they refused. All volition left him. The tendril rose almost to his face, taunting him with an evil odor of spoiled eggs and sulphur and turning his skin clammy with fear.

Sebastian felt an alien presence burrow into his soul. Words from a strange language spilled about the edges of consciousness, threatening to consume him.

For a moment, the scene around Sebastian shifted, and he was once again in the castle halls of his family. These were not the walls of his home as he remembered them, however, for the very stones of this place weeped with shame and dread. From somewhere ahead came the sounds of a child sobbing. Sebastian shuddered at the sound, for it filled him with loathing. But though he recoiled from the thought of confronting the child, still he found himself stalking the halls toward the source of the crying. His shadow, flung forward by the torches on the wall, bobbed and weaved ahead of him as if eager for the hunt.

Before he could locate the sound, however, a sudden breath of air passed over the bridge. The merest suggestion of a breeze, it brought with it a hint of meadow grasses and farmland lying somewhere beyond the hill. Soft as it was, the gust was sufficient to disperse the tendril of mist. It vanished wraithlike in the slow moving, heavy air.

Sebastian blinked his eyes to clear them. He hadn't felt such emotional and physical exhaustion since . . . but he didn't want to remember. Perhaps, he thought hastily, he had felt such exhaustion when, as a boy training for knighthood at his uncle's estate, he first faced the dreaded quintain. Now he looked again at the stream beneath the bridge, seeing only cool, clear water bubbling over mossy rocks. Nothing remained to account for the nausea and terror he had felt a moment earlier. He leaned over the wall, trying to peer along the banks beneath the bridge to see if some waterfowl had left its nest of eggs to decay in the heat of the season. But he saw nothing and was reluctant to approach the water to investigate.

Refreshed by the breeze, Sebastian went on his way. The episode on the bridge disturbed him at first, but the memory it left was too uncomfortable and ill defined to dwell on long. By the time he followed the roadway beside the stream another mile or two, Sebastian dismissed it. Only much later did he have reason to recall the incident.

Soon he was whistling again. Before him, the dirt road wound between a pair of low hills, following the river down from Pomme de Terre. As he neared the hills, a small caravan rounded the bend, coming toward him rapidly. Sebastian stepped to the side of the narrow road and waited for the travelers to pass, intending to ask how far he had yet to go.

The caravan consisted of a four-wheeled covered wagon drawn by horses in tandem, evidently the property of some wealthy merchant. An armed man with the golden spurs of knighthood rode beside the wagon while two foot soldiers with spears trotted behind.

Sebastian noted the knight's spurs, envying the noble birth and martial accomplishment they signified. But he reminded himself of his present lowly condition and hailed the driver of the wagon as if a mere merchant were his equal.

"*Pardon, monsieur*, how far is it to Pomme de Terre?" he called out, waving at the wagon.

The fat merchant only glared at Sebastian and crossed himself before urging the horses to greater speed. Beside him sat his wife, dressed in a colorful silk coat with fur trim and ornamented with jewels. She averted her face hastily from Sebastian. The knight, swathed in arrogance, never even noticed him, while the foot soldiers were too busy keeping up to waste their breath on talk.

Sebastian stopped in mid wave as anger born of injured pride swept fiercely through him.

"French dog," he shouted to the retreating wagon. "Your mother never knew your father's name!"

Still, he received little satisfaction from the insult, having switched from French to the more familiar Saxon English of his forefathers so the merchant's men wouldn't understand and seek their vengeance upon him.

Then dust from the caravan's passing swirled around him, leaving Sebastian coughing and choking. After the air cleared, he brushed himself off and wondered whether anything about his appearance warranted such spite. True, his tights and tunic were plain, and the long pointed shoes that were the style tended to droop at the toes after a day of hard travel. But his blouse was colored gaily enough and only beginning to smell from the journey. His face, which he had shaved the previous day in preparation for this trip, was solidly formed, with a firmness to the jaw and a fineness to the features that was not displeasing to the young ladies he had met.

Finding nothing about himself that might account for the treatment he had received, Sebastian dismissed it as insolence on the part of the merchant, who apparently was trying to emulate an aristocratic aloofness appropriate only to those of truly superior social rank.

What a mockery such a boor made of himself, acting above his class!

Sebastian rounded the curve and passed between the hills

through which the caravan had come to find Pomme de Terre
spread out in a small valley below him. The town was nestled in
the foothills of the Pyrenees, which rose serenely in the late
afternoon sun behind and to the right of Pomme de Terre, sunlight glinting off peaks still white with snow.

A modest size town, Pomme de Terre was the center of politics
and commerce for the province, a minor flower of its time. From
his vantage point, Sebastian saw a town spilling beyond its walls
to develop new additions to the community in the shadows of
the old. Overlooking the town and forming the area's political
hub was the castle of the duke, the reigning noble of the independent fiefdom of Gardenia.

The duchy de Gardenia lay on the eastern fringe of an area
which had for three hundred years been fought over by England
and France. Gardenia's situation had grown worse during the
current series of conflicts that had been going on for seventy
years now and threatened to continue for decades. Constant
warfare had brought economic ruin to both nations and had
devastated the land and population of much of France.

In the early decades of the present war, the English, led by
Edward the Black Prince, once more took possession of the lands
from Gardenia west to the sea. Sebastian's grandfather had
served under the Black Prince and, in recognition of his service
to the prince and the king, was given lands within the duchy to
hold in vassalage to the English crown.

When the fortunes of war shifted again and France reclaimed
Gardenia for its own, Sebastian's grandfather stayed in the duchy
to maintain his holdings. A pragmatic Saxon, he considered
Charles V of France no worse a sovereign than any so-called
"English" king descended from that Norman usurper, William
the Bastard. He decided it was better to remain in Gardenia
where he now owned lands and to change his allegiance as necessary, rather than keep the same king and be forced to return
to England where he owned nothing.

Control of Gardenia continued unsettled into Sebastian's father's time, when France at last pushed the English into the west.
But France as a nation was demoralized and incapable of exerting
control. Civil war broke out over rival claims to the crown between the houses of Burgundy and Orléans. The English used
this opportunity to again rampage throughout northern France
as well as renew the fighting in Gascony and Aquitaine.

During the period of civil war, and acting out of disgust as much as any urge for political autonomy, the Duke de Gardenia followed the lead of several other nobles in the region just north of the Pyrenees and proclaimed Gardenia an independent fiefdom. It was a move France would be unable to challenge for almost two hundred years.

With independence, the merchants and peasants of Gardenia anticipated an era of sweeping change. Rumors of rising power among the lower classes had been trickling out of Italy for years, and many in Gardenia expected these new ways to take root in the duchy as well. But under the duke, Gardenia returned instead to staunch adherence to medieval values and culture. Renewed stability strengthened the traditional feudal economy of Gardenia, and many nobles began rebuilding fortunes lost during the war.

Unfortunately, the fortunes of Sebastian's family had not paralleled those of other nobles of Gardenia, and the holdings his grandfather received, his father eventually lost. So it happened that Sebastian was now forced to look, along with the peasant and merchant classes, to the future for any hope of raising his family from the disgrace into which they had fallen.

Even from here, Pomme de Terre seemed to strain the limits of medieval feudalism. If ever a place was ripe for change, he thought, this was it. For him, the stultifying days at the abbey were forever gone. Life beckoned. Even the prospects of apprenticeship seemed suddenly enticing. If the merchant on the road could get fat and rich in Pomme de Terre, why couldn't Sebastian do at least as well? Perhaps this was his destiny, after all. Eagerly, he slung his pack onto his shoulders and quickened his pace toward town.

So anxious was he that he hardly noticed the cold, hostile stares from serfs in their fields or the averted eyes of the few straggling travelers who hurried past as they fled Pomme de Terre. Sebastian waited impatiently for a peddler to clear the gates with a laden cart, then dashed around it to get inside.

A guard stepped into his path.

"Halt," growled the man in French, dropping his halberd in line with Sebastian's stomach. "Who are you? *Quel est votre nom?* And what's your business in Pomme de Terre?"

"How dare you!" Sebastian demanded. He knocked the halberd aside with a sweep of his arm and drew himself to full height, acting out of reflex rather than reason. "Step aside, churl, for the rightful heir to the Château d'Oignon."

"Ah, *un anglais*," the guard said, taking no offense. He swung the halberd back to Sebastian's stomach as he added in halting English, "Hail, English cur, your sister sleeps with pigs." Then he beamed, pleased with himself.

Sebastian started to cuff the guard for his insolence, but the halberd tip against his belly dissuaded him. *"Que dis-tu?"* he asked instead in low, threatening tones.

The guard's smile vanished. *"Pardon, monsieur.* Didn't I say it right?" he asked in French. "I'm sure that's how they said to greet an English nobleman."

"Who? Who told you that?"

"Down at Le Bourreau Joyeux. Some of us have been learning English. They say possibilities will open up for a man who's good at languages once the wars come to an end."

Sebastian fingered his throat unconsciously on hearing the tavern's name. The Jolly Hangman—how repulsive! But what else could he expect from foolish peasants like this who believed they could advance beyond their class? "Perhaps you misunderstood the proper greeting," he said.

"Peut-être," the guard agreed. He brightened, letting the halberd slip to one side. *"Sang de dieu, monsieur,* languages come hard for me anyway. No, counting's the thing. I've been learning counting so I can use one of those abacuses Marco Polo brought back from Cathay. They say the abacus is going to change the way we barter and sell in the marketplace, and there's money to be made by a man who can use one." He waved vaguely toward the town market somewhere behind him.

"Is that what they say?" Sebastian scoffed.

"Oui, c'est ce que l'on dit."

"What a foolish rumor, *un cafard*," Sebastian said, feeling smug over his handling of the idiom to put the guard in his place, though it seemed a strange use of the word for a duck.

"Un cafard, monsieur? Where?" The guard searched the ground at his feet, then scratched his head. "I think you mean something else."

"I know what I mean," Sebastian snapped.

"Well, perhaps I'm just not familiar with that expression," the guard said. "Nevertheless, what's wrong with common folk making a little money? There are merchants already who're doing it. *Pardieu!* I don't want to be a guard for the city all my life. Although it's better than most work around here." The guard recollected himself and jerked the halberd back into place. "What'd you say you're here for?"

Sebastian stopped himself from knocking the weapon aside again, reminded of his purpose in Pomme de Terre. His shoulders slumped. His voice became a whisper. "I've come to be apprenticed to—"

"*Comment?* Speak up, I can't hear you."

Sebastian took a breath. "I'm to be apprenticed—"

"*Un apprenti*, eh? What a surprise, my young 'noble' friend. Trying to rise above your place, are you? Well, no matter. Your master will straighten you out soon enough, I imagine. But you certainly chose a bad time for coming here, what with the plague and all."

"*La peste?*" Sebastian stepped back. "Has the Black Death returned?"

"No, no," the guard assured him. "Not at all. This plague doesn't kill its victims, just leaves them mindless and drooling like old Jacques, the town idiot." He thought a moment, then added, "When they're not turning violent, that is."

Sebastian shivered, understanding why the travelers he had seen had all been so anxious to leave Pomme de Terre. "Violent? How violent?"

"They speak in tongues, and attack anything around them." The guard shrugged. "*C'est la vie!* Funny you haven't heard about the plague, though. It's been going on here for two or three fortnights now." He thought a moment. "You're not a spy, are you?"

"*Un espion?*"

"Yeah, for the English. Or even the French, now that Gardenia's independent."

"No, I'm not a spy," Sebastian said. "I'm only here to be apprenticed—"

"Oh, *c'est exact*. You said that. Where are you from?"

"L'Abbaye de Sainte-Tomate in Justienne." Sebastian mumbled the words. "I'm to be apprenticed to—"

"Sainte-Tomate, you say?" The guard looked to see if anyone was listening, then leaned forward. The halberd dragged in the dust. "It hasn't started there yet, has it?"

"The plague?"

"Of course not, you fool!" the guard hissed. "The new order. *L'une d'Italie!*"

Sebastian started to bristle at being called a fool, then thought better of it. He shrugged, the movement almost lost against his slouch. "No, it hasn't."

"Oh well, I was just hoping," the guard said. "They said things were going to change in Pomme de Terre back when the duke made us independent. But nothing happened. I just thought maybe it had started in Justienne by now, what with the abbey being closer to Italy and all." Then, almost as an afterthought, he nodded. "You may enter. But beware that you lead a righteous, unsullied life within the gates of this God-fearing town and pursue no unlawful activities that might bring you to the attention of the guard."

As Sebastian started past, the guard winked and grinned. "And if you should develop a thirst while in Pomme de Terre, try the wine at Le Bourreau Joyeux. Tell the landlord I sent you."

There was that tavern name again. Sebastian suppressed a shudder. "I suppose you'll be there," he sniffed, holding his chin high with disdain.

"What with that plague all about? *Non, monsieur!*" The guard's laugh sounded grim and his eyes rolled as if expecting to be stricken from any quarter. "Tonight when I finish my shift and lock the gates, it will be from the outside. Not another day will I spend in this plague-ridden dung heap of a town. I'm off to Italy, where a better life awaits the likes of me. But best of luck to you, *monsieur l'apprenti*, best of luck. You may need it in Pomme de Terre."

Sebastian set his jaw and entered the gates, feeling much more subdued than when he arrived minutes earlier.

CHAPTER 2

Welcome to Pomme de Terre

THE ROAD FROM THE GATES BECAME A NARROW, COBBLED STREET
leading into the depths of town. Sebastian followed it through
the maze of stone and timber buildings, passing several townspeople. None would meet his gaze as they hurried from his path,
eyes downcast. A few made signs to ward off evil, then skittered
to the far side of the road. Unseen faces peered at him from
behind closed shop doors and shuttered windows, in the waning
light, their eyes glittering points of reflection through the cracks,
following his course with baleful interest. All recognized him for
a stranger and, in these fearful times of turmoil and plague,
distrusted him for that alone.

At last, Sebastian reached the open space of the market,
though it offered little more activity at this time of day than the
street. Most venders had long since packed up for the night and
the crude stalls stood empty and silent in the fading light. The
floors of several stalls were strewn with leafy stalks of spoiling
produce, but many stalls appeared unused. Either this had not
been a regular market day for Pomme de Terre, Sebastian
thought, or fear of plague kept many at home.

Still, a few clusters of people remained to haggle over last
minute transactions or exchange the dregs of the day's crop of

gossip. Sebastian approached one of the nearer groups, anxious
for human company. A hawker in dusty, travel-stained clothes
spoke earnestly to four or five dowdy matrons about his wares,
which he displayed on a tray suspended before him. The tray
held several grey, greasy lumps that Sebastian didn't recognize.

"But *madame, mon savon de luxe* is the finest soap there is,"
the hawker was saying. "Far better than you can make at home.
Why, this soap will turn a peasant's rough hands into the delicate
ones of a princess."

"*Ma foi!*" one of the women cried. "Marie, here's your chance
to land a baron for a husband after all."

The women broke into laughter while the one called Marie
dismissed her friend with a wave. "*Par pitié*," she said, giggling
into her apron. "As if I'd ever thought it!"

The hawker grinned, but the glint in his eye was predatory.
He noticed Sebastian at the rear of the group. "*Tenez!* Here's
a lad who could use a washing up. It would be a bit of a job,
but my soap could do it if anything could." He held his nose
with one hand and fanned the air with the other as if to ward
off fumes. "Been on the road long, have you, boy?"

The hawker laughed uproariously at this, and the matrons
joined in, drawing away from Sebastian. Sebastian flushed and
turned aside. As two of the women counted out hoarded copper
coins for the soap, he skulked across the marketplace to a larger
group. In his head, Sebastian could hear his father's voice demanding to know whether Sebastian had it in him to reclaim the
family name and fortune as he had vowed to do. Sebastian cursed
himself for his doubts, trying to drown out the voice.

So lost was he in his thoughts that Sebastian failed to notice
when he jostled a huge peasant. The peasant, dressed in rough,
drab clothes, shoved back, then glowered as he looked Sebastian
over.

"*Quel bellâtre!* Push me again, boy, and I'll point your aristocratic nose even higher, I will," the peasant snarled. Then he
turned back to hear the man addressing the group.

Sebastian backed out of the man's way, muttering apologies
as the sounds of his father's anger raged inside him.

Gradually, the words of the wiry old man speaking from the
stone lip of the fountain trickled into his consciousness. The man
pranced along the narrow fountain edge in ragged clothes, ex-
horting and pleading with the small crowd before him.

"You've waited for years, and you're sick of waiting," the old man said, crouching low and reaching out to the crowd. The crowd surged closer as if to clasp the man's out thrust hand. The frustration of their waiting was a tangible thing, even as Sebastian wondered what it was they waited for.

"You question whether you shall see the day come before you die or whether even your children shall live to see it," the man went on. "Perhaps, you think, it is only a hopeless dream."

A woman moaned somewhere as the crowd began to sway in unison, rocking slightly from side to side with the words.

"Perhaps your children's children and their children after them will live under the duke's repressive tyranny," the old man said, his voice booming over the crowd. "For tyranny is what it is, *mes amis*. Ignorance and superstition which tyrannize the mind and feudalism which tyrannizes the body."

The man paused and drew himself up, lean and scraggly, his angled face imposing with its fanatic inner vision. He looked at each person in turn, and when their eyes met, Sebastian felt stripped to the soul, naked before the world in all his fear and anxiety. He tore his eyes away, hot with embarrassment, yet he couldn't bring himself to leave the crowd.

"But you don't have to live in fear and torment any longer," the man went on softly. "The nobles of Gardenia have tried to hold back that which is rightfully yours, to keep it from you. The duke himself has led the way, paving the path to your repression with his writs and pronouncements and edicts against all you so justly deserve and so earnestly seek. But the moment has come, *mes amis*. The time is now."

The words grew again in intensity, filling the marketplace and drawing cries of support from the crowd.

"Henceforth, edicts or no, a new way of life will reign in Gardenia. It has arrived. *C'est là, maintenant.* It only waits for us to reach out and take it, to pull it into our minds and our hearts and claim it for our own. It is our rightful heritage that no one, not even the duke, can keep from us any longer. So reach out, all of you, and take it. Take the spirit of change into your souls, for this tyranny cannot be prolonged anymore, not even for a single day!"

Sebastian stopped, frozen as he realized what was being said. The chill washing through him tasted sour with fear. Although he himself looked to change for salvation, it was only to restore rightful order to the world. But this misguided fool apparently saw change as an opportunity to upend that order completely and defy the just decrees of his monarch. Regardless of the reasons, the expressed will of a sovereign noble could not be dismissed so lightly. It threatened the very fabric of society.

Around him, others also stirred restlessly. Heads turned to stare about the marketplace. Still, most of the listeners remained. Then a voice next to Sebastian broke the mounting tension.

"Thaddeus is right," said the hulking peasant who had pushed Sebastian aside. "I for one am sick of the duke's wretched sumptuary laws. Why should we be forced to wear nothing but simple clothes of black and brown, while young cock-a-dandies like this wear colored shirts and fancy shoes?" He pointed a blunt finger at Sebastian. "Why can he have what we cannot? Are we not all God's creations, noble and peasant alike?"

Sebastian stumbled back from the man's accusing finger. Then another man spoke, distracting the crowd's attention.

"*Oui*, Platt's right. The guards chased my wife home yesterday and took her embroidered apron and two colored skirts. Said such clothes were only for noble ladies to wear. As if my Emilie wasn't as good as any two of them. Well, here's what I think of life in Gardenia under the duke." The man spat. "I'm with you, Thaddeus. It's time for change!"

"*Certainement*, it is time for a change," Thaddeus replied. "Time for many changes in our lives. And each of you can make those changes come about. But only by acting now and with a single voice, for the hope of the future is ours today at last!"

"What's the point? It's useless!" another voice said roughly. "Thaddeus, you've been saying this for years. My father remembers hearing you proclaim the beginning of a new era when he was a boy. Well, it wasn't true then, and it's not true now. The duke will never let such foreign heresies into his realm!"

Words of frustrated agreement rose from the crowd. Sebastian tried to feel vindicated by their waning hope, but something within him felt lost as well. If change was prevented in Pomme de Terre, how could he regain what was rightfully his?

Then the thought struck him with stunning force—he might have to remain a tradesman all his life!

"I tell you, the time is here," Thaddeus insisted, trying to regain control over the crowd. "The only thing standing between you and a better life is a scrap of parchment, a flimsy royal decree. And why do you think the duke issues his decrees and insists on maintaining Gardenia as a feudal society? Do you think it's for our good that he does this?"

Reluctant cries of no sounded from the crowd.

"Of course he doesn't. And from where does the money come which makes the nobles of Gardenia rich?"

"From us!" a peasant yelled. "From taxes on our goods and businesses and from the muscles in our backs!"

"Some of it, *certainement*," Thaddeus agreed. "But even that ill-begotten wealth is not enough to account for the riches accumulated by the nobility. No, I tell you, the duke and his henchmen are receiving fortunes in gold for keeping change from Gardenia. Someone outside Gardenia, someone with power and wealth, wants the duchy to remain an archaic tyranny as much as the duke himself. And this person or group is paying huge sums to the duke to help him remain in control.

"But I also tell you this: All the decrees and soldiers and threats of the duke himself cannot stop you unless you let them. You must rise up and demand that which is rightfully yours! Make the duke feel the weight of your years of oppression. Don't let him—"

"*Les gardes*!" someone interrupted. "The guards are coming!"

The crowd melted away, bodies swirling around Sebastian and then seeming to disappear from the marketplace. The old man on the edge of the fountain gazed sadly over the vanishing throng. Then rough, muscular hands grabbed him as two guards dragged him from his perch. The captain of the guard stood to one side looking on.

"Come along, Thaddeus," the captain said. "We've got a cell ready for you where you can preach your heresies all day long to the rats." He sneered. "Despite all the warnings, you just had to come back, didn't you? Well, we've been waiting. Take him away!"

The two guards pulled the old man roughly along the street toward the fortress that stood above the town. A third guard nailed a broadsheet to a nearby post. Just before they left, the captain glanced around the empty marketplace, his eyes lingering over Sebastian. His scarred face grinned.

"Think not that I won't remember you," he said.

Sebastian forced himself to stare back calmly across the empty, darkening square. The captain laughed, then turned and strode after his men.

When they had vanished, Sebastian walked over to the document on the post. It was a warning to any who would disrupt the realm by spreading heresies dangerous to the duke's au-

thority. Punishment for offenders began with imprisonment and
went from there to more rigorous measures, depending upon the
severity of the offense. It also required all travelers from outside
the realm, particularly those from Italy, to present themselves
for questioning by the duke's guard immediately upon crossing
the borders into the duchy. All such travelers were further encouraged to set their worldly affairs in order and be duly shriven
prior to questioning.

Sebastian felt lost and alone and very tired. The sun had
dropped behind the town's fortified wall, draping Pomme de
Terre in shadows. Lowering darkness brought with it a chill. The
familiar abbey, even with all its faults and restrictions, suddenly
seemed very desirable. Heaving a sigh, he turned from the decree
to seek the alchemist's shop by the abbott's none-too-certain
directions.

Those directions took Sebastian into an old section of town
near the wall where the streets narrowed until he could have
stepped from the second floor window boxes on one side of the
street to those on the other. The cobblestones became less uni-
form, and he stumbled often in the deepening gloom. Refuse
lined the twisting streets. Soon rats were his only companions as
townfolk sought out safety and warmth indoors, the glow of
candles and firelight piercing chinks in barred doors and shuttered windows, emphasizing Sebastian's isolation.

He followed the streets round and round, seeming to retrace
his steps a dozen times. Finally, he realized he was lost.

An old crone ambled toward Sebastian, crooning to herself.
He stepped into her path and forced her to halt.

She looked up balefully at him with one eye, her head cocked
like an attentive bird. "Out of my way before I give you the evil
eye," she croaked, pushing her leathery face toward his. "Maybe
I'll even give you the plague!"

"Hold on, old woman, I mean you no harm," Sebastian said.
"I'm a stranger here, and lost. Show me the way to the shop of
Master Corwyn, the alchemist, and I'll make it worth your ef-
fort."

He jingled the coins in his purse for effect, carefully concealing
how meager was their number.

The look in the old woman's eye took on a hawkish aspect.
She stared unblinking a moment, holding his attention. Then her
elbow caught him in the ribs. The blow startled rather than hurt
him, but as Sebastian doubled up in surprise, she scampered

away more nimbly than he would have thought possible.

"Looking for the alchemist, *anglais*? And they call me daft!" she cackled, disappearing around a turn. By the time Sebastian straightened up to follow, she was gone.

He went on, even more tired and dismayed. Finally he came upon a beggar, a young man missing both a leg and an arm. "Alms, *monsieur*," the man quailed, stretching forth a battered cup. "*Ayez pitié.*"

The abbott had provided Sebastian with only a small sum, but this wretch was so pitiful that Sebastian dug out a few of his coppers and dropped them into the cup.

"*Merci, monsieur*," the beggar said in the same dry whimper.

Sebastian frowned. "Now you can earn those coins," he said. "Tell me the way to Master Corwyn the alchemist's shop."

There was the merest flicker in the beggar's eye, a look much like that on the old woman's face earlier. Still Sebastian was caught off guard when the beggar sprouted a second leg from behind the rags where it appeared he had none. The beggar sprang up, flinging cup and coins in Sebastian's face, and ran down the street. But Sebastian was faster and quickly overtook him. He grabbed the beggar's wrist and twisted the man's only arm behind his back. A knife clattered from the beggar's hand to the cobblestones.

"Now, my spry crippled friend, since you have experienced such a miraculous recovery you can lead me to the alchemist's yourself."

"*S'il vous plaît, monsieur*," he puled. "I've done nothing. Without me, how would my poor wife and sick children get by?"

"What are you babbling about? I'm not going to hurt you. Not that you don't deserve it. If you call that thieving act of yours nothing, you probably wouldn't regard slitting throats as much more. Now lead on while you've still got one good arm left in its socket." Sebastian gave the man's arm a nudge up his spine.

The beggar shut up and led Sebastian to the entrance of a narrow, dead-end alley. "*C'est là*, the door at the end," the beggar whined, jerking his head toward the alley.

From the darkness at the end of the alley rose a blunt mass of stone far older than the other buildings in town. Its graceless lines were offset by a solidity as indomitable as the earth itself. The iron-bound door opening onto the alley was so small against the building's bulk it had the appearance of an entrance to a mine. Sebastian shuddered at the thought of going inside.

The beggar twisted in his grip. "I brought you here, *anglais*. Now let me go."

Sebastian held him tight. "Not so fast, you slippery wretch. We'll check first. I want to be sure where you've led me. If that's really the alchemist's shop, you can leave. But if any of your cutthroat friends are waiting to ambush me, it's you they'll fall on first." He pushed the beggar toward the alley.

After the incident with the "missing" leg, Sebastian would normally have anticipated what happened next. But he was tired and his mind was slow with fatigue. Suddenly, the beggar turned into the direction of force on his arm, throwing Sebastian off balance, then spun all the way around, the front of his ragged coat bursting apart with the force of his hidden second arm rising from beneath it. His fist caught Sebastian in the face.

Sebastian fell to the cobblestones as the beggar ran back up the alley and around the corner to the street. For a time, Sebastian lay still, more miserable than ever before in his life. He felt cold and hungry and completely forsaken.

When his face and leg began to throb, he checked himself over slowly. His lip was swollen and bleeding, and he had bruised a leg in falling. But otherwise he was still in one piece. He stood gingerly and limped toward the door, wondering what fiend he had been apprenticed to who could raise such fear among his neighbors. The abbot had said nothing to indicate Sebastian should fear for life or soul—but then the abbot had said little enough about anything, mostly being anxious to get Sebastian away from the abbey in the shortest possible time.

Sebastian had been no less eager to leave himself. Now, at the forbidding doorway to the alchemist's shop, he paused, wondering if he had made a mistake. Perhaps it wasn't too late to turn back.

That pause alone saved Sebastian from even further physical abuse.

A muffled crash and a shriek sounded from behind the heavy wooden door, then the door was flung open and a black object hurtled past, narrowly missing Sebastian in its headlong flight. The object sped on, dark garments fluttering out behind, and emitted a bloodcurdling wail. Terror stopped Sebastian's throat as the apparition rounded the corner of the alley and disappeared.

Sebastian understood now why the townspeople were so frightened of the alchemist—he obviously employed the black arts and had just summoned one of the hounds of hell to rampage unchecked through a defenseless world.

Sebastian fled back up the alley before he could be discovered. He peeked around the corner, then hurried into the narrow street. The thought of encountering the demon terrified him, but not as much as the idea of remaining near the alchemist's shop.

He started to retrace his steps at a run, when something made him glance over his shoulder. At the end of the street beyond the alley, a spring flowed into a stone trough, providing the neighborhood with water. Something wallowed in the trough. Sebastian squinted to see in the uncertain light.

Why, it was a man! He had a white beard and hair and was dressed all in black. Each time he moved, he sloshed water onto the cobblestones. Sebastian crept nearer. Perhaps the man had been knocked into the water by the demon and needed help.

Soon Sebastian was close enough to overhear what the man was saying. "Always it must be so. Always, always, oil of vitriol is to be added to water. Never should they be combined the other way around. Oh, when shall I ever remember! *Tenez!* What are you staring at, boy?"

"Who, me?" Sebastian asked. He leaned closer. "*Pardon, monsieur*, but who are you?"

A chuckle rose from deep in the man's chest. "I am Corwyn."

"The alchemist? *Morbleu!* I've been seeking you." Sebastian studied the man, surprised by how short and stout he looked. This was the powerful alchemist and black sorcerer everyone regarded with dread?

"Alchemist, *oui*." Corwyn sighed. "That is, if I still have a shop left. Here, help me out and we'll go see how bad the damage is."

Hesitantly, Sebastian took the old man's hand. Corwyn thrashed his way from the trough, splattering Sebastian. Then he led the way back to the alley, his black cloak clinging wetly and leaving a dripping trail.

"But wait, don't you even want to know who I am?" Sebastian asked, hurrying to catch up.

"If you've been looking for me, I know who you must be—Sebastian, *mon nouvel apprenti*. Well, don't dawdle, boy, there's work to be done."

Sebastian stopped, wondering whether to follow or turn and

run. He swallowed, then started walking again, keeping his distance behind the strange little man.

In a different part of town, Thaddeus the rabble-rouser faced with dread the door through which he must pass. Then the duke's guards unlocked the dungeon cell and shoved Thaddeus rudely inside.

The fetters chaining his wrists and ankles hampered him, and he sprawled in the straw on the floor. The stench of decay filled his nostrils. He tried to rise, but his knee slipped in the slime that covered the stones. He rolled onto his side instead and looked up.

The captain of the guard stared back at him with cruel disdain. "Pick him up," he ordered. "Chain him to the wall."

The two guards who had dragged Thaddeus from the marketplace yanked him to a sitting position and unlocked his fetters, punctuating their work with cuffs and blows.

"*Allons donc*! Hurry up," the captain snarled, his eyes ranging restlessly about the tiny room. "Do you want to stay in here too long?"

The men dragged Thaddeus to the rear wall where one held him up as the other clamped chains to his hands and feet. Thaddeus could almost count the hairs of the man's unshaven stubble or the broken veins of his nose, so close did he stand. But the guard's eyes, like those of his captain, prowled the cell instead of watching Thaddeus, as if the room held some unseen danger.

"That's enough. *Allez vous-en*!" the captain urged, hardly waiting for the last lock on Thaddeus's chains to click tight before pushing his men out the cell door and slamming it shut behind him.

After they left, Thaddeus sagged against the crumbling stones of the cell, suspended by wrought iron manacles in the wall. The iron chafed his wrists, staining his skin with rust. He shivered and wondered, now that it was too late, if his dream of bringing change to Gardenia was worth the price it carried.

As a young man, Thaddeus had escaped the war in Gardenia by fleeing to Italy, where he witnessed the emerging new order firsthand. Merchants and tradesmen, their pockets heavy with the rewards of trade, successfully demanded equal place among the nobles who governed the lands. Thaddeus became drunk with all he saw. Eagerly, he took this vision back to Gardenia, believing he had found a means of salvation from the tyranny of feudal law and the resulting wars.

He returned to find his home an independent fiefdom, and for a time this added to his excitement. But the duke turned the eyes of the duchy to the past instead of the future, and Thaddeus's efforts were doomed. After imprisonment for preaching treason, he spent the next twenty years as a hermit in the desolate wilds of the Pyrenees, tending a flock of goats.

Still, he had never forgotten that vision from Italy, and when his isolated vantage point led him to discover the secret by which the duke maintained his power, Thaddeus again began to preach his dream. He was certain that this time nothing could stop progress from finally coming to his home.

Now, only his jailors would be coming, and they would be coming for him much too soon.

CHAPTER 3

Aquatic Alchemy

SEBASTIAN LIMPED THROUGH CORWYN'S DOORWAY AND EMERGED IN a dark, high-vaulted room. To one side, a dim passageway led into darker shadows. Sebastian heard quick, furtive rustlings from the passage, possibly the scurrying of a rat.

"The walls are certainly thick," Sebastian said nervously as the old man shut and locked the door.

Corwyn nodded, depositing a ring of keys somewhere inside robes wet from his dunking. He sloshed past Sebastian to another door, which opened onto a storeroom and began changing into dry robes. "They're sound and serve to isolate me from the strife and daily affairs of life outside, not unlike the walls of your abbey."

"Former abbey," Sebastian corrected as Corwyn reemerged from the storeroom. Sebastian struggled with himself and the demands of his father's voice, then added, "*mon sire*," in barely audible tones.

"*Sire?*"

Sebastian bowed awkwardly. "I am your most humble servant," he mumbled, lacking conviction.

"I am not your sire, nor are you my servant."

Sebastian straightened with relief. "*Pardon, Monsieur* Corwyn." He smiled down at the man and tried not to appear too condescending. "I feared my true standing as a nobleman might go unacknowledged under the present circumstances. You are very wise to see beyond surface appearances to the true qualities of my birth."

"Surface appearances, are they?" Corwyn said. "We shall soon see what you know of surface appearances, boy. In the meantime, you misunderstand my meaning. I care nothing for your birth. You are my apprentice and I am your master, which is a relationship much different from one involving a servant. And more difficult, perhaps, for you." His face darkened. "For you will quickly learn that as master, I expect harder work, longer hours, and more strict devotion to duties from an apprentice than I ever require from a mere servant. *Comprends-tu*?"

Sebastian stumbled back as if struck. His face burned and his hands clenched as his father's voice thundered at him with rebuke. "Yes, I understand," he whispered.

"Yes, what?" Corwyn demanded, stepping to close the gap between them.

"Yes, Corwyn."

The alchemist pushed himself into Sebastian's face. "Try again, boy. Yes, what?"

"Yes . . . master." Sebastian forced the words through his teeth.

"That's better," Corwyn said, turning away as if nothing had happened. "It will become easier for you as you get used to your new home here with me." He waved an arm to indicate the room.

Sebastian fought to control his own anger as well as his father's. How dare this common man speak to him so? Who did he think he was?

Yet Sebastian knew; Corwyn was his master. The shame of his fate washed away his outrage. He stared about the room, seeking refuge.

The massive strength of the chamber, balanced by graceful arches distributing stone and space to their appropriate places, helped soothe his troubled emotions. He reminded himself why he had come, and the great wealth he expected this apprenticeship to bring, which would enable him to restore his place in life.

Although the ceiling rose so high as to suggest unlimited expanse, the floor of the room was crowded. A heavy table took up most of the space. It was cluttered with strange vessels, candle stubs, odd bits of apparatus, and parchment scraps. A great leather-bound volume lay open at one end of the table, while near Sebastian the table surface was blackened and littered with broken glassware. A wisp of smoke rose from the tabletop, adding an acrid stench to air already pungent with foreign smells.

Corwyn followed Sebastian's eyes and smiled ruefully. "The results of my latest endeavor," he said. "Spoiled by failure to remember fundamentals. I expect my apprentice to do better." He swept the ruin aside, succeeding only in smearing wreckage across the table and soiling his sleeve.

The sharp odors and stuffy air were too much for Sebastian. His head reeled with fatigue. He caught the edge of the table as the room spun out of control.

Corwyn grabbed Sebastian and led him to an end of the room almost entirely given over to a fireplace.

"I have quite forgotten my manners, it's been so long since I had company," he said, seating Sebastian on the hearth. "You need refreshment after your journey."

A fire blazed in the fireplace, warming the room despite the chill outside and adding a homey touch to the unfamiliar surroundings. Sebastian huddled closer to the flames and shivered with fatigue.

Corwyn busied himself at one of the cabinets along the walls, then returned with a chunk of dark bread and a piece of cheese. He looked questioningly at Sebastian.

"*Il fait un froid de cafard,*" Sebastian said, anxious to explain that he was merely cold, not afraid.

"*De cafard?*" Corwyn glanced along the hearth to either side of Sebastian. "Are you sure?"

Sebastian nodded as he took a huge bite of bread. Why did the townspeople of Pomme de Terre have so much difficulty understanding the idioms of their own tongue?

Corwyn cocked his head. "French isn't your native language, is it, boy?"

Sebastian shook his head and tried to answer, but succeeded only in spraying flecks of bread. Corwyn frowned and brushed at the front of his robe. Sebastian swallowed quickly and tried again. "My family is Anglo-Saxon," he said. "We spoke only English at home. And when I was old enough, I was sent to my great uncle's in England to be raised in fosterage."

Corwyn nodded. "I thought so."

"You did?" Sebastian asked. "How'd you know? How come everybody always knows?"

A smile played at the corners of Corwyn's mouth as he drew up a tall stool from the table. "Just a guess, from some of the things you've said. Enough talking for now, boy. Eat up."

Sebastian needed no further encouraging. He ate greedily while Corwyn watched from atop his stool.

When he had finished, Sebastian smiled up at the alchemist perched over him. "*Merci*," he said, then added, "Master Corwyn," the words giving him less trouble than before.

Corwyn slapped his knees and leaped down. "This calls for a celebration. I haven't had an apprentice in well over a hundred years."

Sebastian choked on a fragment of crust, then looked up quickly. The alchemist had turned toward the table. As he cleared a space on its cluttered surface, Sebastian studied his new master. The man certainly looked old with his white hair and beard, the crow's-feet around his eyes, and thin, blue-veined hands that darted like nervous squirrels over the table—but he couldn't be *that* old, could he?

Sebastian felt oddly reluctant to pursue the matter, uncertain he wanted to know the answer.

Corwyn gathered items from the cabinets around the room and piled them in the space he had cleared on the table. Then he climbed back onto the stool and spoke to Sebastian over his shoulder.

"Watch closely, boy. I shall do this once so you can learn how. Hereafter, this shall be your task, so attend carefully."

Sebastian jumped up and hurried to the table, his weary feet and aching leg painful in their protest. He considered pulling up another stool, but Corwyn didn't suggest it and Sebastian hesitated to take any more liberties before his mysterious new master.

Corwyn removed a number of strange black beans from a jar and weighed them in a balance. When he was satisfied with the amount, he ground the beans with a mortar and pestle. Soon a new aroma joined the others in the room, like some exotic herb or spice, powerful yet not entirely unpleasant.

"This is a medicine I learned of long ago during my travels in Arabia," he explained as he worked. "I was little more than a novice myself when I learned of this herb from a very old, wise man.

"Few knew of it then, and not many more have learned of it since, yet I believe the day will come when it will be widely used by all manner of men. It is unparalleled in its ability to restore stamina and rejuvenate the body. Indeed, I have sometimes thought that in this simple herb, I have come close to discovering the elusive 'stone' my fellow alchemists have so long sought."

Sebastian had grown drowsy after his meal, but now he jerked awake. Only the lure of the philosopher's stone—with its powers to turn lead into gold, heal all sickness, and bestow immortality— had overcome his revulsion toward entering a trade when the abbott suggested the idea. The "stone" of the alchemists would be the means by which Sebastian could restore his family to the Château d'Oignon, thereby appeasing his father's voice in his head.

Sebastian looked again at Corwyn. He must indeed be very old. And for his age there could be only one explanation—he had discovered the secret to eternal life through the stone so many had sought for hundreds of years. He alone held the knowledge to life and health and money.

And now that power could become Sebastian's.

"Master Corwyn, have you truly found the philosopher's stone?" he asked, unable to keep the eagerness from his voice.

Corwyn chuckled. "I don't know about its ability to turn base metals into silver and gold, but this herb certainly makes a young man out of me again."

"Oh," Sebastian said, then added uncertainly, "But you said your fellow alchemists search for the stone. You are an alchemist; certainly you seek it as well?"

"In a manner of speaking," Corwyn said, nodding. "In my own way, I suppose I do. But not the same stone, perhaps. At least, not for the same purposes. I'm a specialist, an alchemist involved with the pragmatic aspects of a single element—water."

"Water?"

"*Oui*, an aquatic alchemist. I study water in all its manifestations, particularly the processes by which unfit waters can be purified, revitalized. I seek a transmutation that can restore such waters to beneficial use." He pointed to a flask of water as if to emphasize his words, then set the flask on a stand above a burning candle. "But I also perform other work involving water, particularly for individuals like the duke who are in a position to provide financial incentives in return."

"But you work for the duke, do you not?" Sebastian asked,

clinging to hope. "I mean, you are an agent of the duchy, aren't you?"

"Strictly speaking, I'm not employed by the duke, if that's what you mean." Corwyn grinned. "I work strictly for myself, though others retain my services from time to time. I consult with them on specific matters. But I'm careful to maintain my independence. I guess you could say I . . . consult in aquatic alchemy, whatever that might mean." He laughed.

Sebastian nodded, remembering belatedly to close his mouth. Only now did he discover Father Ptomaine had apprenticed him to a madman, for Corwyn must be mad indeed!

"A consulting alchemist," Corwyn continued, waving his arm with enthusiasm. "I like the sound of that." His arm bumped the mortar and overturned it on the bench. "Specialized consulting is the wave of the future, my boy." He brushed the spilled powder into a pile and swept it into a glass beaker, flicking out bits of dirt with his finger. "No longer will it be the goal of an educated man to know something of a great many things, but to know a great deal about a small portion of a single subject. Such a man can command his own reward. By anticipating this, I'm placing myself centuries ahead of the alchemists against whom I compete. I'll be in a position to respond to new developments long before my fellows even recognize their existence. The opportunities are unlimited."

"What kinds of opportunities?" Sebastian asked.

"Oh, opportunities for many things," Corwyn responded vaguely, turning to the flask where water now boiled.

"I see." After a pause, Sebastian asked, "Master Corwyn, does this have anything to do with what's been happening in Italy?"

"Ah, you mean the Renaissance."

"What?"

"The Renaissance," Corwyn said. "That's what they'll call it some day. An important event in history, though I only give it a hundred years at best. My boy, there's no economic future when each man strives to master every subject. If all men know the same things and possess the same levels of ignorance, where's the security? While if one person knows all aspects of a subject no one else has studied, he'll be indispensable to men whose fortunes depend on knowledge contained within his narrow discipline."

Sebastian hesitated. It seemed ill-advised to antagonize a madman. "But what if an area of knowledge is *too* narrow? What if no one's fortune ever depends on what a person learns? What then, Master Corwyn?"

"Rest assured, my boy, the more narrowly you define what you know, the more certainly your knowledge will be in demand. For the more specific it is, the less anyone else will know about it and the easier it is for you to convince them you possess knowledge they absolutely cannot do without. It is one of the guiding paradoxes of what I do."

Corwyn smiled over his shoulder. "You've only been with me a short time, and already I've given you one of the most powerful secrets of my trade." He winked, then turned back to his work.

Sebastian's answering smile felt like a grimace.

Corwyn poured boiling water into the beaker of black powder. The water immediately darkened. Corwyn stirred the mixture to keep the powder suspended. When the process reached some conclusion only he could perceive, he poured the mixture through a finely woven cloth. The cloth retained the sodden powder, allowing only the dark liquor to pass through. He filled two clay mugs with the liquor and handed one to Sebastian.

Steam carried the aroma of the elixir to Sebastian's nostrils. He hesitated to drink anything so potent, particularly when made by a man so obviously demented.

Corwyn watched him.

Suddenly, Sebastian realized he was being tested. It left him giddy with relief. Evidently the old man hadn't decided whether to accept Sebastian as his apprentice. Sebastian's only hope of passing the test was to make the right response. But what response? Should he drink the potion?

He steeled himslf for a gulp and almost gagged. It was the bitterest, most revolting substance he'd ever tasted. He forced it down and swallowed several times to clear the taste from his mouth. "What is it?" he gasped, hoping one mouthful was sufficient for the test.

Corwyn looked startled, then sipped from his own mug. He swirled some around in his mouth, actually seeming to savor the stuff.

"*Très bien*," he said at last. "A most delicious blend. But I sometimes forget it takes getting used to. Maybe this will help." He went to a cupboard and returned with honey and a small crock of milk. He ladled cream from the milk into Sebastian's mug until the liquor became a rich, soft brown. Then he added a large dollop of honey. "Now try it," he said, returning to his stool.

Sebastian reluctantly tried the substance again. To his surprise, it was somewhat improved. "That does make it more palatable. *Merci*, Master Corwyn."

"I was certain you'd enjoy it," Corwyn said, grinning and nodding. "A most stimulating drink." He took another big swallow, making Sebastian shudder, then went on. "Father Ptomaine told me very little about you, Sebastian. How did you come to enter the priesthood and why did you leave?"

Sebastian shrugged, feeling the answer to the first question was self-evident and not wanting to talk about the second. "I'm a second son. Even under the best of circumstances, a second son must often take holy vows to obtain a position in life."

"But yours were not the best of circumstances?"

"No." He sighed. "As I told you, my father sent me at an early age to his uncle's estate in England to be raised in fosterage and learn the ways of a knight. My father hoped that by winning my spurs, I could achieve a place for myself among the landed nobility, much as his own father had.

"I was treated well enough at my great uncle's manor, I suppose, but they never really accepted me. They were Saxons, like my grandfather, and they considered me French rather than Saxon, more French even than the Normans they despised for conquering England."

"You must have been unhappy there."

Again Sebastian sighed, flooded by painful emotions long suppressed. "*Oui*. I considered running away. I missed my home and family." He also remembered the humiliation of the training field, where he had discovered to his shame that he had little aptitude for knighthood. He continued hurriedly, skipping that part.

"Just before I planned to sneak away, my mother sent word that I was to return to Gardenia. Naturally, I thought she meant the château, where my father was lord. But when I got there, I found most of the estate had been lost and my family was living in the forester's cottage.

"Being a lord is expensive, Master Corwyn, between the costs of the manor and the retinue of vassals and servants and men-at-arms one must support. Taxes and rents were already more than our serfs and peasants could pay, yet even that wasn't enough. My father knew that a lord must support his estate by

winning the spoils of war, but how could he take part in a war
in which his friends and peers fought on one side and his relatives
from his former homeland fought on the other?"

"Your father was discovering for himself the inherent limits
of a feudal economy, I'm afraid. But go on. What then?"

"My father entered the grand melee at the tournament in
Toulouse, hoping to win the purse and repay his debts. Have
you ever seen a grand melee, Master Corwyn?"

Corwyn nodded.

"Then you know how brutal they are. Real battle could be no
worse than the melee in Toulouse that year. Father died of his
wounds a few days after. . . ."

Sebastian's voice, already a whisper, now failed. Even that
other voice he so often heard was absent. Silence filled the laboratory, drawing the vast arches closer. The only sounds came
from the crackling fire.

"There must have been other mortgage holders with their eyes
on the purse that day," Corwyn said after a while to lighten the
mood.

Sebastian nodded, his face toward the fire. He swallowed a
gulp of potion from his mug, struggling for control of his voice,
then drank again. "We tried to go on, but the debts were too
high. We sold wine from our remaining vineyards until we were
forced to stop." He turned to Corwyn, his face twisting with
anguish. "As nobles, we weren't allowed to engage in commerce.
But why is it the duke can sell his wine while his vassals cannot?
Why is it not commerce for him when it is deemed so for us?"

"Because the duke makes the laws in Gardenia, and therefore
sets the rules under which all the others here must live," Corwyn
said.

"Well, it's wrong."

"*Oui*, it is. What can be done about it?"

Sebastian gazed up into the dark arches overhead. "*Pardieu*!
Something has to change. . . ."

Corwyn said nothing, studying the young man closely.

Sebastian shrugged, still staring at the ceiling. "My older
brother, Bartholomew, left for the Crusades, hoping to remove
the shame that hung over my family and win enough treasure
from the Saracens to repay our debts. But he never came back."

"Many young men died needlessly on both sides in the stupidity of the Crusades," Corwyn said gently.

"He didn't die," Sebastian snapped. "We learned from one

of the returning knights that Bartholomew married an infidel and settled down with her in Constantinople. He trades, Master Corwyn. He is nothing now but a common merchant, dealing in figs and dates."

"What is the harm in that? He met a woman he probably loves, and he made a life for the two of them—"

"Loves? How can he love her, nothing but a common wench? And a Saracen at that! What of his family, Corwyn, his duty toward us? He deserted us for an infidel whore! When I think of my mother when she learned what became of him . . ." Sebastian choked on memories too painful to recall. He took another swig from his mug and discovered he was getting used to the stuff. It tasted much less awful than before.

"My sister went into a convent," he said when his voice steadied. "I tried to work what little land remained, to support my mother in the manner of a lady. She was losing her mind, and believed we still had servants and an estate. Every day she waited for my father's return, fretting over his absence and complaining bitterly about the servants' neglect. She couldn't understand that her husband was dead and the servants never came when she called because there were no servants left.

"I worked the fields, tilling them like the lowest peasant. Except even a peasant can work by daylight. I had to conceal my efforts under darkness, for it is against the code of nobility to work one's own land. That is for peasants and servants and serfs. A noble must starve before he dirties his hands with common work." The anguish of being torn between standards he believed in and actions necessity forced him to commit ripped at Sebastian's words, lending them a vehemence that echoed in the stone chamber. He stared at his hands, suddenly hating them for what they had had to do.

"When every other hope was extinguished, I took vows for the order at Justienne. My mother had enough presence of mind left to beg me to rise in the clergy and regain some prominence through the Church, that she might not live in shame any longer." Sebastian turned toward Corwyn, ignoring the tears that slid down his face. "She doesn't know I had to leave the abbey and come here. I'm afraid to tell her, afraid what this last failure might do."

"Is it so bad, being apprenticed to me?" Corwyn sounded hurt.

"Oh, it isn't you, Master Corwyn," Sebastian assured him. "It's just the ignominy of being reduced to this state."

It was Corwyn's turn to stare at the embers in the fireplace, pursuing his own thoughts.

"When Father Ptomaine approached me about taking you as an apprentice, I had deep misgivings at first," he said at last. "You were a good lad, he assured me, and blessed with a quick mind. But you were also a noble, and so burdened by the foolish attitudes and prejudices of your class."

He turned to Sebastian. "At last I agreed, and so you are here. But hear me well, boy. You'll learn new attitudes toward work and life, and curb your eagerness to judge others by the false standards of your youth, or I shall turn you out. For I'll not tolerate your petty contempts in my shop. Do you understand me, boy?"

Sebastian leaped to confront him. "How dare you speak to me so? I demand respect!"

"Then earn it."

Sebastian's face burned and his father's voice flared again in his head. He considered giving the man the beating he deserved, but it was a fleeting thought. Instead, he sunk onto a stool as he realized this was now his lot.

"As for the change you mentioned, the Renaissance still to come," Corwyn went on, "you do well to look to it for your future. But be aware that it is the merchant class which you despise that shall rise to prominence in that rebirth. The merchant class which I, as an alchemist, represent and to which you, as my apprentice, are now heir. Your inheritance here may be much greater than you could ever have hoped for on your father's estate."

Sebastian drained the dregs from his mug, grimacing at the taste.

"You show much promise, boy," Corwyn said gently. "But you are a mass of contradictions, of attitudes and beliefs at war with themselves. To make the most of the time to come, you must learn which of your impulses to follow and which to leave behind."

"If this Renaissance as you call it is ever allowed to reach the duchy," Sebastian said, directing his anger toward a less dangerous target.

Corwyn looked startled. "What do you mean?"

Sebastian paced the floor, suddenly restless. His mind was working with unusual clarity. Problems were more sharply defined than normal, their solutions obvious. He went to take another swig from his mug, forgetting he had finished his drink.

"Things should have changed in the duchy years ago," he said. "People are beginning to wonder if the duke will ever let Italian ideas in."

"*Ma foi!*" Corwyn exclaimed. "The Renaissance does seem overdue—"

"What?"

"I said the Renaissance does seem—"

"No, before that. You said '*foie*.' I don't understand what your liver has to do with the Renaissance."

"I didn't say *foie*. I said *ma foi*—"

"There, Master Corwyn, you said it again."

"But it's not the same word, it just sounds the same. They mean different things."

"Oh." Sebastian hesitated. "Then what does '*ma foi*' mean?"

"Which one?"

Sebastian felt bewildered. "What do you mean, which one? You said, '*Ma foi*, the Renaissance seems something or other.' What does that '*ma foi*' mean?"

"Oh, that one. 'My faith,' that's all."

"So what does your faith have to do with the Renaissance?"

"It doesn't have anything to do with it," Corwyn cried. "It's just an expression!"

"Well, no need to get touchy about it," Sebastian said. "I was just asking." He waited a moment, then asked, "What was it you were going to say?"

Corwyn glowered at him. "About what?"

"About the Renaissance."

"I don't remember," the old alchemist spat.

"Oh." Sebastian thought back over the conversation. "Maybe we should speak English. My family—"

"We'll not speak English!" Corwyn roared. "This is France. We're not at the Château d'Oignon, and you're not in the bosom of your family. You'll learn to speak the local language if it kills me."

"You mean if it kills me, don't you? After all, my learning the language couldn't possibly pose any threat to you."

"I'm not so sure about that."

"Ah," Sebastian said, trying to make it sound as if he understood. He played nervously with the instruments and glassware on the table, anxious to steer the conversation back onto a safe

topic. "You said something about the Renaissance seeming overdue."

"Ah, yes. It does seem that it should have reached Gardenia
by now. But the Renaissance's delayed arrival doesn't mean the
duke's purposely keeping change out of Gardenia. Why would
he do that?"

Sebastian drummed his fingers on the tabletop. "I don't know,
Master Corwyn, but he has been keeping it out. In the marketplace some old hermit named Thaddeus said it had something
to do with money the duke receives for preventing new ways
from reaching the duchy. But the guards dragged him away before he could explain."

"Thaddeus taken prisoner?" murmured Corwyn. "I'm sorry
to hear it. I knew him well once, many years ago. He was an
eager prophet of the coming age."

Sebastian walked around the end of the table and back, his
pulse pounding. "Well, it doesn't look like anything will change
after all. The duke's determined to keep Gardenia a feudal fiefdom forever. Say, this potion's pretty good," he added, holding
out his mug. "Is there any more?"

"I have much to remember about introducing new apprentices
to powerful elixirs," Corwyn said, studying the depths of his own
mug. "Perhaps next time half a mug will do, at least till you get
used to it."

Sebastian circled the table, picking up items at random and
setting them down again. He couldn't keep his hands busy
enough.

Corwyn frowned and moved to rescue a fragile looking piece
of glassware from Sebastian's hands, replacing it on the bench.
"Please limit your handling to less breakable pieces of apparatus," he said. "That one took me two days to construct."

"Two days?" Sebastian drew the piece toward him for a closer
look. It appeared to be nothing more than a series of bulbs blown
at regular intervals along a straight tube of glass. "What was so
difficult—"

Corwyn gurgled inarticulately as he again plucked the glass
from Sebastian's inquisitive fingertips. "Don't touch!" he
snapped, cradling the piece to his chest.

"Oh, *pardon*," Sebastian said. He shrugged and tried to remember what they had been talking about. "Master Corwyn, if
you're that anxious for this Renaissance to arrive, it must not

be you who's paying the duke to keep things from changing within Gardenia's borders."

"Of course not," Corwyn said, placing the piece of glass on the table well out of Sebastian's reach. "What a ridiculous notion! Did Thaddeus say I was?"

"No, I just thought that, with you being an alchemist, the duke must be getting his gold from you."

Corwyn stared. "Do you still believe I can actually achieve such a transmutation?"

Sebastian met the old man's eyes with confidence. Yes, I believe you can, he wanted to say. Otherwise my coming here was a waste and there is no hope of redeeming my family's honor.

"I passed the test, didn't I?" he said instead. "Don't you trust me yet?"

"Test?"

"Drinking the elixir you prepared. Seeing beneath the surface appearances to know it wasn't poison, and realizing there's no truth to the nonsense you were telling me about aquatic alchemy and not being employed by the duke. Why, I had begun to think you a madman."

"So you recognized the test, did you?" Corwyn asked after a time, his voice sad.

Sebastian tried not to look smug. "Of course. I'm no fool, Master Corwyn."

"That remains to be seen." Corwyn strode to one of the cabinets and returned with a small, heavy vial. "We might as well begin your training. After the draught you consumed, it'll be a long night anyway. Here, you'll turn this mercury into gold, while I undertake a different preparation. After we've finished, you tell me which demonstration was the more significant. Then we'll see how well you perceive beyond the surface of things."

Sebastian stood dumbfounded, the vial in one hand and a crucible Corwyn thrust at him in the other. Corwyn busied himself at the table.

"Master Corwyn?" Sebastian ventured at last. "Master, I don't know how to transmute this into gold." He hefted the vial.

"Of course you don't," Corwyn retorted. "I haven't shown you yet. If you already knew how, what would be the point of being apprenticed?" He raised his eyes to the ceiling. "Heaven save me from idiots and fools."

Sebastian almost snapped a response. But he reminded himself that he wasn't a noble any longer, at least not for the present.

Besides, Corwyn was about to show him the true secrets of alchemy.

"First, pour the mercury into the crucible," Corwyn said.

Sebastian did so, watching the silvery, liquid metal spill from the vial and shatter into tiny balls in the crucible. Gradually, the balls slowed their frantic motions and coalesced in a shimmering pool.

"Now add some of this red powder," Corwyn said, handing Sebastian a clay jar. "It's the philosopher's stone which will effect the transmutation."

Sebastian's heart beat wildly as he realized what he held. "Then you've found the true stone after all?" he cried.

Corwyn's brows drew together and his face darkened above his beard. "Is this an example of why Father Ptomaine told you to leave the abbey? I gave you an instruction, boy. Carry it out! And don't question me again."

"Yes, master." Sebastian hurriedly added a small amount of the powder to the mercury. The red dust floated on top of the silvery pool.

Corwyn turned back to the table, where he was doing something with a piece of charcoal. While his back was turned, Sebastian sneaked a handful of the red powder into the almost empty money pouch at his belt. His heart thundered with fear the old man would see him. But he had to have the stone, and he might not get another chance.

Corwyn turned and Sebastian jumped, certain he'd been caught. But Corwyn merely handed him several pieces of charcoal. "Here, place these in a mound over the mercury." When Sebastian had done so, Corwyn handed him another, heavier piece. "Put this one on top and set the crucible atop the hottest coals on the hearth. When the charcoal burns away, you'll have transmuted the mercury into gold."

Sebastian hastened to comply, hardly able to believe his good fortune. His first day and already he was learning the old man's most guarded secret. His father would have been pleased.

"Come," Corwyn called. "While you wait, I want you to watch what I do. Then tell me which procedure is more important, yours or mine."

Sebastian returned to the table already certain of the answer. What could be more important than turning mercury into gold? And yet, what if the alchemist was about to reveal something even greater?

"This is a procedure I devised," Corwyn said as he partially filled a tall-necked flask with water. "I call it the alchemical destruction test, and it requires greater skill than the simple process you just performed. Therefore, I shall do it this time myself. Soon, however, this too shall be part of your duties here. Watch closely and learn it well."

Corwyn added a reddish liquid to the water in the flask. "This is the elixir, the philosopher's stone which effects the transmutation in this particular test," he explained. "Now oil of vitriol." He poured a clear, viscous fluid into the flask, swirling the vessel to mix the contents. As the oily liquid touched the reddish water in the flask, the water bubbled and fumed.

"As with the transmutation of mercury, we must now bathe the mixture with heat." Corwyn set the flask over a candle, propping the long neck so the liquid wouldn't spill.

After a while, the flask began to boil. Steam rose into the neck, condensed on the glass, and dripped down again. The color of the liquid changed from red to bluish-green. It made a pleasing display, but Sebastian was eager to check his own work at the fireplace. He glanced anxiously over his shoulder, trying to see what was happening in the crucible. Corwyn acted as if the creation of gold was so ordinary to him that it had lost all interest. He settled on his stool and watched his flask with satisfaction. "A most wonderful process, is it not?" he asked.

"Oh, yes, master," Sebastian said with feigned enthusiasm. "Most wonderful indeed." He glanced again at the fireplace. "*Mon dieu*, the charcoal has burned away. It's done!" He hurried over and pulled the crucible from the fire with a pair of tongs. The crucible overflowed with grey ash, which Sebastian gently blew away. Then he gasped. "Gold! Master Corwyn, I've created gold!"

"Is that what you have done?" Corwyn asked.

"Yes, look!" Sebastian grabbed for the solidified gold puddle in the bottom of the crucible, then jerked back his hand with a gasp. "*C'est chaud*!" he cried, sucking his fingers.

"Of course it's hot. That's why you're holding the crucible with tongs."

"But I did it," Sebastian insisted, shoving the crucible closer so Corwyn could see.

Corwyn peered into the crucible. "It certainly appears so."

"I made gold," Sebastian said to himself, breaking into a grin. "I actually did it!"

"Exactly what have you done?" Corwyn asked.

"Why, I made gold. The red powder and the heat transmuted the mercury."

"You are sure?"

"*Oui*." Sebastian was confused by Corwyn's questions and unconcern.

"It couldn't be an illusion? This transmutation actually took place?"

"*Oui*. I mean, no, it isn't an illusion." Sebastian examined the burns on his fingers to reassure himself. "I transmuted mercury into gold. It's real, it happened. I did it."

Corwyn gazed steadily, almost sorrowfully into Sebastian's eyes. "My boy, what you did is commit a hoax."

Sebastian started to protest, but Corwyn stopped him.

"You did it unknowingly, but it was a hoax nonetheless. You're too willing to believe what you see, what you think is real. You must search beneath appearances to discover truth, for it rarely reveals itself as openly as a nugget of gold. That which has true value is often seen by many, but overlooked by all but a few."

"But the mercury," Sebastian objected. "I put it there, and now it's gone."

"Boiled away in the fire."

"And the philosopher's stone?"

"Any worthless red powder will do."

Sebastian touched the purse at his belt with his free hand. It hung full and heavy with the stolen "philosopher's stone," his dream of regaining the family estate shattered. Words of self-recrimination echoed in his head. "And the gold?" he asked.

"Ah, the gold," Corwyn said with a tight smile, retrieving the small lump which had cooled in the crucible. Corwyn held it to the light, watching its glittering reflections. "That is my seed gold, by which I occasionally make my fortunes multiply. When you weren't looking, I pushed this gold into a small cavity in the last piece of charcoal and sealed it in place with blackened wax. When the charcoal burned away, the gold melted and ran to the bottom of the crucible."

"So that's how the *villein* did it," Sebastian mumbled.

"How who did what? Speak up, boy, so I can hear you."

"Near the end, when my father saw his fortune dwindling, he tried to recover it by investing in an alchemist who claimed to have the secret for turning base metals into silver and gold. The man demonstrated his skills much as you had me do. My father, anxious to pay off his mounting debts, gave the man such money as we had left to set up a laboratory and buy equipment. We never saw the thief again."

"Hmmm," Corwyn said, stroking his beard. "I never worked this scheme near your father's lands, so it couldn't have been me. But this technique is sometimes essential for subsidizing legitimate work when honest funds run low. That is how I developed this."

Corwyn returned to the table, where he took the tall flask from its stand and blew out the candle. After plunging the bulb of the flask in a bucket of water to cool the contents, he added a few drops from a small bottle. Then he poured another clear liquid into the flask until the contents suddenly turned from blue to red again. Corwyn smiled and jotted down on a scrap of parchment how much of the last liquid he had added to make the color change.

"There," he said. "It's finished."

"Oh," Sebastian said. "But master, what did it do?"

"Do?" Corwyn looked puzzled.

"Well, the color changes were very . . . pretty." Sebastian hesitated. "But did anything else happen? Perhaps something I failed to see?"

"Why, from this I can determine to what extent a body of water has become corrupted, fouled, unsuited for use."

"Ah," Sebastian said. It was that water madness again, that "aquatic alchemy." The old man was quite insane after all. "Why, this process must be wonderful, a boon to all mankind."

"Yes, it is." Corwyn beamed at the flask. "The only difficulty has been applying it in a way which is financially rewarding. After all, my time and effort in developing this procedure must be repaid. It was an investment in the future. I haven't yet been able to use the test in a manner which is profitable as well as functional."

"So that's aquatic alchemy," Sebastian said, staring at the flask and trying to sound excited. "Little did I dream I was coming here for this." Evidently, the potion he'd consumed was wearing off, for he again felt overwhelmed with fatigue.

"You're fortunate, boy, to be in at the beginning of what is to come," Corwyn said. "But this isn't all there is. Come, there's more. I'll show you."

Corwyn lit a pair of candles, then led the way across the room to the passage Sebastian had noticed earlier.

As Sebastian followed, he thought he heard something rustle again in the shadows, but he couldn't be certain. He was so tired he might only have dreamed it. Or perhaps it was a rat.

He and Corwyn walked in overlapping pools of light. After a short distance the corridor turned, running parallel to the town wall. Doors were set into the passageway, leading into the wall itself. Corwyn stopped at one of them. He produced his ring of keys from inside his robes and turned a key in the rusty lock.

"Welcome to my incubatorium," he said, waving for Sebastian to enter.

It was a small chamber, once a storeroom of some kind. The ceiling timbers were low and massive, and Sebastian stooped to keep from hitting his head. But the air in the room was surprisingly cool and fresh after the closeness of the main laboratory.

A small table filled with apparatus stood to one side of the chamber. The far end of the room was taken up by a trough from which a gurgling sound emerged. As they stepped closer, Sebastian saw the sound was caused by water flowing through the trough.

"Where does the water come from?" he asked.

"From a small tributary of the River Ale. It passes near the town on its way to join the Ale a few miles downstream. Nobody pays the smaller stream much mind because the Ale flows through town, making it a more convenient source of water. But for my work, I need flowing water close to its source."

Corwyn used his candle to light a pair of sputtering, smoky torches set in sconces on the wall, then continued.

"My assistant and I dug a tunnel under the wall to a bend in the stream and channeled it here. The water flows through each storeroom along the passageway, then back out to the stream. This provides me with water for drinking, cooking, and washing, as well as for my experiments. More importantly, it also provides the physical and spiritual essence of the stream itself, characteristics that play a critical role in another procedure I've perfected."

Taking his candle, Sebastian crossed the room and sat on the low stone wall of the trough. The dark water glittered with reflected candlelight. He let his free hand flutter in the current. Then his fingers touched something hard and smooth under the surface. He jerked his hand out and held the candle higher.

ALCHEMY UNLIMITED   47

Water from his wet hand ran down his arm, making him shiver
as he searched the uncertain shapes in the current. Finally, he
made out the outlines of several bottles resting on the bottom
of the trough, the glass almost invisible in the water. Reaching
into the stream, he felt the smooth, cold glass of one of the
bottles and lifted it out.

"What's this? Why do you hide these in the water?"

Corwyn smiled. "That's my new procedure, the one I just
developed. It's another way of measuring corruption in water,
and it complements the alchemical destruction test you witnessed
a little while ago."

Sebastian felt disappointed as he realized the bottle was more
foolishness. He had hoped its being hidden meant it contained
something of importance. He held his candle closer and peered
through the glass, but could see nothing more than water inside.

"What does this procedure do?" he asked without really caring.

"It measures the breath of demons."

Sebastian almost dropped the bottle. His heart pounded, sending energy surging through his veins. He stared at the bottle in
horror, fully awake.

"There are demons in here?"

"Careful," Corwyn cried, rushing to take the bottle from him.
He carried it to the table and set it down. "This bottle represents
the latest stage in a great deal of work."

"But what about the demons?" Sebastian demanded, jumping
up from the trough.

Corwyn inspected the bottle to be sure it wasn't compromised,
then carried it back to the trough and replaced it under the water.
Hitching up his robes, he sat on the wall of the trough, laced his
fingers over a knee, and leaned back.

"Alchemy is based on certain fundamental truths," he said.
"Central to these is that all matter is the same. It receives specific
form only through the spirit or breath which inhabits it."

Sebastian tried to listen, but there seemed little relationship
between Corwyn's lecture and the spirits he kept bottled in the
stream.

"With this breath or spirit, and an appropriate seed to guide
the material form, any matter can be transmuted into any other.
Everyone knows that. That's how my fellow alchemists seek to
turn base metals into silver and gold."

These words pricked Sebastian's interest again.

"Living things take their spirit from the vast ocean of life breath which surrounds us, using its influence to transmute ingested matter into living flesh. Even the fishes and animals of the waters require this spirit. That's why streams are compelled to gurgle and why oceans must pound against the shores—to infuse the life spirit into the waters where it can be inhaled by the living things dwelling there."

Sebastian was confused. As his initial fear left him, fatigue again took hold, and he slumped against the stone wall, his mind numb. What did this spirit of life have to do with transmuting base metals into precious ones?

For a time, Corwyn listened to the water burbling in the trough, infusing itself with life spirit from the room. Then he continued.

"In addition to those living things which we see in water, I believe there are other living things which we cannot see, lesser demons, primarily the sprites and nymphs which prefer the water or are washed into it from the soils and vegetation surrounding lakes and streams. I believe this is so because the breath of life is consumed even in natural waters which bear no obvious forms of life. There must be agents present we cannot see to account for this.

"These sprites and nymphs consume little of the life spirit, and my alchemical destruction test measures the limited extent of their influence on the waters they inhabit.

"But there are also more powerful demons, certain undines and sylphs and even some salamanders, which occasionally inhabit waters and corrupt them, consuming the breath of life and multiplying voraciously at the expense of any lesser demons or other living creatures present. When this happens, the waters are overwhelmed and will sicken anyone who drinks them.

"In this case, too, my alchemical destruction test measures how corrupted by demons a water has become. But the breath of demons test lets me know how powerful and dangerous are the demons in a water, and what future harm they will cause that water as they consume the breath of life in order to multiply. The lesser demons will consume only small amounts of the life spirit, leaving enough for fish and other creatures to inhabit the water with them. But the sylphs and undines and their like are greedy and will consume all the spirit at the expense of any other creatures present.

"So the two procedures work together, to let me know how corrupted a water is now, as well as how corrupted it will become if the demons are not exorcized."

He sat forward then, eyeing Sebastian as if waiting for some question or remark.

Sebastian was too tired to care whether his confusion was resolved. He sagged hopelessly, so that only the wall behind him kept him upright.

"Can all demons be detected by these tests?" he asked at last, feeling stupid with fatigue but compelled by the alchemist's silence to say something. "I mean, are there any demons too powerful or subtle for you to measure . . . ?" He stopped, wondering what he was trying to ask.

Oh, what does it matter? he thought. Just let this ridiculous discussion end. He needed sleep. In the morning he could think what to do about being apprenticed to a madman.

Corwyn looked startled. "Very astute," he said. "You surprise me. In fact, there is a possibility of demons remaining undetected by the alchemical destruction test." He shuddered at the thought. "But they'd have to be powerful demons indeed, and malevolent. I think they'd still be detected by the breath of demons test, but I hope never to have an opportunity to test that belief."

"Oh," Sebastian said, unable to think of any other response, even a stupid one. He slid to the floor in exhaustion.

Just then, the rustling noise sounded in the passage again. Sebastian stared into the passage, trying to force the darkness to take shape.

Corwyn turned toward the passage, apparently hearing the sound for the first time. "That must be Oliver, my assistant. I wondered where he was." He stepped into the doorway, blocking Sebastian's view. "Oliver? *C'est vous?* Where are you?"

Corwyn walked along the passageway, calling for Oliver. Nothing emerged from the darkness and Sebastian didn't hear the rustling again. Finally, Corwyn came back.

"He's hiding. You must pardon Oliver. He's very shy. Come along, it's late and you're tired. I'll show you to your room."

Sebastian nodded, suddenly unwilling to be separated from Corwyn. Madman he might be, but that was preferable to the unknown horrors roaming these halls.

For in the brief moment before Corwyn stepped to the doorway and blocked his view, Sebastian had seen something against the deeper shadows of the passage, something that scurried away.

He wasn't sure what he had seen, but one thing was certain. Whatever it was, it wasn't human.

CHAPTER 4

Another Man's Possession

AFTER CORWYN SHOWED SEBASTIAN TO THE FOOT OF A LONG spiral staircase, and after Sebastian reluctantly left the alchemist to climb those stairs to his room in the tower high above, and even after Sebastian finally slid into a fitful, dream-plagued sleep, someone else in Pomme de Terre waited—awake and watching—far into the night.

For Thaddeus, terror was a powerful stimulant, keeping his eyes open and his mind alert even though he longed for the blessed escape of sleep.

So he waited, straining to hear the first scrape of hobnailed boots outside his cell, the first creak of a key in the lock.

Waited uneasily for the first sight in twenty years of a man he had come to fear more than the devil himself.

Old Nob was coming for him, he was certain. It was only a question of when.

Still, when a key finally squealed in the lock and the door groaned reluctantly inward, Thaddeus was taken by surprise.

He lurched upright, swaying in his chains.

A boy, no older than ten or eleven, peeped around the doorway. He glanced at Thaddeus, then surveyed every corner of the room before easing inside.

He walked uncertainly to Thaddeus, juggling a pair of manacles and a ring of heavy iron keys from hand to hand as he tried to decide how to get the manacles on the old hermit before releasing him from the wall. All the while, his eyes roamed about the room as if something might be hiding in the shadows.

Thaddeus watched, torn between relief and a curious indignation. Old Nob must be waiting in the torture chamber. This only postponed his ordeal; it didn't cancel it. Yet any delay was a blessing.

But who was this lad they sent to bring him? Was Thaddeus of so little consequence a mere stripling was deemed sufficient to lead him to his fate?

As the boy jangled the manacles and keys and contemplated his problem, the smell of animal dung assaulted Thaddeus, overwhelming the cell's odors of rotting straw, filth, and moldering stone.

The boy must be fresh from the stables, Thaddeus realized. That was as insulting as the lad's youth!

"What's your name, boy?" Thaddeus asked.

"Simon, *monsieur*." He reached some resolution and unlocked Thaddeus's wrists, then brought the hermit's arms together in front of him. "Now hold them there," he commanded, wrestling the manacles into place.

Thaddeus considered grabbing the boy and strangling him. With the keys, he could unchain his feet and escape.

But it was no use. He couldn't get out of the dungeon without alerting the guards. Besides, the boy was too young for Thaddeus to kill in good conscience. Simon might work here, but he didn't belong in this place.

Thaddeus had devoted his life to making clear the way for a new, more responsive social order. Though Old Nob might rend him, Thaddeus couldn't violate everything he'd worked for merely to avoid that anguish.

So Thaddeus complied, watching Simon, who was too young to realize his own mortality, go about his task unaware that death had approached and passed him by. Full of youthful confidence, it never occurred to Simon that Thaddeus might do anything other than what he was told.

"What do you know of torture?" Thaddeus asked.

"Not much," Simon answered, leading Thaddeus across the cell.

"How long have you been at this?"

"Since this morning." The boy halted Thaddeus at the door and peered in both directions along the passageway before urging the hermit forward again. "I worked in the stables before this."

Thaddeus smiled. The smell clearly indicated where the boy had previously spent his time. "Have you ever tortured anyone before?"

Simon turned to Thaddeus with a horrified look. "Oh no, *monsieur*."

"Have you ever seen anyone tortured?" Thaddeus asked, disarmed by the boy's unhesitating honesty.

This time Simon kept his attention on the stone passageway through which they walked, but Thaddeus saw the boy shudder at the question. *"Que non!"* came the whispered reply. "Never."

Thaddeus felt saddened by the cruelty Simon would be expected first to observe, then to inflict on others, and how hardened the lad would become in time. He might even learn to enjoy causing pain.

That was the harsh tragedy, Thaddeus thought, of the medieval society in which they lived. A tragedy that could be so easily avoided—or at least lessened—in a humanistic culture.

Thaddeus was silent for a while as Simon led him through the corridors beneath the duke's castle. The stone walls seeped moisture from the nearness of the river and the dungeon's depth, making the floor slippery with puddles and slime. A stench that didn't seem entirely due to stagnant water permeated the passageway. Thaddeus wrinkled his nose.

"What's the smell?" he asked.

Simon shook his head. "I can't smell a thing after working in the stables."

The boy began whistling softly to himself, much as someone might when walking by a graveyard at night to keep the ghosts at bay. Echoes of his tune blended eerily with the sound of water sloshing at their feet and dripping from the walls, distorted into something ominous and evil.

Occasional torches lit their way, the flames flickering off oily slicks in the water and casting long wavering shadows as they passed. Finally, the corridor turned and opened onto a large stone chamber lit by a score of smoking torches.

Thaddeus stopped at the entrance, clammy with the remembered horrors of this place.

Instruments of torture, some with traditions a thousand years old and all representing the peak of their art, lined the walls and littered the floor. A rack stood against one wall of the chamber, while ropes with weights and pulleys hung from the ceiling in a corner. Elsewhere were whips and rods, stocks and presses, wooden horses, thumbscrews, and iron slippers. In the middle of the room, a fire blazed on an open hearth, heating other devices by which men had learned to inflict agony upon their fellows.

Simon surveyed the room, just as he had Thaddeus's cell and the passageway before entering them. Satisfied, he started in, then stopped when Thaddeus stood frozen behind him.

"Entrez!" Simon urged with youthful impatience, pulling on Thaddeus's manacles. But Thaddeus resisted, shaking uncontrollably.

Simon sighed and sat at the hermit's feet in the corridor. "I know what you mean, *monsieur*," he said. "I never wanted to be apprenticed as a torturer anyhow. I enjoyed working in the stables. The animals all liked me." He looked up at Thaddeus with round, sad eyes. "But we're supposed to do this, and we've got to get on with it, *monsieur*."

Thaddeus took a breath of fetid air and steadied himself. He moved half a step closer and peered through the doorway.

"Where's Old Nob?" he whispered.

Simon jerked his head to indicate the direction from which they'd come. *"Voilà."*

Thaddeus spun around, terrified of finding Old Nob grinning at him from behind. But the corridor was empty.

"Where?"

"In one of the cells," Simon said. "With the others, most of them."

"The other prisoners, you mean?"

Simon nodded. *"Oui*, and the ones who worked here. They're all locked up together." The boy's open face took on a frightened look and he leaned close to whisper. *"C'est la peste!* It's taken almost everyone who worked here. We've had to lock them in the cells with the prisoners."

Thaddeus stared at the boy sitting on the floor. "You mean you're the only one left?"

Simon shook his head. "No, there are a few more. But most of us are new at the job. Shorthanded, they were. So they sent me down and told me I was an apprentice, whether I wanted to be or not."

Thaddeus looked into the chamber again. "Then who is to torture me?"

The only response was a snuffling from the floor. Tears ran down Simon's cheeks.

"C'est moi, monsieur."

"Oh," Thaddeus said. He sat by the boy, ignoring the slime on the floor, and let out a sigh of his own. "Oh, my."

Simon looked up at him. "I'm sorry, *monsieur.* I don't want to, really I don't. But they said I've got to do it." He sobbed again.

Thaddeus tried to put an arm around the boy, but the chain connecting his wrists made it impossible. He patted Simon's shoulder instead, waiting for the boy to stop crying. "That's all right, son. I understand." After a while, he stood up. "We'd better go in. Someone might come along."

The boy raised his head but didn't get up. "Are you going to show me how to use those things?" He jerked his chin to indicate the instruments in the torture chamber.

"No."

"I don't want to learn, but I'm scared of the others. If I don't do it, they'll lock me up as well."

"I have an idea for getting around that."

Reluctantly, the boy followed Thaddeus into the chamber. "What are you going to do?"

"You'll see."

"I won't hurt you, *monsieur.* I can't!"

"You're a good lad, Simon." He led the way to the rack, suppressing the dread the machine aroused. "You don't actually need to hurt anyone. With so few jailors here, and all of them new, maybe they won't notice if you play a little trick on them."

For the first time, Simon looked hopeful. "What kind of trick?"

"You'll pretend to torture me, as you've been told to do. If any of the other jailors happen to come in, I'll appear to be suffering the agonies of the rack. But all I'll really experience is a little discomfort to fool the other jailors."

Simon grinned, entering the spirit of the game. "How?"

"Here, I'll show you." Thaddeus sat on the rack and swung his legs up. He locked his ankles into a pair of iron clamps and lay down with his arms extended above his head. His stomach knotted at having to touch the terrible machine, but he felt a grim satisfaction knowing he and Simon were making a mockery of Old Nob's prize.

"Take off my manacles and lock my wrists with the chains from the winch," he told the boy.

Simon complied, touching the machine gingerly. "Now what, *monsieur*?"

"Now tighten the winch," Thaddeus said. "Gently."

Simon turned the crank, slowly taking up the slack in the chains. As he turned, a clicking ratchet on the winch held the tension.

The boy stopped as the last link of chain lifted from the table.

"More," Thaddeus said. "A little tighter."

"Oh, *monsieur*, it will hurt," Simon protested.

"No it won't. Not much, anyway. But the chains have to look tight if they're to fool anyone."

Simon turned the winch another couple of clicks. The tension increased in Thaddeus's ankles and wrists. Suddenly he felt too terrified to go on. But just as he started to scream at Simon to stop, the boy appeared again at his side.

"Are you all right, *monsieur*?" the boy asked. "I haven't hurt you, have I?"

Thaddeus tried to calm the spasms shaking his body. "No, son," he whispered. "I'm all right."

"Do you want me to loosen it a bit?"

Slowly Thaddeus relaxed, startled at the absence of pain. As long as he didn't panic and struggle against the chains, he could tolerate the discomfort.

He let out a sigh. "No. I'm all right," he repeated, surprised to realize it was true.

Simon hesitated. "Maybe we don't need to do this at all. No one's going to come down here—"

He was interrupted by the sound of hobnailed boots in the corridor.

"There's your answer," Thaddeus said, his voice low. "Now to sound convincing." He moaned, trying to repeat noises he had uttered unconsciously years before.

From the corner of his eye, Thaddeus saw another jailor appear in the doorway. The man's piggy eyes squinted as he stared into the room.

"Ah, getting on right well your first day, aren't you, boy?"

"*Oui*, Master Grubb," Simon replied.

Grubb nodded. "I knew you would, boy. Now, come upstairs

and give us a hand. Old Jessie got the plague, and we need your help locking him up."

Grubb turned back to the passageway, but Simon stalled. "I'll be there just as soon as I get this one back to his cell, Master Grubb."

"Ah, leave him be," Grubb snorted. "He'll keep. He's not going nowhere."

Simon glanced at Thaddeus as the hermit moaned in feigned anguish. Thaddeus winked at the boy, never ceasing his pleas for mercy.

Simon grinned, then assumed a sober look for Grubb. "I'm coming, Master Grubb. I'm right behind you."

Thaddeus kept up his noises until he was certain the two were out of earshot, then burst out laughing. They'd done it!

Finally he lay still, panting. His smile remained. It was a small victory, but it felt good.

Then he settled into waiting for Simon's return.

How silent the room was, he realized after a while. He'd never heard silence in this chamber, for the room had always been filled with misery. Now the only sound came from water dripping off the walls.

The discomfort of having his arms stretched overhead grew. Even without the bone-rending tension, it was surprising how disagreeable the rack could be.

When would that boy return? It seemed an eternity already!

Thaddeus closed his eyes and tried to recall the smell of clover, the drone of bees, and the taste of honey thick from the comb. For a time, he almost succeeded, could almost feel himself drawn back to his youth.

A sudden stench shattered his memories. It was the same foreboding odor he'd noticed in the corridor, but intensified.

His eyes flew open, and he turned his head as best he could, trying to see around the room. But there was nothing to account for his fear.

Then something moved in the corner. Something indistinct and wraithlike pulled into itself where moisture seeped from the wall, congealing into a half-seen vision of evil.

The apparition drifted closer, riding the fetid currents of air. Suddenly Thaddeus was overcome with an overwhelming sense of violation as something pilfered the relics of his memory, examining and discarding one personal incident after another until it found what it was looking for.

Now the wraith wore the form of Old Nob.

"*Alors!* If it isn't my old friend Thaddeus, the self-appointed savior of Pomme de Terre," Old Nob scoffed. The voice sounded thin, more like sounds remembered than actually heard, and a babble of words in a foreign tongue at the edge of Thaddeus's consciousness distracted him. But the terror he felt at seeing Old Nob was like being thrust awake into his worst nightmare.

The torturer hovered over him, grinning evilly and jabbing a finger in his face. "Yes, Thaddeus. Now and forever, you are mine."

"No!" Thaddeus screamed.

The stench of the wraith burned in Thaddeus's nostrils. Its tendril, looking like Old Nob's hand, flicked closer. Thaddeus held his breath. The tendril spread to cover his mouth and nose. The image of Old Nob laughed. Thaddeus's lungs ached until the need to breathe overwhelmed him.

He exhaled in a single, violent burst of air that briefly shredded the tendril. But as Thaddeus gasped for air, the wraith slipped inside.

"Oh, Gardenia," Thaddeus wailed in his final moment of consciousness. "So much remains undone!"

He wondered numbly if anyone would continue his work after he was gone. Perhaps there really would never be any change in Gardenia after all.

Then a new look settled over his face, and what now controlled Thaddeus settled back into waiting. The discomforts of the rack bothered it not at all. It was patient and enduring. It always had been.

Its time would come soon enough.

Simon returned whistling cheerfully, eager to release Thaddeus so they could share their private joke.

Master Grubb had been pleased with Simon's progress. In view of the continuing shortage of men in the dungeons, he had even promoted Simon to journeyman torturer. Simon could hardly wait to tell Thaddeus. The old man would laugh at that.

But Simon felt bad that it had taken so long, for when he and Grubb had reached the upper levels, they discovered Jessie wasn't the only jailor who needed locking up. The plague had claimed two more victims—a prisoner and another boy not much older than Simon who'd also started work in the dungeon that morning.

Thaddeus was curiously silent as Simon entered the torture chamber, perhaps suffering real pain from the rack. Maybe someone had tightened the winch while Simon had been off with Grubb. He hurried to release the chains.

Then, for a moment, Simon hesitated. Thaddeus was watching him with oddly predatory eyes. The look chilled Simon's spine. He hadn't realized before that Thaddeus had yellow eyes. A smell penetrated the barnyard odor Simon carried, a smell he had encountered only a short while before.

Simon's hand knocked the ratchet loose and the tension eased from the winch. He came around to the side of the hermit, now limp on the bed of the rack.

"Are you all right?" he asked, reaching for the shackles on the old man's wrists. *"Tenez!* Let me undo these."

The shackles fell open as Simon unhooked the catches. He started to turn toward Thaddeus's feet to open the ankle clamps just as he remembered where he had encountered that odor before. It hung in the air around each person who had succumbed to the plague.

Simon paused with his fingers on the clamps. An abrupt motion registered in the corner of his eye as Thaddeus jerked to a sitting position.

Simon leaped back from the rack just as the hermit's hands slashed through the air at him, clutching like claws as they tried to reach his throat with their powerful, choking grip.

CHAPTER 5

Castle Calls

SEBASTIAN AWAKENED TO SUNSHINE STREAMING THROUGH THE archer's slits in his room atop Corwyn's tower. He groaned and squeezed his eyes against the light.

It had been a long night, partly due to anxiety, and partly the result of that beverage Corwyn brewed, that *kawphy* as he called it. Now that the elixir had finally worn off, Sebastian wanted nothing more than sleep.

But still sleep eluded him. The straw pallet poked him, the coarse wool blanket scratched his skin, and the sunlight on his face made red splotches swim inside his eyes. He rolled over, but the dusty straw and ancient flooring tickled his nose. At last he sat up and went in search of Corwyn.

Sebastian started down the circular stairwell, turning until his sense of direction became confused. His thoughts wandered. The night before, Sebastian had tried to count the steps to his room, but had lost track after the first hundred.

A slight rustling snapped his mind into focus.

There it was again, just around the turn. It sounded like the noise Sebastian had heard the night before. The irritations of the morning boiled up inside him.

"All right, Oliver or whatever you are, come out and face

me!" he bellowed, lunging down the next several steps.

A rat glanced up, eyes glittering. Then it was gone, disappearing into a chink in the wall. Sebastian stared at the empty stairs, his anger unsatisfied.

He found Corwyn in his laboratory. The old alchemist sat at the table peering at parchment sheets and writing in the huge book Sebastian had noticed the previous night.

"Ah, *mon nouvel apprenti*," Corwyn said when he noticed Sebastian. He shoved a wooden plate in Sebastian's direction. "Here, boy, eat up. The morning's half gone and I want to show you something at the castle. I wouldn't have saved breakfast, but Oliver made it for you himself." He grinned. "I think he's beginning to like you."

Sebastian shuddered at what passed for food on the plate. If Oliver's laboratory skills were as bad as his cooking, no wonder Corwyn needed an apprentice.

Then Corwyn pushed a steaming mug in his direction and Sebastian's spirits rose. "Is that *kawphy?* I'll settle for it. I'm not a very big eater in the mornings."

This wasn't entirely true—at the abbey Sebastian had been known as the "archbishop of breakfast," for he presided over that meal more eagerly than many a curé over his parish. But Sebastian felt reluctant to criticize Corwyn's strange assistant.

"Why are we going to the duke's castle?" he asked as he ladled cream and honey into his mug. "I thought you didn't work for him."

"I said I'm not one of his vassals or servants," Corwyn corrected. "But I have been commissioned by the duke to develop a system for bringing water inside the castle. Construction is finished and the system's ready for testing."

"That can't be difficult, Master Corwyn," Sebastian said, taking a sip from his mug. "Just channel water into the castle from the river, like in your incubatorium."

"*Très bien*," Corwyn said dryly. "Less than a day as my apprentice and already you're an expert."

Sebastian's ears burned as if it were his father who chided him. "I just meant it didn't sound hard to do."

"And how do you propose to get water up the hill and into the upper chambers of the castle?"

"I hadn't thought about the hill." Sebastian was quiet, his mind turning over Corwyn's words while he drank. The warmth of the liquid made him feel better. "Why into the upper chambers? Why not into the kitchen instead?"

"Oh, water will go into the kitchen, and many other places besides. But it must also reach the upper chambers because they are where the duke and duchess live, and it is to be readily at hand for drinking, washing, bathing, or any other purpose the sovereign couple might envision."

Sebastian's mind whirled at this idea. Why would anyone care whether water was that easily available, particularly when there were servants to bring the water if it should be needed? He started to ask, then decided against it. The man had a fetish about water.

"Won't there be problems with having so much water in the castle?" he asked instead, thinking of how many chamber pots would need to emptied. "There'll be puddles under all the windows, and the flooding will leave some areas of the courtyard unsuitable for use."

"*Bien, bien!* You're learning." Corwyn beamed as if he were responsible for Sebastian's natural wit. "But part of my system includes pipes and drains to carry spent water back to the river again."

Sebastian shook his head, baffled by the inventiveness his fellow nobles exhibited when it came to ostentatious displays of wealth. It angered him to realize what that money could have meant in his father's efforts to retain the family manor. "Couldn't you just put the water under a spell to get it up to the royal chambers?"

"I have yet to hear of a spell for making water flow uphill," Corwyn said. "Besides, alchemists do not deal in spells or magic. We use natural processes to understand and control the world around us. Ours is a practical tradition."

Sebastian nodded, although measuring the amount of life breath consumed by demons didn't sound very practical. It bordered on the black arts. "What're you working on?" he asked to change the subject, nodding toward the leather-bound volume.

Corwyn smoothed the pages of the book. "These are my alchemical methods for studying virgin and corrupted waters. I have to revise them every hundred years or so just to keep up with new techniques. The field changes that rapidly."

Sebastian drained his mug and twisted around to read the parchment sheet Corwyn had been working from. "What's this?"

Corwyn frowned. "It is part of your master's work, that's what it is. Is that any concern of yours? I hope I shall not be constantly called upon to remind you of your place."

"Oh, I'm sorry, Master Corwyn," Sebastian said with exaggerated deference. "I didn't mean to pry." He was silent until his curiosity got the better of him. "But what does it mean? As your apprentice, is it something I should learn?"

Corwyn picked up the sheet. "'With the rain which wetteth not goeth the word which lacketh all understanding, and that which is writ remaineth unread,'" he read softly. "'Seek ye here for thine answer.'"

The silence stretched as long as Sebastian could bear it, then he burst out, "But what does it mean?"

"It's a fragment of an old alchemical text I stumbled across once, written by someone who must have been a true master of the royal art. In the usual manner of alchemical writing, this passage alludes to a mystical journey, which in turn stands for a physical process. But what that process is, as well as its significance, eludes me. It is an enigma, yet from other passages this same author wrote, I believe it is of great consequence to my own work. I can only hope I will unravel its mysteries when the occasion for understanding arises." He set the sheet down and looked at Sebastian. "Are you ready? Come, let us go to the castle."

Sebastian hitched his breeches over his growling stomach and pretended enthusiasm. "I'm ready, master."

Leaving Corwyn's shop, they walked along the winding side streets Sebastian had wandered the evening before. It was broad daylight now, but Sebastian still saw few townspeople, though several doors closed as they approached. People they did encounter treated Corwyn and Sebastian with fear rather than respect. A young man crossed the street to avoid them, breathing through his scarf as he passed. A stout matron counted her rosary as if her life depended on it. Others simply covered their eyes and hurried by. Yet Corwyn nodded and smiled to them all.

Sebastian wondered what the old man could have done to engender such hostility. He seemed foolish, but otherwise harmless enough.

"Why is everyone afraid of you?" he asked at last.

"They don't know me, and people fear and distrust what they do not know. Especially in these days of plague. Many think I am a necromancer or evil sorcerer who has brought the wrath of heaven down upon them." Corwyn pointed to a beggar girl

who was making arcane signs in the air at them. "See. They
resort to ignorant superstitions to defend themselves against the
plague." He snorted. "As if such foolishness has ever been successful against ailments of the flesh."

"But you live here," Sebastian objected. "Why don't they
know what you really are?" He wondered uneasily if they did.

Corwyn shrugged. "Until recently, I lived in seclusion. It suited
me. After one has outlived as many friends as I, forming new
relationships sometimes seems a tedious and unnecessary occupation.

"Then, just about the time I began to seek out companionship
again, the plague struck. Many people naturally associated my
sudden appearance among them with the advent of their misery.
I am hoping that the knowledge I have to offer will eventually
convince them of their mistake. This project for the duke is my
first real effort along that course."

Sebastian wondered how the peasants would react to such a
lavish project, constructed with their taxes for the idle luxury of
the duke. Then he caught himself, shocked at his own indiscre-
tion in thinking ill of how the duke chose to exercise authority
in his own domain.

Corwyn and Sebastian soon reached the marketplace. On this
morning it bustled with activity as farmers sold their produce
and craftsmen hawked their wares. Still, Sebastian noticed people nervously made way for Corwyn.

Corwyn either ignored their reaction or was oblivious of it.
He stopped to read the proclamation Sebastian had seen the
previous evening. Someone had smeared it with mud, but it was
still legible. The alchemist said nothing for a time, his face wrinkled in thought as they walked.

Pomme de Terre sprawled over a low, wide hill, with the duke's
castle perched on an adjacent, more commanding prom-
ontory. Between the two hills flowed the Ale River. Though it
now ran cold and swift with spring runoff, it wasn't much as
rivers go. The city wall crossed it in two places to join the higher,
thicker walls of the castle. Iron grilles extended down into the
water to keep attackers from swimming under the walls and into
the city.

A channel had been cut to form a moat, creating an artificial
island upon which the castle stood. The only access to the castle,
other than secret tunnels, was by drawbridge. They had just

reached the middle of the bridge when suddenly several knights rode out of the castle.

Sebastian jumped aside to avoid being trampled and collided with a friar's donkey. The frightened animal brayed and kicked, catching Sebastian with a hoof. Sebastian collapsed at the edge of the drawbridge while the friar tried to calm the beast. The knights thundered past, surreal and untouched in their plumage, leaving a tangle of people, animals, and upset goods in their wake.

Peasants and merchants stumbled to their feet and gathered scattered belongings. Sebastian lay unmoving, his wind knocked out. His head and arm dangled over the water.

A greenish vapor rose from a backwater near the bank. It climbed silently, hidden by the drawbridge, wending its way through the air toward Sebastian.

For a moment, Sebastian felt his mind invaded as it had been on one other occasion. But he was groggy from the fall, and before he could puzzle out where he had experienced this previously, everything shifted and he was again in the halls of the Château d'Oignon, tracking the sounds of a child crying. As before, the walls around him suffered from shame and dread. This time, however, the child sounded closer. Sebastian pursued the sounds doggedly, haunted by the burden exuded from these walls, repelled by the weakness he heard in the child's crying. His shadow leaped ahead of him.

He rounded a corner and discovered a boy, not more than six or seven, cowering in a shallow niche in the wall. The boy lifted his face and pleaded silently with Sebastian, tears smearing the crusted blood from several cuts and bruises.

Sebastian was disgusted by the boy's frightened expression, and anger swelled in him to a terrible rage. He wanted to lash out against the boy, and the feelings the boy's anguish evoked within him. But before he could act, a heavyset woman on the drawbridge leaned on Sebastian in an effort to get up. She forced the air violently from his lungs, dispelling the vapor and hurling it to the river below. The vapor swirled in the water, then was caught by the current and swept downstream.

Sebastian slowly became aware of Corwyn pulling him away from the edge. He sat up, holding his head. The world reeled and his mind was numb with remembered fear and anger. He opened his mouth to speak, but the words got tangled with his tongue. He shut his mouth, licked his lips, and tried again.

The words came out thick and strangely accented, as if he was unused to them. "I feel awful. What happened?"

Corwyn checked him for broken bones. "You took quite a spill."

Sebastian shook his head to clear it, then stopped when it felt like his skull was sliding off. "I've never fallen like that before. There was a terror to it, and something else. Almost like..." His voice trailed off. "I've felt it before, but can't remember where. And when I tried to talk, the words that came to my tongue were foreign."

"Foreign?"

"*Oui,*" Sebastian said, then added hastily, "I couldn't remember how to speak, not French, not even English." He glanced at the water, where several ducks were swimming, but saw nothing else. "*Ce n'est qu'une couvée des cafards.*"

Corwyn's eyebrows arched. "*Des cafards?* In a covey?" He squatted down to look under the drawbridge. "This I have to see for myself."

Sebastian frowned, wondering why Corwyn was looking on the slimy underside of the wooden planks instead of at the birds swimming in clear view on the water. Perhaps covey was the wrong term to use with ducks. Sebastian's anger rose anew as he realized the old alchemist must be ridiculing his French, but he felt too drained to pursue it.

When he stood up again, Corwyn said nothing, but studied his apprentice questioningly.

They crossed into the castle grounds making an incongruous pair, Corwyn half supporting an unwilling Sebastian who towered over him and made them both stagger. But the ill effects of his fall quickly wore off and Sebastian resumed walking on his own.

When they entered the castle grounds, Sebastian was startled by how much construction was being done. Even more surprising was how little of it served any military purpose. Sculpted gardens, ornate pavilions on a new tournament field, and stonework facades for the interior buildings were poor investments of a limited economy. Next to such abuses, Corwyn's project might appear benign indeed!

Finally they reached the great hall, the rear of which adjoined the wall encircling the castle. Corwyn led Sebastian to a small door near the back. As the alchemist searched for the right key on his ring, Sebastian wandered, still dazed from his fall. Corwyn opened the door and motioned to Sebastian, who started to follow until a flash of color caught his attention. He stared at the back of a turret rising from the great hall.

Three gaily colored windmills stuck out from the turret. The first was at the turret's base, just above the castle wall. The second was halfway up the turret, while the third perched precariously at the top. The cloth sails, each a different color, caught the breeze above the castle and slowly revolved on their axes.

"What are those?" Sebastian asked.

"They supply the power for my water pumps," Corwyn replied. "Beautiful, aren't they?"

"So that's how you get water up there," Sebastian said, avoiding the question. "Why three windmills? Wouldn't one do as well?"

Corwyn stood with legs apart, his head upturned to stare at the gaudy contraptions. "A single windmill can't lift the water that high. Each machine lifts the water part way, filling a reservoir at each stage. The first windmill draws water from the Ale, the second gets water from the reservoir of the first, and so forth. Water from the reservoir at the top then flows through conduits throughout the castle."

Sebastian was strangely impressed by the old man's engineering. "I have seen windmills for grinding and milling, but who would have thought of using them to lift water?"

Corwyn snorted, but his eyes looked pleased. "In the lowland countries, they're using windmills to drain marshland for farming. Someday, they may even harness the wind to push back the sea."

Push back the sea with the wind? Sebastian tried to imagine such a thing. No, it was impossible; Corwyn was exaggerating. Still, the idea added to a growing awe Sebastian felt toward the alchemist.

Could this be the same man who had carried on last night about the breath of demons, transmuting impure waters, and other nonsense?

"The workmen were told to start the system this morning." Corwyn motioned toward the door. "The reservoirs should be full. Come, I'll show you the rest of the system."

The air inside was musty with disuse, smelling of ancient stones. Dust lay everywhere. Another door opposite the one they entered led into the interior of the castle. Sebastian started toward this door as Corwyn locked the outer door behind them.

"No, not through there," Corwyn said as Sebastian tried the

rusty latch. The alchemist pointed overhead. "Up there." He started up the stairs, leading the way.

Sebastian looked up the stairwell into the darkness of the tower, thinking dismally of the stairs to his own room above Corwyn's shop. The world seemed based on endless stairways, all leading through persistent gloom. Sebastian hoped if change ever reached Gardenia, it would bring level structures where people traveled sideways instead of up and down. That, and better light.

He sighed and plodded after Corwyn.

At the second floor landing, another door led to a mezzanine over the great hall. From here, official ceremonies and affairs of state could be watched by servants and other nonparticipants. Sebastian paused to catch his breath and was about to open the door to peek into the hall when Corwyn called impatiently from above.

The alchemist was waiting on the next landing. Beyond, the stairwell narrowed to a tight spiral for its ascent into the tower. From the dim heights came the creaking of wooden gears and pulleys as the windmills lifted buckets of water on long loops of rope. The buckets showed briefly as silhouettes against a pair of archers' slits in the side of the turret, entering through one slit with their watery burden and returning empty through the other on their way back to the Ale, far below. Several brass tubes descended from the top of the tower to the landing where Corwyn stood, then separated to follow various paths along the wall.

The landing smelled of damp stone and wood, and moisture sprinkled Sebastian's face as he stared into the darkness of the tower. He tried to see where the conduits originated and how water passed from reservoir to reservoir, but couldn't. He started up the steps again, his dislike for heights forgotten in his new-found eagerness to uncover the mysteries overhead.

"No, no," Corwyn said. "In here. I know you're anxious to learn how the system works, but I want you to witness the miracle of water available on demand. Follow me."

He led Sebastian into a corridor where elaborately framed portraits of dukes and duchesses past lined the walls, unsmilingly regal as they stared from their canvasses of dark and cracking paint. The polished hardwood floor was strewn with rugs stolen from their Saracen owners during the Crusades. The far end of the corridor opened onto the stairway by which members of the duke's family descended in elegance to grace functions in the

hall below. Part of the stairway's marble balustrade rose from
the cavernous depths of the hall into the corridor.

But the feature which dominated all others was a stained glass
window in the far wall. In shards of color, the window portrayed
a ragged man with the halo of a saint, casting out a demon from
the unconscious body of a young noblewoman. The demon was
departing the girl hurriedly, looking back over its shoulder at
the uncouth saint with evident distress. A respectful distance
away stood a crowd of onlookers, while overhead hovered a flock
of angels.

Before Sebastian could admire the window, Corwyn urged him
to a large door at the end of the corridor. Just as the alchemist
was about to knock, the door opened and a shrunken peasant
woman backed out carrying a pail of water in one hand and a
bundle of wet rags in the other. She was so busy trying to haul
the door shut behind her that she didn't see Corwyn.

"*Attention!*" she cried as she backed into the alchemist.
"Watch where you're going!"

"I'm sorry, old mother," the alchemist said. "Is the duke in
his chamber?"

The woman set the pail down and pushed back strands of hair
that had slipped across her face. "Do you think I'm daft, trying
to clean his room with him still here and complaining of specks
of dirt all about? He's gone to see one of his mistresses, I suspect,
and good riddance, too."

She turned to struggle with the door again, still trying to drag
it shut. "Off he goes to visit his whores, and him with a good
wife here who dotes on him, God knows why. And her a beauty,
too. But I never pretend to understand noble folk, I just clean
up after them and keep to my own *Tenez, garçon!*" she said to
Sebastian. "Why don't you help an old woman with this door?"

Sebastian was too shocked to move. All he could think of was
the penalty for treason, and what might happen to him if he was
caught listening to this old wench.

The woman turned to Corwyn. "Can't he talk?" she asked,
jerking her head at Sebastian.

"Oh, he can talk. He's just not used to hearing what common
folk think of nobles," Corwyn said. "Careful what you say, old
mother. He comes from the nobility himself, and still thinks
himself one of them."

The woman glowered at Sebastian. "Well, he's welcome to
them for all I care." She tugged at the door.

"Hold on, old mother." Corwyn put a hand out to stop the door. "We're here to check the new water pipes and fixtures."

"Ah, that!" The woman lifted her pail with effort and held it for them to see. "Carrying this has been good enough for me, and for my mother and grandmother before me. Why, women of my family have been hauling water and cleaning for the nobles of this castle through rape and pillage for generations now, and no upstart quack of a chemist who invented those windmills is going to change that."

"I'm the one who invented them," Corwyn said, his voice strained. "And that's 'aquatic alchemist,' not 'quack of a chemist.' Now, may we go in?"

The woman shrugged sagging shoulders and stepped aside. "Go ahead. If anything's missing, they'll blame me anyhow. But don't mess up the floor. I just got it clean."

Corwyn nodded and started in, but Sebastian held back. To take his mind off the villainy of the old woman's words, he had been staring at the stained glass window. From this closer vantage point, he noticed many of the onlookers and angels were holding their noses or fanning their faces, and all were in discomfort.

"What is that?" he asked, pointing to the window.

He was addressing Corwyn, but the old woman squinted at the window and answered instead. "Dirt, probably. But I don't do windows."

"No, I mean what's it a picture of?"

Again she shrugged. "Who knows."

Sebastian stared down at her with all the contempt his outraged sense of class propriety could muster. "And who cares, right?"

"If you don't care, why'd you ask?" the woman demanded, glaring back. She cocked her head. "Say, are you English?"

Sebastian drew himself up. "My grandfather was a Saxon. Why?"

The old woman reflected a moment, then said in halting English, "Hail, English—"

"Yes, yes, I know. 'Hail, English dog.' I've heard that slander before."

The woman looked puzzled. "I thought it was 'pig,' not 'dog.'"

"You must be taking lessons from the same fool who taught the guard at the city gate," Sebastian sneered.

"Call me a fool, will you?" She snapped, flicking the wet rags at him. "I'm the one who taught young Charles, down at Le Bourreau Joyeux. For that matter, you could do with a few lessons yourself, boy. And I'd give them to you, too, for the price of a bottle or three." She looked Sebastian up and down coldly. "Your English is dreadful!"

Corwyn stopped Sebastian's sputtering by grabbing his arm and pulling him into the chamber.

Inside, Corwyn crossed to a small table where a brass conduit from the tower led into a basin. Sebastian wandered to the bed and sat, unable to resist its softness.

The duke's chamber was more ostentatious than the corridor, with fine tapestries on the walls, a silk canopy over the bed, and down pillows and quilts. Everywhere glittered gold and silver ornaments set with jewels.

Beside the bed was an inlaid table of foreign design, probably spoils of war. On it lay a handsomely bound book bright with red and green lacquered lettering and the seal of the duchy embossed in gold. Sebastian read the cover, then grabbed it up. The book contained the names and coats of arms of the noble families of Gardenia and neighboring realms. He flipped the pages, searching for his family's name. He found it stricken from the list with a bold stroke of ink. He searched the pages again, slowly, for his father's coat of arms. At last he realized the page was gone, torn out when his family fell from grace.

Sebastian closed the book bitterly, feeling damned to a life among the lower class.

He returned the book to the table and noticed a pair of thin volumes which had been hidden underneath. They were poorly copied on that new paper which was so much cheaper than parchment. The first several pages of one had been folded back. He picked it up, anxious for any diversion. He skimmed a page, then reread it carefully. He turned back the cover page to see the title. *The Pretty Peasant Maid's Cruel Master*. He picked up the other book. *Revels of a Lusty Knight*.

Hastily, he replaced both books, then stood and smoothed the bedclothes.

"Does the duchess share this chamber with the duke?" he asked, rejoining Corwyn.

"No," Corwyn said from under the table with the basin. "She has a chamber down the corridor, next to her physician and personal advisor. It's more convenient for the duke."

Sebastian thought of the two volumes and what the old woman had said about the duke's whoring. He arched his eyebrows, wondering what kind of witch the duchess must be. Probably old

and ugly, with too few teeth and too little hair but fat enough
for three normal maidens.

Corwyn crawled out from under the table and gestured to it.
"You see before you a marvel. Even though the duchess's advisor
encouraged her to substitute cheaper fittings than I had planned,
this invention still ranks as a wonder."

Sebastian looked at the table with the basin set into it. The
conduit ended above the basin in a wooden tap from a beer
barrel. A second conduit led from a hole in the bottom of the
basin back to the tower.

"Not through agriculture or government does man become a
civilized being, but by this: water flowing freely on demand,"
Corwyn said. "Only when man harnesses the vagrant waters of
the earth and channels them to his use does he truly rise above
the barbarian. My boy, you see before you the birth of true
civilization!"

Corwyn turned the spigot. The wood squeaked, opened part
way, and stuck. A gurgle from the conduit was followed by a
slight gush of water. The trickle faltered and stopped. Corwyn
tugged on the handle. The tap opened further and water flowed
out. Corwyn beamed proudly at Sebastian.

Sebastian thought of the windmills turning outside, of buckets
bringing water from the Ale River far below, of the brass tubes
wending through the castle's depths, and was awed. How could
he have doubted the sanity of the man behind such an invention?
Silently, subtly, water was being brought to man, wherever he
might live, to serve his needs. It was as if the whole of human
progress had suddenly lurched forward by some momentous
amount.

The majesty of the moment was shattered by a man's scream
from the corridor. "The jewels! Great Charlemagne, it's gobbled
the jewels!"

A woman's voice followed, rich and controlled even in distress.
"Do something, Dr. Tox. Do something!"

Corwyn ran for the door, gathering up the skirts of his robe
and racing ahead of Sebastian, who hurried to keep up. They
dashed into the corridor, then through the open door of another
chamber.

This room was small and sparsely furnished. A canopied bed
with sheets of plain linen, a few wooden stools and chairs, a
chest or two, and a simple wooden table were the only furnishings. The room looked altogether barren after the lavish decor

of the duke's chamber. Yet the stark simplicity only served to highlight the beauty of its inhabitant.

The duchess possessed that rare combination of fragile grace and childlike innocence that turns courageous men weak and foolish men eloquent. She stood unself-consciously in her white dressing gown, clutching papers of state with one hand and running fingers through her long, golden hair with the other. Her round, blue eyes were wide with concern, yet she stood composed and regal; and though she was shorter than any in the room save Corwyn, her manner was such that she towered over them all.

"Your ladyship," Sebastian breathed, bowing and wondering if she could be older than sixteen.

"Monsieur Corwyn," she said, ignoring Sebastian as she bade the alchemist rise. "You must have been sent by Providence to help us."

"I will do what I can, milady," Corwyn said. "What is the difficulty?"

The other person in the room shuffled forward, a gangly, awkward man with stringy black hair and long, bony fingers that fidgeted endlessly.

"That—that infernal thing of yours," the man stuttered, indicating a basin and flowing water tap similar to those in the duke's chamber. "It's stolen milady's jeweled necklace!"

At the sheer horror of it all, the man's hands flitted from his face to his elegant hat, then to the front of his ermine-lined coat and back to his face again. All the while, he stared at the basin as if his dreams had vanished down its drain, which in fact they had.

Sebastian studied the man. Could this be the duke? The idea of the duchess being married to such a fop was revolting!

The duchess indicated the fool with a delicate gesture. "Master Corwyn, you know my physician and personal advisor, Dr. Tox?"

Corwyn nodded, his mouth grim. "We've met, milady." He turned to the table, where water still flowed from the tap. The basin was almost full. Corwyn started toward it. "Quickly, we must turn it off."

Dr. Tox lunged at the basin ahead of Corwyn. He gave the tap a savage yank, breaking the wooden handle off and sending him tumbling backward. Water gushed all the harder from the tap.

Dr. Tox turned to Corwyn, his face pasty with fear. "This is your vile invention. Do something!"

Corwyn eyed the broken tap and the now overflowing basin. "I'm afraid you already have." He took the wooden piece from Dr. Tox and attempted to reinsert it, but the flow continued. Corwyn stood back. "You'll have to summon one of the craftsmen, milady," he said.

"But it's your invention!" Dr. Tox screamed. "You fix it!"

Corwyn shook his head. "I only designed it. Construction was handled by carpenters and smithies from town. The wooden taps resulted from changes you insisted on making to save money. I told you all parts should be brass."

Water spilled from the basin and pooled on the floor. Dr. Tox shifted from one soggy pointed slipper to another, his face purple. "You refuse to stand behind your work?"

"Not when some pompous fool interferes," Corwyn said, his fists clenched and face red.

The duchess stood in silent anguish. "Please, we have no time for this," she said at last. "We must get my necklace back."

She spoke softly, yet Corwyn and Dr. Tox reacted as if they had been slapped. Corwyn bowed apologetically while Dr. Tox bolted for the door.

"Yes, milady, it shall be done," Dr. Tox cried. "I'll summon a craftsman personally." Then he was gone, running down the corridor with the peculiar gait of a man outracing his own legs.

Corwyn and Sebastian shifted from one foot to another, gradually stepping back from the expanding pool of water. The duchess remained perfectly still, ignoring the water like some unfortunate breach of taste which threatens a social affair. Her poise seemed invincible until Sebastian looked at her eyes. Behind her youthful, wide-eyed innocence stalked unbearable terror.

She caught Sebastian staring, yet acted as if he had demonstrated no impropriety. "You must understand, monsieur, that we have to regain those jewels. They must be pawned to pay for the tournament our husband is holding next month."

Sebastian glanced at the papers the duchess still held in her hand, then at the books and other papers on the table nearby. Slowly, understanding pervaded his mind. They were financial accounts and ledgers. His eyes swept the room, seeing it anew. Other records and legal documents lay scattered about, seeming to occupy accustomed places.

The significance of the room's sparse furnishings struck him. The duchess kept the duchy's books and maintained the treasury. While the duke lived in splendor, the duchess's room was scarcely furnished. She was preparing to hock her necklace that the duke might hold his tournament. What was it the old woman in the corridor had said, that the duchess doted on her husband? And what had Corwyn said the night before about the limits of a feudal economy?

Of course the duchess was terrified, if she loved the duke so much she would go to such lengths to finance his traditions and elaborate castle, all while hiding the true costs from him. The duke probably didn't even realize the sacrifices she was making to keep Gardenia from going bankrupt.

But then what about what the hermit, Thaddeus, had said in the marketplace about vast sums being paid to keep change from reaching Gardenia?

Sebastian didn't know how this piece fit into the puzzle, nor did he care. He knew only that he had to do whatever he could to save the duchess from misery.

"I'll stop the water," he said, hurrying to the basin. "I'll save the necklace for you!"

"Sebastian, wait," Corwyn cried, jumping to intercept him.

It was too late. In his eagerness, Sebastian tried to block the flow with his palm, but the force of the water was too great. For a moment it seemed to stop, then a great spray of water shot past him. Oblivious to the duchess's cry of surprise behind him, Sebastian struggled with the flow until Corwyn dragged him loose.

"But Master Corwyn, I've got to save her necklace!"

Without a word, Corwyn turned Sebastian around. To his horror, he saw the duchess had been drenched by the spray. Her hair hung in dripping strands over her shoulders, while her dressing gown clung to her wetly, revealing her body with unseemly intimacy. Sebastian stared at her breasts, her loins, then tore his eyes away.

"I'm sorry, milady," he mumbled.

The young duchess trembled slightly, her lips pouting and her eyes filling with tears. But she did not cry. She forced herself to resume an air of calm, dignified detachment.

A handsome, grey-haired man strode into the room. He noted the flowing water, the pool on the floor, and the individuals present, then let his eyes return to the duchess, his gaze almost tangible as he lingered over her.

"*Ma chère,* how lovely you look today." His voice was suave, but his manner revealed an underlying contempt. "Your lack of attire becomes you."

Sebastian started to strike the stranger for his impertinence, then stopped as the duchess curtsied. Corwyn bowed gravely. This was the duke! Sebastian dropped to a hasty bow.

The duchess smiled at the duke despite her embarrassment. Was she so desperate for attention from her husband that she would accept humiliation at his hands? Sebastian wondered.

"*Ma chère,* we have just returned to find our library flooded," the duke said, his eyes still caressing her. "The ceiling is positively raining. This must stop or it will ruin our valuable books."

The duchess winced, and Sebastian wondered what books the duke kept in his library.

"Yes, milord," she said, curtsying again. "A craftsman has been sent for to stop the water."

"Very good, *ma chère.*"

"I should like to see your library some time if I might, milord," Corwyn said, distracting the duke from his wife's condition.

"Oh, are you also a student of the . . . the exotic in literature?" the duke asked.

"I've had an opportunity to peruse a manuscript or two in my travels. I'd be most interested in seeing how your collection compares with others I have encountered."

"*Bien*! By all means, you must see our collection. It's quite extensive. We have seventeen books."

Even as Sebastian followed their conversation, he was struck by the incongruity of the man whose appearance was so much at odds with his conduct and tastes. Where was the pillar of strength and virtue Sebastian envisioned as the ruler of Gardenia?

Water lapped at the duke's boots, making him step back. "Now is not the best time for visiting our library, however," he said, still addressing Corwyn. "Monsieur alchemist, we trust that floods will not occur frequently with this system of yours."

The duke's soft voice failed to hide the sharp edge of his intent.

"No, milord," Corwyn said. "They will not."

"*Très bien.*" The duke turned away as if they had ceased to exist.

"Milord," Sebastian called out, seizing his opportunity. "I am Sebastian, son of the former lord of L'Oignon. Might I speak with you about my family's estate—?"

"Monsieur alchemist," the duke interrupted, "when your work

brings you to our castle in the future, you will leave this . . . this . . ."

"He's my apprentice, milord."

"You will leave your apprentice in your shop where he belongs."

"Yes, milord." Corwyn bowed again.

Sebastian stood, too stunned to speak. He barely heard the duchess call out as the duke headed for the door.

"Milord? Will we be graced with your presence tonight?"

The duke let his eyes drift over his wife. "*Ma chère,* are you asking to be bedded by us?"

The duchess blushed. "*Oui,* milord. If you will."

"Perhaps we shall, *ma chère,*" the duke sneered. "Perhaps we shall."

"Thank you, milord." She curtsied again, but the duke was gone.

Enraged by his own humiliation, Sebastian found the duchess's plight a justification for his anger. He vowed to avenge her, sending a chill through him that made him shiver. He thrilled to its tingle. But the chill continued after his emotional surge faded. He looked at his feet and found them ankle-deep in cold water.

Corwyn sloshed about the room and hummed to himself, testing the depth of the flood. The pointed toes of his shoes dragged in the water at every step, and the hem of his robe floated out behind.

The door to the chamber swung open again and Dr. Tox ushered in a heavyset, stubble-faced man in a stained leather jerkin.

"Your ladyship, may I present Tom the Fat, master craftsman from Pomme de Terre?" said Dr. Tox, hurrying to keep up.

Tom the Fat ogled the duchess, but had the sense to pretend otherwise. He executed a curt bow and began whittling a stick, which he then hammered into the water pipe, plugging the hole. The water stopped; the basin slowly emptied. With a bent piece of wire he snagged an elegant jeweled necklace from the drain.

Tom the Fat handed the necklace to the duchess, who snatched it up with a cry of joy. The craftsman turned to Corwyn, smiling broadly. "This is an ingenious system of yours, monsieur alchemist. I may take up repairing it entirely. It could be much more profitable than metal working or carpentry."

Corwyn turned red and started to respond, but the duchess interrupted.

"We thank you, master craftsman," she said. "You have been
of great service to the realm."

It had the sound of dismissal, but Tom the Fat stood his
ground. "You're most welcome, your ladyship. But I'm a free-
man and a member of the guild. I should like my fee before I
go."

"You shall be adequately repaid, master craftsman. In due
time." The duchess tossed her head. "Dr. Tox, enter an appropriate amount in the ledger."

Dr. Tox sprang to one of the books on the worktable and
made an entry with a quill pen. Tom the Fat stood a moment
longer, then turned on his heel and stormed out, leaving the
door open. Corwyn propelled Sebastian through it as well, bowing and backing from the room as he pulled the door shut behind
him.

Corwyn backed right into the old hag who had earlier admitted
them to the duke's chambers.

"Cursed pipes and windmills," the woman muttered, pushing
past the alchemist with her burden of pail and rags. "Make more
work for a body and all for what, I ask you, for what?" She
stopped with her hand to the door and glared at Corwyn over a
stooped shoulder, then snorted and entered the chamber to clean
up the flood.

As Corwyn started for the stairs by which they had arrived,
Sebastian stared in the direction of the stained glass window.

"A saint," he sighed. "A perfect saint."

Corwyn looked around. "That's St. Eberhard the Unwashed,
a hermit who never bathed. Some say his success at casting out
demons resulted more from his smell than from religious devotion."

Sebastian looked in confusion at the alchemist, then shook his
head. "No, I mean the duchess. She's a saint to suffer for the
duke the way she does."

Corwyn laughed and guided Sebastian down the corridor.
"Boy, you've just been fooled by appearances again. For all her
beauty and eagerness to please a husband she didn't choose, the
duchess is no saint. She bleeds her subjects dry to pay her husband's debts. When she can wring nothing more from them she
flings them aside, sentencing them to the dungeon or death as
penalty for having nothing left for her to steal. If Tom the Fat
is wise, he won't press her for his fee." Corwyn snorted. "For

that matter, I'm beginning to doubt I'll be paid for my work here as well."

Sebastian wrenched away, appalled at this blasphemy. He could hear his father demanding action. Sebastian swung without thinking.

Corwyn reeled and clutched his face. Sebastian could only stare helplessly, shocked at what the voice in his head had goaded him into doing. Was he possessed?

"Boy, I shall forget your transgression this once," Corwyn said as he regained his composure. "But mark my words, if you ever do that again, it'll go harshly for you. Very harshly indeed!" He turned and strode down the hall.

Sebastian hurried to catch up, ashamed of facing Corwyn and afraid of being left behind. At every step, his father's voice taunted him for his weakness.

What a terrible world Sebastian had entered when he left the gates of the abbey.

As a repentant Sebastian followed Corwyn down the stairway to the castle grounds, he unknowingly passed another entity in its ascent to the reservoir high overhead.

Earlier, the wraith Sebastian encountered on the drawbridge had been swept downstream toward the Ale. The wraith lay upon the water like a vile stain. The current was too strong and turbulent for it to separate from the flow, but the creature was patient. All rivers become quiescent eventually, and a sluggish backwater near shore was all it needed to coalesce and take to the air in search of a suitable host.

But as the wraith floated past the great hall, a bucket plunged into the water and lifted the creature from the moat. The wraith traveled through the archer's slit into the tower, driven by a windmill on the tower's side. Then it was dumped into the first reservoir of Corwyn's water system.

The wraith began to congeal above the water's surface, but another bucket scooped it up and began the second stage of its journey. Eventually it reached the top of the tower, where a conduit sucked it from the reservoir. For hours it descended through a maze of tubing, dragged by occasional surges of current as one or another tap within the castle was opened and then turned off.

Corwyn and Sebastian returned to the alchemist's shop for their midday meal, then spent the afternoon collecting samples

from the Ale and initiating them into the rites of aquatic alchemy.
Daylight ebbed as night took its place. In the castle, the duchess
picked at her dinner at one end of a long table. At the other
end, the place set for the duke remained unused, and the duchess
resigned herself to another night of disappointment. The stars
emerged for their trek across the void. The duchess blew out the
candle beside her bed, extinguishing her hopes as well as the
flame. A sliver of moon cut itself free of the mountain peaks and
joined the starry sky just as the duchess's door creaked open,
then closed again. Her squeal of surprise at the duke's arrival
soon shifted to other, more urgent sounds, then trailed away
into the soft noises of sleep. The duke snored beside her and
dreamed of new conquests in the day ahead.

As the pair slept, water dripped from the broken tap. Each
drop swelled at the base of the plug, engorging until it fell with
a splat in the basin. Then another drop would take its place. But
as the cycle continued, a haze seeped from around the plug,
obscuring the drops. Like an obese, greasy vapor the haze con-
gealed until it too fell into the basin. Instead of sliding down the
drain, however, it oozed over the side and rolled onto the air.
It writhed and stretched until it reached the royal bed. A tendril
extended from the wraith toward the duke's nose.

Just before the vapor reached him, a look of terror gripped
the duke as his dream turned into a nightmare. Then the tendril
insinuated itself into his nostrils and the mist slipped inside. A
hideous grin settled on the face that once had been the duke's.

CHAPTER 6

Sign of the Reluctant Virgin

SEBASTIAN CRACKED HIS SKULL ON THE LINTEL AND STOPPED TO swear, clutching his head. The day which started out so badly had only gotten worse. He blinked back tears of pain and looked for Corwyn, who was already halfway across the crowded tavern.

The sign that had distracted Sebastian and caused his accident hung above the tavern door, showing a voluptuous woman emerging Venuslike from the sea. Her hands were positioned as if modesty directed them, but her eyes leered with anticipation. Her only reluctance was in remaining a virgin a moment longer.

Sebastian shook his head. At the abbey, his artistic education had been restricted to Biblical themes rendered in the flat, dyspeptic style of the times. Realistic art was a novelty, especially when connected with commercial endeavours such as taverns. He wondered if the woman on the sign worked at the tavern. Perhaps coming here wasn't a bad idea after all.

Inside, however, a glance around confirmed the suspicions Sebastian had formed on the street. The room was dim and smoky, and reeked of wine and sweat. Years of soot had darkened the low rafters; old straw covered the floor, littered with bones and refuse. But most intimidating were the tavern's in-

81

habitants, racked and crippled by every scourge known to man. Others, though bodily fit, bore witness to deficiencies of the spirit. Several seemed likely candidates for the ruffian free companies that terrorized the countryside. One table even appeared to be recruiting youths to join a brigand band. Peasant lads crowded around, listening to a massive, scarred ruffian and gawking at the two aging prostitutes who sat on either side. The prostitutes, their clothes inside out to show their profession, purred obscene, improbable offers to the youths.

The ruffian gave Sebastian a wink and invited him over with a wave. Sebastian looked away and tried to follow Corwyn. But people made way for the alchemist as readily here as in the streets and marketplace. For Sebastian, passage was more difficult.

He managed to get as far as the ruffian without mishap. The big man yawned and stretched a booted foot into Sebastian's path. As Sebastian stepped over, the recruiter tripped him with his scabbard. Sebastian stumbled, tried to regain his footing, and crashed into a table.

"Sang dieu! Watch out," growled one of the table's occupants as he pushed Sebastian aside.

"Hey, he spilled my wine!" another man cried. He started toward Sebastian, his face full of malice.

"Ah, shut up," said a third, dragging his companion back to the table. "Leave the boy be; you spilled your own wine half an hour ago. And it's your turn for the drinks. Are you going to buy us a round, or do me and Armand have to slice off your ears instead?"

Through it all, the ruffian recruiter laughed uproariously. The youths around his table joined in and the prostitutes guffawed with open mouths.

Sebastian reached Corwyn's table and slid onto a stool. His shoe displaced a rat which ran chittering through the straw to another table. He leaned against a post which supported the roof and sighed, his mind wandering.

On the way back from the castle that afternoon, Corwyn had stopped on the drawbridge to fill a pair of small glass bottles from the river. Sebastian held back, wary after the incident earlier.

But nothing happened this time. Corwyn and Sebastian took the bottles to the laboratory, where they used one of them for an alchemical destruction test. The other bottle they used to set up a breath of demons test.

Corwyn appeared perplexed by the initial results and sent Sebastian to take more samples from other parts of the river. Then they repeated the tests. The longer they worked, the more Corwyn frowned.

"What's wrong?" Sebastian had asked when they finished. "What do the results mean?"

Corwyn had started to reply, stopped, then said, "In a few days. We should know something definite then." He nodded as if to reassure himself, looking at the trough where bottles for the breath of demons test rested in the stream.

"But what about the other test?" Sebastian had asked. "Doesn't it tell us something now?"

Corwyn frowned. *"Oui, peut-être."* The frown deepened. "It might. I must be certain first."

He would say nothing more, despite Sebastian's attempts to question him.

Completing the tests had taken longer than expected. Oliver was still keeping out of sight, which irritated Corwyn. The alchemist relied on Oliver in setting up the tests, he explained. Sebastian, however, was relieved his introduction to Oliver was delayed again. He tried to make up for Oliver's absence by assisting Corwyn, wanting to get back into the old man's graces after striking him.

Unfortunately, his efforts were misguided, with spilled chemicals and broken glassware the result. It was after dark when they finished the tests and cleaned up the wreckage. Corwyn had announced that he, for one, could use a mug or two of wine and a bite to eat. Sebastian had agreed, but when Corwyn turned in at the sign of the Reluctant Virgin, he balked.

"I need information," Corwyn had explained. "Information I can only get in a place like this." He smiled for the first time since they'd left the castle. "Besides, I think you'll find reason enough for coming here, once we get inside. The Reluctant Virgin contains one of Gardenia's few real jewels."

"A jewel? *Voici*?" Sebastian snorted.

Corwyn's smile faded. "Not all jewels are found in golden settings, boy." He went in, leaving Sebastian to follow.

Now, from the safety of his stool at Corwyn's table, Sebastian looked around the tavern for the jewel. It must be well hidden, he decided. The men in this room would kill for such a treasure.

Corwyn turned to him suddenly. "You never told me why Father Ptomaine asked you to leave the abbey."

"I witnessed too many practices my father wouldn't have tolerated, and I became critical of the order."

Corwyn studied him. "Do you always do what your father would have done?"

"Not always." Sebastian looked away. "Sometimes I'm incapable of being the man my father was."

"He carries great weight with you, doesn't he?"

"He was a great man, worthy of esteem."

"Yet it's a grave burden to continue another man's life for him. It requires giving up your own," Corwyn said. "Would your father have been proud of having such a devoted son?"

"I'm not giving up my own life," Sebastian said angrily, avoiding the real issue Corwyn had raised. But he couldn't avoid the memories.

As a boy, it seemed he had always stood in his father's shadow, tugging on the hem of the great man's tunic in hope of being noticed. Yet when his father did notice him, it was only to chastise him for his inadequacies. Sebastian grew up knowing he lacked some mysterious quality his father expected a son to possess.

And now, Sebastian's father was with him still, as a disembodied voice in his head, and Sebastian was forever trying to appease the criticism he had heard in that voice, as a child. But he could never live up to the demands of that voice, and his failure was the source of his shame.

He shrugged. "Eventually, Father Ptomaine suggested I'd be better off somewhere else."

Corwyn stared, and for a moment Sebastian was afraid the alchemist would question him further about his father. Tears of outrage had welled in his eyes. He balled his hands into fists until his fingernails bit into his palms.

"What was so objectionable about the order?" Corwyn asked at last.

"They were more interested in accumulating wealth for the order than in spiritual growth and saving souls," Sebastian said, relaxing slightly.

"Surely it wasn't as bad as that. Isn't wealth and personal advantage what you wanted in the first place, and what you now hope to acquire through me?"

Sebastian's face went hot. "That's different. My family was unjustly deprived of its position. All I seek is to correct that wrong." He leaned back. "Besides, it's one thing for an individual to pursue wealth or earthly advantage. It's altogether

different when those pursuits become the Church's consuming
passion."

Corwyn nodded. "Perhaps you're right. The Church's obses-
sion with property and status at the expense of moral health has
caused widespread spiritual decay. It may even lead to religious
fragmentation in upcoming years."

"Fragmentation of the Holy Church?" Sebastian looked
around to see if an officer of the Inquisition might have overheard. "Surely you're not serious? It's heresy to even suggest
such a thing!"

"But isn't it already occurring on a smaller scale?" Corwyn
continued. "Isn't that what happened when you left Justienne?"

"Peut-être." Sebastian pursed his lips in thought. It was a
frightening prospect, like suggesting the world might roll off its
axis and plunge from the spheres of the cosmos.

"Do you know what novitiates call the order at Justienne?"
he asked after a time. " 'The Holy Order of Greed.' That's how
we referred to it among ourselves."

Corwyn laughed.

"You think it's funny?" Sebastian pulled a leather purse from
inside his blouse and began searching through it.

"No, no, it's all right," Corwyn said. "I wasn't laughing at
you."

"Ow!" Sebastian yanked his hand from the purse and sucked
a finger. He dumped the contents of the purse onto the table.
Out spilled a large splinter of wood, a short piece of stem from
a thorny bush, and a long, heavy iron nail, thick with rust. "Here,
look at these."

Corwyn examined each item in turn. "What are they?"

Sebastian held up the splinter. "A piece of the true cross on
which our Lord was crucified." He picked up the stem with his
other hand, holding it carefully to avoid the thorns. "A piece of
the crown of thorns He wore on His way to Calvary." He added
the nail to the items in his hands. "One of the nails by which
He was affixed to the cross."

"I see," Corwyn said, his expression neutral. "But what have
these to do with leaving the abbey?"

"The brothers of the order sell these and other relics, Master
Corwyn. No matter who your favorite saint might be, they can
produce a piece of his bones or a scrap of his clothing guaranteed
to protect you from earthly harm or spiritual tribulation. They

sell these items not only at the abbey, but all over Europe by means of wandering friars."

"Many clerics offer relics, Sebastian," Corwyn said. "Often it's done in the best of faith. But you mustn't be taken in by claims that these relics are true ones." He took the piece of wood. "This, for example, may only be—"

"A splinter from an old beam at the abbey," Sebastian interrupted. "Or it may have come from any number of other sources, things too old and broken down for any better use." He indicated the thorny stem. "We grew these bushes outside the refectory for just this purpose. And the nails came from our own smithy." He flung the items to the table. "All sold as religious relics, Master Corwyn, and not a true one in the lot!"

"Ah, I see," Corwyn said, filtering the words through his fingers as he played with his moustache. "How very, uh, enterprising of Father Ptomaine."

"Enterprising!" Sebastian sat back in disgust. "Master Corwyn, we weren't allowed to throw away the bones from meat at dinner because they could be sold as the remains of saints!"

"Father Ptomaine's zeal for increasing the wealth of the order obviously offended you."

Sebastian snorted, then withdrew from his blouse a crumpled sheet of the new material, paper. He unfolded the rough sheet lovingly and handed it to Corwyn. "Here, this is what I tried to do at the abbey."

Corwyn read the short text on the sheet. "It's a prayer, rather common. *Je ne comprends pas*. You wanted to work as a copyist or perhaps an illuminator?"

"No, no. Look at the formation of the letters." Sebastian leaned across the table to tap the sheet for emphasis. "Don't you notice anything unusual about them?"

Corwyn peered closer. "The lettering is crude, but otherwise I see nothing of significance."

"Aha! Now who's failing to see beyond superficial appearances?"

Corwyn set the paper down. "Don't gloat, boy. If you have a point, I suggest you make it."

"I'm sorry, Master Corwyn. But notice how there are irregularities in the lines unlike those in normal lettering? And the letters themselves aren't properly aligned. I didn't letter this by hand. I printed it on a press from individually assembled letters."

Corwyn looked up sharply. *"Comment?"*

"I printed this page and many more like it in minutes. I carved the letters from bits of wood and combined them to form the words."

"Amazing! I've seen printing before, of course, even as far back as my travels to Cathay. But this refinement is remarkable." Corwyn looked at the paper, then back up at Sebastian as if seeing him for the first time. "Why, this could transform the world!"

Sebastian's spirits dropped. "Well, it might have, if it was used for the right purpose. Printing could replace skilled copyists laboring for months by hand." Sebastian grabbed the sheet and waved it. "It might even have been used to print the Bible. But all Father Ptomaine wanted to do was reproduce popular prayers and bits of religious text to sell at town fairs and markets. To him, it was just one more opportunity to fill the abbey's coffers!" He slumped against the post again, defeated.

"A short-sighted view," Corwyn agreed. "Think of it—whole books printed a dozen copies at a time!"

"Father Ptomaine said no one could use that many books," Sebastian scoffed. He refolded the sheet and stuck it in his blouse, then returned the fraudulent relics to his purse. The whole time, he felt Corwyn's eyes watching him.

"Boy, I don't know what to make of you. In many ways, you seem locked within the follies of your class. Yet just when I begin to think there's no hope, you surprise me with something like this." He shook his head. "For as long as I have lived, I have yet to truly understand another human being."

Embarrassed but pleased, Sebastian turned his attention to the tavern, where a plain, middle-aged woman in a dingy apron filled mugs from a pitcher of wine. Watching her, Sebastian realized how hungry he was. "Mmmm, *un cafard*!" he exclaimed, leaning back on his stool and thinking of the ducks he had seen earlier on the river. "My, that would taste good tonight."

Corwyn grimaced and hunched forward, but a man at a table next to Sebastian spoke up before the alchemist could say anything. *"Un cafard, monsieur?"*

Sebastian eyed the man haughtily. *"Oui, un cafard sauvage,"* he replied, *"au jus."*

The man turned to his companions and elbowed one in the ribs. "Did you hear?" he cried. "The Englishman wants *cafard* for dinner." He laughed so hard tears came to his eyes and he gripped his belly. "A wild one, with gravy."

The man's companions joined in the laughter and spread the news of Sebastian's request to other tables. Corwyn sat back, a half smile playing about his lips, while Sebastian glowered. Soon, he was the focus of attention, with guffaws and stares greeting him from all parts of the tavern.

Fools, Sebastian thought. These peasants would stoop to eating frogs and snails, yet they found the idea of dining on wild duck amusing.

The man who had spoken to him leaped from his stool and scooped something from the rushes on the floor. Bowing elaborately, he stepped up to Sebastian. "*Un cafard, monsieur*," he said, and opened his hand to display a cockroach. "A wild one." Then he smacked his hand on the table in front of Sebastian, squashing the insect against the wood. "In its own juice," the man cried, laughing until he could scarcely stand. "A specialty of the house. Enjoy your dinner!"

Sebastian's haughty self-assurance crumbled under a torrent of laughter. He turned to Corwyn, who was biting his knuckles and snickering. "*Canard*," the old alchemist gasped. "That's the word you want. A duck is *un canard*. *Un cafard* is a cockroach."

Sebastian nodded curtly and thought back to the other times he'd used that word, starting with the guard at the city gate and twice more with Corwyn. Finally he understood the strange reactions his use of the word had elicited. But if the humiliation he faced from the tavern's patrons was painful, the cold fury he endured from the voice in his head was worse.

What kind of language was this, he wondered, where the word for cockroach was so similar to the word for duck? Yet he knew the real problem wasn't the language. The voice in his head assured him of that.

Sebastian's real problem was the innate deficiency he knew existed within himself.

Suddenly, the confusion stopped and attention shifted to the far end of the room. A serving maid had emerged from the kitchen with a pitcher in either hand. She moved from table to table, refilling mugs and tankards with unhurried grace. At each table she had a smile or wink for the grinning, boisterous patrons who greeted her. Her hair tumbled from a white peasant's cap in auburn waves that bounced as she walked. Patches of freckles highlighted her cheeks and her dark eyes crinkled with laughter. She wore her plain brown smock as if it was the finest dress, enhancing its simple lines with well-proportioned curves. On long legs she crossed the room in easy strides.

The noise resumed at greater volume, accompanied by whistling, stamping feet, and cries of "*Oui*, Gwen, over here, *ma chère!*" and "Ah, Gwen, how about a toss in the moonlight with me tonight?"

Sebastian found he was holding his breath. She was lovely, though in an earthier way than the untouchable beauty of the duchess. Here was the ripeness of apples, the colors of a peach, the firmness of a golden pear hanging heavy on the bough. Here was a girl, he found himself thinking, a man could hold onto.

At least for a night, he amended quickly, his father's voice reminding him of the difference between her place and that which was Sebastian's by birth. Still, highborn youths often dallied with peasant wenches for a while, though Sebastian lacked such experience.

Her route took her near the ruffian recruiter, who grinned and patted her with familiarity as she passed. Annoyance shadowed her face. She swatted his hand, much to the big man's amusement, and swept past to a more distant table.

"Ah," Corwyn said, "here is the jewel of which I spoke."

"*Monsieur* Corwyn," the serving maid cried with delight, and wound through the tables to his side. "It's been too long since last you graced our hearth."

Corwyn chuckled, smiling at her like an adoring pup. "Gwen, you're one of the few inhabitants of this town who's always pleased to see me. It warms an old man's heart."

Sebastian coughed into his fist, anxious to be noticed. This pretty wench might be just what he needed to divert his mind for a time. And maybe relieve him of his innocence.

"Patience, boy, I'll get to you," Corwyn growled. "Gwen, meet my new apprentice, Sebastian."

She smiled.

Sebastian, still smarting after the incident with the cockroach and goaded by his father's voice, leered at the girl. "Looks like hard work," he said, pointing to the pitchers.

"*Oui.*" She set one down and brushed hair from her face. "They're a thirsty lot."

She certainly was comely. Sebastian could almost feel her in his arms. He mimicked the casual intimacy of the tavern's other clients and asked, "Do you have any time of your own after you're through serving here?"

She laughed. "When I finish here at night, all I want is to go to bed."

Excitement surged through Sebastian at the implication of her words. *"Délicieux!* Then perhaps I might keep you company and warm your bed tonight?"

The corners of her mouth turned down. She glanced at Corwyn, then back to Sebastian. "I'll have Mama bring you wine and something to eat." She walked away, ignoring the cries around her.

Sebastian turned to Corwyn. "Did I say something wrong?"

A slap was his only answer. The alchemist's hand was thin with age, but it struck with surprising force. Sebastian lurched to one side and the stool toppled beneath him.

He righted the stool and sat back down, filled with rage. "Why'd you do that?"

"Fool!" Corwyn hissed. "Arrogant young idiot! As well throw pearls before swine as introduce her to you. She's a rare treasure, but why should I expect you to recognize that!"

He turned to stare sullenly across the room.

Sebastian looked the other way, the voice in his head thundering with rage. Why had Corwyn and the girl been offended? She was only a serving wench. She must be used to such offers, and probably accepted them often enough. Besides, how often does a peasant girl get to sleep with a noble?

His reflections were interrupted as the middle-aged woman plunked mugs on the table and hurried away with promises of food to follow.

Sebastian drank heartily, then started to resume his thoughts. But again he was interrupted, this time by a blast of air from the door. A tall, gaunt man insinuated himself into the room.

The newcomer was dressed in worn cloth and leather. He pulled his wide hat brim low, encasing his face in shadows. The fire on the hearth flickered from the blast of air, making shadows leap on the wall as if he were pursued by demons.

He closed the door and studied the room, his eyes glittering in the hollow darkness under his hat. Most of the tavern's clients turned away, pretending not to notice. The giant recruiter grunted and nodded. The stranger returned the nod as if acknowledging a fellow professional. Then he slipped to a table near enough to the fire for warmth, but far enough away to keep his face in shadow, and sat facing the door.

"String John," Corwyn murmured. "I must talk with him."

Before Sebastian could ask who String John was, Corwyn was gone. He spoke to the traveler, who nodded to an empty stool across the table. Corwyn sat hunched over the table to keep the conversation low.

Through it all, String John's eyes kept scanning the room, as if any corner might harbor treachery.

Sebastian tried to overhear, but they were too quiet. Suddenly he became aware of someone standing beside him.

It was the middle-aged serving woman.

"What do you want?" Sebastian demanded, his voice gruff to cover being startled.

The woman twisted her apron nervously. "Nothing, *monsieur*, it isn't really anything, and I probably shouldn't even mention it, except I noticed there's something special about you. An air, perhaps. Like maybe you're somebody important after all, and I thought that maybe you should know."

Sebastian straightened self-consciously, pleased she recognized his true status. "Know what?"

The woman leaned forward. "It's about her," she whispered, tilting her head to indicate Gwen who was serving String John.

It irritated Sebastian to have that wench brought up again. "What about her?"

"She's not what she appears." The woman paused and straightened. "Might I sit with you a while, *monsieur?*"

"I suppose." Sebastian indicated Corwyn's stool. "What do you mean, not what she appears? Who is she?"

"You're not what you appear, either, I'll warrant," the woman said with coy grandeur. "I think you're a nobleman."

"True," Sebastian said. "You're to be commended on your perception. Would that others were as astute as you."

"Huh?"

"Get on with it."

The woman recollected herself. "Well, it's about Gwen, *monsieur*. She also is noble." The woman leaned back and added archly, "Her lineage may be even better than yours."

Sebastian jerked back, then laughed. "What nonsense is this?"

The woman pressed her lips tight and straightened her apron. "Perhaps I shouldn't say. A gentleman wouldn't laugh."

She waited for him to urge her on, but Sebastian was tiring of her game. "If you shouldn't say, then don't."

"Oh, but I'm sure you won't tell anyone. Her secret would be safe with you, wouldn't it, *monsieur?*"

Sebastian stared until the woman flinched. *"Eh bien!"* she said petulantly. "Gwen's a lady of nobility, a princess."

Sebastian frowned and turned away.

"But she is, *monsieur*," the woman insisted, plucking at his arm. "I'm not her real mother, I just raised her. She was left with us when she was very young, for her own protection. All of her family was slain save her, and her life would be worthless now if the truth were ever known."

In spite of himself, Sebastian leaned forward again, thinking of the turmoil of the past seventy years. Long, bloody struggles for control of France had destroyed several powerful families. "Was it a fight over who should inherit a title? Is she heir to one of the great baronies?"

The woman nodded.

"Which family is she from?"

The woman hesitated. "I'd best not tell. I've said too much already."

"Pardieu! You can't stop now! Who's her family? What's her rightful title?"

The woman glanced around and spotted Corwyn returning. She stood hurriedly.

"But wait . . ."

"Not now," she whispered. "Another time."

Before Sebastian could object, she was gone. Corwyn resumed his seat, looking from Sebastian to the departing woman. "What did Old Meg want?"

Sebastian started to tell him, then changed his mind. Corwyn undoubtedly knew. That was why he favored Gwen, and why he'd been furious when Sebastian invited himself to her bed.

Cold horror swept Sebastian as he realized what he'd done. He'd behaved frightfully toward a lady of nobility, a lady who'd had to endure peasant life to keep from being slain.

A princess, the woman said!

How could he have been so stupid? Sebastian heard his father demand. He dropped his head in shame. "She didn't want anything," he mumbled. "Just chatting, that's all." He forced a smile.

Corwyn stared, but let the matter drop.

"What were you and String John talking about?" Sebastian asked to change the subject. "Did you find what you wanted to know?"

Corwyn shrugged. "Maybe. I'm not sure. I asked if he'd seen

anything unusual in the duchy recently, anything out of place."

"Had he?"

"A pair of peasants have been leading mule trains through the mountains at night. Nobody knows what they're hauling or who it's for. The strange thing is, they're never bothered by brigands, although free companies sometimes roam the area."

"Why's that important?"

"Because wherever these two pass, people behave strangely afterwards."

Sebastian gasped. "*La peste . . . ?*"

The alchemist nodded.

"*Morbleu!* Who are these two?"

"String John didn't know, but he's finding out. He'll bring me word here tomorrow."

"How odd," Sebastian said. "Thaddeus said someone was interfering with Gardenia, though that involved payments in gold to help the duke maintain control and prevent change in the duchy."

Corwyn looked perplexed and fell silent.

Old Meg served them, curtsying and twisting her apron as though she feared for her life. They ate in silence, lost in separate thoughts. As they finished, Gwen again approached. Her smile had returned, but she ignored Sebastian. "*Monsieur* Corwyn, I hope you won't stay away so long this time before you return."

"Ah, Gwen, *ma chère,* you know how to keep an old man coming back. But it's only been a week since last I was here."

She pouted prettily. "I'm sure it's been longer."

"You'd pretend it was even if I'd eaten here at midday."

She grinned. "Try it and see."

"Perhaps I shall, *ma chère.* Perhaps I shall."

She started to leave. Sebastian couldn't bear for her to depart still angry with him. "Gwen, wait," he cried.

She half turned, questioning.

"Milady, I'm sorry." He bowed. "I didn't know."

Gwen looked from Sebastian to Corwyn and back, her eyes wide. "What do you mean?"

Just then, a voice thundered through the room, distracting Gwen with a demand for wine. Sebastian dropped to his knee to regain her attention and grasped her hand. "Your highness, can you forgive me?" he whispered, kissing her fingers.

She wrenched back her hand as if bitten. "Do you mock me, apprentice?"

"Mock you? Why, no, milady, I would never mock you—"

"I said, more wine!" demanded the voice, louder this time.

Gwen glanced over Sebastian's shoulder. "Why're you doing this to me? Get up, I beseech you." She tugged at his sleeve, her attention vacillating between Sebastian and the man calling for drink.

"Hey, *ma chérie*, are you deaf?" came the voice. "I want wine! And then you can sit on my lap to keep me company while I drink." He laughed, sending titters through the tavern.

"Oh!" Gwen cried. "Why doesn't Mama get it?" She looked for the older woman, then bolted toward the voice.

For once, Sebastian's own instincts matched the voice in his head. He grabbed her.

"Let go!" she hissed, pushing his arm.

"No, milady." Here was a chance to make both his father and Gwen proud of him. He got to his feet. "Let me take care of this. To convince you of my sincerity."

Gwen hesitated. Without waiting for an answer, Sebastian turned to confront the speaker.

It was the ruffian recruiter. The man grinned—a hideous expression. "Ah, *l'anglais*. Did you enjoy your fresh *cafard*?" He lumbered to his feet, stooping to avoid the low ceiling. The two prostitutes and nearby patrons scurried for cover.

Sebastian sucked in a breath. His heart beat with something other than courage. Why couldn't it have been anyone but the ruffian? he wondered to himself. But he forced himself to walk toward the hulking fighter.

He stopped a few paces away and hunched his shoulders, rocking onto the balls of his feet. Then he sidestepped, studying the man for weakness.

The giant laughed and turned lazily. He didn't bother to take a fighting stance.

Part of Sebastian's shame was that he'd never excelled in the martial arts of knighthood. He'd never been even moderately adept, and laughter from his Saxon cousins had frequently chased him from the practice field, a fact which his unseen voice never let him forget.

Now, his old Scottish fighting instructor's oft-repeated advice came to mind: "When ye're outmanned, laddy, yer best course is to strike first, hard and fast."

Sebastian dove under the man's elbows and pummeled his massive belly with both fists.

It was like pounding on rock.

The ruffian laughed and pushed Sebastian back. *"Eh bien!* Now it's my turn." He feinted with one shoulder, then swung at Sebastian with the opposite fist. Sebastian flung up an arm to ward off the blow.

The recruiter's fist slammed into Sebastian's forearm, smashing both fist and arm into his face. Sebastian sprawled across a table—which collapsed, throwing him to the floor amid spilled food and drinks.

He sat up and shook his head. A smear of blood glistened where his arm had struck his face. But the pain was nothing compared to the disgrace he felt.

Several men pulled Sebastian to his feet and pushed him toward the ruffian. The ruffian grinned and motioned him forward. "Now it's your turn again, *anglais.* You hit me."

Shakily, Sebastian brushed food from his clothes. Beneath his blouse, the fake relics pressed against his chest.

Another piece of advice from his fighting instructor flashed into Sebastian's head. "If all else fails, and ye canna run away, dinna be afeared to cheat."

Sebastian thrust out his hands, fingers spread. *"Attenez vous!* I concede."

The recruiter's grin widened.

"At least, this part of the fight," Sebastian added quickly, reaching inside his blouse for the purse.

The man's grin faded. "What do you mean, this part?"

Sebastian leaped to a nearby table and grabbed two platters. Ignoring the protests from the men at the table, he dumped the remnants of their meal on the floor and held the platters aloft.

"I challenge you to an eating contest," he cried so all could hear. "The one who finishes first wins the fight."

The recruiter eyed Sebastian with disbelief. "Not eating cockroaches, I hope."

Sebastian shook his head and hurried to another table where he grabbed a loaf of bread.

The ruffian's grin returned, splitting his massive face. *"Eh bien, anglais,* what do you have in mind?"

Sebastian broke off two hunks of bread and placed them on the platters, making sure everyone in the tavern could see.

What they couldn't see was the wooden splinter Sebastian had palmed. Under cover of his other movements, he shoved the splinter into one of the hunks of bread.

He carried the platters to another table and hacked two pieces from a wheel of cheese. As he placed the cheese on the platters, he surreptitiously pushed the thorny stem into one of the pieces.

The cheese was followed by a portion of meat apiece, with the nail going inside one portion. Then Sebastian crossed to the recruiter, offering him a platter.

The recruiter looked at the platter Sebastian was presenting him, then at the one closer to Sebastian's chest.

"This one's got bigger pieces," he growled, pushing it aside.

Several patrons shouted their support, objecting that the first platter *did* hold larger portions. The ruffian waved them to silence and grabbed the second platter with its smaller portions. "I'll take this one instead."

"Very well," Sebastian said. "The first one finished wins." He started cramming food in his mouth, keeping an eye on the ruffian.

The recruiter shoved the entire hunk of bread in his mouth and began chewing. He paused when he hit the splinter, then went on more slowly. "Thish bread hash quite a crusht," he mumbled through a full mouth.

Even after slowing, the ruffian finished his bread ahead of Sebastian. He shoved the cheese into his mouth and bit down. The thorns made him wince, but he kept chewing. "Well aged," he said. "I like a cheese with bite."

The ruffian and Sebastian grabbed for their meat at the same time, urged on by roars from the crowd. Again, the ruffian's piece went in whole. A loud crunch sounded as he closed his mouth. The ruffian held his jaw with one hand and struggled to chew and swallow the nail.

"*Sang dieu*, what a bone!" he gasped, swallowing his portion just behind Sebastian. He reached into his mouth and withdrew a broken tooth while the crowd cheered Sebastian. Stunned by defeat, the ruffian stumbled to his table and stared at the tooth in his hand.

Sebastian belched and grinned, striding toward Gwen and Corwyn. Gwen gasped when she saw his face. "You're hurt. Sit down and let me look at you." She lifted a corner of her apron to wipe away the blood.

"It's nothing," he said, more satisfied than he had ever felt in his life. "I'm all right." But he let her minister to his wounds, enjoying the feel of her fingers.

"No one's ever risked his life over me before," she said, sounding pleased.

Sebastian bowed. "It's an honor to fight for you, your highness."

Gwen stared at him with round, hurt eyes. "You are callous after all, *monsieur*. And cruel. Why do you hate me?"

"But milady, I don't hate you," Sebastian protested. He knelt again, wincing in pain.

She shook her head. "Yet you must despise me, to humiliate me so." She fled to the kitchen.

Sebastian turned to Corwyn, who watched with a questioning frown. "What did I say that upset her?"

Corwyn didn't answer as he hastened Sebastian out into the chilly night. Sebastian moved slowly as they walked back toward the alchemist's shop, his body aching.

"Sebastian, where did all that nonsense come from, with you treating Gwen as if she were a lady?"

"Meg told me. She said Gwen's a princess," Sebastian said, staring at the cobblestones. "But you already knew that, Master Corwyn."

Corwyn stopped. "Old Meg said what? And what do you mean, I already knew?"

"You told me Gwen was a jewel, a treasure. You knew she was really a princess, hiding to save her life. I just didn't understand at first."

Corwyn sucked his teeth unconsciously as he considered Sebastian's words. At last he resumed walking. "Old Meg told you that, did she?"

Sebastian nodded.

"And when you heard it, you realized Gwen really was someone special?"

Sebastian nodded again.

"That made her important, didn't it? Important in a way she couldn't be otherwise?"

"Of course," Sebastian said, looking at Corwyn in surprise. "She doesn't belong in that tavern. If it wasn't for the danger, she'd be living among nobility as befits her station."

"Like you," Corwyn said.

"Yes, like me. Not that I don't appreciate being your apprentice, Master Corwyn," he added hastily. "This is important if I'm ever to regain what's rightfully mine. But if there were justice, I wouldn't be condemned to live as I am, and neither would Gwen. We were born to better than this."

"I see." Corwyn increased his pace and said nothing more. Stealing a glance at him, Sebastian was surprised by the hurt look on the old man's face.

They walked in silence, the night air stimulating after the closeness of the tavern. Sebastian sighed, realizing how embarrassing it must be for Gwen to have someone remind her of her true position and the degradation to which she had descended to save her life. Then a frightening thought struck him—perhaps he had endangered her. What if someone saw him bow to her, heard the way he addressed her? What if they were even now taking word to her enemies?

Fool! The word roared in his skull, and Sebastian hung his head as he realized that his unthinking actions could cost Gwen her life. If she died now, his father's memory assured him, it would all be Sebastian's fault.

CHAPTER 7

Strangers in the Night

"A DRAUGHT OF *KAWPHY* WOULD BE GOOD ON A NIGHT LIKE this," Corwyn said as he bolted the shop door behind them.

"Excellent idea, Master Corwyn," Sebastian said, shivering with cold and misery. "But tonight only half a mug for me. I don't want to repeat last night's error."

Corwyn went to the table and began assembling his notes. Sebastian stood uncertainly, wondering when Corwyn was going to brew the drinks.

"What're you waiting for?" Corwyn asked at last. "Get started."

"Oh," Sebastian said, flustered. "*Oui, monsieur. Tout de suite!*" He busied himself with the ingredients, hoping his red face wouldn't show.

As Sebastian ground the dark, aromatic beans into powder, Corwyn came to observe his technique.

"Master Corwyn, I know very little about you," Sebastian ventured as he worked. He risked a sideways look at the alchemist. "Would you tell me about yourself?"

"What do you want to know?"

"Where were you born? How did you come to study alchemy? And what brought you to Pomme de Terre?"

Corwyn examined the powder, then sat on a stool. "Inquisitive, aren't you?"

Sebastian didn't answer. He was aware of having disappointed Corwyn at the tavern, and hoped that showing an interest in the old man would return him to his master's good graces. Besides, something about the alchemist genuinely intrigued Sebastian.

"Well, curiosity is a good attribute in an alchemist," Corwyn went on. "And natural in any apprentice. *Très bien!*" He checked the water Sebastian was heating, then leaned back.

He had been born in Britain, Corwyn explained, at the beginning of the Roman withdrawal. His father, a scribe for an imperial magistrate, anticipated the disorder which would follow and moved the family to Rome, then Alexandria, where Corwyn grew up amid men and women of learning. Later, he studied at the great University of Alexandria, helping combine Greek philosophy with Egyptian technology to create alchemy, or *chemeia* as it was known. Corwyn had tried to introduce a practical, experimental approach to this new science, but in this his efforts were rejected by his colleagues.

Then the university had been destroyed and one of the last flickers of learning in the ancient world went out. Corwyn had fled to his native Britain, where he came under the influence of the last Druids and Celtic thought. Their reverence for the natural world altered his view of alchemy, making its overall goal—perfecting all things according to their essence—more specific. His focus narrowed to perfecting the natural surroundings, especially water, to the highest potential.

After finally differing with the Druids over the matter of Arthur, Corwyn left Britain for Arabia, where the rise of Islam had brought a return of learning. The Moslems were receptive to alchemy, as well as to other ancient arts, and Corwyn was appointed by the caliph to teach at the University of Baghdad. Later, when interest in learning revived in Europe, he wandered north, translating Arabic texts into Latin and Greek. But his own efforts had long since shifted from traditional alchemy, and he remained convinced that water was the most important element of the four. He had therefore modified the three goals of alchemy to fit the needs of aquatic applications.

"What three goals?" Sebastian asked, removing the beaker of water from the flame and adding the powder.

"Conventional alchemists seek a substance which will turn base metals into gold and silver, a method of curing all bodily ills, and a means of conferring immortality. I merely found suitable parallels in my own field. I seek a substance which will instantly transmute polluted water into drinkable water, and a universal analytical procedure for measuring any aquatic contaminant or characteristic."

"What about the third goal?"

Corwyn grinned. "Ah, for the third goal, I seek a means of prolonging financial support from my patrons indefinitely."

Sebastian handed Corwyn a mug of *kawphy,* wondering whether his master was serious or jesting. He poured half a mug for himself, adding cream until it was white and the mug nearly full. He gave it a couple of dollops of honey and tasted it, made a face, then took a hefty slurp from the mug. All the while, he studied Corwyn.

The face was ageless, lined and white bearded like an old man's, but with the sparkling eyes of someone younger. His hands were much the same—lined and spotted, yet deft and firm.

"But you can't be that old, Master Corwyn," Sebastian blurted at last. "Why, you'd have to be ancient!"

"I am," Corwyn said.

"How can you be?"

Corwyn's grin faded. "In Alexandria, when I was already an old man, a visitor came to the university. He was a scholar from the east, and had received from his master, Pao Pu Tzu, an elixir capable of bestowing immortality. Before leaving, he gave a vial of this elixir—enough to prolong one person's life—to the head of the university in appreciation for use of the library. The head of the university, a colleague and friend of mine, shared the potion with me, though neither of us believed the stranger's tale. We considered it a pleasant distraction from the concerns that pressed upon us in those times." Corwyn's eyes sought something long past and sadness crept into his voice. "Years later I traveled east to Cathay, searching for the scholar who had visited Alexandria. I never found him. I'm not certain he survived the journey back to his home."

Corwyn's voice dropped. Sebastian strained to make out the words. The fire, which had crackled fiercely when they arrived, glowed softly as the embers died. Shadows climbed down from distant corners of the ceiling, claiming the vast room for their own. Sebastian sipped his drink, the sound startlingly loud in the receding light.

"What happened to him?" he asked. "Your friend in Alexandria, I mean."

"Her," Corwyn said, and for a time it seemed that was all he would say.

"She was a woman, intelligent and beautiful. Hypatia was her name. At thirty, she headed the greatest academy of learning the ancients produced. A brilliant mathematician, astronomer, and physicist, she was leader of the Neoplatonic school of philosophy. But she was lonely and beset by enemies. We were going to drink the potion and spend the rest of time together. My age worried her, and she was afraid I'd die before her, as well I might have, leaving her truly alone amid her enemies in a deteriorating society.

"Over the next few years, neither of us grew older and we realized the truth of the elixir. We joked to ourselves, wondering since we had shared the contents meant for one person, what half of forever would be. You see, I can expect to die sometime, as all mortals can. But what's half of immortality?

"But for my lovely Hypatia, the end was near. Even an elixir of eternal life cannot stand before acts of violence. When parishioners of Cyril, Archbishop of Alexandria, pulled her from her chariot and stripped her flesh from her bones, they killed not only the one woman I've ever truly loved, but they also quenched the flame of learning in the West for three hundred years."

Sebastian let the remnants of heat from his mug seep into his skin. "I'm sorry," he said at last.

Corwyn shook his head with a wan grin. "That was long ago. I must be getting truly old at last to slip back through the centuries that way." He slapped his knees and held out his mug. "That was good, Sebastian. I'll have another."

Sebastian leaped from his stool, pleased by the compliment. "Tell me, has there been no one then, no friend or companion to share the years with you?" he asked, pouring more hot water through the sodden powder he'd used earlier. The aroma of the brew drifted on the air, but not as pungent this time.

Corwyn watched water drip through the filter. "There has been one," he said. "For a long time after Hypatia's death and the collapse of the university of Alexandria, I was very lonely. My friends and colleagues were dead and there was no one to share the joys and frustrations of my work. But I acquired considerable skill during those years. At last, I resolved to create a life, a creature who'd be a friend and companion." He paused, then added, "I'm not sure I did the right thing."

The shadows grew ominous and oppressive. Sebastian hunched closer to the dying fire, his eyes peering into the gloom. "Oliver," he whispered.

"*Oui*, poor Oliver," Corwyn said, taking a sip from his mug.

"But where is he? When will I see him?"

Corwyn smiled. "When he's ready, he'll appear. I'm sure he's watching, making up his mind about you. He's slow to trust. You'll understand when you meet him."

"*Pourquoi*? Is he some kind of monster?" Sebastian laughed, but it came out shrill in the advancing gloom.

"Don't ever say that!" Corwyn hissed. Sebastian jumped, startled at the alchemist's intensity. "Whatever your feelings on meeting him, guard yourself well. He's terribly sensitive and quick to take offense. Despite his years, he's a child confronted by a hostile world. So take care what you say and never underestimate his abilities."

Sebastian nodded, still peering around the room. "He's deformed, huh? Don't worry, I won't say anything."

"Not so much deformed as aberrant. But you'll see." Then, resuming his normal voice Corwyn asked, "How did you manage that eating contest?"

Self-consciously Sebastian began telling him about the relics hidden in the ruffian's food. Then, as Corwyn chuckled, he went on with enthusiasm. Finally, both men were laughing too hard to speak.

"Well done, my boy," Corwyn gasped at last. "That's probably the best use to which those relics have ever been put."

Sebastian sobered. "I wish Gwen saw it that way. Something made her angry. Perhaps she prefers champions who can win an honest fight."

"Perhaps she doesn't want a champion at all," Corwyn said. "Perhaps she'd prefer a companion who accepts her as she is."

"Oh, I could never presume such familiarity with someone of her status," Sebastian said.

"Don't sell yourself short," Corwyn said, "or place her on too exalted a level. It gets lonely that high up. Even a princess wants a warm, caring man beside her in her battles, a man who respects her as his equal."

"But I'm not! At least not yet, though I hope eventually to be."

Corwyn shrugged. "You may be closer than you realize, boy. Reminds me of a woman I once knew who claimed to be the sultan's niece." With that, Corwyn launched into a wildly improbable tale of intrigue and adventure in the Arabian deserts. The woman, although beautiful and seemingly of royal blood, turned out to be a commoner. In the end, however, she fell in love with and married the sultan's favorite warrior. Sebastian only half believed the story, but was absorbed by it nonetheless.

For a while the room seemed friendly again. Sebastian even forgot Oliver, watching from the shadows. He and Corwyn laughed and joked and traded lies until Sebastian's eyelids drooped and their conversation was punctuated by his yawns.

"My young apprentice, you'd best be off to bed," Corwyn said at last. "Even youth needs sleep sometimes."

Sebastian nodded and stumbled toward the vaulted passage, taking up a candle to light his way. He paused to watch Corwyn open his book of alchemical analyses. "What about you? Don't eleven-hundred-year-old men need sleep?"

Corwyn smiled sadly. "Sometimes the dreams of eleven-hundred-year-old men are best avoided."

Sebastian nodded and went out.

Shadows shifted eerily on the stone walls as his candle flickered in the vagrant drafts. He gripped the candle holder tightly, sweating despite the chill. He was fully awake now, his mind alert to imaginary horrors.

So terrified did he become that it was some time before he noticed a dry, swishing sound, barely audible in the still air, that followed him in the corridor.

Sebastian stopped to listen. The sound stopped, too. He started walking again slowly, straining to hear over the roar of his breathing and the pounding of his heart.

The rustling resumed, just out of sight. Sebastian walked faster. The sound continued, maintaining its distance. When he slowed and finally stopped again, the sound also stopped.

Summoning his courage, Sebastian forced his feet toward the sound.

After a moment's hesitation, the sound retreated. Something flickered at the edge of visibility in the weak candlelight. Before Sebastian's eyes could bring form to it, the thing was gone. He walked faster. The stranger matched his pace in retreat.

Sebastian ran, the candle guttering in the wind. Suddenly, he burst into the main room of the laboratory.

Corwyn half rose from his stool in surprise. Sebastian sought wildly for his prey. At first he saw nothing; then a movement caught his eye.

The improbability of what stood before him, wavering in indecision, almost made his mind reject what his eyes perceived.

It was a gnarled stalk of wood, chest high to Sebastian and sporting a pair of withered branches, each of which ended in a cluster of twigs. Its base was swathed with brush.

Sebastian stared.

"Ah, at last you two meet," Corwyn said as he approached.

"This is Oliver?"

"Of course. Oliver, shake hands with Sebastian."

There was a moment's hesitation, then one of the branchlike appendages raised, the twigs stretched toward Sebastian.

Sebastian kept his own hand at his side. "Shake hands? With that?"

"Sebastian," Corwyn hissed, "remember what I told you."

Fear suddenly melted in a wave of relief. Sebastian burst out laughing. "Why, it's nothing but a broom!"

The proffered branch froze. The stalk began to tremble. "Oliver, no," Corwyn commanded, but the creature sprang away and ran down the passage, the brush at its base rustling as it swept the thing away.

"Sebastian, how could you do that?" Corwyn said. "I warned you. Now you've hurt his feelings."

"But it's only an old broom," Sebastian insisted, suddenly angry. He'd been terrified by an abomination which turned out to be a broom, then chastised by an odd little man who claimed to be eleven hundred years old, all after defending an ungrateful princess from a giant. He felt tired and foolish and ached all over.

What madness had he fallen into?

Without another word, he stalked down the corridor. "Sebastian, wait," Corwyn called, but Sebastian ignored him.

He had better things to do than play the fool in this diabolical comedy. Tomorrow he'd return to the abbey. If Father Ptomaine wouldn't have him back, he'd figure out something else to do. After all, he was young and healthy. He'd survive. But it wouldn't be here.

His anger still burned hot as he tramped up the stairs to his room, but his thoughts were eventually interrupted by rustling just around the bend. This time, he didn't even pause. "Oh, come on out, Oliver. I'm not afraid of you." He held the candle higher as he continued around the spiral stairwell.

A flurry of twigs and brush exploded in his face. Sebastian stumbled backward, fighting to keep his balance on the precarious steps. One hand clung to the candle while the other scrabbled at the wall for support.

Pressing his advantage, Oliver dove between Sebastian's legs, catching Sebastian behind one ankle. Oliver flung himself around to clip the other ankle, prying Sebastian's feet from the step. For one dizzying moment, Sebastian was aware of the candle flying away into darkness behind him while his arms beat the air to no effect. Slowly he fell backward into the depths.

His initial terror was quickly overcome by pain and disorientation as he tumbled down the stairs. At last he came to a stop at the base of the tower. Blackness pressed around him. The candle, somewhere on the stairs, had blown out in the fall.

Sebastian shifted to a sitting position, checking his limbs for breaks. Fortunately, nothing seemed broken—nothing but his self-esteem.

After his breathing slowed, he began crawling up the stairs. He didn't dare stand upright in his present condition. Several times he stopped to rest, wondering if some spell had transformed the stairs into an endless passageway.

At some point, he heard Oliver again in the dark, coming down the stairs ahead. Sebastian dropped flat, protecting his face from attack with his arms. But there was only a brief flurry of brush over one hand as Oliver scurried past.

"I'll get you, Oliver," he shouted after the creature. "I'll chop you into kindling and use you to start a fire!"

His threat was full of confidence, but even after he had bolted his door behind him, he felt no better.

A man he could face, he told the voice in his head. But how did one fight the fury which inhabited that broom?

While Sebastian crawled up the darkened stairwell, and while the duchess's water tap seeped something more sinister than water, two other figures stealthily made their way through the darkness. Hand over hand, the pair scaled a steeply angled rope across the moat and up the side of the duke's great hall.

The smaller figure in front climbed as effortlessly as a rat.

Behind, a larger man heaved himself up the rope, grunting with effort. The only other sounds came from the creaking of windmills and the splash of buckets scooping up water for the long journey to the top of the tower.

The two stopped once, waiting for a guard to pass on his rounds along the castle wall some thirty feet away. When it was safe, the pair resumed climbing.

At last they neared the crenellated top of the great hall, where the rope ended in a grappling hook wedged between two merlons. The smaller man looped an arm through the opening of the crenel to secure himself and stopped. He didn't look down and he made no effort to pull himself up onto the stone wall. His instructions had been to climb to the top of the rope. That done, he waited.

The heavy man did look down. His heart pounded and his stomach turned to ice when he saw how high they had climbed, but he forced himself to keep looking until he spotted a small leaded window in the wall a few feet below and to one side of him.

Panic turned to anger as he realized the window was out of reach. "Now look what you've done," he complained to the smaller man. "We're too far away. It's all your fault."

The small man said nothing. Of course it was his fault. Mistakes always were, as Kwagg was quick to point out. Successes, however, were always Kwagg's doing. So the small man ventured no opinion, simply waiting for instructions.

"Don't just hang there, Meier," Kwagg hissed. "Turn around so you can lower me to the window."

Meier swung his feet over the crenel and stretched full length upon the rope until he could just reach Kwagg. Kwagg turned around so Meier could reach his feet. It was tricky work and started the rope swinging dangerously. At last, Kwagg was in position, hanging headfirst down the rope. He closed his eyes and tried to ignore the moat below. "Now grab my feet," he called over his shoulder.

The small man complied, gripping Kwagg's boots with both hands.

"All right, hang on," Kwagg said. "I'm letting go."

He released the rope and swung toward the wall. The effect was like letting go of a pendulum at the top of its arc. Kwagg, suspended from the rope by the smaller man, smashed against the stones with a sickening thud. For a time he hung motionless, then shook himself weakly, pulling his blouse loose. It fell away from his belt to hang down over his head.

"You're going to catch it for that," Kwagg muttered, the sound muffled by the shirt around his face. "Just see if you don't! Slamming me into the wall like that."

Despite the threat, the small man was relieved to find Kwagg conscious. He watched anxiously as Kwagg inched across the stone wall toward the window. Kwagg was heavy. The smaller man's arms and shoulders ached from holding him, and his feet, which anchored them to the battlements, were numb.

Meanwhile Kwagg, blinded by the inverted shirt, could navigate only by the faint glow of candlelight from the window. He crawled over the face of the stone wall like some fat, upside-down spider until he reached the panes. He tapped on the glass, hoping the occupant in the room was alone.

The occupant was alone, and none too happy about it. Dr. Tox sat miserably at his desk, ostensibly studying the book before him. But his mind was filled with lust for the duchess and resentment toward the duke for displacing him from her bed tonight. Not that Dr. Tox had ever been able to insinuate himself into the duchess's bed, but he always had hope. As her ladyship's closest confidant and personal physician, it was only right that he, Dr. Tox, should be the one to comfort her through the night.

It was all the fault of that alchemist, Corwyn! If it hadn't been for that water system of his, and the flood which brought the duke to the duchess's room, Dr. Tox might have had the chance to achieve his dearest ambition by sharing her bed this night.

His thoughts were interrupted by a noise from the window. A shirt fluttered outside like some ghostly moth. Then it raised a spectral arm and tapped on the windowpanes.

A chill ran up Dr. Tox's spine and raised the hairs along his neck. He crossed himself and muttered a Hail, Mary, then threw in a curse against evil.

"Dr. Tox," the thing at the window wailed. "Dr. Tox, are you there?"

Dr. Tox approached the window on unwilling feet and flung it open.

The apparition twisted violently. "Dr. Tox, is that you? Blast, I can't see a thing!"

"Kwagg?" Relief flooded Dr. Tox like hot spiced wine. "What are you doing? Where's Meier?"

The shirt pointed skyward. "Up there," came the muffled voice. "Holding my feet."

Poking his head out, Dr. Tox saw Meier silhouetted against the starry sky.

"You two shouldn't be here," he said. "You're supposed to be in Spain. The next shipment isn't due for a fortnight."

"The schedule's changed," said Kwagg. "Got a letter for you here someplace." The shirt arms fumbled at the big man's belt pouch overhead. "We'll be bringing loads more often."

"But you can't!" Dr. Tox whined. "I'm already having trouble covering for you. Somebody's going to get suspicious. That alchemist's a problem as it is. We have to stick to the schedule."

"The schedule be hanged," Kwagg snarled. "Or Monsieur Phobius may hang you instead." He thrust the letter at the wall, thinking he was handing it to Dr. Tox.

Dr. Tox leaned out to take the soiled, wadded sheet and read it in disbelief. "You mean . . . this comes straight from Hydro Phobius?"

"Look at the seal," Kwagg said. He tried to wave at the letter, unaware he was pointing across the moat instead. "Phobius wants to take a closer look at things in Gardenia. Wants to know where all the money's going that he pays the duke to keep up this charade.

"He says people in Gardenia are getting awful restless for change, and that isn't what he wants. Let in new ideas and people start thinking all kinds of thoughts. Might lead to questions about where this plague is coming from. Might even threaten the stability of Gardenia.

"Now, Phobius seems to think someone's keeping the money he pays instead of seeing it goes into the proper purse. So if you've got problems with his new schedule, Dr. Tox, I'm sure he'd be interested in hearing them."

"Mais non!" Dr. Tox felt faint. Did the Black Knight really suspect him of keeping the money for himself? How much did Hydro Phobius know? "I mean, I'll manage. Somehow."

"That's the spirit," Kwagg said, then laughed so heartily he almost dropped. "Get it, Dr. Tox? That's the *spirit*?"

"Yes, yes," Dr. Tox said, his attention on the letter. "Very funny, I'm sure." How could he meet this schedule? It was impossible, particularly with conditions in the duchy as delicate as they were. Kwagg was right about that; too much attention was being paid to the plague. Not to mention the growing demands for change among merchants and peasants alike, despite the duke's efforts to stamp out such talk. And that fool, Corwyn— always poking around the waters in the area. He'd stumble onto something eventually, if he didn't already suspect!

Dr. Tox shivered. Somehow, he had to manage. He couldn't tell Hydro Phobius he'd failed. Especially if the Black Knight was already concerned about how his money was being spent.

There was no justice, Dr. Tox decided. How was he to have known the duke didn't have enough money to support his fief? There hadn't seemed any harm in secretly channeling Hydro Phobius's money into an Italian bank. The duke was already doing what the Black Knight wanted, without extra funds. But then things in Gardenia began to fall apart. And that meddling alchemist only added to the risk.

Maybe Corwyn would catch the plague. That would take care of him and distract everyone's attention from the economic plight of Gardenia for a while.

The plague! An idea formed in Dr. Tox's brain. He looked at the letter again. Maybe there was a way out after all. A way that would occupy public attention in the duchy de Gardenia while the new schedule was met, keep Hydro Phobius happy, and take care of that alchemist, all at once.

Dr. Tox smiled. Without another look at Kwagg he closed the window and returned to his desk. All he needed was an appropriate incident, something he could use to sway the duchess against Corwyn. That shouldn't be too difficult, since she already objected to the expense his water system required. Then Dr. Tox could have the alchemist imprisoned for causing the plague and solve his own problems in one neat maneuver.

His smile broadened. So consumed was he with his thoughts that he never noticed Kwagg, who'd been struggling to get back onto the rope, suddenly plunge headfirst into the moat. Nor did he see the smaller figure of Meier work his way down the rope to the distant bank, his progress hampered by Kwagg's empty boots, still clutched firmly in his hands.

CHAPTER 8

Dungeons and Demons

SEBASTIAN FLATTENED AGAINST THE WALL AND CAUTIOUSLY peered around the corner. Nothing. He darted down the hall.

At the incubatorium, he squeezed into the shallow recess of the doorway to study the route ahead. He focused particular attention on the deeper shadows, looking for any sign of Oliver. His hand gripped the short sword that was one of the few items his family had held onto during their fall from nobility. He hefted the sword and grinned, thinking how he would use it to hack that broom to splinters.

He dashed to the next doorway and froze, blending into the darkness. Again he watched the gloom ahead, ears alert for the slightest rustle. Again, nothing. Only one more doorway stood between him and the end of the passage where it opened onto the laboratory. Sebastian leaned against the rough wooden door, steadying himself before continuing.

Hours earlier, in the grey light before dawn, Sebastian had watched from his room as Corwyn hurried down the alley below. For a long time, Sebastian had remained there, watching for Corwyn's return and plotting his escape. He would abandon his apprenticeship and leave Gardenia forever. Italy offered the best prospects; France and England held nothing for him now.

But first, his grudge against Oliver must be settled. Before going to sleep, he had promised his father to repay the broom for the last night's attack on the stairs.

All the way down those stairs and into the corridor, Sebastian had expected to encounter Oliver. But so far he'd seen and heard nothing. His nerves were frayed. He let the door behind him take his weight while he switched his sword to the other hand and wiped his sweaty palm on his tunic.

Suddenly the door flew open. Sebastian tumbled backward to sprawl on the floor, his sword clattering across the stones. He stared up to find Oliver looming over him.

He rolled to his hands and knees and sought his sword. There it was, on the other side of Oliver! Sebastian crouched, weighing his options. If Oliver went for the sword, Sebastian would run to the laboratory for another weapon. But for now he waited.

But the broom seemed indifferent to the weapon. In fact, it seemed as surprised at Sebastian's entrance as was Sebastian.

"Parfait! We're all alone now, Oliver," Sebastian said, trying to goad the broom into a hasty action which could be turned to his own advantage. "Corwyn's not here to save your wretched, splintery little neck." But the broom only looked disdainful, placing its hands where its hips should have been and tapping a brushy foot on the floor. This made Sebastian more wary. "Unless Corwyn's back." He glanced around the storeroom into which he had fallen. "Where is Corwyn, anyway?"

At this, the broom became animated, jumping up and down and waving its arms.

"You're not scaring me off," Sebastian said. "I have a score to settle."

Oliver's actions became more frantic. Sebastian bit his lip, trying without much success to stifle his laughter. Soon his sides shook and tears filled his eyes.

Oliver stopped and made an effort to control itself as Sebastian wiped away his tears.

"Mon dieu!" Sebastian choked. "You're so funny. Now I understand why Corwyn keeps you."

At that, Oliver stamped a tuft of straw and pointed at Sebastian.

"Me?" Sebastian asked. "What about me?" The broom kept pointing. "You don't expect me to apologize, do you? That is what this is about, isn't it? My laughing at you?"

The broom dropped its arm and swished from side to side.

"If that means no, then perhaps it's what I said. But all I said was that Corwyn—"

Oliver bobbed up and down.

"Corwyn? You're trying to tell me something about Corwyn?"

Oliver bobbed more vigorously.

"If my former master wanted to make you truly worthwhile," Sebastian said, "he'd have made you so you could speak. Very well, what about Master Corwyn?"

Oliver pointed at the door, then marched in place, its two straw tufts pumping like stubby legs, its arms swinging at its sides.

"Corwyn left? Yes, I watched him leave. But where'd he go?"

The broom clutched itself in a ridiculous caricature of modesty.

"The Reluctant Virgin?"

Again Oliver bobbed.

Sebastian's interest stirred at the thought of Gwen. "But why would Corwyn go to the Reluctant Virgin at this time of day?"

Oliver shrugged, then ran to a table and grabbed an hourglass. He came back, pointing to the instrument.

"He went to see their hourglass?" Sebastian asked.

Oliver swiveled from side to side.

"He went to see what time it was?"

Again Oliver swiveled. The creature grabbed the timepiece in both hands, turned it over once, then back again.

"Even poor, befuddled Master Corwyn would not go to the Reluctant Virgin simply to turn over their hourglass," Sebastian said, tiring of the game. The hourglass reminded him how little time he had for dealing with the broom and slipping away before Corwyn returned.

At Sebastian's remark, Oliver hurled the glass. Sebastian ducked and the instrument smashed behind him. He straightened slowly, his anger hot again.

But Oliver ignored him. Instead, the creature held its hands in the air, separated by the space of an hourglass. It inverted the imaginary glass, inverted it again, then a third time.

"Three hours," Sebastian ventured reluctantly. "Corwyn left three hours ago?"

Oliver nodded.

"Je sais cela," Sebastian growled. "I told you, I saw him go."

The broom held out the imaginary glass, started to invert it, then swished from side to side in a stiff-necked attempt to shake its head.

"He wasn't supposed to be gone more than an hour?"
Oliver bobbed.

"What concern is that of mine?" Sebastian said. "I won't be
here when he returns." He inched toward his sword, his attention
on the broom.

Oliver stamped its foot and pointed at Sebastian.

Sebastian hesitated. "You want me to go after him?"

Oliver practically jumped up and down, it bobbed so excitedly.

Sebastian eyed the broom. There might never be a better
chance, his father admonished him. Yet he held back, reluctant
without knowing why.

The fact that Corwyn had gone alone to the Reluctant Virgin
saddened him, and he wondered if the old alchemist was as
anxious to dissolve the apprenticeship as he was. Not that Sebastian had changed his mind about leaving, but he wanted Corwyn to miss him when he was gone. And somehow he couldn't
bring himself to deal with Oliver while the broom's only concern
was for the safety of another. It wouldn't be right, he told his
father, for the broom to appear more chivalrous than he. There
was more to it than that, Sebastian knew, but his point was
sufficient to decide the matter.

Besides, he added silently, maybe this way he could also make
up for his mistakes with Gwen before leaving Pomme de Terre.

"*Bien!*" he said aloud. "I'll find Corwyn. But I'll be back to
deal with you, and after that I'm going. Corwyn can find someone
else to be his apprentice."

He stooped to retrieve his sword, but the broom blocked him.
"If Corwyn's in trouble, I'm not going unarmed," Sebastian
snapped.

Oliver moved aside slowly. Sebastian sheathed his sword and
left the laboratory, feeling foolish at having engaged in a one-
sided conversation with a broom.

The Reluctant Virgin was almost as dark by day as it had been
by night. Sebastian peered about, surprised to discover it empty.
He had expected to find Corwyn exchanging gossip, unaware of
the hour or the concern he'd caused.

Sebastian made his way through overturned stools and tables
to the seat he'd occupied the night before and called out, hoping
Gwen would emerge from the kitchen.

But the next person to enter came not from the kitchen but
from the street. The door opened and a long, thin shadow
wrapped itself around the lintel. String John studied the room,

then threaded a broken path to Sebastian. *"Monsieur Cafard?"* he asked in a low whisper.

"What?"

"Your name. *Monsieur Cafard?"*

"Who told you that?" Sebastian demanded.

"Not important." String John hesitated. "Strange name though. It means—"

"I know what it means," Sebastian growled. "What do you want, anyway?"

String John wrapped himself around a seat across the table and hunched closer. "You Corwyn's man?"

"I suppose," Sebastian answered doubtfully. "I'm his—"

String John cut him off with a gesture. *"C'est inutile.* Ears, you know. Can't be too careful." He leaned forward and dropped his voice further. "Message for Corwyn. Tell him. I found the source of the problem."

"You mean the plague?" Sebastian whispered. "You found what's causing it?"

String John nodded. "Kwagg," he said. "Meier."

"Quag"—Sebastian repeated slowly—"mire?"

Again String John nodded. He sat back, his message apparently finished.

"That's it? Quagmire?" Sebastian persisted. "That's everything you came to tell him?"

The nod again, a brief, businesslike gesture. "Sorry to be late," he added. "Detained by brigands."

"You're late? You mean Corwyn was supposed to meet you here earlier?"

Another nod.

"I don't believe this," Sebastian said. "Corwyn arranges a meeting with you, leaves his laboratory hours ago, disappears along the way, and all you tell me is 'quagmire'?"

String John looked apprehensive. "Corwyn? Missing?" He glanced about the room.

"Why, yes. Actually, I came here looking for him—"

"No time," String John said, pushing to his feet. "I'll have more in three days. One day there, one to observe, one day back." He began creeping sideways across the floor. "Three days. Tell Corwyn. If you find him." Then he was gone, gliding out the door into the street.

Sebastian stared at the door. Corwyn moved among the oddest assortment of characters—human and otherwise—Sebastian had ever encountered. Life at the abbey had been dull compared to this.

His musings were interrupted as Old Meg's flushed face peeped from the kitchen. "Oh, it's just you, *monsieur,*" she said, sounding relieved. She scuttled toward him. "I thought I heard voices."

"*Oui,* it's only me," Sebastian answered sarcastically. "I was talking to myself, Meg. Now what do you think of that? It seems I'm the best company I've found in Pomme de Terre. At least I can count on myself for sanity."

Old Meg looked at him as if that sanity might be in question. She fidgeted beside the table, her hands busy with her apron. "How might I serve you, *monsieur?*"

"Meg, do you know my name?" Sebastian asked on impulse, rankled by what String John had called him.

"*Mais oui!* You are *Monsieur* Sebastian—"

"Well, at least someone here knows my name."

"Sebastian Cafard," Meg finished. "One of the patrons told me the last part later." Her expression became thoughtful. "It's an unusual name. Did you know that it means—"

"I know what it means," Sebastian said. "And it's not my name." He drew himself up. "I am Sebastian d'Oignon."

Meg frowned. "Sebastian d'Oignon? That's not much better." She brightened. "But speaking of *l'oignon,* if you're hungry I could fry up some with *le foie.*"

"*La foi?*" Sebastian was momentarily confused. "Why would you fry onions with faith?"

Meg drew back. "Oh, *le foie!*" Sebastian exclaimed, remembering. "Of course! You mean liver with onions, not faith with onions."

"*Oui, monsieur.* How can anyone fry onions with faith? Although the curé assures us that in faith, all things are possible." Meg risked an uneasy laugh, watching Sebastian's face intently.

He shook his head. "No, Meg, I'm not here to eat. I came looking for Corwyn. His broo—, that is, his assistant said he came here three hours ago. Have you seen him?"

"He hasn't been here." Meg's face relaxed. "Such a kind man to my Gwen, he is. Strange, mind you, and I'm not one for those who act strangely. And I don't like what folks say about him being a necromancer. But Master Corwyn's always been gentle to my Gwen, nonetheless."

Sebastian looked around the tavern, recalling its clients from the previous night. What did Old Meg consider strange and what normal?

"He's the only man my Gwen—that is, her highness"—she shot Sebastian a sly look—"the only man she trusts. She's had a hard life here, Gwen has. When she was young, she trusted everyone and let herself get hurt. The peasant boys are too rough for such a fine lady, and the occasional nobleman who comes never thinks twice about her except to try to share her bed."

Sebastian managed a look of sympathy, aware that his own thoughts toward her had been just as low.

Old Meg tossed her head. "They don't know who she really is, but they'll see. Someday they'll all know what they missed. Meantime, you don't let her ways get to you. If she seems sharp tongued or difficult at times, it's only because she's afraid. Afraid you'll hurt her, too, just like all the others. You remember that, monsieur. She's friendly enough with the customers, but if she likes a man, she'll never let it show."

"I'll remember," Sebastian said. "And I won't hurt her, I swear. But what about Corwyn? Have you heard from him?"

"Not since he was here with you last night." Her hands worried her apron frantically. "You don't suppose something's happened, do you? *La peste,* perhaps? Seems everybody's being struck down by it these days."

"Oh, knowing Corwyn, I imagine he's all right. Just got distracted and forgot is all." But as he said it, Sebastian wondered how well he did know Corwyn. What was keeping the alchemist so long?

The door swung open and banged heavily against the tavern wall, interrupting his thoughts. In stepped Gwen, her hair disheveled, her eyes wild. For a moment, Sebastian thought she'd fallen victim to the plague, so crazed did she appear. Then she seemed to gather her wits. "Oh, Mama, isn't it awful?" she wailed.

"What, child?" Meg hurried over to comfort her. "Whatever is wrong, *chérie*?"

"Haven't you heard?" Gwen's words were muffled by Old Meg's bosom. "The duke succumbed to the plague. It happened during the night."

"*Alors!*" said Meg, patting Gwen's shoulder. "Still, it's hardly a matter for such concern. Unfortunate, but then, he wasn't a very good duke. And we didn't know him well."

"No, you don't understand," Gwen cried, pulling back.

"They're blaming Corwyn. The duchess and that dreadful Dr. Tox have imprisoned him. They say Corwyn's been working black magic and used his water system to poison the duke. They say he's responsible for conjuring up the plague to bedevil Pomme de Terre. They've declared him guilty of heresy and treason and ordered him broken on the rack. After he confesses, he's to be burned at the stake. Oh, Corwyn!" Gwen dropped to her knees and sobbed.

Sebastian was shocked. Foolish, the little man might be, but he was no sorcerer.

The voice in Sebastian's head told him to abandon this fool quest to save Corwyn and to flee the duchy. Sebastian wavered, uncertain how to refute his father. Finally, Gwen's anguish decided him. He hurried to her side and executed a sweeping bow. "Don't worry, milady. Upon my honor as your champion, I swear I'll save him."

Gwen looked up, tears streaming from her eyes, then buried her face in her hands and cried all the harder. "How despicable you are, *monsieur*. Even in Corwyn's hour of need, all you do is mock me!"

Corwyn wondered how long he'd been in the cell. He might have been hanging from these chains long enough to have missed Gabriel's trumpet. But since the turnkeys had yet to bring him his daily allotment of foul water and moldy bread, he assumed a somewhat smaller, more finite interval of time had actually passed.

The dungeon had been excavated too near the river and water dripped from one wall of his cell. A small channel cut in the rough stone floor drained the accumulation, but its flow had become blocked by straw, creating a pool over much of the floor. From the slime on the stones and the fetid smell of the pool at his feet, Corwyn judged the seepage had been going on for years.

To his surprise, a change occurred. A slight fuzziness developed around each drip oozing from the wall, a vague green haze that obscured the boundary between water and air. For a time he couldn't see the change by looking directly at the drops, but only when he looked away. The eerie haze began to haunt his peripheral vision.

Horror gripped Corwyn. He couldn't take his eyes off the drips as they formed. A stench weighted the air, adding to his discomfort. With a shock, Corwyn recognized it as the same odor which had lingered after Sebastian's peculiar fainting spell on the drawbridge.

The drips became the only measure of passing time, a sequence of water beading up, swelling into greasy drops that slid down the wall and joined their stagnant cousins on the floor.

After a while, Corwyn found himself recalling ancient guilts and deathbed promises made to friends long since in their graves. With each drop that ran down the dungeon wall, another image would rise unbidden from the recesses of his mind. They were memories he'd thought safely forgotten ages before, and their reappearance now troubled him.

He shifted in his chains, seeking to escape the memories. A man could accumulate quite a store of regrets in eleven hundred years.

The hypnotic effect of dripping water and recollected faults was shattered by a key grating in the lock. The door swung inward and boomed against the wall. Corwyn shivered at the sudden draft. He hadn't realized how much he'd been sweating. The air from the corridor was dank and stale, but he couldn't remember anything so refreshing.

A slightly built boy with terror in his eyes peered in before entering the cell. Bruises discolored his throat. From the smell, Corwyn decided he must have come to the dungeons by way of the stables, for he reeked of animal dung. But even that odor was welcome after the stench that had dominated the cell moments earlier.

The boy's eyes rolled as he approached, trying to watch every corner at once. He even regarded Corwyn with suspicion, as if the alchemist might break loose and attack him. He set a bowl of watery gruel and bread crusts at Corwyn's feet, then backed away.

"Wait," Corwyn cried, terrified of being abandoned.

The boy sprang back, his hand at his throat. *"Oui, monsieur?* What do you want?"

"Who are you?" Corwyn asked gently, thinking the lad couldn't be more than eleven.

"Me, *monsieur?"* The boy checked to either side to see if Corwyn was addressing someone else. He took a half step forward and halted unsurely. "I'm Simon."

"And what are you doing here, Simon?"

"I'm a master torturer," he mumbled. "At least, that's what they say. When I came here this morning, they said Master Grubb had fallen to the plague, and I'm not an apprentice or even a journeyman anymore, I'm a master. They told me I'm in charge of this whole level of the dungeon now, on account of there being no one else left to do the job."

"But you're so young," Corwyn said. "When did you become apprenticed as a torturer?"

"Yesterday." He brightened. "I worked in the stables before that. I liked working with the animals, and they liked me." He looked smug. "I could tell. They liked me better than the others because I was good to them and used to sneak them treats."

"They sent you here because so many people have come down with the plague?"

Simon's face fell. "*Oui,* including most of the guards and torturers. They're all locked up now, from that nice old hermit to the duke himself."

"Hermit? Do you mean Thaddeus?"

"*Oui, monsieur,* that's the one." He stopped, staring at Corwyn and touching his bruises as if remembering something. He backed toward the door.

"Wait." Corwyn's chains rattled as he reached for the boy to reassure him. "You must help me. Please, let me loose."

Simon shook his head. "I'm sorry, *monsieur*, but *he* was nice to me, too. And then he tried to kill me."

"But I can help stop the plague."

Simon shook his head more firmly. There were tears in his eyes. "No, *monsieur*. I can't let you go." He reached for the door.

"Don't go! Please. Something's in this cell. If you leave, it'll get me, too."

"I'm sorry, *monsieur*," Simon wailed. "I can't. Please, don't ask me to."

"Simon!"

The door closed with a dull thud. Simon's footsteps faded as he ran from the cell. Then there was silence. Corwyn watched the water drip from the wall, certain it carried something evil that would soon return to claim him.

A vague but familiar odor began to burn in his nose. He watched in horror as the water on the floor gave birth to a yellow-green vapor. The smell became overwhelming. The vapor assumed roughly human shape, making a mockery of the form. Corwyn's eyes burned, but he couldn't turn them away or even blink them for comfort. The chains held him like a ready sacrifice.

The thing moved unhurriedly toward him, its empty eye sockets seeming to penetrate his soul.

Then the dark memories returned, and he shivered as he realized what portent they held. Even as the thought came to him, the creature's appearance altered. Soon a man stood before Corwyn to present his claim against Corwyn's soul, a man in reality long since dead. Behind him waited others in turn, forming an endless line of grievances and accusations. Corwyn swept his eyes down the row of grim, silent faces and knew they were only memories brought forth to haunt him. Yet he could not escape the hold they had over him, for he himself had given that power to them. Each one represented some moral obligation he'd been unable to fulfill, and for which he'd already judged himself and found himself lacking.

"Pssst."

Simon, having learned minutes earlier that he was an apprentice guard as well as master torturer and well on his way to running the entire dungeon, spun around so fast he almost lost his balance.

"Pssst," the voice repeated. "Over here."

Simon peered into the gloomy side corridor. "Don't come any closer," he said, tightening his grip on a bucket of gruel for the prisoners. Then he saw the black-robed figures staring back at him from the shadows. *"Mon dieu!"* he cried, clutching his head and dropping to the ground in fright.

One of the intruders hurried to him. The figure was robed entirely in back and a cowl swathed the face in darkness. Simon moaned louder, certain that Death and his minions were stalking him. He tried to roll away as the figure advanced, but it caught and held him. Simon's hands were pulled away and his face forced toward the torch on the wall.

"What're you doing?" asked another figure as it stepped into the light. To Simon's surprise, it wasn't Death, but a young man dressed as an alchemist in ill-fitting clothes.

"Tiens! He's just a boy," the figure holding Simon said in a woman's voice. She sat down and pulled Simon closer.

Her cowl slipped as she examined him and Simon saw a face wreathed with flowing auburn hair. She was beautiful. Hastily she readjusted the robe to cover her features.

"If he's just a boy," said the young man, "let's tie him up and get on with this."

Simon whimpered and huddled against the woman. She twisted to look at her companion. "You'll do no such thing. Can't you see he's frightened?"

"Oh, all right." The young man turned to Simon. "I am Sebastian, master alchemist, and I've come to offer you more wealth than you've ever dreamed of."

Simon eyed Sebastian's clothes. "You don't look like a master alchemist to me."

"Until recently I was under a spell which made me appear short and fat," Sebastian replied, his voice taking on an unpleasant edge. "Only through mastery of the alchemical arts was I able to free myself."

Gwen choked, then tried to cover it with a cough. Simon looked from one to the other uncertainly.

"Never mind that," Sebastian went on, scowling. "The point is, I can offer you everything you want in life."

"All I want, *monsieur*, is to go back to the stables."

"But I'm offering a life of luxury, boy. You won't have to work again. You can lead the life of a nobleman, enjoying the finest foods, spices from the East, elegant clothes, servants." He glanced pointedly at Gwen. "Women."

"I don't know, *monsieur*. I miss the stables. The animals liked me."

"You could have your own animals!" Sebastian said. "Don't you have any imagination, any ambition? Buy a castle and turn it into one huge stable!"

Simon grimaced with the effort of thinking. "I suppose that would be all right. But how could I do it?"

"With this." Sebastian opened a leather bag to show the boy the red powder he'd stolen from Corwyn. "The philosopher's stone."

Simon looked blank.

"The key to the alchemist's dream," Sebastian said. "The quintessential element."

Simon shrugged, content with the warmth of Gwen's lap.

"Surely you've heard of the search for a substance that will turn mercury and lead into silver and gold?"

"Ho ho, *monsieur*, you jest with me! Who'd ever believe such a thing?"

Sebastian threw up his hands in despair.

"It's true," Gwen cut in. "With the powder Master Sebastian holds, one can do that very thing. Why, you yourself could produce a fortune that would be the envy of any king."

Simon looked at her, his eyes full of innocence. "Really, mi-lady?"

Gwen hesitated, pursing her lips, then nodded.

Simon looked at Sebastian, his eyes narrowing again. "Prove it."

Gwen threw back her hood, bringing sunlight to the gloomy hall. "Master Sebastian will do exactly that." She glanced at the shadows and nodded.

From the darkness emerged a third individual, shorter than the others and very timid. His face was hidden by his cowl and his sleeves fell over his hands. His robe dragged the floor, covering feet which made a rustling sound. The robe draped over him in heavy folds.

The little fellow carried a smoking brazier at arm's length. He set it down and quickly backed away.

Sebastian flung his arms over the brazier. "Behold! Fire, one of the four elements." He reached behind him and the skinny assistant put a shallow dish in his hand. With his other hand, Sebastian produced a small flask from under his robe. The bag of red powder still hung by a thong from his wrist.

"Mercury," he cried, holding up the flask. "One of the base metals." He poured it into the dish and placed it on the brazier. Then he stacked charcoal over the dish.

"Now observe as the alchemical elixir performs its transformation." Sebastian emptied some of the red powder from the bag into his hands. "From common mercury I bid you turn into royal gold!" he cried, flinging the powder into the fire.

Flames shot up, singeing Sebastian's hands. Smoke billowed from the brazier and filled the corridor. Sebastian stared in disbelief until the smoke forced him back, coughing. Then there was a crash and a scream as someone tripped over the brazier. Flames burst out again, glowing fiendishly through the smoke as the straw-covered floor caught fire. Sebastian cursed and groped for something to put it out.

Gwen found something first. Carrying Simon's bucket, she made her way through the smoke to where the boy lay and emptied the gruel over the embers. When the fire was out, she helped Simon up and examined him again. This time, however, she held him at arm's length as he stood dripping with gruel.

"He'll be all right," she said. "He's not hurt."

"He should be," Sebastian growled, kicking at the soggy mess. "Now what do we do?"

Simon limped toward a stool. "Ow!" he cried, stepping on a hot coal. Something in the charcoal fragments crushed by his foot caught his eye. He picked it up, hot though it was, and gasped. "Gold!" He bit the nugget to be sure. "Solid gold!"

A slow smile spread across Sebastian's face.

"What happened?" Gwen asked, slipping up to him. "How'd you do it?"

"The fool," Sebastian whispered, his voice masked by Simon's shouts of delight. "The wonderful fool stepped on the piece of charcoal with the gold hidden in it."

Suddenly, Simon stopped, eyeing Sebastian warily. "You said I could have the powder that made this?"

"*Oui.*"

Simon stuck out his empty hand, the other clutching the nugget to his chest.

"Ah, but I must have something in return," Sebastian said.

Simon jerked back his hand. "I knew it," he said. "Well, you'll not get my soul, *monsieur diable*. Not for all the gold in Gardenia!"

"I don't want your soul," Sebastian said, "and I'm not a devil. You have a prisoner here, name of Corwyn. I want him."

"Corwyn? That's all?"

"Yes."

Simon looked at Sebastian in disbelief. "Why?"

"He's our friend," Gwen pleaded. "We must free him."

Simon considered it, then nodded. Without taking his eyes off Sebastian, he untied the keys at his waist. Then he handed the keys to Sebastian in return for the bag of red powder.

"*Monsieur*, you are a fool," Simon said as he ran up the corridor leading out of the dungeon. "I'd have gladly let you free every prisoner in this dreadful place, even without the gold. But I thank you for it, *monsieur*, nonetheless."

"Wait," Sebastian called. "Keep the powder, but give us back the nugget. And where's Corwyn?"

It was too late. Simon was gone.

Sebastian started after him, but Gwen held him back. "Let him go. He's a poor peasant, and that nugget's more wealth than he's ever seen. He's welcome to it for letting us have Corwyn. Besides," she added, wrinkling her nose, "he smelled too strongly of the stables."

"As you command, milady," Sebastian grumbled. He turned away from the path Simon had taken, unaware of the hurt look on Gwen's face. He motioned to Oliver and headed into the depths of the dungeon.

The passageway grew gloomier and wetter. They slipped on the slimy stones. Cockroaches squirmed under their fingers as they clutched the wall for balance. At last they reached the lowest level—a dim passage, dank and fetid with stagnant water. Somewhere ahead, they heard moisture dripping.

They hurried to the first cell. Sebastian peered through a small grate to see who was inside. Oliver grabbed the keys from him and unlocked the door.

"Wait," Sebastian said, lunging for Oliver. "We don't know who's in there."

Oliver evaded him and ducked inside. Sebastian followed more slowly, waiting for his eyes to adjust. Then he saw the Duke de Gardenia shackled in the corner. Oliver stood just beyond the duke's reach.

"*Eh, señor,*" the duke implored, holding up his chains for Oliver to see. "*Desapreto me, por favor?*"

Sebastian cursed his poor understanding of French, then realized that wasn't the language the duke had spoken. He turned to Gwen, who shrugged. Oliver fumbled with the keys and inserted one in the duke's shackles. Sebastian rushed to stop him. "No, Oliver!"

Oliver jumped back. The duke leaped at Oliver with a roar, but his chains brought him up short. He paused to turn the key dangling from the lock at his wrists. Once free of the manacles, he grabbed Oliver by the neck to choke him. Straw flew as the duke shook the broom. Oliver beat at him with spindly arms. The duke laughed at this, then shrieked with rage as his crushing grip failed to subdue the stick figure. He hurled Oliver aside and strode from the cell, knocking Sebastian down.

Sebastian lay crumpled in a pile of straw, his back against the slime-covered wall. He heard Gwen enter the cell, but didn't move, embarrassed at having been caught off guard by the duke.

"*Mon dieu!*" Gwen whispered. "Are you all right?"

Sebastian groaned and sat up. "Yes, I'm fine. Just dazed. . . ." He stopped, realizing she'd been talking to Oliver on the other side of the cell. Sebastian pushed himself up and brushed away bits of straw, muttering under his breath.

Gwen glanced at him from where she was helping Oliver to stand. "Did you say something?"

"Nothing," he snapped. "Nothing at all."

"Are you hurt?"

"No, I'm fine. Just fine." He stalked out of the cell and on to the next, where he had to wait for Oliver to bring the keys. He saw no sign of the duke.

Oliver unlocked the second door and stood aside. "After you, *milord*," Gwen said to Sebastian, giving the word a savage emphasis and mocking him with a curtsy.

Sebastian kicked at the door in fury, picturing how abashed she would be if she knew his true status. Although even *that* might not impress her, so consumed with her own importance did she seem.

The door opened onto an empty cell. The next one was the same. At the fourth, Sebastian stopped Oliver as the broom started to turn the key. *"Attendez!"* Sebastian sniffed the air. "Something's wrong."

"Hurry!" Gwen pushed them aside and flung open the door, then stopped.

"What is it?" Sebastian shoved past her, then he too froze.

The smell hit them first, unsettling their stomachs and turning their muscles to water.

Corwyn hung in his chains, staring fixedly at a greasy, yellowish cloud that floated before him. "Hypatia," he said in an anguished voice.

A thin tendril from the cloud had reached to within striking distance of the alchemist.

Sebastian took a faltering step, ignoring the voice in his head that called him a fool for risking his own soul for the sake of Corwyn's. He stopped when the apparition turned its attention toward him.

—And he was back yet again in the halls of his childhood home, following his shadow around the corner once more to the hiding place of the boy who wouldn't stop sobbing. The boy looked up. Sebastian's anger flared again at the child's weakness, and he raised a hand to slap the boy.

Then, for the first time, Sebastian really saw the boy's face. He stumbled back in horror, breaking the apparition's hold over his mind. The image vanished, but the awareness remained.

The boy was Sebastian.

Sebastian stared at the hovering phantasm, hating it for what it had shown him. Wildly he searched for a way to erase the apparition's mocking grin.

A breath of air from the door blew cool across the the sweat on Sebastian's cheek. Eyes burning, he watched the breeze rustle the outlines of the yellow-green cloud. The thing held still, watching him.

"Oliver," Sebastian said, "come here. Slowly."

Oliver crept up to Sebastian, uncertain whether to keep his attention on the vapor threatening his master or on the young man who had tried to hack him to pieces.

Sebastian reached for Oliver, his eyes never leaving the apparition. Suddenly he hurled the broom at the vapor, concentrating all his rage into one fierce motion.

The phantasm shattered, torn into quivering blobs that fell to the floor like the snows of hell. Sebastian kicked at the fallen blobs, then strode to Corwyn, who hung almost unconscious in his chains. He unlocked the shackles and dragged the alchemist across the cell while Gwen again helped Oliver to his feet. The broom was hysterical. "You've frightened the poor thing almost to death," she said. "How could you be so cruel!"

"I was trying to save Corwyn," Sebastian snapped, aware that wasn't the whole truth. He wondered if she had seen the boy. "The broom's all right. Nobody got hurt."

"Nobody got hurt!" Gwen looked at the floor, still pulsing faintly with flecks of the phantasm. "How can you be so insensitive, *monsieur*? Think what poor Oliver went through!"

Sebastian, sick with what he had seen and bewildered by her concern for a mere broom, dragged his master into the passageway. Having seen to Oliver, Gwen now hovered over Corwyn. Despite his anger, Sebastian watched with an aching heart, wishing he could win her attention too.

As they reached the stairs, Corwyn regained consciousness. "*Arrêtez,*" he gasped. "Sebastian, quit tugging on me. I must find Thaddeus."

"I'm not tugging on you, Master Corwyn." Sebastian pulled the alchemist up the steps. "I'm saving you. Everyone down here must be possessed by the plague."

"But that's just it," Corwyn pleaded. "I must talk with him to learn more about it." He looked confused as he allowed himself to be propelled upward. "There was something I almost understood as that thing started to consume me. I can't remember what it was, but it's important."

Sebastian shook his head. "*Mais non!* You wouldn't survive another encounter with one of those . . . those things." He shivered. "Besides, another guard may come along at any time. We've got to get away while we can."

Corwyn nodded weakly and turned to the arduous task of climbing the stairs.

"Where will we go?" Gwen asked. "The guards will be looking for us when they discover Corwyn gone."

"We must leave Pomme de Terre," Sebastian said. For once, the voice in his head agreed.

"But where will we go?" Gwen persisted.

"I don't know. Maybe we'll hide in the woods. Give me time, I'll think of something." Sebastian glanced back and saw the expression on her face. "Well, I've done all right so far."

Gwen didn't answer. Her look made it unnecessary. They marched on in silence, each wrapped in private fears, the sound of dripping water receding slowly behind them.

CHAPTER 9

Highway to Escape

SEBASTIAN ARGUED FOR LEAVING POMME DE TERRE IMMEDIATELY.
To his surprise, Gwen agreed.

"It's not safe here, especially for Corwyn," she said.

"No," Corwyn responded. "We must stop at my laboratory
first. After what happened in the dungeon, I believe my recent
work may shed light on this plague." He patted her hand. "Then
we will go, *ma chère*, wherever you wish."

Though weak from his captivity and his near possession, Corwyn forced a brisk pace, taking back streets and alleys to avoid
being seen. Once inside his shop, he led the others to the incubatorium where he and Sebastian had set up the breath of
demons test.

"You don't mean to waste time on that foolishness?" Sebastian
demanded. "Our lives may be at stake."

"That is precisely why I must complete this test," Corwyn
answered. "For the sake of not only our lives, but the citizens
of Pomme de Terre as well." He motioned to Oliver to gather
the bottles from their resting place at the bottom of the trough.

Sebastian snorted and started pacing. He was ashamed of the
vision of himself he'd seen in the dungeon, and was afraid the

others might also have seen it. His only refuge seemed to be to adopt his father's anger.

That anger rose within him, demanding an outlet. Corwyn drew it like a steeple in a lightning storm.

While Oliver pulled the bottles from the trough, Corwyn netted minnows. They arranged the bottles along the table and broke the wax seals, then Corwyn placed a pair of fish in each bottle, replaced the stoppers, and waited.

The fish swam vigorously at first, but their motions quickly became lethargic. Their mouths worked frantically to pump water through their gills. One after another, they turned belly-up and floated to the tops of the bottles. Corwyn recorded the times required for each death. Then he motioned for Oliver to clear away the bottles.

"I was afraid of this," he said.

"Of what?" Sebastian snapped.

"Whatever causes this plague is reaching Pomme de Terre through the water. That's what killed the fish. It's extremely voracious to have consumed the breath of life from each of these bottles in only a single day. Yet it cannot be detected by ordinary physical means such as the alchemical destruction test we performed on the samples yesterday."

"This is meaningless to me," Gwen said. "What does it tell us?"

"We now know that the agents causing this plague are not of the ordinary world—not the sprites and nymphs common to natural waters," Corwyn said. "Had they been of this world, we would have detected them yesterday, and there would've been enough life breath remaining for the fish to survive much longer in the test you just witnessed."

"But if they're not natural, what are they?" Sebastian asked in spite of himself. Then it struck him. "They're supernatural!"

Corwyn nodded. "This plague is a result of demonic influence of a far more serious kind than any ordinary sprites and nymphs—these are powerful, virulent demons present in unheard of numbers and capable of causing widespread infection."

"But we knew that already," Gwen said. "That was obvious in the dungeon when we rescued you from that . . . that creature."

Corwyn smiled tolerantly. "You may have suspected it, but you didn't know for certain. Not without alchemical proof. And without this test we wouldn't have known how extensive the

demonic presence has become. Besides, now we know these
demons are reaching the duchy through the water rather than
through the soil or air or by some other means. Such knowledge
marks the first essential steps toward stopping this dreadful
plague."

"Why talk about stopping it?" Sebastian asked. "Let's make
our escape and the duchy be hanged!"

Gwen's mouth tightened and her chin lifted. With a pang of
regret, Sebastian realized she cared about the citizens of Pomme
de Terre who had protected her, the way noble families always
cared about those who served them well.

"I'm sorry—" But before he could finish his apology, a crashing noise cut him off. He ran to the laboratory with the others
and discovered it was the sound of something being rammed
against Corwyn's door. Sebastian opened a shuttered grille in
the door.

"We're too late," he said, peeking out. "There's a crowd of
townsfolk trying to break in. We're trapped."

"Word of the charges against me must have spread quickly,"
Corwyn said.

"They think you're guilty of witchcraft," Gwen said. "The
townspeople suspected as much before, but now they have the
duchess and Dr. Tox assuring them it's true. They're anxious for
the hangman to free them from the dangers of your evil work
and to spare them from the plague."

"Unfortunately, my friends," Corwyn said, "you will all share
their charges with me unless we can find evidence of our innocence. Without it, our lives here are forfeit."

The beam smashed against the door again. Oliver darted to
the far end of the room and returned with a small mallet. He
tapped vigorously at the door, trying to straighten the timbers
as they cracked.

Corwyn studied the door absently. "There may be a way," he
said. "A passage Oliver and I constructed. I'm not sure it's
possible to get through it alive, but we must try."

"If you and Oliver built the passage, why aren't you sure
whether we can get through?" Sebastian asked.

"Because it wasn't made for escape." Corwyn glanced back
at the door. Torchlight flickered through the cracked planks but
the wrought iron bands still held it together. "Come, Oliver,
let's see what we can find to slow them down once they get
inside."

Oliver dropped the mallet and joined Corwyn, who rummaged through the cabinets lining the laboratory.

"Ah, this should help." Corwyn pulled out a large glass vessel. "Oil of vitriol. They'll begin to have their doubts when their shoes start to smoke. After it eats its way through to their feet, they'll dance in the streets getting clear of here." He dragged the bottle to the door and tipped it over. The floor bubbled and blackened where it came in contact with the stuff.

Oliver emptied other vessels throughout the room. Sebastian and Gwen joined in, tossing every jar and bottle they could find into the room. Varicolored smokes twisted from the wreckage. Corwyn trailed the last drops from his great bottle as he retreated from the door. Then he dropped the bottle, smashing it against the stones. Oliver hurried to the alchemist and guided him to safety through the debris.

"I wish I could have saved some of it," Corwyn said, peering from the corridor through the acrid haze that filled the laboratory. "The *kawphy*, at least."

The door shuddered under another blow and the beam finally broke through. A shout of triumph arose from the crowd and torches pressed closer.

"Come," Corwyn said. "They'll soon have an opening wide enough to squeeze through."

He hurried them to the incubatorium and barred the door as the crowd burst into the laboratory. There were shouts of victory that quickly changed to cries of astonishment, then pain and confusion.

"They'll soon find a way through the laboratory," Corwyn said. "We must leave quickly."

"But how?" Sebastian asked.

Corwyn pointed to the end of the trough. "From here, the water flows through an underground channel to the stream and emerges in a rocky pool."

"You mean we have to swim?" Sebastian asked.

Corwyn nodded.

"But what about the demons in the water?"

"They're in the Ale, yes, but not this tributary. If they were, my experiments would have detected them long ago. Come, there's no time to lose. Strip off your outer clothes and tie them in a bundle with this cord. Drag the bundle behind you as you swim through the channel." He turned to Gwen. "I'm sorry, *ma chère,* but you must take off what you can. Otherwise your clothes will weigh you down and you'll drown."

"C'est bien," she said. "I understand."

Sebastian, still staring at the trough, backed away. "You three go ahead," he said, drawing his sword from its scabbard. "I'll guard the rear and come after you."

Corwyn nodded, wadding his outer robe into a bundle with his pointed hat. Gwen turned away and started removing her skirts and blouse, then paused to study Sebastian. He was watching the door, his facial muscles working nervously.

Soon Gwen was clothed only in a long cotton chemise. The other items she tied into a neat package which she placed on the rim of the trough.

"Let's be off," Corwyn said. "Why, Sebastian, you haven't begun."

"Huh? Oh, you three go ahead. I'll be right behind you."

"Sebastian, I'm surprised at you," the alchemist said. "This is no time for false modesty. Look at Gwen. Oh, sorry, *ma chère.* No, don't look at Gwen. But she understands the severity of our situation and has readied herself for the undertaking, despite any embarrassment it might cause her. Certainly you could do the same."

"I will, I will," Sebastian said, his voice rising. Inside his head, his father cursed him for getting himself into this situation. Running feet sounded in the corridor outside the incubatorium, followed by shouts as one of the storeroom doors was breached. "Hurry, Master Corwyn, don't wait for me. I'll be along. Now go!"

Corwyn nodded and helped Oliver into the water. "Come, dear Gwen. Sebastian, don't tarry too long."

"I'll be right with you," Gwen said. "You go ahead."

Corwyn watched them both uncertainly, then swung his legs over the trough. "Whew, it's cold!" he said. He took a couple of deep breaths, held the third one, and sank into the water. His legs kicked, splashing water, then he was gone.

"You'd better hurry, milady," Sebastian urged. "Please, there's no time to waste."

Gwen cocked her head. "You're a most unusual man, Sebastian. I fear I've underestimated you. Where I thought you mocking, perhaps you were only being gallant, after all." The noise from the corridor grew louder, drawing Gwen's gaze, then she turned back to Sebastian. "You can't swim, can you?"

He shook his head, swallowing hard. His eyes never left the door.

Gwen held out her hand. "Come on."

"It's too late to learn now! Save yourself, milady! I'll keep them from you as long as I can." He shifted his stance and cut the air in practice strokes with his sword.

"Stop being a fool and come on!"

Sebastian looked back at the water. "I can't."

"Hold on to me. You'll be all right."

Sebastian took a step toward the trough as someone pounded on the door. Quickly, Gwen helped him out of his clothes, adding them to her own. The pounding grew louder, then stopped. Gwen drew Sebastian into the trough. Water swirled above their knees, bitterly cold. Sebastian's teeth chattered and he clung to Gwen.

"Not so tight," she said. "Take a couple of breaths and let them out." Sebastian did so as the pounding was replaced by the sound of an axe biting into the wooden door. "Now hold this one," Gwen told him, gulping in a breath herself and pulling him into the water.

Panic rose in him as water closed over his head. He tightened his grip on Gwen, now unseen in the maelstrom that propelled them forward. Around him was nothing but black, watery chaos. But worse was the fear that threatened to overwhelm him.

His heart pounded and his lungs screamed at him to breathe. The need to empty his lungs and suck in a full breath of life-giving, refreshing air grew until it consumed him. Nothing else was real anymore beyond that need.

At last light glimmered ahead. He fought to hang on for a few yards more. Then, just as his will gave out and he succumbed to the need to breathe, they burst through the water's surface. Choking and clinging to one another for support, they stood up in the pond.

After a time, Sebastian grew aware of the twilight glowing softly around them, the chirp of birds on a nearby bank. Most of all he became aware of Gwen as she leaned on him for support, breathing more easily now. She shivered against the cold, and Sebastian pulled her closer. She held back at first, then melted against him. He wrapped his bare arms around her and watched her face in the purple light until their mouths met. When at last they relaxed their embrace, Sebastian pulled back slightly.

"Merci," he said. "For saving my life."

She nuzzled his neck with her lips. "Is that all you wanted to thank me for?"

"No," he said, and kissed her again, stroking the wet hair from her face.

They were startled back to reality by a polite cough from the bank. Corwyn, looking more like a wet rat than a master alchemist, watched them with a bemused expression. "For a pair that seemed so painfully modest only minutes ago, you two warmed up to each other quickly," he said. Then, as Sebastian and Gwen hastily dropped their arms and drew apart, he added, "Oh, not that I mind. But just now, I believe embraces should wait while we focus on the problem at hand." He indicated the woods behind him, away from town. "Shall we be off? They'll soon be after us again."

Sebastian and Gwen stumbled from the pool and followed Corwyn. Oliver scampered ahead, the only one of the group unaffected by the dunking. The others dripped and shivered and tried to find their way in the fading light.

At last it was too dark to go any further.

"We must be nearing the point where this stream joins the Ale," Corwyn said. "We should be far enough from Pomme de Terre for now. Let's find a place to spend the night."

Oliver discovered a depression at the base of a rock bluff. It was too shallow to be a cave, but adequate for the night. An overhanging ridge provided protection from above while the roots of a massive oak, toppled in some long ago storm, made a natural enclosure around the spot. Corwyn attempted to light a fire, but the tinder they found was too damp.

They untied their bundles of clothing and draped them over the upturned tree roots to dry. Without food or fire, little was left but to get what sleep they could. Oliver, who needed no sleep and had proved the only member of the band unhampered by darkness and difficult terrain, took up watch on the ledge above. Corwyn sat alone for a time, his thoughts far away. Gwen lay on the mossy ground near Sebastian. Nothing was said for a long time. Sebastian wondered again if Gwen had seen the crying boy in the dungeon, and if she had recognized him as Sebastian.

The night breeze picked up. It moaned like an echo of the boy Sebastian had been and left him feeling cut off from the others. Then Gwen's teeth began to chatter. The sound, so ordinary, brought Sebastian back to the present. The wind became only the wind again, not a memory from the past. Sebastian wriggled closer.

"Are you cold?" he asked before realizing the obviousness of the answer.

Dimly, he saw her nod. "And afraid," she whispered.

That surprised him, for he hadn't considered that she too might know fear.

"Hold me," she asked.

Sebastian wrapped her in his arms. She felt cool against him, chilled by the remaining dampness of her chemise. But where they touched, his skin threatened to burst into flame. He rubbed her vigorously until her shivering stopped, then continued caressing her more slowly. Gwen didn't seem to mind. She snuggled into his embrace, her breath tickling the hairs on his neck. She lay so still she might almost have been asleep.

Sebastian was far from it. Gwen's breasts nestled too softly against his chest, her form too closely molded to his own for slumber. His thoughts were disordered. It was wrong, he thought, to have such desires for a princess. His should be a purer form of love. But with excited embarrassment, he felt his body respond and press against Gwen's in unbidden intimacy. If she was awake, she must be aware of his touch. Yet she made no effort either to pull away or to further it. Sebastian held still so as not to disturb her. Besides, he reminded himself, Corwyn and Oliver were too near in the surrounding darkness. He mustn't act in an unseemly manner.

So he held her, and was content. Senses heightened, he listened to the breeze playing through the oak and beech leaves nearby and counted the few stars to be seen beyond the overhang. But most of all, he thought about the beautiful princess in his arms and how good it felt to be with her, despite the dangers which had driven them to this place or the unknown perils ahead.

He thought his father would have been pleased.

After a while, a subtle change in Gwen's breathing told him she had at last truly fallen asleep. Soon Sebastian joined her.

The night was long for them all. Sounds from the woods sent Oliver scampering back for safety so often that Corwyn finally ordered the broom to stay in camp. But Oliver couldn't settle down. He fidgeted and skittered about like an anxious pup, disturbing their sleep. Then about midnight the wind increased, gusting through the inadequate shelter. Light clouds whipped across the sky, obscuring the stars. The clouds became denser and the air smelled damp with rain. The three humans gave up all hope of rest. As the first fat drops spattered through the leaves, they scurried to retrieve their clothes, almost dry now, before the downpour soaked them again. Lightning threw harsh shadows around them and thunder jarred them. Oliver, who hadn't minded the rain, now fled to the safety of the humans as if they could protect him from the fiery bursts of light and noise.

Then the storm was over, leaving the four huddled miserably at the rear of their shelter as the first grey light of false dawn streaked the sky to the east.

Sebastian watched in perverse fascination as Corwyn's features took shape in the growing light. The alchemist's eyes were red and sunken, his face as droopy as old grey candle wax. "What I wouldn't do this morning for a mug of *kawphy*," he groaned, meeting Sebastian's gaze. Sebastian tried to smile. Then he saw the night had been as merciless to Gwen. He smoothed the puffy circles under her eyes with a finger.

"I'm so tired," she said. Sebastian watched with sorrow, frustrated by his inability to relieve her suffering.

"We had best determine our course and proceed as soon as possible," Corwyn said.

"But where can we go?" Gwen asked. "What are we going to do?"

"We're going to discover the mystery of the plague, *ma chère*," Corwyn answered. "We're going to clear our names and at the same time free the duchy of this vile pestilence. The kind of demon which causes it is not unknown in isolated cases. But it is strange indeed to encounter them in such epidemic proportions. We must find out why this is occurring here. Perhaps in the process, we'll also discover a way to turn this unfortunate affair into a bit of profit for ourselves."

"But what can we possibly do about either the demons or the plague?" Gwen asked.

Oliver tugged on Corwyn's robe, trying to get the alchemist to play. Corwyn brushed the creature away. "We must do something," he said. "And to stop one, we must stop them both, for they are the same. What we've already learned from the breath of demons test gives us a start. The demons are carried in the water, dispersed much as salt is when dissolved. But when the water becomes quiescent, the demons emerge again, coagulating

in the air in the form we saw in the dungeon. It's in this form
that the demons are capable of possessing a human soul. What
we must find is where the demons first enter the water. Obviously, our course lies somewhere along the river. I suggest we
proceed at once into the Pyrenees to the headwaters of the Ale.
There I believe we shall find the source of the demons causing
the plague." He shook his head mournfully. "If only they hadn't
destroyed my laboratory. Our search for the source of the plague
would be much easier if we could run more breath of demons
tests."

As Corwyn talked, Oliver approached Gwen, still hoping to
find a playmate. She held him on her lap and picked dried mud
from his straw tufts as she listened to Corwyn.

"Is there a marsh near the headwaters?" Sebastian asked,
suddenly remembering something.

"The ground would be quite wet in places, but it depends on
what you consider a marsh," Corwyn said. *"Pourquoi?"*

Sebastian shook his head. "Unless there's a definite marsh,
we shouldn't go upriver. We must find a bog or marsh, perhaps
a body of stagnant water. The man in the tavern was quite emphatic about that."

Corwyn's head shot up. "What man?"

"The one you talked to in the tavern the other night. String
John, you called him."

"You saw String John?"

"Yesterday, after you disappeared. Oliver told me you had
set out for the Reluctant Virgin, so I went there to find you.
String John came in, and said to tell you that what you seek lies
in a marsh. Soon after I talked with him, Gwen brought word
of your arrest. I forgot about the message after that."

Corwyn rubbed the bridge of his nose. "I can't imagine that
the source of our problem could possibly lie downstream. The
demons would have to travel against the current, which I thought
was impossible. But if String John told you a marsh . . ." He
rolled his eyes at Sebastian. "You're certain he said that?"

"Oui, certainement. He said it had something to do with a
marsh or bog. I can't remember the exact word he used, but it
was definitely that kind of place."

Corwyn frowned, then shrugged. "Well, String John's seldom
wrong. And if he doesn't know about a thing, he'll find it out."
Corwyn stared at the Pyrenees, the peaks glowering like forbidding monarchs. "Downstream it is, then. I didn't really want to

climb those mountains, anyway. There's a place out on the plains of Gaul some distance from here where the Ale widens and grows sluggish. That could be where String John meant. I've never been there, but I've heard about it."

"I've heard about it, too," Gwen said. She stood up, brushing bits of dirt from her lap. Oliver, tired of being groomed, darted away. "That marsh is on the other side of the Valley of Despair."

"Yes, it would be," Corwyn agreed.

"Then we'd have to go through the valley to get there," Gwen persisted.

Corwyn was slow to respond. "I suppose we would," he said at last.

Gwen said nothing as she stared at Corwyn, who shifted uncomfortably under her gaze. "Well, what else is there to do?" he asked. "We must find the source of the demons, for our own sakes as well as the sakes of others."

Sebastian, who'd been trying to follow their conversation, finally interrupted. "What's the Valley of Despair?"

"You tell him," Gwen said to Corwyn.

"Well, uh, yes." Corwyn stroked his beard. "It's been the subject of many folk tales and idle rumors, none of them ever actually substantiated. Not definitively."

Gwen snorted. "Why prove something definitively that we already know full well to be true?"

"Now, let's not be hasty," Corwyn said. "After all, we don't actually know that what they say about the valley is true. Not really. Only independent observation will verify that."

"Must we be the ones to prove it?"

"Will somebody tell me what this is all about?" Sebastian interrupted again.

"I think Corwyn had best be the one to explain it to you," Gwen said, her eyes on the alchemist.

"Well, I don't wish to unduly influence the boy's perceptions by filling him with a lot of useless conjecture." Corwyn turned to Sebastian. "It's really nothing, and if it should turn out to have some validity after all, you'll know soon enough once we get there. Now I suggest we start on our way."

"Master Corwyn, what are you talking about?" Sebastian demanded.

But Corwyn refused to say anything more. Instead, he retrieved Oliver, who was stuck after trying to follow a squirrel up a tree. Then he set off through the forest, leaving the others to fall in behind. Gwen, her mouth set in a scowl, would say nothing. She walked behind the alchemist as if on her way to the gallows. Sebastian brought up the rear, with only Oliver for occasional company as the broom darted back and forth between the humans and various distractions along the way.

They followed the tributary to where it joined the River Ale. The trail, if it could be called that, led through a tangle of underbrush that snagged their clothes and frequently sent them sprawling. The path wandered, occasionally doubling back on itself. A couple of hours of this left them hot and sweaty. At last the undergrowth opened up and the trees pulled back. A rolling meadow spread before them, green and lush. To their right flowed the tributary; ahead lay the Ale. Looking upriver, Sebastian saw the bridge he'd crossed on his way to Pomme de Terre only three days ago. Suddenly he recalled what had happened on the bridge. His knees felt weak with remembered terror, and he realized how well founded that fear had been.

They drank from the tributary before it flowed into the Ale. "From here on, we must be careful of the water," Corwyn said. "We know the Ale carries demons, and must assume it to be completely corrupted with them. Drink only from streams before they reach the Ale, where they may still be pure." He frowned. "Although if the demons travel upstream, no waterway is safe. Still, we must drink somewhere."

They set off again, following the Ale but keeping away from its banks. Corwyn was particularly concerned about shallows and slow moving portions of the river, for here he said the demons were more likely to coalesce and infect the air. They reentered the forest, but were hard-pressed to find a path. The need to follow the river while keeping their distance from it made progress difficult.

They trudged north and somewhat west as the Ale angled toward the distant sea. A great buttress of land rose far to their left, a vast ridge extending north from the Pyrenees and crossing their route somewhere ahead. Then the trees grew more dense and they lost sight of the ridge.

By mid-afternoon, they were exhausted and lost. They could no longer find the Ale, and their course had become a confused meandering. Finally, they reached the base of the ridge they'd previously seen reaching out from the Pyrenees to angle across their path. Presumably, the ridge forced the Ale into a more northerly course around the higher ground. Their own course, if they were to find the Ale again, must follow the base of the ridge, pushing further north into Gaul.

Corwyn called a halt to rest. He stretched out on the forest floor and soon was snoring. Gwen dozed with her head in Sebastian's lap. Tireless Oliver sought imaginary playmates in the nearby trees while his flesh and blood companions rested.

Sebastian forced himself to remain awake, not trusting Oliver to warn them of danger. He leaned against a tree and looked at Gwen's sleeping features thinking how beautiful she was even now, with her hair tangled and her face scratched by branches. Of them all, Gwen seemed oddly contented. Sebastian recalled what Old Meg had said about her reluctance to trust men and hoped that was beginning to change. Since their escape from Corwyn's laboratory, her attitude had softened. Somehow, he thought, he must win her affection despite his lowered social status, and despite what had happened in the dungeon when they rescued Corwyn. He would prove himself worthy by being the perfect chivalrous protector.

Gwen opened her eyes and caught him staring. She smiled, and stroked his face. "My poor hero, so scratched and clawed," she said.

"Anything for my lady, Gwen," he said.

She looked pleased, her face still groggy with sleep. "Your lady. How nice that's beginning to sound."

As she spoke, Sebastian thought again about what Old Meg had said. "Gwen. That isn't your real name, is it?"

"Of course it is. What do you mean?"

"You can tell me. Your secret will be safe, I swear. Besides," he added smugly, "I already know about it. Old Meg told me."

Gwen listened wide-eyed. "Told you what?"

Sebastian shrugged. "About you being a princess and your real family having been slain."

Gwen scarcely breathed, so intently did she stare at him. Then she dropped her eyes. She sat up and poked in the mulch with her finger, exposing the black soil underneath. "What else?" she asked offhandedly. "What else did Meg tell you?"

"That you were brought to her when you were a child, to be raised as if you were her own. That you're forced to live as a common peasant because your family's enemies would kill you, too, if they knew you were alive. And that there are still hopes you might someday regain your rightful lands and fortune." Sebastian hesitated, then asked shyly, "Are you the missing sister of the slain dauphin?"

Gwen seemed lost in melancholy reverie.

"It's all right," Sebastian urged. "I won't tell anyone. Whoever you really are, I want to be your champion in the fight to regain what's yours." He grasped the hilt of his sword.

Gwen choked trying to suppress a laugh. Sebastian blushed, aware that the short sword was woefully inadequate for any real battle. Gwen looked into his eyes and held him with her gaze. "Sebastian, *mon petit chou*, there are things you must understand."

He bristled at being called a little cabbage, then laid a finger across her lips, afraid of what she might say. If she actually put into words the fact that he was now only an alchemist's apprentice, his fate might be too real, too complete to ever be undone. And it was true, his father's voice reminded him, he'd sunk too low in life to be the champion of a princess. But the words mustn't be uttered. It might be only vanity, Sebastian thought, but he had to keep his hopes alive.

"Shhh," he whispered. "I know what you're about to say. But my family is of the nobility, too, so perhaps it can still be all right. I'm going to regain my father's estates and restore my family name. Let me be your champion, Gwen. I've been trained as a knight."

Sebastian felt a surge of guilt as he recalled his humiliations on the practice field. Only his brother, Bartholomew, had actually completed the training for knighthood. But it seemed best not to mention that just now.

Gwen stared at Sebastian as if seeing him for the first time. "So you're a noble?"

He nodded, sensing hostility in her voice without knowing why.

"And what better means of regaining your family's fortunes than by marrying a princess?"

"What? Gwen, what do you mean?" The voice in his head warned him to calm her suspicions. She mustn't be allowed to think Sebastian was interested in her only for her true position and power.

It was beginning to feel, Sebastian thought, like he was courting Gwen with his father watching, coaching him on what to say and how to behave.

Gwen sighed. "You're apprenticed in the wrong profession, milord."

Sebastian's heart leapt at this sign that she understood the difficulty he was in and recognized his proper position. "I hope to use alchemy to regain what is mine."

Her eyes narrowed. "Well, you have a long way to go to master the craft. Right now, you seem better suited to the reverse of alchemy."

"What do you mean?"

"I mean you have turned the golden hero of my dreams into a mere counterfeit of brass."

"I don't understand."

"Don't you, *mon petit chou?*" She gave the expression a savage emphasis this time. "Well, then, if your skills at alchemy truly are no better than this, perhaps you would have a greater chance of realizing your ambitions by marrying a princess after all, rather than through any expertise in your chosen profession."

There she was, calling him names again! Sebastian was hurt by the continued insult, while the voice of his father berated him for handling the situation so poorly.

She suspected the truth, Sebastian thought miserably, realizing how mercenary his interest in Gwen had been. No wonder she was calling him a cabbage. Yet it was only because she was a princess that his father's ghost put up with Sebastian's efforts to win her at all.

"It is for the sake of my father's memory that I do this, as much as for my own," he said, risking honesty in an effort to explain. "If I can become even half the man he was, I will have earned my rightful place in the world."

His voice cracked as he said it, for he stood little chance of amounting to so much.

"I could almost hate you for that," Gwen said. "If only I could. How much simpler it would be."

"Of course, that's not my only interest in you," Sebastian added quickly. This was difficult terrain, trying to balance both his father's and Gwen's expectations. "It's just that helping you regain what is rightfully yours might also enable me do the same for my own family."

"Of course."

Gwen fell silent. The tension grew. Sebastian thought back anxiously to the original topic of this uncomfortable discussion. "Milady, what is your real name, *s'il vous plaît?* You still haven't told me and I must know what to call you, if only when we're alone together. Is it really Gwenevere?"

Gwen turned to him, her face impassive. "Is it really so important, then?"

"Yes, milady. It is to me."

She nodded. "Gwendolyn," she said at last, her voice flat. "You can call me Gwendolyn."

"Gwendolyn," he whispered. "That's lovely."

"More so than plain 'Gwen'?"

"Oh, *mais oui,*" he said hastily, anxious to reassure her.

"I thought so." She lapsed into silence again, staring beyond his shoulder. Sebastian studied her, wondering what he had done wrong now. Suddenly she stiffened. Her eyes grew wide. "Oh," she said, sitting up. *"Ma foi!"*

"What is it?" Sebastian stood, spun, and dropped into a crouch, extending his sword before him. "Where is it?"

"On the ridge," Gwen replied. "It's beautiful!"

Sebastian looked up. There, in a break between the trees high up on the ridge, stood a white, four-legged creature bathed in sunlight. From its forehead emerged a single gleaming horn.

"A unicorn," Corwyn mumbled, rubbing the sleep from his eyes and coming to stand beside them.

The unicorn struck a majestic pose, gazing toward the unseen horizon. From where they watched, its form seemed a balance of strength and grace. It swung around to look the other way, its mane floating in the breeze. Halfway through the movement it stopped, stared at the little group for a moment, then stepped off the ridge and started down.

It was coming straight toward them.

CHAPTER 10

The Valley of Despair

GWEN SIGHED WITH ECSTASY AS THE UNICORN DISAPPEARED IN the underbrush on its way down the slope. "Wasn't it magnificent?"

Sebastian watched her, irritated without knowing why.

"The symbol of absolute purity," Corwyn murmured, his voice still thick with sleep. "For all their importance in alchemical philosophy, I've seldom seen a living unicorn. Certainly not for several hundred years. I'd begun to think them extinct."

Sebastian scowled. The changing mood of his and Gwen's discussion had been like the atmospheric shifts that warn sailors of oncoming storms: more was at stake than was evident on the surface. He wasn't sure what had happened, but he resented the unicorn for intruding. And he was angry at Gwen for allowing herself to be distracted by the creature like some idle peasant gawking at an affair of state.

He started to walk away, feigning indifference to the animal's arrival, but was stopped by an inrush of breath from Gwen and Corwyn.

"*Quelle pitié!*" Corwyn gasped.

"Corwyn," Gwen asked, "what's wrong with him?"

Sebastian turned to see the unicorn emerging from the trees.

It paraded into the clearing, head high and strutting. But at this range, the creature wasn't magnificent: its gait was uneven, its coat moth-eaten, stained and matted. It was overweight and its back was bowed. Its hooves were overlong and splintered. Even the tip of its horn had chipped. Between its hind legs hung an organ like a second horn, establishing the animal as definitely male.

Sebastian snickered. "Looked better from a distance, didn't he, *mon petit brocoli*?" he whispered to Gwen.

Gwen stared curiously at Sebastian, then turned back to the unicorn. "Take a good look, my tarnished hero," she said. "That's naught but your own reflection you see."

Sebastian, already sorry for taunting her about the unicorn's appearance, was stung by her remark. He wondered if he would ever understand Gwen's mercurial shifts of mood.

The unicorn, meanwhile, ignored everyone but Gwen as he swaggered across the clearing. He stopped in front of her and bowed, knees creaking. Gwen jumped back to avoid his horn, then leaned forward, her hand extended as the creature labored to rise again.

After much grunting, the unicorn got himself upright. "I am Petronius," he said in an age-worn baritone. "I sense you are a maiden in distress, and therefore in need of being serviced."

Gwen blushed and let her arm drop. She started to speak, but Sebastian edged in front of her. "Just what do you mean by 'serviced'? Gwen's not any common maiden, I'll have you know. She's a princess!"

"Sebastian, *vraiment!*" Gwen said. "I'm sure he didn't mean what you think. Not everyone's motives are as tainted as yours."

This hurt, but Sebastian was determined not to show it. "Is that so, *mon petit céleri?*"

Gwen stared at him with questioning eyes.

"Gwen," Petronius mused. "A lovely name for such a lovely lady. Forgive me for not recognizing your nobility; my senses aren't what they used to be. And now that I find your voice is as pleasing as your name and appearance, kindly use that voice to instruct this fop of an Englishman not to interrupt his betters." He waited a moment while Sebastian spluttered. *"Eh bien, ma chère!* How might I be of service to you? To you, that is—not this riffraff with you." He thrust himself between Gwen and her companions, his equine face leering into hers.

Sebastian looked to Corwyn, who frowned. "Most disappointing," he muttered. "This isn't at all the way they're supposed to behave."

Gwen stepped back from Petronius. "Uh, thank you. We do seem to be lost. If you could help us find our way, we'd be most grateful." She paused, then hurried on. "But at the moment, I'm more concerned with getting something to eat. Can you help us? We're famished!"

Petronius closed in again. "And just how grateful would you be for my help, *ma petite chère?*"

"What do you mean?"

"Oh, never mind for now," Petronius said with a toss of his head. "All in due time. Let's take care of that second matter first, shall we? I can offer you a gourmet selection of seeds and grasses, and perhaps a morsel or two of tender bark."

"Don't you have anything more sustaining?"

"Like what?"

"Well, like meat."

Petronius's nostrils flared and he snorted through lips pulled back over worn, yellowed teeth. *"Alors!* Please do not discuss the repulsive eating habits of your kind with me, maiden. I realize humans eat animal flesh, and I accept that fact with what grace I am able. But I, too, am an animal, albeit of a far loftier and more noble kind, and it is my miserable, undeserving cousins of the forest you propose to devour. I must ask you to consider my refined sensibilities in this matter and set any further talk of eating them aside."

Gwen covered her mouth with a hand as she realized her mistake. She reached her other hand to the unicorn. "Of course, Petronius. Oh, I'm so sorry. I just didn't think. Please forgive me."

The unicorn's expression flowed from indignation back to a leer. "Don't worry, maiden, you'll find a way to make it up to me, I'm sure."

To Sebastian, it was inconceivable for a beast to rebuke a princess. He started to step between them again, but Corwyn dragged him back. "It's all right, boy. She can handle herself. Besides, I don't think she wants your help."

Sebastian tried to shake off his master's arm. "But Corwyn—"

Corwyn drew himself to full height, almost reaching Sebastian's shoulders. "Boy, I said leave it be."

"Yes, master," he mumbled.

Having little experience with jealousy, Sebastian felt bewildered by the violent emotions which gripped him. All he knew was that Gwen had slipped farther from him than ever, and this ill-mannered unicorn was complicating matters. The animal deserved a severe lashing. Yet when Sebastian tried to defend Gwen from him, both she and Corwyn treated him like a misbehaving child.

Corwyn cleared his throat. "Petronius, we're looking for a marsh which lies somewhere beyond this ridge." He waved a hand at the land mass Petronius had descended. "We must reach this marsh quickly. Do you know the place, and can you lead us there?"

Petronius turned his long, equine face to Gwen. "Is he with you, too?"

"Oui." She sounded prepared to be stubborn.

Petronius blew through his nostrils in a horsey sigh. *"Très bien!* Yes, I know the place. The river makes a wide circuit around this ridge, which blocks most travel. But there is a way past it, a little-known pass which would take you through the valley at the center of the forest and on to meet the river again. There, the river opens up and slows, flowing into an ancient lake almost silted up and overgrown with weeds." He paused, reminiscing. "I grew up near that lake, when it and I both were young. I held trysts with many a willing peasant girl along its shore. Ah, but I was so inexperienced back then. Not at all the way I am now." He stared meaningfully at Gwen.

Gwen pursed her lips, apparently too lost in thought to notice. "You say you know this region well. Is it true what they say about the valley at the center of the forest?"

"The center of the forest?" Sebastian said, too curious to remain quiet any longer. "Is that the Valley of Despair you and Corwyn talked about earlier?"

Petronius ignored him. *"Oui,* it's true what they say. But that's the shortest way to where you want to go."

"Just what do they say about this valley?" Sebastian persisted. "And who are 'they' anyway?"

"Perhaps we should take a different route," Gwen said.

"Gladly. But the only other way is to follow the river, which adds at least two or three days to the journey, traveling at the water's edge through every meandering bend and turn along the way."

"The water's edge!" Corwyn interrupted. "No, we mustn't get

that close to the river. Besides, we can't afford the time. Think
of the poor folks of Pomme de Terre."

"What?" Sebastian was determined to be acknowledged.
"Corwyn, those 'poor folks' would have killed us!"

"Nonetheless, what else can we do?"

Gwen studied Sebastian a moment, then turned away. "You're
right, Corwyn, of course. Through the valley it is."

Sebastian pushed forward. "*Tiens!* What about me? Don't I
get a say in all this?"

"It's really better this way," Corwyn reassured him. "We can't
afford the extra days of travel, and we must avoid the river."
He shook his head solemnly and started walking toward the
sloping ridge.

"I wish somebody'd tell me what's going on," Sebastian
growled, falling in step behind his master. But no one paid him
any mind.

Gwen started to follow, but Petronius swung his hindquarters
around to block her, then lowered himself to the ground. "My
bower is on our way, maiden. It's quite homey; I'm sure you'll
love it. Climb up and I'll take you there. Then we can discuss
the, uh, dispensation of your indebtedness to me."

Gwen frowned. But when she noticed Sebastian's angry stare,
she seated herself sideways on the unicorn's back. Petronius
heaved himself to his feet, forcing Gwen to grab his mane and
lean into his neck to keep from falling off.

"That's it," the unicorn said in a husky whisper. "Hold close.
It's more fun for both of us that way." He trotted to the edge
of the clearing, passing Corwyn and Sebastian.

"*Adieu, messieurs,*" he called over his shoulder, giving them
a knowing wink. "Take your time. We may be a while."

"No, no!" Gwen cried. "They have to come with us."

"We certainly do," Sebastian agreed grimly.

Petronius sighed again. "*Très bien!* If you must. But you'll
have to keep up. Don't expect me to dawdle on your account."

Oliver had watched the unicorn's approach from behind a tree.
Now, emboldened by seeing Gwen on the creature's back, he
flitted nervously over to Corwyn.

"Out of my way, twigling," Petronius snapped as the broom
skittered by. A dainty hoof shot out at Oliver and missed. "Creatures of magic, ugh! Make my flesh crawl. I've chewed the bark
off bigger trees than that one will ever be." With that, Petronius
took off at a brisk trot, skirting the base of the ridge.

Sebastian and Corwyn were hard pressed to keep up. The old alchemist puffed and sweated profusely as they followed the prancing unicorn. Sebastian, worried about Corwyn, would have stopped their foolish chase had it not been for Gwen, hanging onto the unicorn's neck and begging him to slow down. So they ran, stumbling over rocks and crashing through brush. Oliver, with his stubby legs of brush, soon fell behind. After a while, Corwyn dropped back as well. Only Sebastian kept up the chase, although he too was gradually being outdistanced.

At last Petronius pulled up in a shaded glade. Sebastian stumbled in behind him with all the grace of a lumbering bear. He threw himself to the spongy ground to wait for Corwyn.

"Well, I see you managed to keep up," Petronius said. He tried to sound casual, but Sebastian noticed the unicorn was out of breath and his coat was frothy with sweat. Sebastian smiled grimly, pleased to realize Petronius had done his best to lose him and failed.

Corwyn limped into the glade as Gwen was dismounting. Her face was anguished when she looked at the old alchemist. With a shock, Sebastian recognized that look. It was the expression of someone who has accidentally done something unforgivable. It was the same expression he'd seen on his own face down in the dungeon.

"Oh, Corwyn, I'm so sorry," she sobbed. "He kept running so fast and I couldn't make him stop."

Corwyn nodded and patted her hand, too out of breath to talk.

Gwen looked around. "Where's Oliver?"

"Back . . . there," Corwyn puffed. "Have to . . . go find him . . . when I catch . . . my breath."

Petronius snorted. "Not much of a loss, if you ask me. Odd little creature, anyway." He turned to Gwen. "While these two underexercised gentlemen recover from their unaccustomed activity, how would you like to see my bower? It's right this way. You'll find it very cozy."

She turned on him. "I'm too furious with you to do anything right now!"

"Oh, but a little *tête-à-tête* does so much to help one get over such petty concerns," Petronius whispered. "You'll find yourself substantially refreshed by indulging in robust pleasure."

Gwen threw up her hands with a cry of frustration and stalked to the far side of the glade. Sebastian rolled onto his back and stared at the leaves overhead, waiting for the thundering of his heart to subside. After a while, he heard Corwyn get to his feet and move away.

Alone with Petronius, Sebastian found himself thinking again about the vision he'd seen in the duke's dungeon. He recalled the anger he'd felt while stalking the boy through the castle halls, before discovering the boy and he were one. No wonder the child's weakness had enraged him, for the crying that had led Sebastian on was merely the outward sign of his own inadequacy. It hurt so much to realize this that the sorrow of it tore at him.

If only he had been born more like his father, he thought bitterly. Then he might have become a man, instead of remaining a sniveling boy whose only hope was to masquerade as one.

When Sebastian finally sat up, Corwyn and Gwen were nowhere to be seen. "Where's Corwyn?" he asked Petronius, who was still staring at something beyond the glade.

The unicorn shrugged, his attention fixed on whatever he was watching. "I think he went looking for that stick creature. Maybe they'll both get lost."

"And Gwen?"

Petronius jerked his long head to indicate the direction he was looking. Sebastian peered through the trees, then saw her, wandering forlorn outside the glade. Her face, moving in and out of sight behind the thin trunks, wore an anguish that pulled at Sebastian's heart. He wanted desperately to ease her sorrow, but was helpless to know how.

Twigs snapped behind Sebastian and he looked around to see Corwyn return. "Did you find Oliver?" he asked.

Corwyn shook his head wearily. "Not a sign." He sat down near Sebastian, his eyes sweeping the glade. "Where are Gwen and Petronius?"

"Huh?" Sebastian spun back around, startled to find the unicorn no longer there. When a white flank glinted briefly through the trees beyond the glade, Sebastian knew Petronius was pursuing Gwen. He scowled, but didn't know what to do about that either.

A little later, Gwen's voice drifted through the trees. Sebastian couldn't make out her words, but the tone sounded sharp. He and Corwyn looked at one another. Suddenly Gwen's voice grew louder. "Don't do that," she said. There was a muffled response from Petronius, then Gwen, louder still: "I said don't do that!" The discussion ended with a smack audible through the trees.

Gwen stomped into the glade, straightening her clothes.

"Corwyn, I think it's time to leave," she said. Without waiting for a reply, she started across the glade.

Sebastian's anger flared up again. "What's the matter, *mon petit radis?*" he asked sarcastically. "Didn't you like Petronius's bower?"

Gwen stalked into the forest without a reply, leaving Sebastian to regret his remark. To make matters worse, he caught Corwyn staring at him, a puzzled look on the alchemist's face.

Before Sebastian could say anything, however, Petronius entered the glade. One side of his face was puffy and his eye had swollen almost shut. "She certainly has a strong right arm," the unicorn said cheerfully. "I like a woman with spirit." He grinned at Sebastian. "I have to hand it to you, you do know how to pick them. But I know how to pluck them."

Sebastian swung, aiming for Petronius's other eye, but the unicorn dodged lightly aside. "Come along," he said. "We must catch up with that delightful girl, then I'll take you part way on your quest. Who knows, perhaps she'll come to her senses. After all, consider my competition." He looked Sebastian and Corwyn over disdainfully.

Just then, Oliver stepped into the glade. "Ah, what timing," Petronius said. "Too late to be used to make a fire, too skittish to be used as a walking stick. Oh well, come along with the others. I'm sure you would anyway." With that he bounded into the forest, leaving the others to follow as best they could.

Corwyn, Sebastian, and Oliver came upon them a few minutes later. The unicorn was urging her to climb on his back again and promising impeccable behavior.

"I'll wager you say that to all the maidens you find, before carrying them off to violate them," Gwen snapped, trying to step around him. He moved to block her way. Just then she noticed Sebastian huffing toward her, Corwyn and Oliver trailing behind. The muscles tightened along her jaw and she turned back to Petronius. "Kneel," she said. "And don't move until I say so."

Petronius lowered himself to the ground while Gwen strode over to Sebastian. "Give me your sword."

"What?"

"You heard. Give it to me."

Hesitantly, Sebastian did as she commanded. She returned to Petronius and straddled his back, pulling her skirts above her knees. She wound one hand in his mane while the other held the sword. "One false move, you old goat, and I'll geld you. Now get up!"

Petronius stood quickly, his eyes wide and rolling back in an effort to watch his rider. Gwen glared at Sebastian, ignoring the shock on Petronius's face. She led the unicorn off, this time careful that he set a slower pace.

Sebastian was relieved by the moderate rate, for Corwyn's age showed after the past two days. Even for Sebastian, the going was difficult. Only Oliver was unaffected by the difficult journey.

Petronius led them west toward the top of the ridge. The trail, if indeed there was one, couldn't be discerned by Sebastian. Eventually, the trees thinned and the way grew rocky, making progress treacherous. Gwen's earlier comment about Petronius seemed to have some basis in fact, for he danced across the rocks with the surefootedness of a goat. Corwyn and Sebastian stumbled along, and even Oliver had difficulties on the ridge, for his brushy legs were too short for most of the stones that protruded from the thin soil.

Late in the afternoon, a mist rose, obscuring the landscape. Petronius continued to prance ahead, halting occasionally while he urged the others on as if the trip were nothing to him. But Sebastian heard Petronius's labored breathing and realized the climb wasn't as effortless as the unicorn wished it to seem. Soon after, Gwen told him to set her down and she joined the others on foot. Petronius protested, though not strenuously.

Sebastian tried to get close to Gwen once she was afoot, but she seemed just as determined to avoid him. He swore under his breath at the vagaries of royal blood.

The ground to either side rose, forming a canyon. Down the middle tumbled a mountain stream which forced them to scramble along the canyon wall. Just when Sebastian began to think they couldn't possibly continue, Petronius took them through a narrow gorge at the top of the canyon. Finally, they crested the ridge. They had climbed above the mist and stood bathed in late afternoon sunshine. Even the cold wind couldn't diminish Sebastian's exhilaration. From here they could see the forest awaiting them on the plain beyond the ridge. To the northwest, the Ale swung toward the sea, a gleaming silver snake. He could even make out where the river widened in the distance, opening into the broad, shallow lake that was their destination.

Petronius pointed his horn in the direction they must take. "Just down there is the heart of the forest. It's a high mountain

valley lying in the angle between this ridge and a smaller spur
that strikes off from it. You must pass through that valley, for
the way to either side is impassable."

He struck off again, leading them down and to the west. They
passed through another canyon, and eventually came to a bend
where the canyon veered around a sheer face of stone to funnel
through a notch in the opposite wall. Petronius paused.

"We're there," he panted, head hanging between his forelegs
with fatigue.

Sebastian stole a glance at Corwyn. The old man looked just
as tired. Even Gwen, who'd ridden much of the afternoon, was
haggard from climbing. Sebastian wanted only to sit and rest,
but the unicorn showed no sign of letting them stop despite their
weariness.

"The valley lies just beyond this bend. Be prepared as we pass
around the stone face and do not let the weight of this place
slow you down. You must remain light of foot and quick of wits
to make it across the valley, for if the despair drags too heavily
at your heart, the valley will get you before you can cross. Watch
your footing as you go, be wary, but hurry. And do not let
darkness find you still in the middle or all is lost. Once you get
to the other side, you can make camp for the night."

"You mean you aren't going to help us across to the other
side?" Corwyn asked.

Petronius looked at the alchemist with scorn. "This is the
Valley of Despair. The edge is as far as I go. I won't attempt to
cross it—not for you, not for her." He flicked his tail at Gwen.
"After all, even lust has its limits."

They each gulped the chill evening air, then Petronius ushered
them around the stone face. The canyon walls dropped away
and the ground lay broad and open before them. It should have
been an idyllic setting, a beautiful mountain meadow.

It should have been, but it wasn't. Instead, the entire valley
floor was one enormous midden heap. It stank of rot and filth,
it shifted and groaned under the combined weight of acres of
garbage mounded high on every side. There were empty bottles
and smashed pots, worn out shoes and cast off boots, shattered
swords, rusted armor, broken hoes and plows and rakes, ragged
coats and ruined carts, toothless combs and twisted pikes—every
useless tool and worthless implement of any shape and size and
sort. And there were other things: piles of bones, both human
and not, heaps of rotting animal wastes and spoiling vegetable

matter, and decaying mounds whose origins could no longer be recognized.

All the accumulated debris and excrement from civilization's centuries of hurried passing seemed cast aside in this awful place.

But there was something else here as well: a vile presence oozing through and over it, obscuring the outlines and blending individual bits of rubbish into one living, breathing, restless whole. It was a foul presence that permeated the very stones and pulled at their hearts, clutching at them with its weary whisper of despair and the inevitability of defeat. It called to them to quit their vain pursuits and give themselves up to putrefaction.

Sebastian, in the lead, came to an abrupt halt at the edge of the heap, forcing the others to do the same. Petronius urged him on, but Sebastian stood, frozen. He stared over the sea of trash, glowing blood-red in the fading light. "This is it?" he demanded. "This is what you were frightened of?"

Corwyn groaned and crouched beside him. The nearest edge of the heap seemed to surge slightly in an attempt to engulf him. "Such hopelessness—it's even worse than I feared."

"Horrible, " Gwen agreed.

Sebastian shook his head in bewilderment, but the motion dizzied him. "I don't understand. What were you so afraid of? It's ugly and villainous, certainly, but there's no danger here." He sighed, feeling an almost overpowering need to wander across the mounds and yield himself up to them. "Come on, let's get to the other side."

Corwyn jerked him back as Sebastian started to step onto the nearest mound. The mound, which had been waiting to receive him, writhed in fury as Sebastian's foot swung past its heaped trash and came down instead on solid ground. Or was it just an illusion of the shifting wind that created this impression in Sebastian's mind?

"Once again, boy, you see the surface of a thing and think you know its underlying reality," Corwyn said, holding Sebastian firmly. "Remember the lesson in the laboratory your first night? Well, there's more here than you're ready to admit. You feel it, but you dismiss its warning. Don't presume to see this place only with your eyes. Sense it also with your heart."

"What're you talking about?" Sebastian asked, trying to free himself from Corwyn's grasp.

"Don't you feel it?" Gwen asked. "Can you be so blind?"

"Feel what?" But already he sensed a shadow falling across

his heart, a cold, malevolent darkness anxious to strangle him. In his initial outrage at having been misled, he'd failed to notice the nature of the place, the way it sought to snuff his will and devour him. Now he opened himself to it and it threatened to overwhelm him. An unspeakable malignancy inhabited this place, a grotesque and mindless purpose as insensitive as any mold or slime, and just as inevitable. It sucked at his soul, attempting to pull him into the muck and ooze of the dump. He fought it, yet it dragged at him relentlessly, a chilling and silent war beneath the visible reality. The world around him blurred. Sebastian felt tired and sick. He longed to give in to the remorseless ache of the place.

"What is it?" he asked. "What's happening?"

"Now you feel it," Corwyn said. "You don't yet completely understand, but at least you're beginning to."

"Master?" Sebastian clutched the alchemist's sleeve. "What is this place? What's it doing to me?"

"What you sense is one of the greatest dangers threatening not only Gardenia, but eventually all of mankind. It's a danger because it's so easily overlooked, just as you first did, and yet it's so pervasive. It's our own insensitivity to the world we depend on, turned round and coming back to choke us."

"But it's just a midden heap," Sebastian protested, no longer believing it.

"And still you do not fully understand," Corwyn said. "It begins as such, but once it passes a critical point, it assumes a vital force of its own, compelling it to feed, to grow, to multiply. It was born with the first apple core Adam tossed unthinkingly over his shoulder, and it grows greater by the day. As civilization spreads, so does this virulence. But it grows faster. It feeds off the wastes and debris and poisons we so casually dismiss. And one day, if we don't learn to control it first, it'll destroy us all."

"What does it want?" Sebastian croaked. "Why can't we just go across and leave it be?"

"It's been here a long time," Petronius said, lifting his head to join the discussion. "It was formed two or three years ago and then abandoned, and all this time it has waited unfed. Now it senses our presence. It is hungry, and if you do not cross with care, it will feed on your bones tonight."

Sebastian backed away as far as the stone wall behind him would allow. "How did it get here?"

"A couple of peasants used to collect refuse from around the duchy and haul it away," Corwyn said. The alchemist was talking out of nervousness, Sebastian could tell. "They convinced various towns and individual citizens in Gardenia to pay them for doing it. They only received a pittance, hardly enough to justify the work. Still, they kept it up and Gardenia looked and smelled much better for their efforts. The duke even hired them to dispose of the dead after some of his battles. No one ever bothered to ask what the two were doing with the garbage they hauled away. Nor did anyone care why two idiot peasants were willing to do such hard work for so little reward."

He waved an arm at the reeking valley. "This is where they carted that garbage. And here it remains."

"But how'd they do it?" Sebastian asked, revolted at the thought of bringing so much foulness into a place that must once have been beautiful. "And why?"

"Eventually, someone discovered the two peasants were using a tribe of Germanic gnomes as slave labor. The gnomes had fled the Rhine to escape persecution by princes of the Holy Roman Empire. The gnomes tried to keep their presence in Gardenia a secret, but the two peasants stumbled across them and threatened to expose them unless the whole tribe hauled refuse. They convinced the gnomes they'd be treated with equal cruelty in Gardenia if their presence were known, and that the duke might even turn them over to the German princes for a reward. So the gnomes worked hauling refuse and the peasants kept the money."

"I remember," Gwen said. "The peasants were imprisoned for a while, but later were released. A jailor who used to come by the Reluctant Virgin once intimated money had changed hands to gain their release, but I never heard anything more about it.

"The peasants have a pig farm out in the country now, but there have been rumors the farm is just a masquerade to cover up some new scheme." Gwen frowned, trying to remember just what she'd overheard at the tavern. Hadn't someone seen them recently, somewhere in the Pyrenees where they had no business being?

"Who are these two?" Sebastian asked, breaking into her thoughts.

"One's Kwagg," she said. "His partner's Meier. An unwholesome team if ever there was."

"Kwagg?" Sebastian's knees felt weak. He sat down suddenly.

" Meier?" He looked over the valley, where the trash was fading from sight in the departing glow of sunset. "Quagmire?"

Behind him, Corwyn and Gwen listened with dawning comprehension. Then they too sank to the ground to watch the light fail, twinkling occasionally on the remnants of things now faded, shattered, and torn. They could feel the dark presence of the midden heap waiting patiently to claim them.

There followed a silence which no one broke for a long, long time.

CHAPTER 11

Midnight Dumpers

SOMETHING WOKE SEBASTIAN FROM A DREAM IN WHICH HE'D BEEN hiding in a passage beneath the Château d'Oignon, crying with fear. He forced himself to lie still and listen.

He heard only the breeze rustling through acres of garbage, and Corwyn's soft snoring nearby—nothing to account for his being jerked from his sleep.

Sebastian slid his hand to the hilt of his sword. He tried to find Corwyn, but all he could see was an indistinct shape on the ground.

The shape snorted, rolled over, and resumed snoring on its other side. Sebastian smiled, relieved to find Corwyn sleeping. He'd been worried his master might have pushed too hard on their journey. From the time they discovered Sebastian had misunderstood String John's message until they'd lain down to sleep a few hours later, Corwyn had said nothing. He just huddled in his robes and stared across the valley, his face tormented.

But if Corwyn was silent, the voice in Sebastian's head was not. While the group had prepared for night, no longer needing to risk their lives crossing the midden heap, Sebastian's father had thundered at him. How could he have been so stupid!

Ah, Gwen, he thought. What have I done?

Sebastian uttered an anguished cry—half sob, half groan. It was a sound from his dream, or like the child he'd seen while rescuing Corwyn. This further evidence of their sameness shamed him, and he fidgeted on the hard ground in an effort to escape his own derision. At last he checked the stars overhead for something to do.

He was wide awake and too filled with self-reproach to sleep. Soon the waxing moon rose above the ridge and spread its stingy glow on the valley. He could just make out the dark shapes of Gwen and Petronius where they slept. Then he scanned the dark mounds in the valley, but all lay quiet—as quiet as the eerie malevolence of the place could ever be.

The ashes of their fire were a darker shadow against the ground. That fire and the meager meal it represented had been the one redeeming aspect of their evening. While they sat immobilized after Sebastian's discovery that Kwagg and Meier were peasants and not a geographic feature, Oliver had gone back into the canyon to play. He'd come upon a rabbit there and, to his own surprise as much as the rabbit's, caught it. The broom returned proudly displaying his find.

At first, Gwen and Sebastian had looked to Corwyn to explain their need for food to Oliver. But the alchemist paid them no attention, so Gwen had undertaken the delicate task instead. Oliver was upset when she explained she wanted his rabbit for dinner, but Gwen insisted. In the end, Oliver couldn't refuse her and had given the rabbit up, but he sulked about it and soon wandered off. He hadn't returned since.

Sebastian dispatched the rabbit with his sword, then skinned and dressed it for cooking. But it was Petronius who grudgingly provided a fire, striking sparks from a stone with his hoof as if he'd been shod with iron. The unicorn was grim-faced as he did it and kept his attention diverted from the waiting rabbit. Then he too left them long enough for the meal to be cooked and eaten. Since returning, he'd treated Gwen with greater reserve than before, even though she had apologized and explained how badly they needed food.

It had also been Gwen who managed to get Corwyn to eat a little, though he never responded to her questions.

The breeze rose in the darkness, stirring the ashes from the fire and dropping them again closer to the edge of the midden heap. In time, Sebastian realized, the ashes would join the rest of the debris in the valley, contributing in a small way to the presence lurking there. He squeezed his eyes shut to block out the thought and tried to go back to sleep.

He'd almost succeeded when the disturbance came again, only half heard in the dark. Instantly Sebastian was awake, listening. There it was again, the sound of voices arguing nearby.

With a start, he realized Petronius and Gwen were gone from the places where each had bedded down for the night. What Sebastian had taken for their shapes were only denser shadows of rocks.

He rolled to his feet and crept toward the sound, short sword ready. Ahead loomed the rock face they had rounded when they emerged from the canyon. The arguing grew more distinct as he approached. It seemed to be coming from the other side.

Sebastian leaped around the rocks and alighted in a fighting stance, ready to challenge whatever threatened Gwen and Petronius. Ahead, Petronius scuffled with a shadowy assailant. There was no sign of Gwen. Before Sebastian could reach the unicorn, he heard a thud as something struck soft flesh, followed by an outrushing of air from Petronius. The dark figure of the unicorn froze. Petronius's assailant squirmed from under him and stepped aside.

The unicorn stumbled toward Sebastian, his legs shakier than ever. Short gasps burst through his gritted teeth. He shambled past Sebastian without appearing to notice. The unicorn's hind legs kept crossing, giving him a curiously crablike gait.

Petronius shuffled in a wide circle that took him to the canyon mouth. A moment later, Sebastian heard the unicorn's hooves dragging across the stony canyon floor, growing higher as Petronius climbed. Then there was silence except for sobbing from the darkness where the unicorn had been attacked.

Sebastian crossed quickly, looking for the assailant. But he saw only Gwen, huddled on a low rock, crying. She gasped and jerked upright at Sebastian's sudden appearance.

Sebastian peered into the darkness, feeling awkward. He had the odd sensation that he'd intruded on her privacy.

"I'm sorry, milady," he said. "I thought something was wrong." Then he realized something *was* wrong or she wouldn't be crying. "What happened to Petronius?"

Gwen lowered her head. "He left," she said, her voice cold. "Let him go. We're better off without him."

"He left? But why?" Sebastian looked around helplessly. "Why would he leave us stranded? And who attacked him?"

Gwen didn't seem to hear his questions. "I told him," she said. "I told him I wasn't what he believed me to be."

Sebastian crouched beside her and tried to take her hand, but she pulled away. "What do you mean?" he whispered.

She pushed the straggling hair from her face, then fixed him with a curious stare. Tears glittered on her cheeks in the moonlight. "I'm not a maiden," she said.

"Huh? *Je ne comprends pas.* What do you mean?"

"Exactly that. I'm no maiden, no virgin untouched and untaken. I have loved whom I willed, and no one ever held it against me." The breeze fluttered her hair around her face and she pushed it back again impatiently. "Now do you understand?"

Sebastian was too shocked to think. "I . . . but, Gwendolyn . . ." He stopped.

Gwen dropped her eyes. "I thought you would," she said.

Sebastian knelt in a surge of compassion and tried to draw her to him. She pushed him away. "Gwen, I forgive you."

She laughed, but it was an ugly sound. "I didn't ask you to forgive me. Only to accept. I'm not repentant for what I've done."

Sebastian sat back on his heels. An uncomfortable silence fell between them. In his head, the voice of his father was quick with judgment. "So Petronius spurned you," Sebastian said at last.

Gwen looked up sharply. "Spurned me? *Mais non!* If only he had, it might have been easier. He said he was glad I wasn't a maiden, that he found the whole virginity matter tedious. He said it was a malady afflicting too many young women—a malady that is readily cured."

Sebastian waited, but Gwen seemed unwilling to go on. "Then what?"

"Then we scuffled and I kicked him."

Sebastian winced. Much as he despised Petronius, as a fellow male he couldn't help but sympathize with the unicorn over his fate.

"Why'd you tell him?" he asked.

Gwen's eyes were two black, glittering stones in their unflinching appraisal of him. He shifted under her stare and added petulantly, *"Alors!* You know unicorns only aid virgins."

"I can't stand relationships based on deceit."

"But you kept silent this long. Couldn't you have waited a little longer, at least until he'd led us out of here?"

"Would you have me continue a lie?" she demanded, her voice rising.

"Well, no." Sebastian squirmed between pragmatism and principle. "Not exactly. You didn't have to actually lie. You didn't have to *say* anything. You could have just let him believe what he wanted to."

"It was a lie, Sebastian." She flung the words at him like an accusation.

"All right then, have it your way, *mon petit navet!* Yes, it was a lie. And, yes, in this case you should have kept it up. It was for the good of us all. Gwen, sometimes you act more like a common serving wench than a princess!"

Sebastian found himself shouting at her the way his father's voice so often shouted at him.

Gwen stood and Sebastian followed. They stared at one another with open hostility.

"So you think our need for him justified my silence? I wonder."

She gave the final two words a peculiar emphasis that made Sebastian feel cold. But before he could ask what she meant, they were interrupted by Corwyn's voice from the other side of the stone wall.

"Children, please! Do you think you might discuss whatever it is a little more quietly? Or better yet, save it till morning. It was a long day and I'm very tired."

The tension drained from Sebastian abruptly as he realized they had disturbed the old alchemist.

"I'm sorry, Corwyn," Gwen said. "We didn't mean to interrupt your sleep. God knows, any rest you can get is well deserved. We won't talk anymore tonight."

Sebastian started to turn away but she caught him with a sharp jab in the ribs. "Just don't think the matter rests at this," she hissed, stalking off.

Sebastian remained until he heard Gwen settling down to sleep. Soon Corwyn was snoring again. Sebastian let out his breath, surprised to find he'd been holding it.

Gwen's final words held a bitterness Sebastian didn't understand, but there were tears in her voice as well. Something he said had hurt her, but what? Was it because he had given voice to his father's anger? And why did he and Gwen always end up arguing? Just thinking of her made Sebastian's heart miss a beat and his throat catch. How did he always manage to do or say something that cut him off from the tenderness she so willingly gave to others?

Sebastian wanted to talk to Corwyn about it, and many other things besides. But the alchemist was so tired. Concern for Corwyn seemed the only thing he and Gwen agreed on.

Indecisive and unable to sleep despite exhaustion, Sebastian wandered to the edge of the midden heap that covered the valley. He stooped occasionally and picked up pebbles to fling at odd bits of trash, listening to the breeze sighing through the debris. If demons truly breathe, he thought, as Corwyn's test seemed to prove they did, it must sound as forlorn as this. Then, irritated by his own restlessness, he folded his hands and forced himself to stand quietly for a time. He'd almost determined to lie down again and try going back to sleep, when a flicker of movement registered out of the corner of his eye.

Turning, he saw Oliver approach around the perimeter of the field, carefully picking his way past the clutter. Oliver stopped abruptly two or three yards away, suddenly aware of Sebastian. The spindly creature started to turn away, avoiding Sebastian as he'd done since the night they met when Sebastian had laughed at the broom.

Sebastian felt saddened. "You don't have to run away, Oliver. I won't hurt you. Not anymore."

Oliver stopped and turned with feigned indifference to look across the desolate field. He came no nearer, but he didn't leave either. Sebastian felt almost content as they stood in the breeze together waiting for the darkness to pass.

To the south, at the massive, iron-bound entrance to the deserted workings known as the Goblin Mines, Dr. Tox also waited, though impatiently.

In the more credulous times of ages past, goblins had sometimes been seen in the Pyrenees, extending a labyrinth of tunnels just below the crest on the French side. From here, they mined precious metals and jewels. Then, as the relative enlightenment of a newer age replaced strict credulity in the medieval mind, belief in the goblins faded. Encounters with the creatures grew rarer, until they'd finally stopped altogether ten or twenty years back. Now people knew the goblins had never actually existed, that they were the superstitious inventions of a bygone era. But although the goblins had vanished (or rather, had never existed), the empty mines remained. People didn't bother to explain this discrepancy, but they didn't go too near the mines, either. It seemed prudent not to push the limits of one's understanding by venturing too near a fact which never should have been.

This accounted for only part of Dr. Tox's unease, however, for he also knew what the mines now contained, and it terrified him. Besides, dawn was near and his task was best completed in darkness.

And that thought reminded him of Hydro Phobius's concern about the funds intended for the Duke de Gardenia. Dr. Tox wondered how much his master suspected. Did the Black Knight realize the money intended for stabilizing the economy of Gardenia and bolstering the duke's authoritarian rule was going instead into Dr. Tox's personal account? Probably not, but he must suspect something or he wouldn't have come up from Spain to oversee the operation in Gardenia. Previously, he'd been willing to leave relations with the duchy to Dr. Tox.

Dr. Tox swore with forced bravado and resumed pacing.

Below him, tailings from the mines spilled down the mountainside, dim in the light of a thin moon. The tailings formed a broad scar across the landscape, obliterating vegetation where the mineral wastes had poured from the bowels of the earth. Only in isolated spots were a few straggly growths beginning to take root again.

Such persistence was ill-suited to Dr. Tox. He was anxious to escape from Gardenia as well as from the mines. Nothing about this operation was going right.

His plan to eliminate Corwyn had gone awry when the alchemist escaped. Now Corwyn was not only free to interfere, but also he probably realized there was more to this plague than the pernicious will of God.

Then there were all the mundane difficulties involved with managing an operation of this size, while at the same time keeping it secret. And worst of all were the two peasants upon whom Phobius had bestowed the job of freighting shipments from Spain to the mines.

A wisp of cloud obscured the moon, then blew past. Dr. Tox glowered at the sky and noticed more clouds advancing from the east. The threat of rain added to his unease.

A creaking harness and muffled shouts from the forest to his left signaled Kwagg and Meier's arrival from Zaragoza on the Spanish side. Dr. Tox judged they had just enough time to dispose of this load before it began to rain or daylight exposed their activities to any prying eyes. There was little chance of being seen at the Goblin Mines, even in daytime. But with the job they were performing, Dr. Tox wanted that chance reduced to none at all. Too much was at stake. Besides, despite its remoteness, he'd had the feeling they were being watched on previous trips up here.

Slowly Kwagg, Meier, and the mules emerged from the darkness as they climbed the hill. At each switchback the barrels tipped precariously, threatening to drag the animals over and dump their contents on the ground. Kwagg and Meier countered each threat energetically, Kwagg providing verbal assaults while Meier kept the loads upright. At last they reached the final turn, and the mules stopped near the entrance to the mines and waited to be unloaded.

"You're late!" Dr. Tox snapped.

Kwagg shrugged. "Couldn't be helped. Some tall, bony fellow from Pomme de Terre was spying on us."

"Oh, no! What happened?"

"Well, I think he found what he was looking for," Kwagg laughed. "One of the barrels cracked and we had to leave it behind. The fool crept up for a better look, then went skipping down the trail singing children's rhymes."

"You're lucky it wasn't you," Dr. Tox said. "I can't understand how you and Meier always come through these accidents unscathed."

"Guess we must live right." Kwagg sniffed and wiped his nose, then added, "Though I don't consider falling in the moat and catching the grippe as unscathed." He started loosening the lead mule's harness.

Dr. Tox hurried to help, mentally shutting his nose against the smell of pigsty. Previously, he had avoided becoming involved in this part of the operation except for overseeing final disposition of the cargo. But the clouds to the east were moving closer, driven by the rising wind, and dawn pursued them. For once Dr. Tox lent his muscles to the job at hand.

Meier loosened the harness of the lead mule and tossed a barrel to Kwagg. Dr. Tox cowered and flung an arm over his eyes, expecting the barrel to smash.

"*Soyez prudent!*" he whined. "Those mustn't come open outside the mines."

Kwagg shrugged and tucked the barrel casually under one arm before starting up the slight incline between him and the entrance. With every sneeze along the way he jostled the barrel and made Dr. Tox flinch.

As always, Meier ignored Dr. Tox. He'd found it best to pretend the miserable physician didn't exist. Meier unstrapped another barrel and swung it onto his shoulder. Dr. Tox stood, arms outstretched, waiting, but Meier pushed past him as if he wasn't there. Staggering slightly under the weight of the barrel, Meier followed Kwagg up the slope.

Dr. Tox trotted to the mule and grabbed at a barrel, intending to swing it onto his shoulder the way Meier had done. The barrel seemed anchored to the pack. Dr. Tox checked the harness to be sure it was loose, then heaved at the barrel again. He grunted and strained until his vision swam, but the barrel refused to budge.

Kwagg returned and brushed him aside, then lifted the barrel effortlessly and started up the slope as Meier came down, slung another barrel onto his own shoulder, and prepared to follow. Kwagg stopped.

"Tiens! How many times do I have to tell you?" he demanded of Meier. "Quit slacking off! You're supposed to carry two barrels each time. That's the deal. Now get with it!"

Meier hastened to comply, balancing one barrel on each shoulder and stumbling up the slope. Kwagg faced Dr. Tox. "I've got a bad back. Him, he's got no excuse. He's just lazy, that's all." Kwagg shook his head. "I tell you, it's hard to get good help in Gardenia anymore, what with rumors of change all around. Nobody wants to work. Now me, I don't pay any mind to that kind of talk. It just poisons the will of the populace, that's all. Just poisons the will of the populace."

Dr. Tox wondered what tavern Kwagg had picked up that phrase in. But Kwagg looked pleased with himself and started off again, pausing only long enough to admonish Meier to work faster.

Dr. Tox followed the men up the slope, trying not to wince at the casual way they handled the barrels. If an accident did occur, he hoped the garlic around his neck would protect him long enough to get away. He didn't care what happened to Kwagg and Meier. But Dr. Tox knew he was far from civilization and the services of an exorcist. If a barrel broke, he might be eternally damned.

At the top of the slope, he found Meier stacking the barrels in dilapidated ore carts. The carts rode splintery wooden rails that led inside. Dr. Tox stood by, stroking his beard and muttering useless precautions, while Kwagg and Meier finished hauling barrels up the slope and dumping them into the carts. Then Kwagg approached Dr. Tox, sneezing and wiping his nose as he came. Meier hung back, making final adjustments to the carts. Kwagg panted mightily to impress upon Dr. Tox the extent of his exertions and mopped his brow with a sleeve—the same sleeve he had used for his nose.

"Hard work, bringing those kegs up the mountain and dumping them in the mines," Kwagg said. "Know any way of getting that stuff to flow uphill on its own?" He laughed and jabbed Dr. Tox. "Wouldn't that make life easier for us all!"

Dr. Tox rubbed his side, wondering if any ribs had cracked. He jumped back to avoid another poke from Kwagg. Foolish peasant, talking about water flowing uphill. How could Kwagg joke when their souls were in danger?

Then a picture flashed into his mind, a picture of cloth sails turning in the wind on the side of the duke's great hall. Dr. Tox grinned. Maybe Kwagg's idea wasn't so stupid after all. "I know just the man to accomplish it," he muttered to himself. "All it'll take is a little persuasion."

"Comment?" Kwagg asked.

"Oh, nothing," replied Dr. Tox smugly. "I just may be able to grant your wish, that's all."

Kwagg looked puzzled. He'd already forgotten his comment and couldn't figure out what this fop was talking about. Then he brightened. "Almost forgot." He pulled a worn coin purse and a wad of soiled parchment from the pouch at his belt. "Old Phobius wants a record of when each shipment is unloaded here at the mines. He's getting real particular about having everything down on parchment. He says you're to sign and date this to show the shipment arrived on time and that you received the next payment for the duke."

Dr. Tox accepted the wad and opened it gingerly, wondering why messages delivered by Kwagg always arrived in such a state. The parchment sheet whipped about in his hands with the wind. He read the statement, drawn up by one of the clerics working for Hydro Phobius, then tried to push the sheet back at Kwagg. "I can't sign this until the shipment's been consigned to the mines."

Kwagg stared. "If you want to stand around out here after we roll those barrels in, you go right ahead. But me and Meier intend

to get as far away as possible just as fast as we can. There's a
deep shaft just up the tunnel here, and we don't want to be
anywhere around when them barrels hit bottom."

"Well, it really isn't proper," Dr. Tox complained. Still, it did
sound like good advice. He signed the sheet.

Kwagg wadded the parchment back into his pouch and counted
gold coins into Dr. Tox's palm. Then Kwagg yelled to Meier,
"Let 'em roll!"

Meier withdrew the wheel chocks and heaved on the end cart,
setting the ore train in motion. The ancient axles squealed in
protest at being recalled to service. Gradually the carts picked
up momentum as they rolled down a slight grade into the mine.
Kwagg flung open the massive door as the leading cart approached. He waited nervously as the carts rolled by. As soon
as the last cart cleared the door, he slammed it shut and Meier
dropped a heavy beam in place to seal the entrance. Then the
three men scrambled down the slope to the pathway.

Panic crawled up Dr. Tox's back like a tangible being. Without
looking back to where Kwagg and Meier were climbing onto
mules, he fled down the road. Moments later Kwagg and Meier
overtook him, their expressions grim, the gaunt old animals galloping faster than Dr. Tox had believed possible. The two peasants never even paused to offer him a ride. As they passed, he
felt a slight tremor from deep within the earth.

He ran faster, hurtling down the mountain path in the grey
light of a dismal, cloudy dawn. He entered the forest behind the
mule train, slipping in mud their hooves had churned in passing.
Finally, he judged himself safely away and collapsed in exhaustion. As he lay gasping from the pain in his sides, feeling the
mud trickle down his face, he wondered if the money he diverted
from the duke's treasury could possibly make up for the degradation he endured. How much gold was it worth to risk his
life and soul? Why didn't he just go into honest practice like
Corwyn?

But he knew why, and he hated the world for it, for he couldn't
compete successfully in honest trade with the likes of Corwyn.
He wasn't capable enough. And he wanted more wealth than
could be acquired by the scrupulous.

Then he remembered Kwagg's comment, and his own half-
formed idea about making Corwyn accomplish the task. That
would be appropriate revenge to inflict upon the wretched alchemist. And it might help distract the Black Knight's attention.

Phobius was close to discovering the real disposition of his funds.

A leer lit Dr. Tox's dirt-streaked face. Maybe this vile business would be worth the risk after all.

All the way to Pomme de Terre, he embroidered his vision of a pipeline stretching from Spain over the Pyrenees to the Goblin Mines, powered by windmills. Corwyn wouldn't want to cooperate, of course. But Dr. Tox was certain his reluctance could be overcome. Enforced cooperation was a subject the Black Knight knew much about.

This thought lightened his heart. By the time rain began falling around him, Dr. Tox was too gleeful with anticipation to care.

CHAPTER 12

Anhydrous Rain

IT WAS A DISPIRITED GROUP THAT STRAGGLED UP THE RIDGE FROM the Valley of Despair later that morning.

Oliver and the three humans reached the crest under ominous clouds, dark with rain and haughty with chill, damp winds. Already, clouds had swallowed the Pyrenees to the south.

Corwyn stumbled across the saddle. His arms hung limp, his face fixed with dumb resolution as he lurched over the open ground. His fatigue-dulled eyes reflected the slate of the clouds, and his skin echoed their pallor. Finally his legs folded in protest and he sank to the ground.

Sebastian dropped to the grass behind his master and Gwen sprawled on a hummock several yards away. The mood of the elements matched their own sullen outlook, for they were exhausted and sick with hunger. The futility of their journey weighed as heavily on their spirits as did the clouds upon the ridge. Sebastian turned his face into the wind and breathed in short gasps, letting the wet bite of the air restore circulation in his face. It stung his cheeks and dispelled the fog engulfing his brain, but it did nothing to diminish the pain inside him.

Corwyn's presence of mind gradually returned and he studied the slope, searching for the way Petronius had taken when he led them over the ridge the evening before. But there was no indication to the alchemist's inexperienced eyes of where they had passed. He blinked owlishly into the wind, realizing without surprise that the trail Petronius had taken was too indistinct for him to follow. At last he turned to the others.

"Our situation couldn't be much worse," he said, his voice flat. "We're lost without Petronius. We don't even know what we're looking for, except that it lies somewhere in the Pyrenees." He waved a hand vaguely. "Our only help in conquering the plague might have come from String John, but he'll be in Pomme de Terre today to meet me and of course we can't return there until we unravel the mystery of the plague, which we need his help to solve in the first place."

Corwyn paused, befuddled by the circuitous logic of his words. He shrugged, and Sebastian realized how old his master looked, huddled from the wind beneath a lowering sky.

"What should we do?" Corwyn asked at last.

Gwen stared at a blade of grass she was mutilating. "It's my fault," she mumbled. Corwyn and Sebastian leaned toward her and strained to hear, for her words were whipped away as though the very wind delighted in this chance to confound them. "I shouldn't have told Petronius the truth about me." Her sigh was drowned in the greater sighing of the coming storm. Then she lifted her chin to glare at Sebastian. "I thought relationships should be based on truth, not falsehood. Now I know better. It's a mistake I won't make again."

Sebastian felt a surge of shame wash through him. His eyes dropped. The voice in his head demanded that he be angry with Gwen for her admitted wantonness as well as for alienating the only creature who could guide them. But Sebastian heard the anguish in her voice and couldn't be angry with her no matter what his father insisted. "I'm sorry about bringing us here," he said. He struggled to keep his voice under control, aware that it didn't matter, that appearances were vain and useless after the hurt he'd caused.

"Well, I should have known our true course led into the Pyrenees," Corwyn said. He looked for some hint of the mountains under their grey covering, then gave up and returned his attention to Gwen and Sebastian. "I allowed my fear of entering that wilderness to influence me, and that was wrong. But self-recriminations do us no good. We must decide what to do, and how to proceed from here."

Sebastian listened, hoping for absolution. Only chance, and Oliver's intervention, had spared him from abandoning Corwyn during his imprisonment, condemning the old alchemist and Gwen to face this plight alone. Although it might have been better for them if he'd stolen away as planned, Sebastian reflected bitterly. At least they wouldn't have come to the Valley of Despair had he not been along to misinterpret String John's message.

He twisted his face into the wind again to conceal any outward display of the emotions inside him, aware that fatigue had left him at the mercy of personal storms more violent than the elements.

Corwyn and Gwen were discussing the watershed above Pomme de Terre. The source of the plague, Corwyn insisted, had to be there. His breath of demons test, if they could acquire the materials to perform it, would show them exactly where.

Across the meadow, Oliver gamboled after a pair of rabbits. The broom made a comical figure as he pranced, arms flailing, through grass still sere from winter. Sebastian smiled despite his exhaustion. Then he remembered the rabbit they had eaten the night before and wished Oliver would catch one of the creatures. But the rabbits evaded the broom easily, and Sebastian had the feeling Oliver made certain it stayed that way. The little fellow didn't want to sacrifice another playmate to the unaccountable hungers of his companions.

Sebastian chuckled at the sight, interrupting Gwen and drawing her gaze.

"It's Oliver," he explained. "The way he's dancing around with those rabbits reminds me of Thaddeus haranguing the crowd in the marketplace the night I arrived. Thaddeus was almost as scrawny, and Oliver brings the same intensity to playing that Thaddeus did to preaching."

Corwyn and Gwen looked bewildered, and Sebastian dismissed the whole thing with a wave. Then he sobered, thinking of Thaddeus. Being imprisoned and possessed by a demon was an undeserved fate even for a heretic who encouraged change.

Of course, Thaddeus had also accused the duke of accepting payments from someone who wanted him to maintain a feudal tyranny in Gardenia. That kind of talk bordered on treason. Still, what harm could the old man's words have caused that would warrant the punishment he received?

Suddenly, Sebastian stiffened, staring past Oliver into the grey distance toward the Pyrenees.

"What is it?" Corwyn asked, noting Sebastian's change in manner. Gwen also looked at Sebastian, then peered in the direction he was facing as if the answer might be found in what he saw.

"Where did Thaddeus live?" Sebastian asked his master.

"I don't know exactly." Corwyn shrugged. "In the mountains somewhere, with his goats."

"The Pyrenees?"

"Oui, bien entendu! Why?"

"Remember I said Thaddeus told the crowd he'd discovered gold was being paid to the duke to keep Gardenia a feudal tyranny? Gold from outside the duchy? Well, whatever Thaddeus discovered made him come down from the mountains after all those years to bring his message to Pomme de Terre."

"So?" Corwyn asked.

"Don't you see? *Pardieu—*"

"Watch your language, boy!"

"Excuse me," he said with a nod to Gwen, then turned back to Corwyn. "But master, if Thaddeus discovered secret payments were being made to the duke, it must have been because something happened up where he lived."

"What has that to do with us?" Corwyn snapped. "Thaddeus was concerned with the Renaissance; we're trying to find the source of the demons causing the plague so we can stop them."

"Renaissance? Oh, that's what you called the Italian heresy, isn't it?"

"It's not a heresy, boy, and the name refers to this whole period of change and rebirth."

Sebastian wished Corwyn wouldn't bring up his peculiar notions in front of others. He rushed on, trying to direct the conversation back to Thaddeus. "But, master, Gwen said Kwagg and Meier have been seen skulking around there with a mule train. And you yourself maintain the cause of the plague lies within the watershed of the Ale. So doesn't it strike you as odd that the solutions to both mysteries, that of the plague and that of the duke's resistance to new ideas, are to be found in the same region of the Pyrenees?"

Corwyn didn't bother to mask his incredulity. "What makes you think the two are related?"

Sebastian hesitated. It did seem preposterous to connect Thaddeus's comments about the duke with the demon plague which eventually possessed him.

And yet, he felt certain they were. He smiled grimly, but with a trace of self-satisfaction. He'd been wrong so often in recent days, had made so many mistakes in judgment. There was little he could point to in support of his conviction. But he knew a connection existed, if only because it was inconceivable to him that two such bizarre situations, each unlikely enough on its own, could possibly have developed in the same desolate area without sharing a common thread.

Sebastian shrugged, understating his certainty to avoid discussing something he felt was true but wasn't ready to prove. "It's worth some thought."

"Hmmph," Corwyn snorted. "That's about all it's worth."

The first splatters of rain interrupted them. Corwyn pushed to his feet, groaning and pulling his robes tighter. "Come along, children," he called over his shoulder. "We'd best get going. It's a long way from here to the mountains."

"But, master," Sebastian objected, "how will we get there if we don't know the way?"

"I shall leave it to my assistant to guide us," the old man said without looking back.

"Your assistant?" Sebastian considered this, then froze. *"Attendez!* Master, surely you don't mean me!"

"Of course not, you're my apprentice." Corwyn pointed to Oliver. "He's my assistant."

Oliver, oblivious to Corwyn's intentions, skittered about the field bewildered by the disappearance of his wildlife friends once the rain began. He had turned to chasing butterflies after the rabbits vanished some time earlier, but now even the bright insects were gone and Oliver couldn't fathom why. It was frustrating; no one ever seemed willing to play with him.

"But, master—" Sebastian began.

Corwyn drew himself up imperiously. *"Oui?"*

Oui, Sebastian repeated to himself, so tired and discouraged he could scarcely focus his thoughts. . . . *and this little piggy cried oui, oui, oui all the way home!*

"Nothing," he said.

Corwyn let his stance relax. "I thought not."

Sebastian glanced at Gwen, seeing his concern mirrored in her face. She hurried to Corwyn and took his arm.

"Corwyn, *mon chou,* is this wise?"

Sebastian's eyes widened. Gwen was more upset than he'd realized if she was now calling Corwyn a cabbage too.

The old alchemist didn't appear to notice the slight. "What do any of us know of these things?" he said. "Besides, Oliver's made from straw and wood, things of the field and forest. He can do no worse than the rest of us, and may be uniquely suited to do much better." He motioned to the broom.

Gwen hung back. Sebastian tried to catch her eye, but she evaded him and started after Corwyn. Sebastian followed grimly.

Corwyn spoke with Oliver, waving his arms at vague reference points invisible to other eyes. Oliver nodded vigorously, delighted at being chosen to lead. When Corwyn finished, the broom strutted before the three humans, sizing them up and indicating the order in which they were to follow.

"Oliver," Corwyn interrupted, "you are simply to lead. I will still command."

Oliver slumped, but apparently decided it was better to lead without authority than to be powerless and a follower, too. He waved them on and started down the mountainside.

Even with frequent admonishments from Corwyn, Oliver proved a demanding taskmaster. From the first he set a pace the humans found difficult to maintain. He'd end up well in front of them and then stand by impatiently, clacking his long wooden fingers in irritation while waiting for them to catch up. As soon as the three humans closed the gap he'd be off again, quickly outdistancing them.

Often it was Sebastian who lagged behind, lost in thought. He didn't need his father to tell him what a fool he was. In fact, he found he'd grown increasingly resentful of the voice in his head over the past several days, something he'd never felt before. This awareness was uncomfortable, however, so he concentrated his thoughts on Gwen instead. But there were hidden undercurrents at work there as well. Gwen had become very preoccupied during the past two days, and Sebastian was certain it had something to do with him. For some reason, that thought irritated him.

Oliver led them down the ridge and through the forest without hesitation. After a while, they reached the glade where Petronius had stopped with Gwen the day before. Off to one side, Sebastian noticed a dense cluster of vines which had been trained to grow over the lower limbs of two adjoining trees, forming a bower. He was about to say something when Corwyn caught Gwen's arm and indicated the bower, evidently entertaining the same thought of seeking shelter.

Then they heard Petronius's voice, soft and persuasive from amid the vines. This was followed by a very human, very female giggle. The giggle shifted to lustier sounds. Gwen faced ahead stiffly and marched after Oliver.

"What's the matter, *mon petit panais?*" Sebastian asked, unable to resist the barb. "Don't you want to stop for a visit?"

Gwen ignored him, but Corwyn looked at Sebastian strangely. "What are you doing, boy?"

Sebastian dropped his eyes, ashamed of what he'd said. "I'm sorry, Corwyn. It's just the way she behaved with that unicorn," he answered lamely.

"Her behavior wasn't the problem. But that's not what I mean." Corwyn waved the comment away. "What I want to know is why you're calling her these names. Just now you called her your little parsnip, last night it was a turnip. You've been calling her one vegetable name or another since Petronius arrived."

"Well, she started it," Sebastian answered. "She called me a cabbage. She even called you the same thing a while ago."

Corwyn sighed. "Boy, when will you learn? Calling someone a little cabbage is a term of endearment, not an insult."

Sebastian considered this, a sick feeling in his stomach. "It is?"

"And another thing," Corwyn went on, "when you called her these names, why did you use the masculine gender?"

Sebastian was startled. "The vegetable names were masculine, of course."

"Yes, but Gwen isn't."

"I know that!" Sebastian snapped.

"I'm just making sure," Corwyn said. "The way you've been acting, one can only wonder."

"I've made a mess of this all way around, haven't I?" Sebastian asked after a moment.

Corwyn nodded.

Sebastian walked in silence for a while. "Why is it these expressions mean the right thing when someone else uses them," he burst out at last, "but when I use them they always come out wrong?"

Corwyn shrugged. "As I said, one can only wonder."

Sebastian sighed heavily, then trotted up to Gwen. "Corwyn

just told me what it meant yesterday when you called me your *petit chou*," he said. "Oh, Gwendolyn, I'm sorry. I just didn't understand. Please let me be your *petit chou* again."

She didn't respond, but her pace slackened and Sebastian thought perhaps she looked a trifle less grim. He could only hope that eventually she would forgive him.

After they had passed Petronius's glade, Oliver struck off at an angle to head south toward the Pyrenees. Sebastian hoped the broom knew what he was doing. Wherever they were heading, it was new terrain.

The rain, a drizzle at first, grew harder. Soon they all were shivering from the soaking. All except Oliver. He seemed exasperated at the way the three humans slogged along under the trees. The rain neither dampened Oliver's spirits nor slowed his pace as he danced over blackened, sodden leaves. Even with the delays the broom had to make for the sake of his entourage, the band made good headway. Oliver seemed to have an innate sense of direction.

They continued for what must have been hours, following the base of the ridge into the foothills of the Pyrenees until they were roughly even with Pomme de Terre, but in a smaller valley west of the town. Sebastian was long past knowing or caring whether Oliver really knew where he was taking them. All he could think of was food and rest and a warm fire to chase away the chill in his bones.

The soft hiss of rain falling through new foliage on the trees was mesmerizing, as was the effort required to put one foot in front of the other. So Sebastian was unprepared when Corwyn stopped abruptly. He almost ran into the alchemist before he could stop walking. Corwyn glared at him, then looked around, sniffing.

"What's the matter?" Sebastian asked.

Behind him, Gwen also sniffed. "It's drier," she said, her voice tinged with awe.

Corwyn nodded, still sniffing.

"What are you talking about? What's drier?" Sebastian snapped.

"The air," Gwen said, too absorbed to be impatient. "Smell it? It's drier than it was."

"We're in the middle of a rain," Sebastian scoffed. "How can the air be drier?"

But it was. In some inexplicable way, Sebastian realized Gwen was right. The air had turned dry even though rain continued to fall unabated around them.

"Allors!" Corwyn called as he ran to catch up with Oliver. "Hurry."

They sped through the forest, dead leaves crackling underfoot. The trees, which had been bright with new foliage, now looked withered and frail.

The trees came to an end and Oliver and his band emerged into a barren, dusty clearing. Moisture vanished from the air as if burned away. Sebastian's breath scorched his throat.

Before them stood a disordered compound of drab stone buildings surrounded by a high wall. Lacking any semblance of grace or style, the structures dominated the clearing with a dismal permanence strangely in keeping with the dry, lifeless air.

Corwyn ran to a weathered gate in the wall. "The monastery of the Order of St. Mathurin," he said with awe, reading a crooked, poorly inscribed sign over the gate.

"The patron saint of idiots and fools," Sebastian sneered. "We heard tales of the order at the abbey in Justienne. I always thought the tellers exaggerated their stories, but now I'm not so sure."

He scowled at the crumbling wall, remembering tales of the misfits who entered the order founded by the lunatic third century French priest. The brethren were derelicts rejected by the legitimate orders of Christendom. They were the mentally and physically impaired, those afflicted with the "malady of St. Mathurin," as it was popularly known. They had nothing but foolishness, ignorance, and personal limitations to bring to their clerical duties, and so were held in derision by all other orders.

Indeed, the Order of St. Mathurin's greatest achievement was a joke among respected clerics. Where other orders could boast of having preserved the learning of antiquity by copying Greek and Roman manuscripts, the copyists and archivists of St. Mathurin preserved only the lowliest and most mundane details of merchant trade, daily life, and political rule. The brothers toiled over canceled notes for old accounts, receipts for shipments long since made, and writs by which minor nobles had recorded unimportant acts of provincial jurisprudence—all cast away by their former owners as worthless and now tediously maintained and recopied by the illiterates of St. Mathurin in crude mimicry of the illustrated manuscripts of other orders. Here might be found elaborately inscribed copies of a village deed attesting to the barter of one old cow for three bushels of milled wheat and a broken scythe. Or the bill of lading for a merchant caravan from Bordeaux or even Calais two generations back, in the time of Sebastian's grandfather and the Black Prince.

"Corwyn, what happened to the rain?" Gwen asked, interrupting Sebastian's thoughts.

Corwyn peered overhead. Rain still streaked the sky, but something prevented it from reaching the ground. "'The rain which wetteth not,'" Corwyn said in a soft, reverential voice. "I believe we've stumbled upon the place in which to find some answers." He reached for the bellpull beside the gate.

"*Arrêtez!*" Sebastian cried, gripping his master's wrist. "You don't mean to go in there, do you?"

Corwyn frowned at Sebastian's hand and the apprentice dropped the alchemist's wrist. " Although your question doesn't deserve an answer," Corwyn said, "I'll give you one anyway by reminding you of the ancient alchemical text we discussed on your first morning with me. I'm beginning to believe the journey that text referred to may not have been allegorical after all, but a real one with this monastery as its destination.

"Besides," he added, shrugging, "we need food and shelter. We might as well seek it here as elsewhere."

Sebastian said nothing, but gritted his teeth in distaste as Corwyn pulled the rope. A bell clanked inside the compound, making a dull, lifeless sound. Receiving no answer, Corwyn tried again.

"I'm coming, I'm coming. Don't vent your spleen," came a dry, cracking voice from the other side. The gate opened on unoiled hinges. Before them stood a large man in the drab robes of the order. He paused, facing the group without appearing to see them. "Yes, my children, what is it? What may I do for you?" His eyes drifted up and to the left as he spoke.

"We are travelers who seek food and shelter," Corwyn said, his voice thick from the dryness in his throat. "We hoped to find it here."

"Oh?" The man's eyes swung across the group and came to rest looking down and to the right of Corwyn. "You want to come in?" He smiled as if his face were unskilled at it. His parched lips cracked. "There's no precedent for that here, but I suppose it would be all right. No one ever visits the Order of St. Mathurin because of the archives. All those records, you know. And of course, no one ever wants to read them."

" 'That which is writ remaineth unread,' " Corwyn quoted to himself.

"Pardon, monsieur?" the man said, his eyes seeming to see through them without actually settling on them.

"It was nothing," Corwyn said. "I was remembering something I once read. To answer your question, we do wish to enter and to see your archives if we may."

"You do? Well, then, come in, please." The cleric turned part way around and collided with the gate. He felt his way past the obstacle, oriented himself, and started across the compound. "I'm François, chief archivist for the order," he said, barely missing the corner of a building.

Gwen tugged on Corwyn's sleeve. "Is he all right?" she whispered. "He seems to be, well . . . uh—"

"Blind?" François prompted, speaking to the air above them. "Oh, it's quite all right, I'm not offended." He laughed easily, but the sound grated from the dryness of his throat. "Where else but in the Order of St. Mathurin could a blind man become an archivist?" Then he called over his shoulder in the general direction of Corwyn. "You'll have to wait until later to see the archives. Now, it's time for our dinner. You must hurry or we'll be too late."

Sebastian tried to swallow, but his mouth felt full of sand. He looked forward to a meal and something to drink. He was grateful to the monk for providing them even if it meant accepting the hospitality of the Order of St. Mathurin. "I hope our arriving at mealtime isn't an inconvenience," he croaked. "But in truth, *monsieur*, we are famished. And exceedingly dry."

"Ah, *un anglais,*" François said. "Yes, it is dry. That's the problem. It's the effect of the archives. And that's why we must hurry."

Sebastian wanted to ask about the strange dryness, but François would say no more, concentrating instead on guiding them to a large common room furnished with long rows of trestle tables and wooden benches. Several men in the drab robes of the order sat at the tables, but Sebastian hesitated to examine them too closely. Many were maimed or deformed, while others lacked their mental faculties. Most stared openly at the alchemist and his friends.

Sebastian looked along the table where François seated them and saw Gwen sit tensely on the bench, her eyes averted from those around her. Only Corwyn seemed at ease, chatting hoarsely

with François. Sebastian glanced around for Oliver, but the
broom had disappeared.

A burly man stepped up to the table across from Sebastian.
Under his arm he carried a squirming bundle. With a shock,
Sebastian realized the bundle was a man with no arms or legs.
The big man sat his companion on the bench, then took a seat
beside him.

The man with no limbs mouthed something to the other man
without speaking. The big man simply nodded in response. Then
the limbless man spoke across the table. "Eh, François, you have
brought strangers?"

"Pierre," François said. "And I trust Jean is with you? These
people have come seeking aid, and to search among our archives."

Pierre's eyes widened. He mouthed something to the burly
man, the one Sebastian guessed was Jean. Jean's expression grew
startled as well. Pierre turned back to the table. "But, *messieurs
et mademoiselle*, no one ever reads the records in the archives."

"Nonetheless, they have come," François said. "We must
honor their request, no matter how ridiculous it might seem."
He looked beyond Corwyn's left shoulder. "Pierre is the order's
chief copyist."

Sebastian's jaw dropped and even Corwyn looked nonplussed.
"Then surely you read the records, even if no one else ever
does," Corwyn said to Pierre in an attempt to mask his confusion.

"Oh, *monsieur*, that is so funny," Pierre replied, laughing.
Again there was a silent consultation with Jean, who laughed
soundlessly. Pierre turned back to Corwyn. "*Monsieur*, I cannot
read. I am illiterate." He laughed again.

"There do seem to be several people here with various, uh,
disadvantages," Gwen said cautiously. "Doesn't that make it
impossible to do the work of the order?"

"Ah, that is one of the follies of the Order of St. Mathurin,"
François said. "Trying to find utility for that which is deemed
worthless by others. But it's also the order's greatest triumph,
for where else might men such as ourselves find gainful work?
And who but God's afflicted would deign to work at such foolish
tasks in this barren, hostile place?" He smacked dry lips for
emphasis. "As for how well we function, *mademoiselle*, you will
have to reserve judgment until later. Right now, I smell food
being served, so we must discontinue talking."

As François spoke, two youths, one on either side of the table, hurried down its length with buckets, filling mugs with water. As soon as each man's mug was filled, he would grab it up and drain it greedily. Sebastian frowned. While he could understand their thirst, he couldn't forgive their manners.

"François, why don't the brothers wait until everyone is served?" he asked, leaving his mug on the table.

François's face contorted over the lip of his own mug in reply, but he drank until his mug was empty. "Hurry," he gasped, wiping his mouth with the back of his hand. "Drink, while there's still time."

"But surely I won't die of thirst if I wait for my friends to be served."

"Drink, drink quickly," François insisted.

Scowling, Sebastian raised the mug to his lips, only to find it empty. *"Tiens!* Who drank mine?"

"I am sorry, *monsieur*," François said. "You're too late. Now you see why we hurry."

"What happened?" Sebastian studied the bottom of his mug.

"The air here, it's so dry," François explained. "Food and drink must be consumed immediately or—poof." He raised his hands, his fingers springing open. "They dry out."

"It is the manuscripts in the archives, you see," added Pierre. "Nothing in the world is so dry as the records we collect and preserve. When so many such manuscripts are gathered in one place, they devour the very moisture from the air around them. Thus we of the Order of St. Mathurin live in a desert surrounded by lush forest."

Sebastian licked dry, cracking lips, bewildered at the thought of records which sucked moisture from the air like a furnace. "Will I get another chance to drink?"

"At the end of the meal, they'll serve water again," François said. "Already the serving lads have gone to a spring beyond the compound to fetch it. But when they bring it, you must act quickly."

Sebastian didn't need to be told twice. When the soup was served, he dove into it as eagerly as the seasoned veterans around him. Even so, the soup, which began as a clear broth, was thick and gummy by the time he finished. And the bread which followed fell into desiccated crumbs as he ate. At last the two youths reentered the hall, looking harried but curiously devoid of sweat. They ran along the tables again with their buckets and Sebastian drained his portion in a single gulp.

François wiped his mouth again. "And now I'll show you the archives, if you still wish to see them."

Sebastian and Gwen looked at Corwyn, who nodded. François sighed. *"Très bien!* Though I can't understand why anyone would who didn't have to."

They followed him across the compound to the largest building. Jean fell into step behind Sebastian, Pierre tucked under his arm once more. As they crossed the open area, Sebastian looked up to see the clouds giving way to sunshine. He looked around the dusty court. Not a single drop of rain had reached the parched earth within the order's walls.

They entered the building to find themselves crowded into a tiny space near the door. The rest of the vast room was taken up by row upon row of shelves, each filled with books and scrolls and bundles of pages tied with cord. Manuscripts spilled from the shelves to the floor, burying the aisles knee-deep in parchment.

"Here they are," François said, waving an arm. "All the notes, letters, deeds, liens, ledgers, petitions, bills, writs, edicts, proclamations, and pronouncements the order's been able to gather from throughout the duchy for the last seven hundred years."

Sebastian, Gwen, and Corwyn stared in dismay. Dry air assaulted their noses and burned their lungs. A layer of fine dust covered everything.

"No wonder the air's so dry," Corwyn said. "You have so many records, there's hardly room to move."

"I know." François sighed. "We'd like to enlarge the archives, but what're we to do? A greater concentration of such documents would only make the air drier still and push the forest further from the monastery walls. There's no way to safely store so many dry records in one place."

"Where do you list what documents you have and where they're filed?" Corwyn asked.

"We don't."

"Then how are the archives organized?"

"Size," François said, motioning blindly with his hands. "And texture, the way different documents feel."

"But how do you find anything?"

"We don't. I told you, no one ever wanted anything here before."

Corwyn swept the mountains of parchment with a critical gaze. "We have our work cut out for us."

François shrugged. "It is as I said."

Corwyn nodded, then realized the gesture was lost on François. "We'd best get started." He motioned for Gwen and Sebastian to follow as he waded into the room.

"Certainly," François called. "And if Pierre or I can be of any help, please let us know."

Corwyn nodded, again forgetting the uselessness of the gesture as he puzzled out how to proceed. "We must simply search at random," he said, spreading his hands in defeat.

"But what are we looking for?" Gwen asked, echoing Sebastian's thoughts.

"I don't know. Anything that might help us understand how the plague reached Gardenia and what's causing it, I suppose. Perhaps somehow, something might have made its way into an account somewhere that would explain it. . . ." He trailed off, aware how hopelessly vague his words sounded. "We can only try," he said.

The rest of that day and well into the next, they searched the archives. They coughed and sneezed from the dust until their throats ached. Their lips and fingers cracked and bled with drought. Brittle parchment crumbled as they examined the manuscripts, looking for they knew not what. Nor did they seem to be finding anything of use, for Corwyn's head sunk lower on his chest in discouragement with every passing hour. He took to stroking his long white beard and mumbling to himself.

They spent the night in small, Spartan cells in the clerics' quarters, then renewed their search the next morning.

Sometime during the second day, Oliver slipped into the archives. Sebastian had no idea where the broom had been or how he'd entered the compound, but it seemed to have been accomplished without assistance from the brethren of St. Mathurin. Oliver waited until none of the clerics were looking, then scurried to Corwyn. Later he began quietly searching a remote section of the archives by himself.

Sebastian wondered if the little fellow could read, but decided not to ask.

Once or twice, Gwen and Sebastian suggested they abandon the search and continue into the mountains, where answers were more likely to be found. But Corwyn wouldn't hear of it, insisting that the Order of St. Mathurin corresponded too well to the alchemical text to give up. He became so testy that Gwen and Sebastian finally let the matter drop.

Occasionally they uncovered documents that piqued their curiosities or that they recognized, like a copy of the duke's proclamation against spreading heresies dangerous to his authority. It was the same proclamation Sebastian had seen posted in the marketplace the night he arrived in Pomme de Terre, and it reminded him of Thaddeus again. But it also reinforced his belief that the political situation in Gardenia and the plague's appearance were connected. He noticed how often the changes taking place elsewhere entered into the documents he read, whether it was a letter from one merchant to another complaining of high taxes and looking forward to the day when power in the duchy would shift in their favor, or a minor lord's decision on a peasant squabble in which he expressed concern about who would preside over such disputes if the nobles were prevented from acting as local magistrates.

On the morning of the second day, Sebastian was working near Corwyn when Gwen came over with a packet of parchment scraps.

"Look at these," she said to Corwyn. "They seem to be entries from a ledger. But what's this in the margin?"

Corwyn took the slips, and Sebastian sidled up to read over his master's shoulder. When the apprentice saw the size of the entries, all of them deposits and all made in the same curiously crabbed handwriting, his eyes went round with surprise. Why, they amounted to a fortune!

Corwyn squinted at the note scrawled on the top sheet. "Cosimo de' Medici—he's head of one of the great banking families in Florence," he said. He thumbed through the other slips. "Who in Gardenia would have such an account?" He took the slips to François and asked the archivist if he recognized them.

As François felt the parchment, his face twisted in a lopsided smile. "You're in luck," he said. "These arrived recently. I remember them. They came from the duke's castle."

"Are you sure?" Corwyn asked. "The duke hasn't had this much money in years."

"I'm certain, *monsieur*," François responded. "There's an old charwoman in the castle whose son is one of our brothers. She provides us with records from the castle intended for the midden heap."

"How strange," the alchemist muttered as he handed the scraps back to Gwen. "I wonder if the duke has money hidden away that the duchess doesn't know about."

They returned to their work and soon forgot the slips.

Later, as Sebastian flipped through a sheaf of pages, something caught his attention. He looked at the top page. It was an agreement to buy a dozen mules from a local merchant. The buyer wasn't specified, and it obviously had nothing to do with change in Gardenia or with the plague, yet something about the note nagged Sebastian.

He looked at the other sheets, but they were only poor copies of the top page made by someone who'd mimicked the nervous handwriting of the original without comprehending the meaning of the words and letters. The copies could be read after a fashion, but they failed to arouse Sebastian's interest. He went back to the first page. Its significance eluded him. Finally he set the sheaf aside and went on searching.

Sebastian knew his attention was divided. Corwyn insisted what they were doing was important, but Sebastian's mind was on Gwen and the silence between them since the night Petronius left. She spoke little, and almost never to him. When she did speak to him, it had to do only with matters facing the group as a whole, not their personal relationship or her feelings. But whenever Sebastian caught her watching him, the pain in her eyes wrenched at him. He longed to talk with her, to hold her, but she never allowed him to find her alone.

The voice in his head grew impatient with Gwen, with Corwyn, and with this whole foolish quest, but Sebastian refused to acknowledge it. The look on Gwen's face cried out more loudly to him than the voice of any ghost.

Then, late on the second day, Sebastian saw Gwen off by herself in a secluded corner of the building. He crept around the shelves, avoiding the piles of manuscripts on the floor as best he could. He slipped behind her as she scanned one of the books.

Sebastian touched her arm. Like a spark flung in hot oil, his longing burst into flame. From the shudder that passed through Gwen, he knew she felt it too.

"Milady, please, I've got to talk with you," he choked out through the anguish blocking his throat. "I can't stand this. We have to work things out."

She lowered the book she'd been reading, her eyes drifting over the shelves. She didn't turn, but her body sagged as if suddenly released from tension. Sebastian moved closer, slipping an arm around her waist and drawing her to him.

"I've been such a fool since I came to Pomme de Terre," he

whispered. Her hair enveloped his face, still smelling of rain and new leaves. He inhaled its fragrance like a man imprisoned reveling in unexpected sunlight.

"I know I've hurt you," he went on. "I've hurt Corwyn, even Oliver. I was blinded by my need to redeem my family, and for all the pain I've caused, I'm truly sorry. But it won't happen again, milady, I swear. I've learned so much since I arrived."

Gwen let her head fall back against his shoulder. Sebastian nuzzled her neck, elated.

"I've been jealous, you know—even of Petronius," he said, conscious of the way his skin burned where she touched him. His own volatility awed him, and he felt compelled to talk to protect himself against its heat.

"I was afraid others would give you things I couldn't rival. I was afraid of being displaced because I have so little to offer, nothing beyond myself and my family's name. That seemed inadequate for a princess. You're more than I had a right to hope for."

Her breath caught and she stiffened in his arms.

"Not that my interest is due only to your station, milady," he amended quickly. "I'd feel the same for you even if you were nothing more than a minor lord's lowliest daughter, with no dowry to offer beyond the simple heritage of your line."

Sebastian sensed a shift ripple through the cosmos, as if his words were fraught with unseen danger. Gwen held motionless in his arms, suddenly cold and unyielding. The voice in his head hissed a warning.

"Ah, Gwendolyn," he purred, uncertain what direction to take. Where did safety lie, and from what quarter had this threat arisen? Had he made some mistake with the language again? "As soon as this is over and we've stopped the affliction in Pomme de Terre, you and I will ride off together to restore what's rightfully ours. Your enemies will be my enemies, and they'll scatter before us like chaff in the wind. This I swear, milady, upon my honor."

Gwen tore away, clutching herself and doubling over as if struck.

"What is it? What's the matter, my princess?" Sebastian asked, reaching to soothe her.

She wrenched away as if his fingers stung. "And I thought you'd changed!" she cried.

Sebastian fidgeted, afraid what reaction another touch from

him might bring. "Milady, if my words brought forth painful memories or shamed you with reminders of your current state, I'm sorry. You've only done what you had to in order to survive. No one can gainsay you for that."

She spun on him, fury in her eyes. "So you'd love me even if I wasn't a princess, would you?" she hissed. "Just how lowborn would you allow me to be and still make good that promise?"

"Milady, what're you asking?" A thought struck him. "Are you saying that you're not a princess after all?" He moved toward her again, tender with compassion. "But Gwendolyn, your status among the nobility doesn't matter to me. If Old Meg exaggerated, that's all right. I'm still your champion, and I'll fight to regain whatever is rightfully yours."

"You really think that's what this is about?" she snapped, pushing him away. "Nothing but foolish concern over some worthless title, some imaginary claim to wealth?"

Sebastian dropped his arms. "But Old Meg said—"

"Apparently Meg said a lot of things, not a one of them true."

Sebastian held very still. "What do you mean?"

"Meg has always wanted something better for me than she had herself. I guess she wanted it so badly she was willing to lie—even deny her own child's parentage—to enable it to happen. She must have thought telling you I was a princess might encourage you to marry me. And she was right; it worked. Otherwise you'd never have thought any more of me than as a means of warming your bed for a night.

"You swear yourself so easily to me and believe your own words, but what do you really know of a sacrifice like Meg's? For that matter, what do you understand of anything, you son of a . . . a *noble*!

"What you imagined about me is no more true than what I wanted to believe about Petronius, or even about you. Well, I have no title, no estate, no claim to status and wealth—just myself, plain Gwen, a serving girl in my father's tavern. But it's not my birth or my station that shames me, Sebastian—it's you! Take your idle dreams somewhere else. They have nothing to do with a peasant girl like me!"

Gwen covered her face and ran.

"What do you mean?" Sebastian called after her, trying to shut out the torrent of anger in his head. "Gwen, please wait."

It was too late; she was gone.

Sebastian started to follow her, but he tripped over a bundle of documents and crashed to the floor. He cursed and thrashed among the parchment, tearing pages loose and sending billows of dust into his face as he struggled to get up. At last her words sank in and he quieted, unable to suppress the derision hurled at him from inside any longer.

His world was in ruins. Gwen was a peasant.

At the sound of the commotion, Corwyn hurried over. Behind him stumbled François, feeling his way along the shelves to find out what the excitement was. Jean followed, leaving his charge on a table at the building's entrance.

"Alors! Come back for me," Pierre cried from his perch on the table. "Jean, you come back this instant!"

"Sebastian, what are you doing?" Corwyn demanded, ignoring Pierre. *"Tiens!* You've torn pages from these documents!"

"Pages torn?" François cried. His face crumpled. "You're ruining the records." He felt through the debris, scooping up handfuls of loose pages and stuffing them arbitrarily into a manuscript that lay close at hand. He filled the manuscript with as many extra pages as it would hold, then turned and carefully set it on the floor further down the aisle, out of harm's way.

"Master, Old Meg lied to me," Sebastian said from the floor. "Gwen's not a princess as Old Meg said. She's a peasant. And you knew it all along, didn't you? Why didn't you tell me?"

"You mean this disgraceful behavior is all because of that? Boy, get on your feet and help clean this up!"

"So much damage," François clucked, shoving pages into unrelated documents.

Jean watched François, then moved in to help. He squatted down and squeezed a huge mass of documents between his powerful hands. He carried the bundle a way down the aisle and, with casual indifference, let the documents drop. Then he waded back through the parchment sea to help some more.

"But, master, you don't understand," Sebastian said, bewildered by Corwyn's refusal to see what was so stark and clear to the voice in his head. "She has no family, no name—nothing! For someone of my standing to marry her is unthinkable. I'm the son of a nobleman!"

"Sebastian, you don't have any standing, nor is your family still of the nobility," Corwyn said with forced restraint. "You're apprenticed to me to learn a trade, something most nobles would rather die than do. Once you accepted this position, your past glories were lost. You must achieve new ones of your own. I thought you understood that."

"There seems to be a lot I didn't understand," Sebastian said bitterly. He kicked a pile of books aside so he could shift to a sitting position, ignoring François's efforts to save the manuscripts.

"Now, as part of your apprenticeship," Corwyn went on, his voice gathering volume, "you'll pick yourself up off the floor and help restore order to this portion of the universe. As for the rest, I'll leave it to the slow workings of your mind to determine what course to take with Gwen. However, let me tell you that if you allow that girl to slip out of your life, you should consider entering the Order of St. Mathurin yourself!"

It took a moment after the final blast for Sebastian to catch his breath. By that time, Corwyn was gone. But Pierre, in his place on the table, surveyed the damage Sebastian had caused. Then he turned his baleful gaze on the lad. "Do you know how long it takes to copy just one of these pages when you have to hold the quill with your teeth?"

"I'm . . . I'm sorry," Sebastian stammered. No matter how hard he tried, he seemed incapable of pleasing anyone, not his father, not Corwyn, not Gwen—least of all himself. "Oh, God, forgive me for I have sinned and am most truly sorry about *everything*." As he spoke, he carefully raked the nearest documents into a pile and arranged them in a stack at the base of the shelves.

While Sebastian helped straighten the mess on the floor, he was battered inside by the shifting tides of his thoughts. Gwen's revelation came as a devastating blow, and Corwyn's indifference to their social separation threatened the stability of the God-given order. Yet one image kept intruding upon his father's outraged sense of propriety, drowning out the dead warrior's ghost. It was the look on Gwen's face as she fled.

Sebastian didn't know what was right anymore. At last he decided to swallow his pride and go to Gwen, regardless what his upbringing demanded of him. He'd tell her he understood why she'd violated his trust by deceiving him and that all was forgiven. He wasn't sure yet what their new relationship should be, now that he knew the truth about her, but that much he had to do. It would be difficult, and he was glad his family couldn't see; but under the circumstances it seemed the most honorable, manly avenue open.

Oddly, he felt better after making this decision, as if any chance to talk with Gwen was worth whatever sacrifice it entailed. There was a strange glow inside him at the mere thought of her. Even the ever-present voice in his head was subdued by the force of his decision.

He started to set down the manuscripts he'd collected from the floor so he could seek Gwen out again, when he happened to notice the one on top of the stack. A name leaped from the page and he scanned the text quickly, looking for it again. Yes, there it was!

With a yell that brought everyone running, Sebastian called Corwyn.

"The Goblin Mines?" Corwyn said when Sebastian showed him the document. "You called me over just to show me someone has been foolish enough to lease the Goblin Mines?"

"But look who signed the lease," Sebastian insisted, pointing to the page and trying to recall what it was about the oddly crabbed signature that seemed familiar.

"What? Oh, all right." Corwyn peered where Sebastian pointed. Then he, too, saw the name.

It was Dr. Tox.

Corwyn burst out laughing. Sebastian, who had thought the document important somehow in their attempt to understand what was happening in the Pyrenees, felt hurt. "What's so funny?"

"*Tiens!* The duchess has managed to swindle that pompous fool out of a considerable portion of his annual salary for the mineral rights to some worthless mines. He probably heard tales about gold and jewels being taken from the mountains by goblins and thought he'd get rich. But there hasn't been any gold or jewels in those mines since the goblins disappeared. All the wealth vanished with them. The duchess gets back most of what she pays him, and Dr. Tox gets what he so richly deserves—nothing!"

Corwyn laughed so hard he clutched his belly to keep it from hurting.

The humor was a welcome relief, and it proved infectious. Presently, the room was filled with laughter over this evidence of Dr. Tox's latest misadventure. Everyone in the duchy knew of Dr. Tox, and few there were who wouldn't welcome a chance to laugh at the poor physician's expense.

Only one voice failed to join the glee. Gwen, alone on the far side of the vast room, listened through pain to Corwyn and Sebastian and wondered dismally why mention of the Goblin Mines nibbled at her memory. The mines had something to do with a conversation she'd overheard at the Reluctant Virgin.

She shook her head, unable to remember. A tear trickled down her cheek, then evaporated before it reached her chin. Just now, she couldn't seem to care about half-heard words from a distant, smoky tavern.

She clenched her fists, both loving and hating Sebastian in a single moment.

CHAPTER 13

A Woman Scorned

DINNER INTERRUPTED THE SEARCHERS IN THE ARCHIVES, AND IM-
mediately afterward Gwen retired to her room.

The narrow cells in which the brothers of the order slept and
spent their occasional hours to themselves were too austere and
confining for Gwen. She preferred space around her in which to
move and dream. This, she thought as she surveyed the rough,
whitewashed plaster walls and cramped flagstone floor, reflected
too closely the real constraints affecting her life—the limitations
of poverty and social class, of living in an isolated region where
the important events of the world were all too remote.

But she came to the room in hopes Sebastian would find her
in case he wished to apologize.

She tried to sit still. Then, unable to contain herself, she
jumped from the bed and paced the tiny room, angry at herself
for expecting him, furious with him for not coming to her.

It had seemed that Sebastian wanted to talk, that he had almost
started to several times during the meal. But conversation was
awkward in the dining hall with everyone bolting their food
before it dried out and the silence leaving so many ears unoc-
cupied to overhear a private discussion. Or perhaps she was

hoping for too much and had only imagined he had something to tell her.

After the meal he had disappeared, and she had returned to her room to give him an opportunity to speak with her undisturbed, if that's what he was waiting for.

A rap at her door set her heart pounding.

When she opened it, though, Corwyn was standing in the hall. The alchemist shuffled his feet, chatting about the dryness of the archives and the difficulty of their search. He looked over his shoulder at the empty corridor, then whispered, "The brethren of St. Mathurin couldn't have made our task more difficult if they'd tried. The archives are a shambles, and most of the records they've salvaged are trash. The copies they produce are illegible because the copyists can't read to recognize their own mistakes. They copy any scrap of writing no matter how worthless, but their work is as mindless as any beast of the field's."

"Perhaps we'll find something tomorrow," Gwen said, putting a hand on his arm to cheer him up.

Corwyn shook his head. "I don't think so. The archives are too muddled to find anything. Even if the records hadn't been distorted by faulty copying, how could we hope to stumble upon the particular documents we need? Besides, we don't even know those documents exist. No, *ma chère,* I was wrong to bring us here." He paused, then chuckled grimly. "About the only thing we've found worth the effort is Sebastian's discovery that Dr. Tox has leased the Goblin Mines, and unfortunately that has no connection with what we're looking for."

At the mention of Sebastian's name, Gwen's hurt and confusion returned. "What do we do now?" she asked to divert her thoughts.

Corwyn was slow in answering. "I'm no longer certain we can do anything. About the plague, that is. And without uncovering the cause of the plague and stopping it, we can't return to Pomme de Terre." He shrugged. "These last few days, I've begun to feel like the old man I really am.

"Tomorrow, I think we should retreat into the Pyrenees. It'll be difficult for anyone from Pomme de Terre to find us there. I have an old friend who lives over on the Iberian side. He'll keep us until it's safe to return. It's just over the range from the headwaters of the Ale. From that vantage, I can study the watershed and try to uncover its secrets. My breath of demons test may eventually lead us to something. Perhaps, in a year or two . . ." He trailed off, leaving the thought unfinished.

"This friend—?"

"Wygaard." She looked blank. "Smoke?" he said.

Gwen nodded slowly. "I've heard of him." She was silent a moment, then, "Will I be welcome there?"

"You'll be with me," Corwyn answered. "He'll accept that."

"But perhaps not willingly. And over such a long time, there might be problems."

"Peut-être," Corwyn admitted. He lifted his hands, palms up. "I am sorry to have led you into this, *ma chère*. But what else can we do?"

Gwen patted him and smiled. "Dear Corwyn, no man I've ever met has been half so sweet as you. But if you wouldn't think ill of me, I may stay here tomorrow when you leave."

"Leave you?" He looked troubled. "Here at St. Mathurin's?"

"Oui. I'll be all right here for a while."

"I suppose," he said. "I should hate to leave you, but I do understand."

"Merci." She bent to kiss him. "I shall miss you, Corwyn."

"And I you," he mumbled, starting to leave. Then he turned back. "He's my apprentice, Gwen. I can order him to apologize."

She shook her head. "If he does come, it must be of his own volition. Otherwise it would mean nothing."

"You're right, of course. But if he doesn't, he's a bigger fool than I thought." He started down the hall, muttering to himself.

Gwen closed the door and leaned on it, hoping Sebastian wasn't as big a fool as that. Oh, when would he come to her!

She thought absently about what Corwyn had said and a slight smile crept over her face at how pleased he'd been to learn of Dr. Tox's foolishness with the Goblin Mines.

Her smile froze. The Goblin Mines! Now she remembered the conversation from the Reluctant Virgin. It had been on the way to the Goblin Mines that someone, she didn't remember who, had seen the peasants Kwagg and Meier headed with their team of mules. But why would those two, who never did anything unless there was a dishonest coin to be made from it, visit a worthless set of mines leased by Dr. Tox? And why would they be leading heavily laden mules *to* the mines, as she'd heard, instead of away from them?

The real message Sebastian had received from String John was that those two peasants were connected with the plague. She couldn't imagine how, but it must have something to do with the mines.

She turned to the door, intending to call Corwyn back, but another thought stopped her. If she was right, and they all went there together, Sebastian would share the credit. Even his mistake in leading them to the Valley of Despair would be vindicated. Worse, his opinion of her would remain unchanged.

As she hesitated, another tapping at the door interrupted her thoughts. But it wasn't Sebastian this time, either. Instead, François stood there, his sightless eyes staring past her shoulder.

"Well, uh . . . ahem . . . yes, well, I just wondered if you need anything."

"*Merci*, François, but no. Nothing anyone can provide."

"No, I suppose not," he conceded. "No one but that apprentice fellow." He turned away from the door, talking as he went. "Just the same, if there's anything I can do, I'm just down the hall."

"*Merci*, François. You're most kind." She paused, then, "I may stay here for a day or two, if you don't mind. Until I decide where to go from here."

"Without your friends? Corwyn said you'd all be leaving tomorrow."

"Without my friends, yes."

François nodded to the wall. "I see. Certainly you may stay, for as long as you like. It would be a pleasure."

Gwen thanked him and closed the door, glad for the emotional support Corwyn and François had offered her, but angry Sebastian hadn't been among them. Then a new thought occurred to her. What if he left with Corwyn tomorrow without ever saying a word? Would she see him again?

If he didn't show up with an apology soon . . . !

There was a footstep outside her door, then a pause before the knock. She flung the door open. "I thought you'd never come—"

"And leave a beautiful maiden in distress?" Pierre answered from under Jean's arm. "Chivalry isn't limited to nobles. In the case of your apprentice friend, the two don't even seem related."

Gwen clung to the door and stared. Would everyone at the monastery come to comfort her except Sebastian? She glanced into the hall to see who else might be waiting even as she answered Pierre, her voice cold with remembered humiliation. "I'm not a maiden. I'd hate for anyone else to labor under that mis-apprehension."

"No?" Pierre's eyebrows shot up, followed by an easy grin. *"Tiens!* So much the better perhaps. It's far too prevalent an affliction. But enough of that. May I come in?"

"Oh, yes. Certainly." Gwen waved them into the room. "Please forgive me."

Pierre thrust his chin to indicate a wide windowsill to Jean, who crossed the room and placed the limbless man on it. Then Jean took up a position beside the window and waited.

"You should forget this Sebastian," Pierre said. "He's not worthy of you."

Gwen shook her head. "I don't think I can forget him."

"Bah! You haven't tried. Look, several of our brothers are staging a new morality play next week. Stay here and see it with me."

"Oh, Pierre," Gwen replied, "I can't. That is, I can't stay here that long."

"I see. It's because of the way I am, isn't it? Because I'm unlike other people?"

"No, of course not," Gwen said hastily, focusing on the man's face rather than his body, aware her answer was at least partially a lie.

"Yes, it is. I can tell." He paused. "Although I wouldn't have thought you'd hold my illiteracy against me."

"Of course I don't," Gwen said. "That's not it. I thought you meant—" She stumbled to a halt, flustered. He grinned. Gwen couldn't help laughing. "Pierre, you had me."

"There isn't a woman I'd rather have," he said, deliberately misinterpreting her meaning again. "And it's good to hear you laugh."

She smiled, suddenly feeling at ease with him. "You're a most unusual man. It would be a privilege to see the play with you." She sobered. "If it wasn't for Sebastian."

"Ah, him again."

Gwen nodded. "I'm sorry."

"So am I." Pierre signaled to Jean, who lifted him up and took him from the room. "If you should change your mind, or if he doesn't come back . . ." Pierre added as Jean carried him down the hall.

Gwen smiled, her eyes full of tears. But she was thinking that Sebastian wouldn't be coming back to her, ever. He'd abandoned her because she was a peasant, even though men like Corwyn and Pierre treated her like a lady.

"Where are the fairy-tale endings—where princes fall in love and marry beneath their class—when a woman needs them?" she demanded of the empty room.

Yet another knock came from her door, a dry, shallow sound. Gwen clenched her fists. "Sebastian, that'd better be you," she hissed, wrenching the door open.

In the hall stood Oliver, shuffling his straw tufts self-consciously. The motion raised swirls of the powdery dust that lay everywhere within the compound. The broom extended a branch, brushing her arm with his dry fingertips. Then he turned and ran as if afraid at having exposed his vulnerability.

Gwen watched Oliver scurry down the hall and vanish around a corner. When he'd gone, she slammed the door. She stamped across the room, turned, and strode back. Then she hammered her fists on the door in frustration.

"Everyone but you, Sebastian," she cried, sniffling back tears that insisted on spilling from her eyes to quickly dry in shiny tracks on her cheeks. "Well, I'll show you, you nobleman's son!"

Her mind jumped back to the Goblin Mines and what she'd overheard about Kwagg and Meier. The mines weren't very far from where Corwyn's friend Smoke was said to live. She smiled grimly. There were advantages to working in a tavern. Otherwise she wouldn't have recognized the connection between Dr. Tox and the curious activities of Kwagg and Meier. Perhaps Corwyn had underestimated Dr. Tox. Maybe he was responsible for the plague somehow. Anyway, it was worth checking, and Corwyn wouldn't be too far away if she needed him.

Her smile became cynical. Wouldn't Sebastian be surprised if she, a poor serving girl from a peasant family, solved the mystery of the plague?

"Sebastian, I'll show you what a peasant girl can do! I'm not staying behind like some discarded wench while you run off, never to return or even think of me again!"

She had few belongings and was quickly ready. A glance through the window told her the moon wasn't yet up. That was good. She must be far away from the compound before moonlight could reveal her intentions. No one must know what she was up to. Corwyn would try to stop her, or at least come along. This undertaking must remain hers alone. By the time they found

out, she'd be well on her way. If she hurried, she could reach
the Goblin Mines by morning.

She ran her tongue over dry, cracking lips. It would be good
to be out in the forest again. Anywhere with moisture had to be
better than the monastery.

Idly she wondered if there would be water at the Goblin Mines.
She was in desperate need of a bath.

CHAPTER 14

The Revenge of Dr. Tox

THE SQUAT, POP-EYED TOAD OF A MAN STARED UNTIL DR. TOX squirmed, his bony fingers playing nervously with his beard, his clothes, and one another.

"Look here, *mon bon homme,*" Dr. Tox squeaked. He cleared his throat and dragged his voice down an octave. "Look here, just tell him I've come on a matter of utmost importance."

The man continued to stare, his harsh little eyes flicking over Dr. Tox. "*Oui,* I'll tell him," he said at last in a voice like gravel. "I'll tell him you've come and see if he's here. Though he's not likely to be, not for you." Then he ambled down the corridor, snickering under his breath.

Dr. Tox went limp with relief at being out from under the gaze of the man who acted as Hydro Phobius's valet, squire, chamberlain, butler, and business advisor. It was impossible to see the master without being humiliated by his servant first.

If only Hydro Phobius had remained in Spain!

After a while, Dr. Tox grew tired of waiting for the valet to return. He wandered down a side passage and through a door into a small courtyard—a sunlit surprise hidden within the gloomy fortress. But weeds overran the garden, debris choked the marble fountain, and broken tiles from the colonnade revealed where the roof had collapsed.

The courtyard was like the rest of the castle: old and dilapidated. Hydro Phobius was always attended by blight. It was the inevitable scar he left behind to mark his passing.

Originally, the castle had been a remote outpost in the struggle between Moslems and Christians for control of the Iberian peninsula. After the Moors retreated to southern Spain, the castle fell into disrepair. Hydro Phobius was able to lease it cheaply from the Spanish nobleman on whose land it stood. With half a dozen mercenaries and a couple of lackwit clerics, Phobius used the castle to keep track of the demon disposal operation.

But the Black Knight himself had stayed either in Spain, where he was too involved with problems at the Inquisition's demon stabilization facilities to be concerned with the disposal site deep in the Pyrenees, or in northern Italy, where Dr. Tox suspected he had some other operation. He left it to Dr. Tox to ensure that the Duke de Gardenia left matters at the Goblin Mines alone. The two clerics at the castle had been occupied with menial record keeping, setting up shipment schedules, and financial accounts. Dr. Tox was able to assume virtual control of the operation in France.

But Phobius's recent arrival at the castle to retake personal command of the operation had changed all that.

Dr. Tox wandered under the colonnade feeling uneasy. He squinted into the bright sunlight and thought about how fine a line he trod in his dangerous gambit. This scheme could cost him more than his life—it could eventually cost his immortal soul.

Dark forebodings pressed upon him from the shaded confines of the walkway. His mind heard fearful whispers of defeat. How much did Phobius suspect about what had become of the gold he sent to support the duke?

His knees started to shake, and he slid onto a low stone bench between a pair of spiral columns. He stared unseeing at a bee struggling to find nectar among the dusty, neglected blooms of a primrose. Dr. Tox was too preoccupied to notice. He was recalling several recent incidents that had seemed unimportant at the time. Now he recognized them as warnings of Hydro Phobius's growing suspicion.

First, there'd been the increasing number of records Phobius had demanded. And then Dr. Tox had discovered his lease to the Goblin Mines and other personal records were missing. He'd thought he'd just misplaced them; but Hydro Phobius's spies must have stolen them from his room. Probably that old char-woman at the duke's castle; she was always sneaking through his things when his back was turned.

Dread swept through him, leaving him trembling and clammy. That lease could be his death warrant. Under the arrangement he was to have made with the duke, a lease would be unnecessary. A lease on the Goblin Mines in Dr. Tox's name would arouse unpleasant notions in Hydro Phobius's mind. Notions too close to the truth.

Suddenly Dr. Tox knew he'd pushed his luck too far. He had enough wealth deposited in Florence to live in splendor for the rest of his life. It was madness to remain in Gardenia any longer. Eventually Phobius would discover what had really become of his money, and all would be lost.

Dr. Tox had just resolved to make his escape and flee to Italy before Phobius learned any more, when the valet reappeared.

"Ah, there you are," the valet said with counterfeit delight. "I thought perhaps you'd left us, but I see we haven't been so blessed. Hydro Phobius will see you now, though I can't under-stand why. Follow me."

Dr. Tox, already halfway to his feet after his decision to flee, started at the valet's unexpected arrival and tumbled into the primrose bush. The bee buzzed threateningly as he extricated himself and loped after the valet.

For now, it was too late to escape. His only hope was to keep Hydro Phobius's attention away from questions of money until an opportunity arose to get away.

The valet reached the double doors to Hydro Phobius's throne room ahead of Dr. Tox. He swung them open and stepped inside. "Dr. Tox has come to grovel before your eminence and beg your indulgence for an audience."

Dr. Tox burst into the room, gasping and trying to pull his disarranged clothes into order. He scowled at the valet, but the man only smirked as he passed, trotting across the room to Hydro Phobius's throne. Dr. Tox followed with what dignity he could muster, tripping occasionally on a loose hem of his full-length, ermine-trimmed silk coat. He remembered just in time to doff his hat.

Hydro Phobius was perched on a magnificent throne atop a raised dais, so that it cramped Dr. Tox's neck to carry on a conversation with his master from the floor at the foot of the platform. Behind the throne hung the room's one adornment, a silk banner emblazoned with the crest of Hydro Phobius—a fish floating belly-up in a stylized body of water. Over the crest arched the Latinized motto: *In pollutis profitum est*.

Hydro Phobius was a huge man, over six feet tall, and the dramatic effect of his presence was enhanced by the full suit of armor he always wore. The armor was lacquered deep black and polished until it gleamed in the darkness of the room. Against its black background were intricate inlays of silver and gold.

As he neared the throne, Dr. Tox recited the ritual the valet had taught him for approaching Hydro Phobius:

> "If you are a fool,
> The greater fool is me,
> For you are the fool
> To whom I bend my knee!"

He bowed and gestured as instructed while reciting, ending in a position of supplication at the foot of the dais, where he waited for permission to speak.

Hydro Phobius stared at him from within his inscrutable mask of a helmet, as remote as ever. Only the valet responded, sitting on the dais beside the throne like a street performer's trained monkey and awarding Dr. Tox a slow, exaggerated grin that stung more than any reprimand.

Dr. Tox fidgeted. The floor was cold and hard, and he'd struck his kneecap on the stones when he kneeled. After a while, Hydro Phobius's helmeted head turned toward the valet. The valet leaned close to Phobius for a private consultation, then spoke to Dr. Tox for his master. "The great Hydro Phobius wonders if you have anything to say or if you have come simply to bask in his glorious presence."

Hydro Phobius peered at Dr. Tox as the valet spoke.

Dr. Tox stood quickly, then thought better of it and started to kneel again. But that didn't seem right either, so he ended in a half-crouch, his legs bent uncomfortably and his head bowed to his chest. "Yes, your worship, I do have something to say. That is, if I might." He added hurriedly, "Not that it isn't enough simply to bask, as you say, in the presence of your gloriousness."

The valet leaned over the edge of the dais. "Dr. Tox," he hissed, "I'm sure the great Hydro Phobius would like you to get on with this. I know I do."

"Uh, yes, as you say." He twisted his head, which was still bowed, looking to Phobius for confirmation of the valet's words. But his black-helmeted master only stared at him. *"Tiens!* It's about hauling all those barrels by mule train to the Goblin Mines. They're so heavy, and the job is much more dangerous than it need be."

"Kwagg and Meier will be glad to hear of your concern for their welfare, I'm sure," the valet said. "But since they do the hauling, what interest is it of yours?"

"Tiens! I wouldn't say they do all the work," Dr. Tox said in a hurt voice, remembering his efforts to carry a barrel from one of the mules to the ore carts at the mines. "I hold up my end."

"I'm sure you do."

"But it isn't very efficient, particularly with more frequent shipments coming up from Spain. Besides, the risk of being seen and arousing suspicion has increased under the new schedule. That could cause serious repercussions in Pomme de Terre."

Hydro Phobius stared coldly. The valet leaned closer, an evil glitter in his eyes. Dr. Tox hurried on, aware of having strayed onto dangerous ground. The conversation must be kept away from Pomme de Terre, the duke, and unrest among the citizenry.

"At any rate, I think I've devised a better way of bringing in demonic wastes," he said. "One that would allow us to operate continuously, yet would not expose anyone to unnecessary danger."

And a way that would bring Corwyn under the influence of Hydro Phobius, Dr. Tox added to himself.

The Black Knight considered Dr. Tox's words in silence while the valet sneered. "Oh, you've devised a better way, have you?" The valet lifted his eyebrows in mock surprise. "I see. Better, I take it, than the present system, which was devised by our great and benevolent master?"

Dr. Tox stumbled back, appalled by this unexpected turn. *"Mais non!* I didn't mean that at all!"

"Exactly what did you mean?"

"Just . . . just a slight improvement," Dr. Tox squeaked. "Not that the way we're doing things now isn't perfectly all right with me. The system probably doesn't need improving, anyway. No, now that I think about it, it most assuredly doesn't, not in the least." He paused, terrified by the answering silence, then concluded lamely, "After all, I'm not one to cause trouble for my master." He looked beseechingly at Hydro Phobius, but the Black Knight ignored him.

Oh, why hadn't he escaped to southern Italy when he'd had the chance?

The valet grinned. "No, I'm sure you're not. Not one to cause problems at all." The grin disappeared. "No problems except for allowing the alchemist to escape. You've let him become a real threat to us, Dr. Tox. Have you found him yet?"

This brought a renewed wave of fear over Dr. Tox. But another feeling rose to drown out the first, a fierce sense of outrage directed at Corwyn.

Corwyn's odd habit of exploring the upper reaches of the River Ale, combined with rumors of his diabolical experiments, had stirred the embers of unrest in Gardenia into flame.

At first, Dr. Tox had tried to use this unrest to direct attention away from the plague and Hydro Phobius's demon disposal operation in the Pyrenees. But the effort backfired. To make matters worse, the duke's reign was showing evidence of decay. There was growing danger of revolt. The merchants and lesser nobles were complaining openly about the duke's inability to assert control.

All this was happening so fast, and it was all Corwyn's fault. Through his pernicious meddling, Corwyn had accidentally jeopardized the stability of the duchy, and now he also threatened the security of Dr. Tox's position with Hydro Phobius.

These thoughts passed quickly through Dr. Tox's feverish brain. "No," he answered hotly, "I haven't caught him—"

"I thought not."

"But I believe I know where he's headed. And Corwyn is very much at the center of my proposal for improving the delivery of demonic wastes to the Goblin Mines." He hesitated, wondering whether to continue, but his anger at Corwyn decided him. "Suppose we had a pipeline into the mountains. The slurries of waste could flow directly into the mines without danger of anyone being exposed. And a pipeline would be so much better suited to the new delivery schedules. Dumping of the wastes could go on continuously, regardless of the time of day or weather."

"I see. A pipeline to the mines," the valet said. "And how do you propose to make the wastes flow uphill to the mines? Put a spell on them, perhaps?" He laughed at the idea.

"No, no, not at all. But I believe it could be done if we used pumps powered by windmills at regular intervals along the pipeline, like Corwyn's windmills at the duke's castle." Then he told them both (for he was no longer sure whether he was talking to Hydro Phobius or to his valet) about the water supply system Corwyn had designed for the duke.

"The duchess, who adamantly opposed the new system at first, has become much enamored of it in recent days," Dr. Tox concluded, thinking how satisfied she'd looked when he spied on her recent baths.

The valet started to speak, then hesitated. Hydro Phobius turned to him, light reflecting from the interlaced silver and gold. Obediently, the valet bent his ear to his master's visor. After a few moments of private consultation, the valet leaned over the front of the dais. "Dr. Tox, you surprise us. For once, a suggestion of yours deserves serious consideration. It just goes to prove that a worthwhile idea may present itself from the most unlikely source."

"*Merci,*" said Dr. Tox, stung by what he could only hope was intended as a compliment.

The valet tugged thoughtfully on a tuft of hair growing from one of his warts. "Most intriguing suggestion. Yes, this may hold possibilities." He grinned again, showing crooked yellow teeth. "You say you know where he is?"

"I think I know where he's heading," Dr. Tox said, giddy with relief, and anticipating of Corwyn's fate. "I spread a few coins and considerable wine among members of the brigand free companies during the past several days. They told me of seeing Corwyn and two or three others traveling toward the Valley of Despair."

The valet frowned. He glanced at his master, but the Black Knight remained impassive. "What's the Valley of Despair?" the valet asked.

Dr. Tox laughed, pleased at being accepted at last as one of them. Even the valet seemed less disagreeable somehow. He told them how Kwagg and Meier had created the Valley of Despair two or three years earlier.

"Fool!" the valet hissed when he was through. "Don't you see? Corwyn suspects that valley is related to the plague in Pomme de Terre."

Dr. Tox tried to laugh, but it came out a cackle. "But they aren't related at all. Except for Kwagg and Meier."

"*Exactement,*" the valet snapped. "And if he knows about those two, he may eventually trace their activities to the Goblin

Mines and us. Corwyn was mistaken in thinking the plague is connected to this Valley of Despair, but his error is nevertheless bringing him closer to the truth." The valet's expression darkened. "Why didn't you warn us about this before now?"

Once again, Dr. Tox felt reduced to insignificance before Hydro Phobius. He hung his head and waited in silence, unwilling to risk saying more.

The valet drummed his fingers on the side of Phobius's throne until Dr. Tox clenched his teeth against the sound. "We have to capture Corwyn before he causes further damage. Besides," and here the valet smiled evilly again, "we must convince him to start that pipeline at once."

Dr. Tox brightened a little. "Do you want me to go after him?"

"Eh?" the valet said, having evidently forgotten the physician's presence. "No, I think not. You've exceeded our expectations as it is. No need pressing our luck by hoping for more." His hideous face became thoughtful again. "This is a task my master and I had best undertake."

"As you wish," Dr. Tox murmured, annoyed at being so callously dismissed, yet relieved not to be called upon to lead an expedition into the wilds.

"As the great Hydro Phobius wishes!" the valet corrected.

Dr. Tox's shoulders dropped and his nervous fingers came to a halt. He nodded, wondering that the valet could presume to know his master's mind so thoroughly while in his very presence. But there was only silence as the Black Knight remained unperturbed.

"Who did you say was with Corwyn?" the valet asked after a time.

"His new apprentice and a tavern wench from Pomme de Terre. And possibly a skinny child," Dr. Tox replied. "The men I talked to couldn't agree on the last. Some said there were only the two others with him."

"Well, either way, they shouldn't present any serious problems." The valet pierced Dr. Tox with his gaze. "Besides, you're to stay in Pomme de Terre. Something's wrong there. The duke isn't as secure as he should be after all the gold Hydro Phobius has supplied. The situation is volatile and becoming worse. Someone seems to be diverting the money before it reaches the duke."

Dr. Tox felt the color drain from his face. The room grew quiet and very distant around him. "What do you mean?" he asked, his voice sounding oddly calm in his ears.

"I mean that someone is stealing those funds, Dr. Tox! And I think I know who."

"Wh-Who?"

"The duchess," the valet whispered with terrible intensity.

The doctor's eyebrows shot up in disbelief.

"Oui," the valet said, nodding. "She's said to be tight with a coin, and it's well known the duke despises her. I think she may be secreting the money away, preparing to leave both her husband and Gardenia. Keep a close eye on her, Dr. Tox. After all, you have access to the royal treasury's accounts. See if the money actually reaches the duke, and find out what that woman is up to!"

"As you wish," Dr. Tox replied, pleased at having fooled Hydro Phobius. Besides, he liberally interpreted this command as granting him further license to spy upon the duchess's baths. Then he caught himself and amended hastily, "As Hydro Phobius wishes."

"The *great* Hydro Phobius!"

"The great Hydro Phobius," Dr. Tox conceded, peering fearfully up at the knight.

"And now, Dr. Tox, this audience appears to be concluded." The valet also glanced at Phobius, then whispered to the physician, "Our great and benevolent lord and master is contemplating the news you've brought him. Either that, or he's drifted off to sleep. Before you try his patience further, I suggest you leave for Pomme de Terre and carry out his commands."

"Oh, *oui.* Certainly." Dr. Tox backed away from the throne, bowing as he went.

"Dr. Tox."

He stopped, frozen in mid-bow. *"Oui?"*

"Please observe the correct protocol as you leave. Our master may have turned his attention to other matters, but he should still be afforded proper respect by his inferiors."

Dr. Tox dropped to his hands and knees and crawled backwards, licking the floor as he went and periodically stopping to proclaim, "Fortunate am I, a lowly and detestable slug of a creature, to be granted the privilege of cleaning the path where the foot of the Black Knight, Hydro Phobius, treads."

The words were hard to force out past the dirt on his tongue. Dr. Tox struggled to keep from gagging as the valet laughed.

Once free of the throne room, the doctor got hastily to his

feet and hurried to the castle gate, anxious to leave his master, the valet, and this latest humiliation behind. He spat several times to clear his mouth and scowled. How he wished he could catch the valet sometime where Hydro Phobius couldn't see. He'd teach the man not to trifle with Dr. Tox! Of course, he added to himself, it'd be best to have a few hired men along, just to ensure justice was really rendered.

He puffed out his chest and took a swing at the air, practicing for the fateful day when he might be granted his wish. Then he realized the guard at the gate was grinning at him. Dr. Tox nodded coldly at the guard, pulling dignity around him like a sodden blanket. His revenge against Corwyn, now that it had been set in motion, seemed less satisfying than he'd expected. All he wanted was to return to the security of the duke's castle and the company of the duke's lovely young wife.

Phobius's gate boomed shut behind him, and Dr. Tox began the long trek over the Pyrenees to Pomme de Terre. Hydro Phobius hadn't discovered the lease to the Goblin Mines after all. His secret was safe.

There wasn't any hurry about escaping to southern Italy now. He had time to collect a few more payments first. After all, he reasoned, an opportunity like this might never come his way again. And this gave him still more time to worm his way into the misplaced affections of the duchess's heart—or into her bed, at least.

Besides, he wanted to stay in Gardenia long enough to see Corwyn ensnared in the Black Knight's web.

Sebastian paced the darkened, quiet monastery, his feet kicking up swirls of dust that burned his nostrils and shimmered in the moonlight. Everyone seemed to have settled down for the night, but he wanted to be sure. There'd been such a confusion of comings and goings earlier.

He wandered aimlessly for a time. Then his feet led him, almost without conscious intent, to Gwen's door. The hallway stretched into darkness in either direction, closed doorways marking the distance along the walls.

He listened for a moment to be sure she was alone. Earlier, every time he'd ventured near her room, it had been to discover someone else was already there.

He pressed his face against the rough surface of the door. His change in status was having repercussions far beyond wealth and social conduct. It changed his most fundamental relationships. Life was proving complex, even among the lower classes. If it hadn't been for the strange hold Gwen had on him, he doubted it would be worth the effort to adjust.

But she held him, whether she knew it or not, and now he was at her door to make whatever apologies he must to regain her affection. All thought of respectability and family pride had been cast away the first time he approached her door. At first, he'd tried to rationalize his actions by explaining them to his father. Finally, he gave up. Dead or alive, his father would never understand or forgive. But it no longer mattered. This, Sebastian did for himself.

Had his brother Bartholomew known the same certainty before marrying the infidel woman in Constantinople? For the first time since learning of their marriage, Sebastian realized how much he missed his brother, and it startled him to think of his brother's wife simply as a woman, instead of an infidel whore. When had this change come about?

Sebastian heard nothing through Gwen's door, although the sounds of someone's restless sleep came from the next room down. He knocked softly and whispered her name, trying not to disturb her neighbors. When she failed to answer, he knocked again, then again harder. No answer. He beat on the door with his fists and cried out for her, no longer concerned about disturbing others. A cold knot formed in his belly. She couldn't be sleeping through the racket he made.

A door some way down opened and François stepped into the hall. "What is it?" he asked of the darkness eternally shrouding him. "What's wrong? Who's there?"

Before Sebastian could answer, the door closest to him opened and a woman emerged, frowning as she pulled on a robe. Sebastian's first glimpse told him she wore nothing underneath. Hers had been the room with the troubled sleeper, he realized, even as it occurred to him to wonder what she was doing in the monastic quarters. Another woman, somewhat younger, appeared behind her, too busy lighting a candle to pull on her own robe. Sebastian tried not to stare, but she was very pretty and he was only partially successful.

François felt his way along the corridor, demanding to know what was happening. The first woman turned to Sebastian, her face framing the same question.

Sebastian started to answer, but again was interrupted, this time by a voice from the room behind the two women. *"Tiens! What is it? Who's making all the noise?"*

The voice was Pierre's.

Sebastian tore his eyes away from the women in horror, realizing the sounds he'd heard from the room had nothing to do with sleep.

The woman with the candle went back into the room, saying something to Pierre. The first woman glared contemptuously at Sebastian, then followed the younger woman in, already untying the cord around her robe.

François hovered along the wall nearby. "Is everything all right?"

Sebastian nodded, then realized his mistake. "Yes." He paused. "I'm sorry. I didn't mean to . . ." He trailed off, uncertain what to say.

"It is Pierre, is it not?" François asked, his voice kind. "Some of his women friends were with him?"

"Oui."

François nodded to the air in front of him. "I thought so. He's still a man, despite the loss of his limbs. Don't think of him as less than he really is." He started to turn away, then added, "Do you know what the women in the village call him? *La langue de Dieu*. It's a term they use with much respect." With that, François began working his way back along the wall to his room.

Sebastian's mind recoiled from the image he was creating, horrified yet intrigued by the possibilities he envisioned within the room.

How could Pierre? For that matter, how *did* he?

The tongue of God, indeed!

Sebastian forced the thoughts from his mind and rapped on Gwen's door again, pleading with her in a hoarse, fervent whisper to let him in.

There was no response from Gwen, but a low moan rose from Pierre's room down the hall. Sebastian tried not to hear.

"Gwen, I'm coming in," he said, opening the door and stepping inside. "I'm sorry, but you've given me no choice. I have to talk to you—"

He broke off as he realized she was gone.

He ran to tell Corwyn and together they checked the compound. Then they returned to her room, examining it by the light of a candle. On the windowsill, Sebastian discovered where Gwen had rested her hands to watch the evening shadows advance over the mountains, the omnipresent dust already obliterating her fingerprints like snow covering tracks in winter. Sebastian studied the prints and knew they'd be gone by morning. He placed his own hands over the imprints, surprised at how small Gwen's hands seemed. Would she vanish from his life as surely as those prints?

"She's gone," Corwyn said bitterly from behind him. Then, as if to convince himself, he added, "Perhaps she's gone ahead for some reason and will meet us at Wygaard's tomorrow."

"Do you really think so?" Sebastian asked, hope rising inside him.

Corwyn stared at him levelly. "You'd better hope so, Sebastian. There's little else beyond this compound for her but cutthroats and thieves and wolves."

Sebastian turned back to the window, unable to look Corwyn in the face. But the darkness gazing at him from the window was just as cold an accusation. Somewhere out there, alone in the forest, Gwen wandered. He shivered, frightened for her.

"When do we leave?" was all he said.

Gwen was cold and lonely. She struggled to keep herself from succumbing to terror as the forest pressed in around her.

She was lost.

For several hours after leaving the compound, she'd climbed into the Pyrenees, using the moon to guide her. But the peaks and landmarks looked different in moonlight. After a time, she began to doubt her direction. Still, she kept climbing, certain that if she reached the peaks by daybreak, it would be a simple matter to work her way to the Goblin Mines.

The climbing became treacherous. Her feet slipped on wet grass, and stones rolled out from under her. Soon her hands were torn and bleeding from her falls. She tied her skirt at her waist to keep it out of the way, but the cloth was already in shreds from snagging on briars and stray branches.

The forest deepened around her until there wasn't even moonlight to guide her. After another hour of tramping through the trees, she had to admit she was getting no closer.

She decided to return to the compound to wait for daybreak. Traveling at night through unfamiliar terrain was simply too difficult. She'd return to her room and wait until Corwyn, Oliver, and Sebastian left for Smoke's lair. Then she'd set out for the Goblin Mines with the sun to guide her.

But the hours since she'd reached that decision had been long enough to retrace her steps several times over, and still she couldn't find the way back to the monastery. There wasn't a trace of dryness in the damp forest air to tell her she was at least coming close. If anything, the air was becoming heavier. Perhaps it would rain; the moon, when there was room enough between the trees to look for it, had disappeared behind clouds long ago.

Soon it did rain, lightly at first, then heavier. Lightning flashed, hitting somewhere close by. The thunder was immediate and overwhelming. Gwen forced herself to keep plodding along, driving all thoughts from her head. There was nothing else to do—she *had* to keep going. Rain plastered her hair and clothes to her body while the forest soil churned to mud that clung to her feet, holding her back. She did her best to ignore her misery. By the time the darkness around her gave way to the grey, dreary light of a new day, she was almost too numb to notice. She was traveling on what seemed to be a faint, narrow track through the forest, hoping it would eventually lead to a peasant's cottage or shepherd's hut where she could ask for a meal and shelter.

In her misery, she didn't notice the two men coming toward her through the forest. But they saw her.

One was a large knight in gleaming black armor rich with inlaid silver and gold. The other was his squire, a squat, heavy man who tramped through the mud on foot leading his master's horse. They stopped when they saw her, barring the narrow, muddy track and waiting patiently for Gwen to come to them.

CHAPTER 15

Shades of the Inquisition

"WHO IS WYGAARD, ANYWAY?" SEBASTIAN ASKED AS HE STUDIED the rock outcropping they were preparing to climb. "Why does he live way up here?"

Corwyn paused with his hands on the rock. "I shouldn't have called him Wygaard. He stopped using that name a long time ago. He prefers to be called Smoke."

"What an odd name. But all right then, who is this Smoke? Why does he live on a mountaintop?"

Corwyn put a foot on the rock and hoisted himself up. It was becoming harder to do as the day wore on. "He doesn't actually live at the top. He lives in a cave over on the Spanish side. It's his lair."

Sebastian sighed, his eyes sliding down from the heights before them to his two companions. Corwyn's robes were dirty and torn from trailing on the rocks. Oliver's straw legs were caked with mud. Sebastian's shoes were worn near through and his clothes were filthy rags. He raised an arm to wipe his face with the sleeve and realized how badly he stank.

They'd left the monastery of St. Mathurin's soon after learning of Gwen's disappearance. For a time, they were able to follow her trail, which had pointed generally in this direction. Sebastian found her course encouraging since it suggested Gwen was indeed headed toward the home of Corwyn's hermit friend. Even though Corwyn found her direction strange and asked rhetorically why she would suddenly go on alone to a destination she'd intended to avoid, Sebastian didn't care as long as they were getting closer. He kept pushing his companions to a faster pace.

But then it had started to rain, and soon not even Oliver could find Gwen's trail. The little broom took it hard, casting about through the forest to either side of them, searching for a sign. But the rain and mud obliterated her tracks. The broom regarded it as a personal loss, as if it were his fault they couldn't find her. Finally Corwyn had called him back and ordered him to stay with Sebastian. Since then, Oliver had shown none of his usual high spirits while in the wilderness. They pressed on toward Wygaard's lair with the unspoken hope that Gwen would somehow be there when they arrived.

Sebastian tested handholds in the rock Corwyn had just scaled and started up after him. "Lair? Nobody lives in a lair." He chuckled. "Except maybe dragons."

"He is a dragon," Corwyn said.

Sebastian almost fell from the rock. He caught himself and swung dizzyingly over the precipice, his feet scrabbling for a hold. When he was moderately secure once again, he glanced up to see the ragged hem of Corwyn's robe disappear over the top of the rock.

"Heh, heh. That's real funny, master," he said. "Even at a time like this, you can still jest." Actually, he found Corwyn's levity lacking in taste.

Corwyn's head popped over the rock. He looked too tired for humor. "Sometimes I wonder why I took you on as my apprentice."

Sebastian held to the rock without moving, dismayed at the remark. "Well, why did you?" he asked after a bit.

Corwyn sighed and moved out of view. "Why did I what?"

"Take me on."

From the sounds Corwyn made as he scraped against the rocks, Sebastian figured the old alchemist must be sitting down for a rest. His voice floated back as if disembodied. "I wanted someone to follow in my footsteps, I guess. To recognize what I've accomplished and perhaps feel the same excitement that's kept me at my work. And for companionship, of course. It's been lonely. The centuries can be very long."

Oliver butted Sebastian from below, urging him onward, but Sebastian ignored him. He had to follow this through. It wasn't something he could ask Corwyn face-to-face and now that the subject had come up, he had to know.

"Are you sorry you did it? Taking me on, I mean?"

Oliver poked him harder and Sebastian risked letting go of the rock face with one foot to kick back at the broom.

"It's hard to tell," Corwyn said, hedging. "You haven't been with me very long, and your apprenticeship was interrupted by this ill-begotten quest before it really began. I don't know how you'll perform in the laboratory under ordinary conditions."

"You know that's not what I mean," Sebastian muttered.

There was the sound of Corwyn's feet shuffling in the dirt above, but the alchemist didn't respond.

"After all, I did help rescue you from the dungeon," Sebastian said. He hesitated, then blurted out, "And I didn't abandon you afterward by running away as I'd planned."

"So you were planning to run away, were you?" Corwyn chuckled humorlessly. "Well, at least you didn't actually do it. And yes, I am grateful to you for rescuing me." There was a long pause. "But as for whether I'm sorry I took you on as my apprentice—*Tiens!* After what you did to Gwen yesterday, and what that led her to do as a result, I'm not so sure. If it's honesty you want, there it is. You'll have to redeem yourself for injuring her before I can ever feel comfortable about bringing you to Pomme de Terre."

Sebastian kicked at Oliver again, stung more by Corwyn's words than by the broom's persistent prodding. Yet Sebastian knew his master's words were justified. He'd already judged himself and come up lacking. Gwen might be a peasant, but she was a jewel among women. It was Sebastian who was unworthy.

Sebastian's other foot came loose as he kicked and for a terrifying moment only his fingertips held him. Sweating and straining, he regained his footholds. Then he inched himself over the top of the outcropping. He rolled onto his side and heaved himself to his feet, relieved to be off the rock face but still unable to look at Corwyn. Instead, he stared over the precipice in the direction from which they'd come.

The land fell away to the north before him, down to a *jasse* they had crossed earlier in the day. Sheep grazed in the small pasture there, but they hadn't seen any shepherds. At the northern end of the *jasse* was one of the innumerable narrow gorges which cut the major valleys of the French side of the Pyrenees into two or three successive steps or level basins. Further down this particular valley, in a larger basin near the plains, lay the monastery of St. Mathurin. Beyond that, the valley disappeared altogether and only the ridge they had crossed several days before with Petronius extended to the horizon, where it too finally flattened on the plains of Gaul.

From those plains to where Sebastian stood, somewhere near the watershed dividing France and Spain, was only a distance of about fifty or sixty miles. But, he reflected wearily, what a difference in altitude separated those miles!

He turned eastward, trying in vain to peer beyond the range into the next valley. Somewhere in that obscure distance of hills and haze was Pomme de Terre. Sebastian wished he could see the town. Better yet, he wished he could return there; he wanted to go to the Reluctant Virgin and find Gwen waiting for him. But that couldn't be. Even if it were not for the plague and Corwyn's troubles in Pomme de Terre, Sebastian knew he'd ruined things with Gwen. The knowledge wrenched at his heart with a physical pain.

He turned to find Corwyn watching him, a slight disapproving frown on the alchemist's face.

"I know I've acted badly, not only to Gwen but to all of you," Sebastian said. He held himself rigid inside, silencing the voice of his father's ghost through force of will. "I'm only an apprentice who's been too busy pursuing vain and petty dreams to see what lay around me. Gwen's the one possessed of true nobility, Master Corwyn, regardless of her station in life. And I love her. I'd gladly foreswear all hope of my family's future and my own advancement to have her safely back again."

"Nice sentiments," Corwyn said. "But they come a little late. Too bad you couldn't have expressed them sooner."

"When we get to your friend's cave, I'll not only tell Gwen how I feel, I'll show her. My actions will be the evidence to prove I've really changed."

Corwyn stood and started off again. "If she's there. I'm not certain that's where she was going. I just can't think of any other reason for her to head in this direction."

Sebastian's shoulders drooped. "She'll be there," he said, half to himself. "Knowing Gwen, she'll already be there when we arrive, wondering what took us so long."

So intent was he on convincing himself that it wasn't until they

were climbing again that Sebastian remembered the earlier part
of their conversation. When he did, it was with a clutch at his
stomach.

."This Smoke—he isn't really a dragon, is he? You were jesting, weren't you?"

Corwyn turned to look at Sebastian. He shook his head and
muttered to himself, but didn't answer.

"Master, this is serious," Sebastian said. *"Ne criez pas au
louche."*

This time when Corwyn turned to Sebastian, he wore a puzzled
expression. "I don't think that's what you meant to say."

"You're right," Sebastian answered. "Instead of wolf, I should
have said don't cry dragon."

Corwyn opened his mouth as if to speak, then waved the matter
off and returned his attention to climbing

"Master, we shouldn't be up here. Dragons have claws and
breathe fire and eat people. Please, Master Corwyn, let's turn
around and get out of here while we still have the chance."

Corwyn stopped. "What about Gwen? You just finished assuring me she's already reached his lair."

Cold shock swept Sebastian. *"Sacré coeur!"* He attacked the
mountainside with newfound fury. "Master, I've heard about
dragons and their taste for beautiful maidens. We've got to hurry.
Gwen may be in danger!"

Corwyn held his pace. "Slow down, boy. You'll kill yourself
before we get there. If Gwen's with Smoke, she's in no danger."

Sebastian's ears burned as he realized his mistake. "You mean
he won't eat her because she's not a maiden?" he asked bitterly.
"That's as absurd as if Petronius had abandoned her because she
wasn't a virgin." In his indignation, Sebastian found it easy to
overlook his own reaction to Gwen's lost virginity.

"I mean she's safe because she's a woman, virgin or not,"
Corwyn answered. "Smoke's tastes, culinary and otherwise, lie
elsewhere." The alchemist paused to look at Sebastian, the weariness in his face dispelled by mischievous glee. "Even with you,
the only real threat he's likely to pose is to your confounded
innocence."

Sebastian let the comment go for a time, concentrating on the
climb and wondering what Corwyn meant. Finally, he could stand
it no longer. "What do you mean about Smoke being a threat
to my innocence?"

The mischief went out of Corwyn's face. "I'm sorry I said that,

Sebastian. It was unkind to you both. Your innocence and Smoke's personal life are none of my concern."

Sebastian thought of Pierre and his women and was uncomfortably certain he knew what Corwyn was referring to, even if he didn't understand what his innocence had to do with Smoke. "Who says I'm innocent?" he demanded. "You don't know that. You can't tell simply by looking at me."

Corwyn kept on as if he hadn't heard.

"Well, can you?"

"Keep climbing, boy. Just keep climbing."

They crossed the watershed—a surprisingly gentle knoll of grass and scree after the difficult climb—and began descending on the Spanish side. Here the mountains grew more rugged and bizarre, a demonic fantasy sculpted in stone. The mountains continued far into Spain in successive ridges that paralleled the main peaks of the Pyrenees dividing France and Spain. On the French side of the chain, the valleys extended northward away from the mountains and into the plains, but on the Spanish side the valleys ran east and west, effectively blocking most travel into or out of Spain. Here, the land was more exposed to the sun, and the waterways became smaller and fewer in number. Vegetation was arid. Sebastian's mouth grew dry with the climb.

They came to a small pasture. Grass was sparse, but adequate for the few sheep and goats grazing there. To one side of the pasture sat a stocky shepherd, snub-nosed and rough in a belted tunic and long hose that was more holes than cloth. He wore a loose blouse and a straw hat to keep off the sun. Beside him sat a peasant woman, her face and figure in the bloom of a youth that was all too fleeting for one of her station. Her skirt was caught up at the belt to free her legs for tramping over the mountains, her hair pulled back with a cloth scarf.

The man encircled the woman's waist with one arm and drew her toward him, whispering something that made her laugh. She offered no resistance as he pushed her back onto the grass. So intent were they that they failed to notice Corwyn leading Sebastian and Oliver across the meadow toward them, until the alchemist coughed softly at their sides. The shepherd turned and scowled at the intruders without getting up. The woman struggled beneath him, trying to free herself of his weight while straightening her skirt. She too glared at the alchemist.

"Please accept my apologies for disturbing you," Corwyn said, "but we're lost and trying to find our way to where a friend lives.

He's a dragon named Wygaard and he lives somewhere around here. Can you tell us how to find him?"

The man scowled deeper and shrugged. He seemed oblivious to the efforts of the woman to get up. She pushed him harder.

"Possibly you know him as Smoke," Corwyn persisted. "Most of his friends call him that."

The scowl continued. This time, the peasant didn't even bother to shrug.

"Tiens! I'm sorry to have bothered you," Corwyn said, bowing slightly and backing away. To a stranger, his voice might have sounded the same as before, but Sebastian heard a trace of sarcasm creep into the alchemist's words. "We certainly appreciate your help."

"No comprende," the shepherd said in heavily accented Spanish.

Beneath him, the woman grimaced with frustration at her inability to get free. She kicked and pushed, then lay back helplessly, panting for breath. *"Desapreto me, por favor,"* she snapped.

The man turned in surprise as if he'd forgotten she was there.

"Ah," Corwyn said, his expression brightening. He thought for a moment, then tried again. "Dragon." He mouthed the word carefully, first in French, then in Latin. *"Draco."*

Understanding lit the peasant's face with a curious sneer. He looked the newcomers over slowly, disdainfully, then said something to his companion. She gave a nasty laugh, her expression one of contempt, then made a vulgar gesture Sebastian needed no Spanish to interpret.

The shepherd guffawed at this. He jerked his head, indicating to Corwyn the direction he should take. Then he turned back to the woman and said something to her that made her snicker as he took her in his arms.

Sebastian was angry at the way the pair laughed at him and Corwyn. He started toward the man to protest, his jaw tight and his fists clenched at his sides. Corwyn held him back.

"Merci," Corwyn said, nodding and speaking carefully as if they were still paying attention. He started walking again in the direction the shepherd had indicated, dragging Sebastian with him.

The sounds of the peasants' laughter cut at Sebastian as he followed his master over the stony field. He could feel the couple's eyes boring contemptuously into his back. "Why'd they act

like that when you told them who we're looking for?" he asked
when they were out of the peasants' sight. "And why'd you stop
me when I tried to cuff that fool for his insolence?"

Corwyn glanced back toward the pasture before answering,
his face rigidly composed. "They're peasants, Sebastian, and
they're been raised in ignorance. They cannot help what they've
been taught." But his voice was strained as he said it.

Sebastian studied Corwyn in silence, disturbed as much by the
alchemist's mild words despite his evident distress as by the peasants' response to Corwyn's request. "Master, what kind of monster are you leading me to?" he asked.

Corwyn spun around, his restrained anger finding an outlet in
Sebastian. "Watch how you talk," he snapped. "Those peasants
are ignorant through no fault of their own. They know no better.
But I won't accept such stupidity from you. Not any longer. I've
watched you jump to ill-founded, hurtful conclusions about almost everyone you've met since arriving in Pomme de Terre,
including Oliver, Pierre, and even Gwen. I don't doubt but that
you've formed similar opinions of me as well. But I'll tolerate
this foolishness no longer. So hold your tongue and control your
ignorant, precious superiority for a change. And just this once,
you might try approaching someone new without judging him in
advance by your own narrow, self-righteous standards."

Without waiting for a response, Corwyn stalked off across the
uneven ground to where Oliver waited impatiently.

"Yes, master," Sebastian said meekly, hurrying to catch up.
Corwyn had cleared up nothing with his speech, but the mention
of Gwen and how Sebastian had hurt her left him unwilling to
pursue the topic further. They walked in silence for a while.

"You know, that peasant woman said the same thing the duke
did when we found him in the dungeon while looking for you,"
Sebastian said at last, looking for a safe topic of conversation.

"You mean you understood her Spanish?"

"No, that's just it. When we came across the duke in the
dungeon, he said something to us we couldn't understand. It was
in a foreign tongue. But when that woman spoke to the man
back there, I realized they were the same words the duke used."

Corwyn froze, then turned slowly. "The duke spoke Spanish?"

"Yes, I guess he must have." Sebastian shrugged. "I didn't
know he knew the language."

"He doesn't." Corwyn resumed walking, though too slowly to
please Oliver. The alchemist stroked his beard in thought. Finally

he chuckled without humor. *"Tiens!* At least we know now where they're coming from," he said to no one in particular.

"Where who's coming from? What do you mean?"

"The demons," Corwyn said. "They're coming from Spain."

"Master, what're you talking about?"

"That wasn't the duke you heard speaking." Corwyn raised his hands to stop Sebastian's protest. "Oh, the words came from his mouth all right. But it was the demon who possessed him that you heard. Having come from Spain, the demon knew only Spanish. The same thing happened to me. When I was in the dungeon before my rescue and that demon was about to possess me, strange words appeared in my head. I didn't understand then what was happening, but I realize now they were Spanish words, the thoughts of the demon as it started to enter my mind."

"Bien sûr!" Sebastian exclaimed. "That's what happened to me, too. On the drawbridge when we went to see your water system! And a couple of other times." For a moment, he thought about telling Corwyn what had happened each time he was nearly possessed. He'd realized during the past couple of days that Gwen and Corwyn probably hadn't seen the vision of him as a crying boy when they'd rescued Corwyn from the dungeon. After all, Corwyn had called out "Hypatia" when Sebastian and Gwen entered the cell, yet neither of them saw anything but the demon.

This assurance that his own vision had gone unwitnessed should have comforted Sebastian, but it didn't. Even as he held back from considering the significance of the vision, he couldn't help wondering why it had so much effect on him. Sometimes he felt he could almost remember . . . something, he wasn't sure what. Nor was he sure he wanted to.

"What are Spanish demons doing in Pomme de Terre?" he asked, redirecting the conversation.

"It's the Inquisition." Corwyn gave his apprentice an oddly vicious grin. "Evidently, the Inquisitors are exorcising demons in Spain on a scale they're unprepared to safely handle."

"I still don't see what that has to do with us."

Corwyn shook his head and sighed. "They can't adequately trap and store so many demons, yet the Inquisition there gathers momentum by the day. So every day they create more of these demonic wastes. They have to rid themselves of the demons somehow, and that means dumping them beyond the Spanish borders—in Gardenia."

"They're dumping them here?" Sebastian asked.

Corwyn nodded. *"Oui.* The demons and other harmful spirits
released by the Inquisition in Spain are being concentrated and
stabilized somehow for shipment out of the country. They're
freighted just over the watershed of the Pyrenees and dumped
inside France, where they eventually work their way into the
headwaters of the River Ale. By that route, the demon plague
reaches Pomme de Terre.

"But who would do such a thing?"

"I don't know. But this makes it all the more important for
us to get to Smoke's lair. He must be very near where this is
happening. From his lair, we can set up the breath of demons
tests to determine where the demons are being disposed. Perhaps
by learning that, we can discover who's behind this hideous
scheme. We have to stop them."

A chill clutched Sebastian. There was something wrong with
the world when a dragon's lair became a haven of refuge from
a horde of demons. He shivered and hoped desperately that
Gwen had reached the uncertain sanctuary of Smoke's cave.

Gwen looked up at the sound of a horse snorting. There, not
fifty feet away, stood a mounted knight and his squire. She felt
a wave of apprehension at being discovered on the road alone,
but that was quickly replaced with anger at herself for allowing
it to happen.

There was hardly a pause in her step as she realized it was too
late to run into the woods and hide. Better to bluff it through
and hope there was nothing to fear. She forced a confidence into
her step that she hadn't felt since she'd realized she was lost.
This was no time to appear the cowering maiden. She looked
each of them in turn firmly in the eye.

The squire was the most repulsive man she'd ever seen, and
she'd encountered some of the worst at the Reluctant Virgin.
But she held his stare just long enough to appear self-confident
without letting it drift into a challenge. Then she looked at his
master.

She couldn't meet his eyes. She didn't know where they were
looking. His visor was down, and it was impossible to tell whether
he was looking at or past her. Rain splattered unnoticed against
the visor grill and slid in shiny rivulets down the lacquered, inlaid
armor plates. She waited for some acknowledgment, then gave
up and returned to the squire. His attention, at least, was still
on her. In fact, he was staring at her in a way that made her

uncomfortably aware how tightly her rain-soaked clothes clung to her skin.

"Are you lost, milady?" he leered.

"No." The word jumped too quickly from her lips. "No, I'm waiting for some friends of mine to catch up with me."

Even as she said it, she wished it were true. She wished Corwyn and Oliver and Sebastian really were following close behind her, about to catch up. Especially Sebastian with that ridiculous sword he drew so readily whenever danger threatened. She wished she'd never laughed at it or at him.

"Ah," the squire said, looking pointedly at the empty path behind her. "These friends of yours, perhaps they've melted in the rain." He laughed, and the sound was as ugly as his appearance.

"They're right behind me," Gwen said, turning to look down the path as if expecting them to appear. "One's a powerful wizard, another's a valiant knight. I'm sure they'll be along any minute." She turned back to the squire, hoping to frighten him with her boldness. "We're on our way to the Goblin Mines."

The effect this produced on the squire was not what she intended. Suddenly, his attention went from languorous perusal to avid interest. He leaned toward her, his eyes sparkling now with something more than lust. "The Goblin Mines, you say? Such a dark and fearsome place. Now what would a charming creature like you want to go there for?"

"I have to . . . that is, we have to get there to stop the plague in Pomme de Terre." She looked beseechingly at the knight, hoping the idea of a noble quest might appeal to his sense of compassion.

"Ah," the squire said again as if this explained a great deal. "It's well known, then, that the plague in Pomme de Terre comes from the Goblin Mines?"

"No," Gwen said, frowning as she wondered if that was what she'd said. "I've only just discovered the connection. But I don't know what's causing the plague, or why it's related to the mines. That's why I must get there—to find out."

In her anxiety to convince the knight of the importance of her task, she forgot to keep up the plural pronoun.

"And your friends?"

"They're going to meet me there. That is, if they don't meet up with me along the way." Again she searched the direction from which she'd come. "I can't imagine what's keeping them."

"These friends of yours, they wouldn't by any chance include an alchemist named Corwyn, would they?"

"*Oui*," Gwen said, brightening. "Do you know him?"

"Only by reputation. But that's sufficient to tell me he's no wizard. Milady, you're a poor liar and I don't believe your friends are close behind." He smiled at her, letting his gaze drift over her body with easy familiarity. "Don't you trust my master and me?"

"*Mais oui*," she said grimly. She wished he'd stop calling her "milady." He gave the word an unpleasant ring. "But you're wrong about my friends. I assure you, they're very close behind."

The squire laughed. "Then perhaps they passed you in the rain. Perhaps they've already reached the mines and are wondering where you are."

"That couldn't have happened," Gwen insisted, beginning to feel frightened. "I would have seen them."

"Only if they were as lost as you," the squire guffawed. "Milady, this isn't even the way to the Goblin Mines." He laughed so hard at this that he slipped in the mud, jerking on the bridle of his master's horse as he fell. He pulled himself up and brushed ineffectually at the mud, still chuckling.

Gwen watched him with a sinking heart, not knowing what to do.

"Tell you what, milady, since you're obviously a noble maiden in distress"—his eyes caressed her with a look that belied the gentility of his words—"and engaged in a most worthy pursuit, my master and I'll undertake to guide you to the Goblin Mines. Then if your friends don't catch up with us on the way, you can wait for them there." He pulled at the mount's bridle, leading his master closer.

"No, that's all right," Gwen said, backing up. "I wouldn't want to trouble you. You're obviously headed the other way."

"Oh, it's no trouble, I assure you," said the squire. "My master's always looking for pretty maidens to rescue. I'm sure he'd enjoy helping you." He stared at the bodice of her chemise, where the wet cloth revealed the fullness of her breasts.

Gwen tried to appear casual as she crossed her arms over her breasts to hide them from his gaze. But the ugly squire only grinned and let his attention wander casually over the rest of her.

"How do you know what your master wants?" she demanded. "He hasn't said anything."

"Oh, I know," the squire assured her. "I know my master's wishes very well." He saw her eyes dart briefly to the trees beside the road and held up a hand. "Don't think of running, milady. Terrible things can happen to a beautiful young maid lost in the woods. If you'll step over here with me, we can be on our way."

"Are you really giving me a choice?"

"Now, don't be that way. We're just helping you reach the mines so you can find your friends."

Gwen knew she was losing, but the menace which seemed to lurk just behind his words made her fling up her head in one final challenge. "Do you know the way?"

The squire laughed again. "Oh, milady, we know the way. And having you with us will make it our most enjoyable journey there in a long time." He turned the knight's horse around and urged Gwen to join him as he led the procession, his hand still on the bridle of his master's horse.

Gwen fell in step beside the squire with unveiled reluctance. "Doesn't he ever speak?" she asked, jerking her head at the knight.

The squire edged closer to Gwen than she desired. "Only to me, and then only in matters of extreme necessity. He's sworn a vow of silence against this sinful world in which we live so as not to be disturbed while he pursues the loftiest of thoughts." He grinned and slipped an arm around her waist. "All baser thoughts, he leaves to me."

Gwen scowled at the squire and shook herself free. He laughed, but let her go. "Perhaps later," he said in a way that chilled her blood.

They walked in silence for a time, the squire huddled deep within his cloak to keep out the rain. He didn't offer to share it with Gwen, not that she wanted to get that close to him anyway. But she wished she were similarly clothed.

They came to a large puddle, which the squire stepped around gingerly. The knight's horse simply clomped on through, its mammoth hooves splattering mud and water everywhere. Gwen looked back in irritation, but the knight just stared ahead, lost in his own thoughts. Like other knights she'd known, he lived on another sphere which contained only himself and the object of his pursuit. Nothing else existed. Gwen had the feeling she and the rain and the mud the horse threw in passing were equally unreal to him.

She'd seen many knights at the Reluctant Virgin. Most were

a rowdy, opportunistic lot who used their noble status as justification for living lawlessly. They drank and wenched, quarreled readily, and ended their frequent arguments with the sword. They took what they wanted with an easy arrogance that would have brought quick death to any peasant presumptuous enough to imitate it. But as long as they were granted all that they might want, and the fragility of their honor went unchallenged, they could be good-hearted, boisterous company. They appreciated a woman who possessed a friendly manner and handsome figure. Gwen knew well how to use their interest to her own advantage, and how to play one knight against another so that she never had to fear one knight's unwelcome advances might go unchecked by his comrades in arms. And on those occasions when she was willing to go to the hayloft or into the stillness of the forest with a knight and receive his more intimate attentions while stars passed overhead, they offered her the skill and grace of practiced, gentle lovers before departing with the dawn—a pleasant experience as long as she didn't expect too much from them after.

But there was another kind of knight, rarer but infinitely more dangerous. He was the knight who believed the myths about the sanctity of his occupation and went off in search of holy, valorous quests. The knight-errant who actually lived by the code of chivalry and swore solemn, complicated oaths of silence, celibacy, and various other forms of abstention as repentance for living in a sinful world. The knight who passed through life oblivious of those around him, and in so doing wreaked more unsuspecting havoc than all his quick-tempered, hot-blooded compatriots put together.

Gwen recognized the knight she was with as one of the latter, and the thought made her uneasy. Reaching him could be much harder than it would have been with the more common form of knight. She would have to discover what motivated him in order to know how to manipulate him to her own ends. Fortunately, she did have an advantage in this task. No knight, regardless how aloof and remote, could ever be quite invulnerable to the wiles of an attractive, cunning woman. Gwen had long survived by using those wiles, and she would readily do so again to gain the aid of this knight.

The thought of her own competence comforted her, and she walked with an easier spirit. The squire would be no problem once she controlled his master.

Finally the rain stopped and the clouds lifted. The sun burst warmly through the leaves to lighten their way. Birds sang and insects lent a multivoiced hum of activity to the forest. The ground rose and became uneven, the trees thinning as they climbed. Gwen caught glimpses of the surrounding countryside as they topped low hills along their way. All the world seemed bathed in the splendor of fresh green. Gwen felt she wanted to sing and twirl her way along the narrow forest path. Even the squire's wicked grins, which he cast her way from time to time, did little to dispel the beauty around her.

But all wonder pales after a time, especially when unsupported by food and rest. Gwen grew weary again and looked forward to the end of the journey. Besides, the sun was creeping nearer to the western peaks. Shadows began to lengthen. She needed to be free of the squire and his unwanted attentions before dark—men were always more difficult to control at night.

They seemed to be descending now more often than they climbed. Gwen glanced back uneasily. Yes, she was certain of it. They had crossed the watershed sometime before and were now on the Spanish side.

"How much further to the mines?" she asked, looking around for tailings or other signs of disemboweled earth.

"Not much further," the squire replied.

"But aren't the Goblin Mines over on the French side?"

"Oui."

"But we've crossed into Spain."

"It's easier to reach the mines by following the contours of the southern slopes rather than cutting across the northern ones." He leered at her confidently.

Gwen said nothing. What the squire said made sense. It was often easier to travel east and west along the range by taking advantage of the direction in which the ridges lay on the Spanish side rather than by attempting to climb directly from one French valley over into another. Yet the look the squire gave her chilled Gwen to the soul.

At the top of the next rise she caught sight of pennants fluttering in the breeze beyond the hill. She frowned. "I didn't think anyone lived this near to the mines," she said. "There are so many superstitions about them."

For once the squire was as silent as his master, though his look spoke eloquently, making Gwen shudder.

She saw nothing more until they topped the next rise. Before them, on the plain of a rocky valley floor, stood a small castle. Its mixture of Moorish and European architecture told of shifting ownership during its formative years, the two styles blending with an uneasiness that had not been reconciled with passing time. The castle had crumbled into disrepair, but the two factions that gave birth to the structure still battled across its face.

They drew near enough for Gwen to make out the design on the pennants above the battlements. It was disgusting, and one she didn't recognize—a dead fish rotting in a putrid pool. But its unfamiliarity was not surprising since there were hundreds of family crests, royal seals, and other insignia within the duchy alone, and the designs flown over this castle were likely to be of foreign origin.

They wound down into the valley and onto a rutted road leading to the castle. As they approached the castle gate, Gwen balked. "This isn't the way to the Goblin Mines. Why're we coming here?"

"It's late," the squire said. "We'll stop here for the night and get a fresh start in the morning."

Gwen stopped. "You had no intention of taking me to the mines, did you?"

"We need Corwyn," he said. "You're going to bring him to us."

Gwen moved toward the edge of the road, but the squire sidestepped quickly, hemming her between himself and the knight. Gwen was trapped. She forced herself to relax as if accepting defeat. A satisfied leer lit up the squire's face and he stepped in to grab her.

"It won't be so bad," he said soothingly. "It's Corwyn we want. We won't hurt you as long as you cooperate."

He reached for her arm. Gwen bolted toward the knight, ducking under the horse. The horse started and skittered sideways, forcing the squire to dart around the beast. Gwen gathered up her skirts and ran for the trees at the edge of the valley. She heard the squire close behind her, but he was a heavy man and not a fast runner. A crossbow bolt whizzed past her head, sinking into the trunk of a tree. The squire paused to bellow at the castle walls not to shoot, that he wanted her alive. The delay gave Gwen an added advantage. She forced herself not to look back, but she heard the squire dropping further behind. If she could just keep going a little further, she might be able to get far enough away to hide in the broken countryside around the castle.

Suddenly, hooves pounded close behind. Despite herself, Gwen spun around to look. There was the knight at full gallop, almost upon her. She jumped aside to keep from being trampled and her foot slipped on a loose rock. She hit the ground rolling. The knight thundered by without a pause, but the squire jumped her before she could regain her feet. He twisted her arm behind her back and laughed between gasps for breath.

"You're a feisty one," he said, dragging her back to the road. "I think I'll enjoy waiting for your friends to arrive."

Gwen gritted her teeth against the pain in her twisted ankle and set her heels in the ground, making the squire work at pulling her to the castle. But he was much heavier than she was and very powerful; her resistance was futile.

As the squire forced her up the rutted road and through the gate, Gwen took a quick glance back at freedom. The last thing she saw before the castle walls obscured the world outside was the black knight topping a ridge, his horse still galloping full tilt. The squire, following her glance, watched his master hurtle over the ridge and down the other side.

"Now look what you've done!" the squire said, scowling. "He's forgotten what we were about. I'll have to go after him, which means it'll be a long time before I get my dinner!"

It was a minor victory, but Gwen gloated nevertheless, hoping the ugly toad was very hungry.

Sebastian hung back outside the entrance to the cave.

"Oh, *allons!*" Corwyn said in exasperation. He took Sebastian's arm and urged him forward. "I'm not going to wait out here on account of your foolishness."

"I'll make a deal with you," Sebastian ventured, trying to resist being dragged. "Let's wait out here, and in return I'll run as many breath of demons tests as you want later."

"I have a different deal," Corwyn muttered. "You do as I say now, and you'll still run all the tests that I tell you to when the time comes. Now move!"

"But, master, everything I've ever heard about dragons tells me we shouldn't do this."

"What a provincial attitude. With that kind of thinking, it's no wonder Gardenia hasn't joined the Renaissance."

"I've been thinking about that, too. I'm not so sure this Renaissance you talk about is such a good thing, after all. Perhaps we should just go back and find another quiet town. You could set up shop as if the plague in Pomme de Terre never happened. What do you say?"

"Keep moving," Corwyn growled, shoving Sebastian further into the cave.

"'Keep moving, keep moving,'" Sebastian grumbled. "That's all I've heard all day." But he made sure Corwyn didn't overhear.

The tunnel was dimly lit by daylight from behind and a glow ahead. Even in the scant light, they had little problem making their way, for the floor was worn smooth and swept clean as if something huge passed through regularly, keeping debris cleared away. The stone walls and ceiling were smooth, except where deep gouges cut the rock. Sebastian shuddered, wondering what kind of claws it took to leave a trail like that.

Sebastian crept stealthily into the mountain. Corwyn clomped after him, the sound of his steps echoing through the passage. Behind Corwyn came Oliver, tapping his wooden fingers on the sides of the cave.

"Shhhh," Sebastian whispered over his shoulder. "À pas de louche."

Corwyn stopped. "With the footsteps of a what?"

"Louche," Sebastian repeated. "You know, a wolf."

Corwyn shook his head and sighed. "Boy, when will you learn?"

"Learn what?"

But Corwyn didn't answer. Instead, he simply took the lead. Oliver fell into step behind him, with Sebastian now bringing up the rear. Sebastian cringed at the noise made by his companions, then quietly drew his sword. It was too small to be much help, but the feel of it in his hand reassured him. At least he would meet his death armed and fighting. But Oliver saw the upraised sword and tugged at Corwyn's robe, pointing out the weapon to the alchemist.

"Put that thing away," Corwyn hissed. "You'll offend our host, and we need his help. Besides, someone might get hurt."

Sebastian sheathed the sword reluctantly. When Corwyn turned away, the apprentice tried to cuff the broom, but Oliver saw the blow coming and danced out of reach.

They emerged into a vast stone chamber, part natural and part—no, not man-made, Sebastian realized. Dragon-made. The thought made his skin prickle.

The air was rich with herbs and spices, as well as some underlying odor Sebastian couldn't identify. He decided it must be dragon. Not unpleasant, merely different, unfamiliar. But his terror of what it signified left Sebastian shivering.

Dried plants hung from the cavern ceiling. The walls were lined with glass and pottery containers, many holding still more kinds of flora. To one side of the chamber, something fragrant simmered in an iron cauldron. The smell reminded Sebastian how hungry he was. His mouth watered and his legs felt weak. He sagged against a low shelf.

"So where is he? Do you think he'll offer us something to eat? I'm starved!"

Corwyn walked to the end of the chamber, where another tunnel led deeper into the mountain. He took a quick look, then returned. "I don't think he's here. At least, no one seems to be in the nearest chambers."

"He can't be far," Sebastian said, his eyes closed to better savor the aroma of food. He waved at the cauldron. "He seems to have left dinner cooking."

Corwyn sat on a low rock. "The next question is, where's Gwen?"

Sebastian straightened, his eyes open. "She must be with him."

Corwyn stared silently at Sebastian, then rubbed his face with his hands. "I hope so."

"Master," Sebastian said quietly, giving voice at last to his doubts, "what do we do if she's not with him?"

Corwyn made no response.

"She could be anywhere out there," Sebastian went on. "She may be lost, even hurt."

"I'm too old for this," Corwyn muttered, his head deep in his hands. "I should have become a recluse centuries ago."

"I won't leave her out there, Corwyn. But when I go to look for her, will you come with me? Will you help?"

Corwyn sighed. "Of course I'll help. I just hope we can figure out where to look."

A slithering sound came from the tunnel, a noise like a thousand snakes writhing against stone in unison. It set Sebastian's teeth on edge. He clenched them to hold down his panic. The sound grew louder. Monstrous sighs rose and fell under the slithering noise with the regularity of breathing. Corwyn looked up without moving from his rock. Despite his master's admonition, Sebastian drew his sword again.

A voice grumbled from the tunnel. "I simply must lose weight. It's frightful the way I put on extra tons. Soon I shall be too enormous to get in and out and then I'll have to give up eating altogether." A dragon's head poked into the chamber, grimacing as he pulled his body through the tunnel. Suddenly he realized he wasn't alone. "Who's there?" He set a large bag on the floor and peered nearsightedly into the room. "You aren't another knight who's come to slay me, are you? That sort of thing's becoming a frightful bother." He squirmed the rest of the way into the chamber, taking up much of the available space.

Sebastian absorbed details of the dragon's appearance and manner. "Know yer enemy," his Scottish fighting instructor had said. Sebastian wondered what good that would do him now, but he followed the old soldier's advice as best he could.

The dragon was enormous, possibly ten or twelve feet tall at the shoulders. It appeared awfully rotund and Sebastian hoped its weight might slow it down in a close fight. Against its bulk, the animal's foreclaws were small and fragile looking, although each was as large as one of Sebastian's legs. When the limbs held still, it was with a certain delicacy, and when in motion, they displayed a studied precision. Two vein-laced, translucent wings, ornamental vestiges useless for flight, arched above the beast and completed the picture. The only thing missing, Sebastian thought, was the requisite puff of smoke trailing from the nostrils of the beast.

But the most noticeable aspect of the dragon wasn't its size or shape, he realized. It was the creature's coloring. The gaudy iridescence shimmering over its scaly hide was stunning to the point of excess. Most of its body was colored in reddish shades that varied from wine to burgundy, with magenta highlights. Toward the extremities, the dragon's limbs, snout, and tail shifted to puce and on into cooler shades of blue and purple. Here and there, particularly along the edges of the scales and spines, flecks of indigo, cyan, and cobalt blue provided opulent contrasts with the rest of his body.

Suddenly, Sebastian discovered that the dragon's coloration had distracted him from the creature's movements. He forced himself to concentrate on any sign that might warn of attack.

The dragon swung its massive head toward the alchemist. "*Alors!* It's Corwyn!" the creature exclaimed. And there was the smoke—two blue grey puffs with a hint of lavender. "What a nice surprise!" Then the dragon noticed Sebastian, sword drawn and braced in a fighting stance. A three-foot grin split the gigantic face, and the creature seemed to simper. "Well, who's this with you? A tasty-looking morsel of succulent young knighthood if ever I saw one!"

Sebastian heard the words like the tolling of his death knell. He tried to remember what his instructor had told him. Was it right foot forward or left? He wished he'd paid better attention when he'd had the chance.

"Now, Smoke, don't start," Corwyn warned. "The boy's my apprentice and I'm responsible for him."

"But, Corwyn," Smoke replied coyly, his saucer eyes still savoring Sebastian, "you know I wouldn't hurt him."

"I know exactly what you have in mind, Smoke. But he's already spoken for."

The dragon frowned. "By male or female?"

"Female."

The dragon considered this, then smiled again. "That could change," he said, dismissing Corwyn's objection with a wave of his claw. "He's probably never even tested the water."

Sebastian noticed with a curious sense of detachment that the foot-long talons on Smoke's waving claw were bright crimson. Obviously bloodstained, he thought.

Smoke edged closer to Sebastian, careful not to crush Corwyn in the process. His tail swished languidly, almost sensuously, from side to side, knocking over furniture. He sucked in his enormous stomach and tried to hold it, but finally had to let it out to breathe.

Then he noticed Sebastian's sword. His smile stiffened. *"Tiens!* You did intend to slay me, didn't you?" he asked with disappointment.

He reached out and plucked the weapon from Sebastian's grip in a motion too fast to follow. Sebastian's jaw fell open, and his sword arm dropped limply to his side. Smoke studied the sword critically. "Much too small," he said. He felt the blade with the tip of a claw. "The steel's too soft to hold an edge." He flipped the sword from one foreclaw to another and sliced the air in a couple of practice strokes. Sebastian jumped back from the humming blade. "The balance is all wrong," Smoke said. He tossed the sword in the air and caught it by the blade, then handed it back to Sebastian hilt first. He smiled again. "It's fortunate you didn't need to use that thing, boy. It would have been the death of you."

Just then, Oliver peered timidly around Corwyn at the dragon. Smoke noticed the broom and his smile broadened. "Oliver, I should've known you'd be somewhere about." The dragon leaned closer to the broom. "Want to slide? It's all right, go ahead."

Oliver shuffled nervously, holding back. Smoke looked hurt. "Ah, Oliver, I've promised never to let it happen again." In an apologetic aside, he explained to Sebastian, "I almost flamed him once by accident. It happens occasionally in the heat of passion or times of emotional distress. Oliver's never forgiven me since."

Oliver hesitated a moment longer, then ran around behind the dragon. He bounded up the long tail and onto Smoke's back. At the dragon's shoulders he turned and slid down the scaly back between the dragon's wings and all the way down the tail to the floor. Then Oliver clambered up to do it again.

"There was another member of our group," Corwyn said as he watched Oliver frolic. "We were hoping she might have reached here before us."

"Hmm?" Smoke replied, his attention still on Oliver. "Someone else still to come? Splendid!"

"*Oui*, her name's Gwen. Have you seen her?"

The dragon frowned. "A woman? Corwyn, you know better. Why are you bringing one here?"

"I know your preferences, Smoke, but we had no choice. She's our friend, and her life is in danger. But she . . . she started out ahead of us and we weren't sure where she was going."

"Have you seen her?" Sebastian asked, stepping forward as he risked speaking to the dragon at last. "Did she get here before us?"

"*Tiens! Un anglais*," Smoke cried. "My favorite!"

Sebastian frowned, wondering why everyone always knew he was English as soon as he opened his mouth.

"This Gwen person wouldn't happen to be the one you're involved with, would she?" Smoke asked, squinting at Sebastian. "Ah, I see. No, I'm sorry, she hasn't arrived. Decided not to come, I should imagine. Fickle, women are. Not worth the bother. I assure you, I can offer you better."

There was a long, awkward silence as the trio digested this. Corwyn looked at Sebastian, but said nothing. Even Oliver halted his game to stare at the uncomfortable apprentice.

Sebastian turned away in what he hoped was a confident stride. But inside, the voice he had held at bay since he'd discovered Gwen's absence started in on him again. "She'll get here. You wait and see. If Gwen planned on coming here, nothing will hold her back."

He didn't believe it himself.

Smoke lifted Oliver from his back. *"Alors!* There's obviously more here than meets the eye. Come, Oliver, that's enough for now. It's time I finished fixing dinner. Your friends must be ravenous."

"Oui," Sebastian said, eager to change the subject. "We are very hungry indeed. *J'ai une faim de la louche."*

Smoke stopped unpacking mushrooms and other wild delicacies from the bag he'd carried into the lair. "You're as hungry as a what?"

"Louche." Sebastian was exasperated at having to repeat himself. "You know, a wolf."

Laughter rumbled from the dragon, shaking the earth and accompanied by billows of smoke. Suddenly flame shot from his mouth and splashed against the stone wall of the cave. "Oh, *pardon!"* Smoke cried, clapping a foreclaw over his snout. "But that was so funny!"

"I don't see anything funny about it," Sebastian snapped, checking his blouse to see if it had been singed by the flame. "It's a common expression."

"To say you're as hungry as a wolf, yes," Smoke agreed, choking back a chuckle. "But you said you're as hungry as a basting spoon. Perhaps instead of calling you *mon petit loup*, I should call you my little basting spoon." With that, Smoke burst out laughing again, still clutching his snout to prevent further eruptions of flame.

"Mon petit loup?" Sebastian asked Corwyn, who was struggling to maintain his composure.

"A pet name," the alchemist said from behind a fist. His face reddened and his eyes filled with tears. "Like that other term of endearment you've had experience with: *mon petit chou.* Oh, Sebastian, you do create problems for yourself with the language."

Sebastian scowled as Corwyn also succumbed to laughter.

"Alors!" Smoke said when he could control his voice again. "I know you too well to believe you're up here just for a visit, Corwyn. You haven't taken a break in a hundred years at least, so this must involve work. What is it this time? Not still that water nonsense, is it?"

Sebastian looked hastily at Corwyn, expecting a sharp retort

to Smoke's remark. But although the alchemist sobered at this
reminder of why they had come, his response was subdued. He
looked his age tonight, Sebastian thought. This quest was proving
too much for him. That, and worrying about Gwen.

Another pang of conscience stabbed Sebastian, and he wished
there was something he could do to atone for his guilt.

"It has to do with aquatic alchemy, if that's what you mean,"
Corwyn said at last. "Or at least it did. I don't know what we'll
do, now that Gwen . . ."

Corwyn's unfinished words and dejected manner were too
much for Sebastian. "We've got to start looking for her, Master
Corwyn. We've got to find her!"

Corwyn started to say something too quickly, then stopped
and cleared his throat. Voice under control, he tried again. "One
old man, a bumbling apprentice, a broom, and an overweight
dragon. Between us, you think we can search this whole portion
of the Pyrenees? Oh, we'll try, all right. But don't be so foolish
as to think we'll actually accomplish anything."

"We'll get help," Sebastian cried, ignoring the sting of Corwyn's remark about a "bumbling apprentice."

"*Bien entendu!* I'm sure the irate citizens of Pomme de Terre
would love to help," Corwyn said. "That way, they could hang
all of us together."

"What about those mines?" Sebastian insisted. "The ones Dr.
Tox leased from the duchy. They're around here somewhere,
aren't they? If Dr. Tox has someone working them, maybe they
would help."

Corwyn snorted. "The Goblin Mines! I wonder if Dr. Tox
realizes yet just how poor a man the lease on those mines will
make him. Those mines haven't yielded anything of value for
two hundred years, and with all Dr. Tox is paying on that lease,
he can't afford to hire anyone to work the mines for him."

Sebastian drew back, defeated. Oh, Gwen, he thought,
what're we to do? How will we ever find you?

"Actually, that's not true about the mines, Corwyn," Smoke
interrupted. "There has been some activity up there lately at
night. A couple of dreadful-smelling fellows with a mule team
have been making occasional trips there, meeting some fop in
fancy clothes."

Mules, Sebastian thought. Now why did the mention of mules
in connection with the Goblin Mines strike a chord in his memory?

Corwyn sat up straight. "Tall, gangly man?"

"With a straggly beard and oily black hair," Smoke said. He grimaced with distaste.

"That's him!" Corwyn slapped his knees and jumped up.

"Who?"

"Dr. Tox. And he's paying someone to work the mines." Corwyn laughed. "He's a bigger fool than I thought!"

"Not quite," Sebastian said, intent on remembering the scraps of parchment he'd seen at the monastery of St. Mathurin. "It's Kwagg and Meier, Master Corwyn. And they're not working the mines, they're carrying loads up to them. Loads of demonic wastes from the Inquisition in Spain."

"What are you talking about?" Corwyn asked. "Dr. Tox isn't capable of organizing a scheme like that."

"When we were searching through the archives, I found a note from someone agreeing to buy a dozen mules from a merchant in Gardenia. Something about the note seemed familiar, but I didn't realize until now what it was. The note was written by Dr. Tox."

"Are you certain?" Corwyn asked, his voice full of doubt.

"It was the same crabbed handwriting as the signature on the lease," Sebastian said.

"That doesn't mean he's hired Kwagg and Meier or that he's the one bringing in the wastes, boy. Anyone can buy a dozen mules, even someone as foolish as Dr. Tox."

"But there was something else, Master Corwyn. Remember that list of deposits to the banking family in Florence? Remember the list came from someone at the castle of the Duke de Gardenia? Well, that list was also written by Dr. Tox."

Corwyn threw up his hands. "But Dr. Tox couldn't possibly be behind a project of this size and complexity. The man's a fool! He's incompetent!" Sebastian said nothing while the alchemist stroked his beard in thought. At last Corwyn went on. "Still, you might be right after all about the connection between the Goblin Mines and the Inquisition wastes. That would be the logical place to dump them. And if Dr. Tox holds the lease on those mines . . ." He shook his head in disbelief. "Hmm, I must run my breath of demons test on the water that drains from those mines."

"But we've got to find Gwen first," Sebastian objected. Then a new thought struck him. "Master Corwyn, if Dr. Tox *is* receiving those wastes from Kwagg and Meier and dumping them

in the mines, and if Gwen stumbled upon the three of them on
her way here . . ." He stared at the alchemist, eyes wide in apprehension.

"Get a hold of yourself," Corwyn said. "We don't know that
happened, and even if it did we don't know where Dr. Tox has
her. He certainly couldn't take her back to Pomme de Terre
with all she knows. No, the way we can best help Gwen now, if
that's what happened, is to learn as much as we can about what's
going on at the Goblin Mines. We must find out whether that's
where the demonic wastes are being dumped. Fortunately, the
breath of demons test will enable us to determine if they are."

The alchemist's words sounded logical and reassuring, but Sebastian heard the worry in his master's voice.

"*Alors!* You can't rush out and do any testing tonight," said
Smoke, who had continued with his preparations while he listened. "It's too dark to travel and you need your rest. Meantime,
dinner's ready."

"Oh, I couldn't possibly eat anything now," Sebastian said,
wondering where Gwen might be. Was she wandering through
the forest, lost and alone, or was she captive in some dank
dungeon? Was she hurt? Was she hungry? Had she had anything
to eat? "What are you fixing?"

"Mushroom cutlets with white wine sauce, steamed broccoli,
and lentils cooked with leeks. And for dessert, *chou à la crème.*"

"Well, I know what that last item is at least," Sebastian said.
"Cabbage with cream."

Smoke grimaced—a terrifying expression. "Cabbage with
cream? Ugh! Why would anyone want that for dessert?"

"It's not cabbage with cream," Corwyn told Sebastian. "*Chou
à la crème* is a cream puff." He scratched his head. "Though I
can't figure out how they came up with cream puff from the word
for cabbage."

Sebastian threw his hands into the air. "Doesn't this language
ever mean what it says?"

Corwyn shrugged. "Not very often, I guess."

"What about meat?" Sebastian asked.

"*Mon petit louche!*" Smoke gasped. "Don't be disgusting! I'm
vegetarian."

"Oh." Sebastian thought despondently of Petronius, then
forced the memory aside as he sniffed the tantalizing aroma
again. "Well, perhaps a little. Just to keep up my strength."

An hour later, Sebastian pulled back from his plate, stuck his feet out, and sighed. Corwyn belched softly and closed his eyes. Smoke looked longingly from the now-empty cauldron to the table, stacked with dirty dishes and utensils.

"Maybe we should have gone to the mines tonight after all," he complained. "The way you two eat, I shall certainly lose weight if you stay."

CHAPTER 16

Captive of the Black Knight

GWEN REALIZED AT ONCE THIS INTERROGATION WOULD BE DIFFER-
ent. After three days of being dragged before the Black Knight
at all hours for questioning, she was familiar with the route from
the dungeon to the throne room and back.

The corridor along which she was now being led was one she
didn't recognize.

Gwen tried to stop. Her ankle hurt where she'd twisted it
during her capture. But the tension on her chains forced her to
keep moving.

"Where are you taking me?" she demanded of the lean, tight-
lipped man who was one of the Black Knight's mercenaries. They
were the first words she'd spoken since her capture, for she'd
resolved to tell the Black Knight and his squire nothing that
might help them find Corwyn.

The mercenary had dark, restless eyes that missed nothing and
a scarred face that attested to a life of battle. He didn't answer,
nor did he slacken his pull on her chains. Gwen was forced to
limp after him into the depths of the dungeon or be dragged over
the rough stone floor.

The mercenary came to an archway cut in the stone and lit
from the other side by smoking torches. The reddish, flickering

glare cast wavering shadows on the walls and shone eerily in the room beyond the arch. The mercenary pushed Gwen inside.

It was the Black Knight's torture chamber.

Gwen went numb with terror as she stumbled into the room. Between the firelight and the instruments of torment hanging on the walls or strewn about the room, she knew she'd passed through the gates of hell. Surely this was her damnation.

The mercenary shoved her toward a corner where the Black Knight waited behind a broken table. He was as regally erect and silent as ever, no more disturbed by his surroundings than if he'd been granting an audience in the great hall.

The squire perched on a stool in front of the table, toying with something in his lap. Gwen fought down nausea. The object he held was an iron boot: its two halves could be clamped in place and tightened to force the sides together, crushing the victim's foot. The throbbing in Gwen's ankle was nothing to the pain the boot could inflict.

Gwen's knees buckled. The mercenary caught her and pushed her onto a low three-legged stool.

"I see you know what this is," the squire said conversationally, holding up the boot. "My master grows tired of waiting. Perhaps this will persuade you to talk." Pause. "Where is Corwyn?" A longer pause. "How much does he know?" Still no answer. "What's he up to?"

Gwen's eyes bulged with terror, but she held her silence, determined not to allow these fiends to catch Corwyn and Sebastian.

The squire stared at Gwen and cocked his head, looking like a hideous bird that pounces on its prey only to find something it can't comprehend. For once, he appeared uncertain, and he got up from his stool to consult with his master. An argument ensued as whatever message the Black Knight quietly conveyed from behind his visor made the squire flinch and shake his head. "No," the squire whispered fiercely several times. "No! Please, master, I can't."

But at last the squire turned to Gwen with a pitying look that chilled her. "Your last chance, milady," he urged. "Please tell him what he wants to know."

Gwen bit her lip until she tasted blood and shook her head, wishing she felt as resolute as she tried to appear.

The squire shrugged and turned his attention to the boot. Firelight cast a sinister gleam on its dull black surface. The squire

frowned at it, then looked about the room, seeking the right
instrument to shatter her will. He set the boot aside and jerked
his head toward the stocks nearby. "Put her in there," he told
the mercenary.

Gwen struggled as the mercenary unlocked her fetters and
forced her feet and hands through holes in the wooden device.
He clamped the restraining timbers in place and left her sitting
on the cold, hard floor, unable to move.

The squire pulled his stool up to the other side of the stocks
where her feet and hands protruded and smeared a thick layer
of lard on the sole of her injured foot. He refused to meet her
eyes as he worked, his expression one of grim determination.
When he finished, he nodded to the mercenary, who brought
over a chafing dish full of burning coals. The soldier carried the
dish with thick, padded gloves that blackened and smoked wherever they touched the dish.

Gwen's heart pounded so heavily she thought it must burst.
She almost wished it would; at least that would deliver her from
her ordeal. But though its thundering beat seemed to shake the
room, her life continued, and when the squire gave her a final
questioning look, the smoking dish now held securely in his own
gloved hands, she had to force herself to shake her head. She
watched, unable to shut her eyes to what was happening, but
the stocks blocked her view.

Something touched her foot. She heard a sizzling noise and
smelled hot, rancid lard. Gwen screamed, anticipating the pain,
as unconsciousness engulfed her.

Sebastian paced the makeshift laboratory. "When are we going
after her, master?"

Corwyn never looked up from the row of bottles on the table
before him. In the bottles, minnows labored through various
stages of asphyxiation. Corwyn recorded their deaths on a sheet
of parchment, noting the source of water for each bottle next to
the corresponding entry for the time of death.

"What would you have us do that we haven't already done?"
he asked.

"*Pardieu!* Go looking for her, of course!"

"Where?"

"I don't know." Sebastian collapsed onto a nearby stool, too
tired to remain standing but too anxious for Gwen's safety to
enjoy the amenities in Smoke's lair. "I don't know where she

might be. I don't even know where she was headed."

"Neither do I. We've searched for her all around the mines and throughout the watershed below. Collecting these samples"—he waved at the bottles—"wasn't our only reason for covering those areas so thoroughly. But she isn't there and I don't know where else to look."

"So we've accomplished nothing," Sebastian said.

"No, that's not true. We haven't found Gwen, but the breath of demons tests prove the Goblin Mines are indeed being used to store the Inquisition's demons, just as you suggested. It's been a tedious, roundabout proof and a lot of work to gather the samples, but performing the tests is much safer than going directly into the mines would be, to see the demons for ourselves."

"But what good is that?" Sebastian gestured angrily at the bottles. "The tests still don't tell us anything useful."

Corwyn shook his head. "When will you ever learn to see what's in front of your eyes, Sebastian? Through the breath of demons tests, we know the demons are leaching from the mines through the groundwater, and into the headwaters of the River Ale. From that we can also infer that Dr. Tox must be involved with this heinous scheme after all. I should have believed you when you first told me that. It makes me wonder if you might also be right that Thaddeus's return to Pomme de Terre and the delay of the Renaissance are connected to the disposal of these demons as well. I can't imagine what the connection could be, but finding Thaddeus's hut so near the mines certainly lends credence to your belief." Corwyn jotted down the time of death for the last minnow, then stood up and walked to his apprentice. He put a hand on Sebastian's shoulder. "We're doing everything for Gwen we can, my boy. Without knowing where she is, or whether she's even been captured, we can only try to solve the mystery of this plague and hope that solution eventually takes us to her."

Sebastian nodded, realizing what Corwyn said was true. He stared at the bottles with their dead minnows. The deaths substantiated at least part of what he'd maintained but been unable to prove. That news should make him feel better, but he was too numbed by grief and worry to be concerned with such trivial matters as whether he'd been right or wrong, or anything else connected with demons and mysterious plagues borne by water. He wanted Gwen safely in his arms. Only her return could lighten the burden of responsibility weighing on his shoulders.

He couldn't watch Corwyn play with his bottles any longer. But what else was there to do?

He stood and paced the cavern again.

Gwen was awakened by a bucket of foul water flung in her face. She spluttered and choked as water ran into her mouth and nose. Her first thought was of her foot, but though her injured ankle throbbed, she felt no other pain. She looked questioningly at the squire, who stood over her with the empty bucket in his hand.

He grinned as he put the bucket down, then picked up a piece of greased leather and pressed it against the chafing dish. The grease sizzled and stank. At the same time, the mercenary touched something hard to the bottom of her foot. Gwen tried to jerk her foot back reflexively, a scream forming in her throat. For a horrible moment, she thought her foot was being burned again.

Then she understood—it never had been burned. "Bastard!" she cried as her vision blurred behind a haze of angry tears.

The squire stooped to cradle Gwen's head, stroking wet strands of hair from her face. She tried to pull away, but the stocks held her.

"Tell him what he wants to know," the squire said, indicating the Black Knight. "Or next time it *will* be your foot."

Gwen shuddered as she pictured herself burned and rent by the Black Knight's lackeys. She'd never withstand it—the pain would be intolerable. But she couldn't betray her friends, either.

She decided instead on another course, one she hoped would appease the Black Knight while still protecting Sebastian and Corwyn. Words tumbled from her mouth as she began babbling, speaking like the crazed woman she felt near to becoming. She told the Black Knight and his squire in endless detail about the quest to discover the source of the plague, beginning with the night Sebastian and Corwyn came to the Reluctant Virgin. She told of Sebastian's first words to her and her reaction, of what Meg told Sebastian and his subsequent fight with the mercenary recruiter. She spilled her hopes and heartbreak at the way Sebastian treated her. She told of Corwyn's capture and rescue from the duke's dungeon. She repeated gossip about the plague overheard in the Reluctant Virgin, on the streets, and in the marketplace of Pomme de Terre. She tried to describe every footstep she'd taken on their long journey to the Valley of Despair.

At first the squire tried to interrupt, attempting to direct her tale to the specifics in which he was interested. But she wouldn't allow it. She rolled her eyes wildly, as if unseeing, and continued over his objections. Finally, he sat and listened, his chin cupped in his hands, his elbows on his knees. He listened, waiting for what he really wanted to hear, and she babbled on, hoping to drown him in a torrent of words.

An hour went by and then a second, maybe a third—she couldn't be sure. She talked until her voice cracked, becoming a whisper. The mercenary carried Gwen back to her cell while the squire and his master stared at the wall of the torture chamber, contemplating what she'd said.

Gwen hoped she'd gotten off with this, but the next day the mercenary returned her to the torture chamber. Then the flow of words began again. All the squire had to do to loosen her tongue was press the greased leather against the chafing dish and her words spilled out uncontrollably. The sizzle and stench of hot lard served as a constant reminder of what she had to fear.

Through it all, the Black Knight listened in patient silence. The squire, however, was neither so patient nor silent as his master. Several times during her monologue, he surprised Gwen with his reactions to details she'd thought innocent when she related them.

"So she didn't steal the gold after all," the squire burst out after Gwen told how the duchess scrimped to support her husband's excesses. "But where did it go? With that much wealth flowing into her husband's coffers she shouldn't have had to pawn her jewels."

The squire was silent for a long time after. Then, when Gwen described the tensions in Gardenia over the duke's resistance to change, he broke into her account in a rage.

"How could the duke have been so stupid?" the squire cried. "I had no idea the unrest was so widespread. How could he have allowed it? How could he have squandered so much money to so little effect? His grip on the duchy should be unassailable by the common rabble. The gold he's being paid should have kept change out for decades to come, yet through his blunderings the duke has virtually invited the rise of the merchant class throughout the realm!"

Gwen was silenced by his outburst, considering what the

squire's words implied. Then she resumed her tale.

The next day, when she told of their trek to the Valley of Despair searching for a bog or marsh instead of for the peasants Kwagg and Meier, the squire chuckled. But it seemed to Gwen there was a nervous undercurrent to his laugh, as if he anticipated the direction the Valley of Despair would eventually lead Corwyn.

Throughout the rest of that day and into the next, the squire listened avidly to her account, tedious though she tried to make it. No matter how many dry, uninteresting details she included, his eyes still lit periodically at references whose importance she could not understand. She began to fear that in telling her captors so many trivial things to hide what they wanted to hear, she was instead revealing more than she intended.

She recounted the trip to the monastery of St. Mathurin, and the squire laughed to hear how they had searched among the records in the archives. But his laugh choked off when Gwen mentioned the strange list of financial transactions they'd found between someone at the duke's castle and Cosimo de' Medici in Florence. He leaned forward, listening.

She babbled on about her last argument with Sebastian and how hurt she'd been when he discovered she was a peasant. Finally, as she neared the end of her tale and was wondering how to prevent the Black Knight from discovering where Corwyn planned to travel next, she told how Sebastian stumbled upon Dr. Tox's lease to the Goblin Mines.

The squire cut her off by leaping to his feet.

"That wretch!" he shouted. "That thieving wretch! So he's the one who stole the gold! *Alors!* He'll soon learn the price of stealing from Hydro Phobius!" He jerked his head at the mercenary, who stood waiting to return Gwen to her cell. "Take her back," he ordered. "We have work to do." Then he turned to Gwen as the mercenary carried her to the door. "When we return, you'll tell us without any more babbling where Corwyn has gone and what he plans to do. My master has uses for the old fool, and he'll not brook any further delays on your part."

Gwen returned to her cell wondering what events she'd set in motion and dreading her next encounter with the squire and his master.

But the following day passed without her being summoned to another session in the Black Knight's torture chamber, and when the squire finally appeared late on the second day, he smiled and handed her a gossamer gown of the thinnest, softest silk.

Gwen stared as he draped the gown over her arm, noting in her bewilderment how its translucence revealed her arm beneath the material.

"My master wishes to express his appreciation for your help," the squire said with a devilish lift to the corner of his mouth. "He wants you to see he can be benevolent to those who help him and thereby enlist your aid. But I'll explain later. Right now, the guard is waiting to take you to bathe. Then you'll appear for dinner with my master, wearing this gown."

Before she could object, the squire bowed mockingly and left.

The bath was awkward because of the ankle, and the mercenary's eyes strayed frequently in her direction as he stood guard. Still, the bath left Gwen more refreshed then she'd felt since leaving Pomme de Terre. And the silk gown made her feel almost like the princess Sebastian once believed her to be. She wished he could see her in it, if only to make him regret his behavior.

She wished she could see him again too. Sometime over the last several days, most of her anger had evaporated, leaving only an aching emptiness inside—an emptiness she doubted would ever be filled now that Sebastian no longer loved her.

She was able to walk, or at least hobble, as the mercenary led her to dinner. She had to bite her lip to keep from crying out against the pain, but the gown was so revealing that she preferred to walk rather than let the mercenary carry her. The way he stared at her left Gwen uncomfortably aware of her vulnerability, for he'd manacled her hands behind her back and placed heavy shackles around her ankles before leading her out of the dungeon.

He led her to a small, ornately decorated room. The floor was strewn with fresh rushes, and in the middle stood a large oak table. The table was intricately carved and gleamed with wax, and it was laden with bowls of ripe fruit, jeweled goblets and carafes of wine, and a wide variety of steaming, fragrant platters of food.

At the head of the long table sat the Black Knight, with neither food nor setting before him. At the opposite end of the table stood an empty chair. Beside it waited the Black Knight's squire, grinning and squirming as eagerly as a pup anticipating a bone. Gwen felt the corners of her mouth draw down as her loathing for the knight and his squire quickened her pulse.

The mercenary left, closing the door behind him, and the squire motioned Gwen to the empty chair. She hobbled over with as much dignity as she could assume. Before seating herself in the chair, she raised her manacled hands behind her.

"Unchain me," she said, her tone calculated to leave no room for argument.

The squire only laughed. "Until we can trust you, you'll wear those whenever you're away from the dungeon. But don't worry about eating. My master has instructed me to feed you."

Gwen scowled. "How unfortunate that you're put to so much trouble."

"Milady, it'll be my pleasure," he said. He guided her gently but firmly into the seat and squatted to attach the fetters from her ankles to the front legs of the massive chair.

"Is that necessary?" Gwen asked, startled that she should be regarded as so important a prize.

"We can't take any chances of your escaping. Not with all you know." His face took on a darker, more malevolent air. "I should hate to see you meet with the same fate as Dr. Tox."

Gwen shivered at the peculiar edge to his voice. "What do you mean?"

The squire dropped the keys to her fetters in a pocket of his tunic. "As a reward for his service to my master, the good doctor now resides with the demons in the Goblin Mines." He laughed, then went on more seriously, "I just hope the damage he's caused can be repaired before the merchants rise to greater power."

With the ankle chains in place, the squire felt secure enough to linger in his crouched position, stroking Gwen's legs. Gwen's stomach tightened. The gown, she realized, revealed too much, was too inviting for a man such as this. She glanced down briefly, noting the way the halos of her nipples showed like soft shadows through the silk, her breasts just barely contained by the tight, low-cut bodice. The gown subtly revealed her every feature, but the shackles left her unable to properly wield the influence the gown provided or to control the passions it aroused.

Her helplessness sickened her. She tried to kick the squire, but the chains restrained her. He worked his way higher, caressing her legs from ankle to knee. She forced her arms to one side behind her back, straining to grasp a lock of his hair, hoping to wrench the strands from their roots. But he was just out of reach. As he stood up at last, only the rough cloth of his tunic brushed her hands. He drew up a stool, too self-satisfied to be aware of her efforts, and sat beside her.

"*Allez!*" he said, pulling the platters of food closer. "What would you like?"

"I'm not hungry," she responded sullenly, her appetite replaced by revulsion.

The squire shrugged and stuffed liberal portions of bread and cheese in his mouth. He followed this with a greedy slurp of wine.

Gwen held herself aloof, her attention on the Black Knight across the table. She stared at him for a time, hoping to make him turn away or somehow respond to her presence. She had to get his attention so he could be made to bring his squire under control.

The Black Knight remained immobile, watching her without apparent recognition.

"What about your master?" Gwen whispered to the squire at last, her hopes crumbling in defeat. "Isn't he going to eat?"

The squire shook his head and tried to speak, spraying food at her. He washed the mouthful down with more wine. "He always eats alone. It's part of his vow. He just wanted to be here while you enjoyed the bounty of his hospitality." The squire patted Gwen's knee, letting his hand rest on her leg. "I certainly commend his taste."

Gwen started to jerk her knee away as best she could, then thought better of it as a vague possibility formed in her mind. She shifted her arms to the side as she'd done when attempting to grab the squire's hair, her heart cold with resolution. At the same time, she casually angled her knee to encourage his touch.

He eyed her suspiciously, then rewarded her efforts with a smug grin. "I hoped you'd respond favorably in time."

Gwen forced herself to lean over and nip playfully at the squire's ear, uncomfortably aware of the Black Knight's gaze. "*Tiens!* It's impossible not to harbor strong feelings toward a man like you," she whispered.

"I thought you'd resent me for what I did. For what he made me do." The squire jerked a thumb at his master, then looked sad. "Most women don't like me."

"Oh, I can hardly believe that."

The squire wriggled with delight. It was all Gwen could do not to choke as she watched. Then his hand ventured more boldly from her knee to her thigh. She smiled at him, then grimaced and stamped her good foot. "My leg," she complained. "It's gone to sleep."

The squire pulled back, suddenly alert again. "*Tiens!* None of that. I'm not unchaining you."

Gwen's eyes widened in pretended innocence. "Oh, I wouldn't ask you to. But my leg's gone completely numb. Won't you rub it for me, *s'il vous plaît?*" She curled her lips in what she hoped he would interpret as a smile.

The squire practically fell from his stool in his eagerness to comply. He squatted beside her and rubbed her calf with both hands. "How's that? Is it feeling better?"

"*Oui, beaucoup,*" Gwen murmured, straining to reach his tunic with her fingers. Fortunately, the table blocked her actions from the Black Knight. Not that he seemed much interested anyway. Gwen had the awful feeling the squire could rape her on the tabletop and his master wouldn't take any notice.

"Maybe I should rub a little higher," the squire suggested, progressing to Gwen's thigh.

"Oh, *oui*," Gwen enthused, her fingers touching his tunic. "A little higher, *décidément!*"

As he raised slightly to reach her, she slipped a hand in his pocket. Her fingernails scraped the iron keys. She wrenched around further, ignoring the pain in her shoulders and the touch of the squire's hands on her leg.

At last, she had them!

Carefully, she withdrew her hands, the keys clutched in her fingers and hidden from sight by the chair.

The squire was too intent on making the most of her latitude to notice the theft. His face was almost in her lap, his hands busily making their way up her thigh. Gwen shifted as sharply as she could and giggled.

"Oh, my," she squealed. "That tickles!"

Her knee was well aimed, for the squire came up groaning and clutching one eye. But he grinned nevertheless. "Since you're not hungry, let's retire to my chamber, just you and me," he panted.

The thought was appalling, but even worse was the possibility that he might start to unlock her and discover his keys were gone. She clenched them so tightly her fingers hurt. Now that she'd stolen them, she didn't know what to do. How could she unlock her chains and get away without the squire stopping her?

"We might go to your chamber," she said, trying to think.

"But first I must eat. I don't want to insult your master."

"You won't," the squire said, stooping to unlock her ankles. "He doesn't care."

Gwen shook her head fiercely. "No! I mean, it wouldn't be right. Not after he invited me to dinner."

The squire started to object, then stopped. Instead, he heaped rushes in a pile near her chair. "All right, I'll just slide you out of your chair and we'll make ourselves comfortable here on the floor. The reeds are soft and fresh enough."

"No!" Gwen cried and shrank from him, aghast. "Please don't. It's . . . it's too unseemly!"

"*Pourquoi pas*? My master doesn't mind."

Gwen was afraid she'd condemned herself to actually coupling with this creature. Why didn't the Black Knight object? How far would he let his squire carry this insanity?

Perhaps he enjoyed watching his squire ravish his captives at his dinner table.

"I must eat first," she said. "I'm ravenous."

The squire scowled. "A minute ago, you didn't have any appetite."

"I do now." The squire hesitated. "Would you want me to faint?" she asked.

The squire seemed uncertain whether this possibility disturbed him or not. Finally he gave in, disappointment clouding his face. "*Très bien,*" he agreed. "But after your dinner's over . . ."

"Certainly," Gwen promised, running her tongue over her lips for his benefit and wondering how long she could stretch the meal. "As soon as I've eaten. My, doesn't that pheasant look delicious!"

Obediently, the squire hacked a slab from the pheasant and held it to her lips. He fed her bites as rapidly as she would take them, his manner impatient at how long it took her to chew and swallow. She sampled various dishes from the table, going from the pheasant to the roast chicken, and from there to the suckling pig. Between meats, she tried the breads and vegetables, occasionally taking small sips of wine to wash it all down. But she was careful to limit her wine, for she had to remain alert if she was to escape.

After tasting each dish, she tried to discuss its merits and how it might have been prepared with the squire, who only grunted in response and shoved more food in her mouth whenever it opened. Gwen grew uncomfortably full and her chatter took on a nervous edge. The time was rapidly approaching when she'd be unable to swallow another bite.

Just when she was sure one more mouthful would bring everything she'd eaten back up again (a possibility she seriously considered, especially if she could entice the squire close enough to be within range), a mercenary entered the room.

The squire refused to acknowledge the soldier's presence as he attempted to force a bite of pear into Gwen's mouth. Gwen, too intrigued by the play of emotion over the squire's face to open her jaw, watched in fascination as he mashed the pear against her teeth. Juice spilled down her lips and chin and fell to her gown, where the drops soaked into the silk. The squire watched the juice fall, and for a moment Gwen was afraid he would lap it up with his tongue.

The mercenary coughed into his fist.

The squire spun on his heels, still in a crouch. His face purpled in fury. "What do you want? I'll have your head for this!"

The mercenary strode over to the squire and whispered. The squire's countenance shifted to one of delight. "Are you sure?"

The mercenary nodded.

"Please forgive me," the squire said to Gwen, "but one of my master's men spotted Corwyn in the mountains over near the Goblin Mines. It seems your alchemist friend has taken up with a certain dragon who lives in these parts." His voice became a sneer. "Frankly, I'm surprised at Corwyn. I didn't think his tastes ran in that direction. But no matter." He waved grandly, dismissing it. Then he leaned forward, chucking her under the chin. "I must leave you for a while so I may attend to my master's business. But don't fear, my pet, I'll return to you as quickly as I can."

He laughed at Gwen's dismay, then followed the mercenary to the door. Before he went out, the squire turned back to her. "By the way, don't think of escaping. My master may be vowed to silence and prone to contemplation, but he has a ferocious temper. If you try anything foolish, he's liable to spring up and slice you through without a second thought."

Gwen shuddered, which sent the squire into more peals of laughter. Then he left, shutting the door on Gwen and her captor.

Gwen held still until she was sure the squire was really gone. She'd only have this one chance and she had to be sure the squire wouldn't return unexpectedly and catch her. But she was also aware that she had to act swiftly. Now Corwyn's and possibly

Sebastian's lives, as well as her own, depended on her getting away.

She had to escape, she thought. She must save Corwyn. And she must save Sebastian, even if he never appreciated her for it.

Gwen looked at the Black Knight, despising and fearing him as she had no man before. But she strove to keep her emotions from her face. So far, the Black Knight seemed immune to her feminine guiles. Yet Gwen remained confident: never had any man been able to resist her determined efforts. Now, with the keys to freedom clutched securely at her back, she had only to lure the Black Knight close for the chance she needed to escape.

"I'm glad we're alone," she said in her most seductive voice.

There was no answer.

She dropped her eyes demurely to her lap. "Please don't hold it against me that I behaved wantonly with your servant," she purred. "I merely sought to distract him for fear he might hurt me. But it's you I really want."

A fly buzzed around Gwen's face. It landed on her nose, tickling her until she blew it away. Then it headed for the table.

Panic rose in Gwen, making her full stomach churn. This knight took his vows more seriously than any she'd ever encountered. For a moment, she considered simply unlocking her bonds and trying to reach the door ahead of him, but she discarded the thought. Even if she could get the chains unlocked before the Black Knight stirred from his reverie, she could never run to the door fast enough. Not with her twisted ankle.

She had to draw him close for what she had in mind. But time was running out. She'd have to try a more desperate measure if she was to rouse the Black Knight before the squire returned.

She squirmed in her chair. "It's very warm in here, milord," she whispered huskily. "Much too warm for clothes, don't you think?" She shifted her shoulders against the ornate carvings on her chair as if scratching her back, conscious of how this pushed her breasts forward to strain against the thin, translucent silk. She paused and asked the knight, "Would you help me, milord? I've developed a most terrible itch."

She waited hopefully, but the only sound in the room came from the droning fly as it sampled one dish after another on the table. Gwen sagged slightly and almost cried.

She knew she had little defense against a fully armed knight. But there was a chance. If she could get him close enough to trip him, force him onto his back, he might be unable to regain his feet. That was the principal danger for a man in plate armor. The weight was such that many a knight was helpless on his back. At the very least, it should slow the Black Knight enough for her to unlock her chains and escape.

She had to get him close! She just had to!

She resumed twitching, still ostensibly scratching herself on the chair back while actually trying to catch a portion of the carving in just the right way. The effort wore her skin raw. She began to despair of ever getting it right when a protruding piece of carved wood slipped under the left shoulder of her gown. Moving very carefully now, she inched to her right, easing the gown off her shoulder. A sudden twist of her torso as if she'd finally found just the right spot for the itch yanked the gown from her shoulder and down her arm. The silk fell away from her left breast and it swayed enticingly, exposed to the Black Knight's view.

"Oh, my!" Gwen gasped, giving her voice the ring of mortified virtue. "Oh, sire, please help me. You must not leave me to be shamed like this." She jerked at her chains, making her breast bob with her struggles. She looked at the Black Knight from lowered eyelids. "Please help return me to my gown, milord, I beseech you. Even if it means you must touch me immodestly."

The Black Knight sat in his chair as if welded.

For a terrible moment, Gwen wondered if she was the wrong sex to interest him. Maybe that explained the Black Knight's strange alliance with his squire. Yet it failed to account for the squire's lust for Gwen.

As she wondered, the fly, gorged at last from its feast at the table, rose heavily into the air and buzzed around the room. The sound was loud in the silent chamber. Eventually the fly landed on the Black Knight's visor. It wandered over the lacquered surface, droning as it went, then passed through the grill to buzz hollowly inside the helmet. Finally it emerged again and droned around the room before returning to the table.

Gwen stared in disbelief. She glanced at her bare breast, then at the foot the squire had pretended to burn in the torture chamber.

"You bastard!" she hissed.

Swiftly she unlocked her wrist fetters, then the chains at her ankles. She took a small loaf of bread and half a cheese from the table, leaving the rest of the meal for the fly. Then, as she was about to leave, she grabbed a knife from the table as well.

Gwen hefted the knife menacingly. "I almost hope you try to stop me, you ugly toad!" she whispered after the departed squire. "I swear, I'll feed your manly jewels to the pigs before you'll ever touch me again!"

Then she hobbled as quickly as she could from the room, seeking a way out of the castle.

CHAPTER 17

The Man Who Wasn't There

SEBASTIAN DREAMED HE WAS CHOKING AND AWOKE TO FIND THE dream was true.

A blanket of gas so foul he couldn't breathe lay upon the air. He gagged and rolled over, eyes streaming from the stench. He tried to get up, but found he lacked the will.

It all came, he thought miserably, from sharing quarters with a dragon. Indigestion in a dragon was said to be life-threatening to mortals. From the evidence, Sebastian was willing to believe the tales.

He coughed violently and sprawled over the edge of the bed.

He had resigned himself to asphyxiation, as helpless as one of Corwyn's minnows in a breath of demons test, when a scuffle sounded in the tunnel outside the chamber where he slept. Sebastian blinked back his tears to see Corwyn, a hand over his nose and mouth, dash toward the front of the cave. The dragon scrabbled through the tunnel behind him with amazing agility for someone of his bulk.

Sebastian dragged himself from the chamber after Smoke and Corwyn.

The tunnel seemed longer than before, but finally Sebastian burst into the early morning air of the Pyrenees. He flung himself onto a rock shelf that extended several yards from the cave and ended in an abrupt precipice overlooking the valley south of the lair. Corwyn and Smoke already sprawled on the rock, gulping deep draughts of air. Sebastian flopped down beside them.

"That was awful," Corwyn moaned. "What went wrong?"

Smoke shook his gigantic head. His coloring was dulled by exposure to the fumes.

"Maybe dinner last night was too rich," Sebastian ventured, trying to console the dragon.

Corwyn and Smoke both looked at him.

"You know, it probably didn't set too well." He jerked his head toward Smoke.

A flush deepened the color in Smoke's scarlet face. "You don't mean . . . ! You think that I . . . ?"

"It's nothing to be embarrassed about," Sebastian said. "It happens to everyone."

"Before you further embarrass yourself," Corwyn said, "Smoke wasn't responsible for what happened in there—"

"You mean you did that?" Sebastian asked.

"—and it was alchemical in nature, not intestinal."

"Then neither of you . . . ?" Sebastian glanced at Smoke, who stared back indignantly. "But I'd heard that dragons . . ."

Smoke scowled and Corwyn shook his head. "Sebastian," the alchemist said, "how many times do I have to warn you about leaping to conclusions when you don't have all the facts?"

Sebastian's head drooped. "I'm sorry, master." He risked looking up again. "What *did* happen in there?"

It was Corwyn's turn to look discomfited. "Just a little alchemical research. Smoke and I were up early, and we decided to let you sleep while we worked.

"A slight miscalculation caused me to add the reagents in disproportionate amounts," Corwyn went on. "The result was somewhat malodorous, I admit, but hardly dangerous."

"Disproportionate amounts, my purple *derrière!*" The dragon snorted, sending twin swirls of smoke from his nostrils. "You failed to mention that you also added them in the wrong order, that at least one of the reagents probably shouldn't have been used at all, and that the whole procedure was highly suspect to begin with. And as for lack of danger, that's true only if you have no fear of death by strangulation!"

"You vastly overstate the case," Corwyn said. "While there was some uncertainty involved—"

"Uncertainty? Corwyn, I've been telling you for a hundred years, alchemy isn't an exact science. It isn't a science at all. It hardly deserves to be called an art. It's a mistake perpetuated by a misconception, a dead end, *de chou*. It'll never amount to—"

"De chou?" Sebastian interrupted. "What does cabbage have to do with alchemy?"

"Nothing, *mon petit louche,*" Smoke said, his attention on Corwyn who was too busy huffing to speak. "Please don't interrupt."

"But that's what you said, isn't it?" Sebastian insisted. *"Chou?* After all, that's one French word I know by now."

"It's just an expression—"

"Certainly not one you're using with endearment," Sebastian cut in dryly.

"An expression that uses cabbage as an example of something having little value. Although to say alchemy has even a little value may be granting it more than it merits. Corwyn, alchemy will never amount to anything despite your valiant efforts to force it to be otherwise!"

Corwyn puffed himself up like a bird ruffling his feathers, preparing to defend his territory. "I'll have you know I'm shaping alchemy into a powerful tool—"

"You've certainly proved its power, Corwyn," Smoke said, waving a foreclaw at the cave and forgetting his own injunction against interrupting, "beyond any shadow of doubt."

"A powerful tool for preserving the quality of the primal elements!" Corwyn concluded heatedly.

The argument went on, as it had the entire time Corwyn and Smoke had been together. Sebastian ignored their disagreements, having quickly realized that the two friends enjoyed the constant sparring. He ventured back to the cave, testing the air cautiously. At the entrance, he caught a pungent whiff that made him step back.

"What were you two trying to do?" he interrupted.

"Corwyn thought he could develop a system for permanently trapping the demons in the Goblin Mines," Smoke said. "Something that would stabilize them for long-term storage. He assured me it would work. I should have known better than to believe him."

"It will work!" Corwyn retorted. "It has to work. We're in a race for the salvation of Pomme de Terre, and we cannot afford to finish *dans le chou.*"

Sebastian waited a moment, his irritation rising, hoping someone would explain. "What does it mean this time?" he demanded at last.

"What?" Corwyn asked.

"You used that word again," Sebastian said. "You said *dans le chou,* and I know you're not talking about cabbage. So what does it mean?"

Corwyn shrugged. "Just what it says. In the cabbage, of course."

Sebastian gritted his teeth.

"To finish last," Smoke said, edging between the alchemist and his apprentice. "That's all he meant, *mon petit louche.*"

Sebastian inhaled sharply, as exasperated by Smoke's pet name for him as he was by the way cabbages were constantly sneaking into the conversation and making a fool of him. "But once we stop Dr. Tox from dumping the Inquisition's demons in the mines, won't that solve the problem?" he asked, again directing the topic away from his mistakes.

"That'll keep new demons from being added to the mines," Corwyn replied. "But we have to prevent the demons already there from seeping into the underground water supply."

"How can we do that?" Sebastian asked. "We can't even go back into Smoke's cave."

Corwyn glared. "For an apprentice, you can be most presumptuous, boy!"

"Presumptuous, he may be, Corwyn, but he's also right," Smoke said. "My cave is perfectly unlivable, thanks to your experiment."

Just then, Oliver peeked out from the entrance to the cave. When he saw who was outside, he strolled out, regarding them curiously.

"Oliver, how could you stand it in there so long?" Sebastian asked.

"Easy," Smoke responded. "He doesn't have any sense of smell. He doesn't breathe."

Corwyn looked startled. *"Bien entendu!"* he said to himself. He turned to the broom. "Oliver, go back to the chamber where Smoke and I were working. There's a vessel on the table there— be careful, it may still be smoking. I want you to bring it here."

Obediently, Oliver returned to the cave.

As they waited, Corwyn and Smoke resumed their argument about alchemy while Sebastian, bored, scanned the countryside to the north, above the cave entrance, and wondered despondently where to look for Gwen today. He'd already searched the most likely areas and was rapidly losing hope of finding her. Either she'd not come this way after all or she'd been captured by Dr. Tox and was being held prisoner. Or perhaps she hadn't survived her journey into the mountains. There were many dangers along her route besides Dr. Tox and his two peasant henchmen.

The voice in Sebastian's head told him both that he was a fool for worrying about a mere peasant wench and that it was his fault she was in danger. No matter what he did, Sebastian thought wryly, the voice was sure to find fault with him.

A hint of movement caught his eye. A small cluster of pines grew beside a boulder several yards from Smoke's lair. Sebastian studied the pines, his face furrowed in concentration. Suddenly, he realized he was looking at a man trying to blend into the shadows of the pines. Sebastian started to alert Smoke and Corwyn when the man stepped from the trees. Sebastian's warning cry turned into a strangled gasp as he noticed the stranger's crossbow aimed at his chest.

At a signal, three other armed men emerged from concealment near the first and fanned out to either side. They carried themselves with the cautious, sinewy grace of professional fighting men.

The first one, a tight-lipped, dark-eyed man whose gaze missed nothing, nodded to Corwyn. "You the alchemist?"

"*Oui.*"

The soldier reached into his travel-stained tunic and pulled out a folded sheet of parchment. He handed it to Corwyn. Corwyn raised his eyebrows, but accepted the sheet. He started to break the wax seal, then stopped as he noticed its design.

"What's wrong?" Sebastian whispered, edging closer to his master but keeping his attention on the armed men. "Who are they? What do they want?"

"This seal," Corwyn said. His voice was flat. Sebastian tore his eyes from their captors to look at his master. Corwyn stared at the seal, which depicted a fish belly-up in the water. "It's the seal of Hydro Phobius."

"Who's that? Do you know him?"

Corwyn shook his head. "I've heard tales, but never met the

man. He claims at times to be a legitimate merchant, at others, a nobleman investing in honest trade. But he deals in whatever corrupts, pollutes, or destroys the achievements of other men, specializing in ventures which concern water. His efforts degrade the element I seek to preserve. He is a worm eating away at the heartwood of civilization and the world in which we live."

"But what does he *say*?" Sebastian asked impatiently.

Corwyn broke the seal and scanned the page. "He wants me. There's a structure of some kind he wants me to design. The note's signed, the 'Black Knight.'"

"The Black Knight!" Smoke said. "Why, I've seen him. Big fellow, all in black armor, heavily inlaid. His squire was with him—an ugly froglike man. I followed them to a castle not far from here, hoping for a better look at the knight." The dragon blushed, adding a scarlet foundation to his other shades, and looked at Sebastian. "It's been lonely up here and I was curious. Besides, one never knows. After all, I've been close to knights from some of the great families in Europe in my time."

Sebastian shifted uncomfortably, then turned to Corwyn. "Master, whatever this Black Knight wants you to build, you can't do it. Don't go with these men. They won't let you back alive. We'll have to fight." Silently, he assessed the odds, then tried to sound encouraging. "With Smoke's help, there's a chance we might survive."

Corwyn let out his breath in defeat. He put a hand on his apprentice's shoulder. "No, Sebastian. It would be death to try. Besides, I *must* go."

"But why?"

"Because he's holding Gwen."

"*Mon dieu*, no!" Sebastian felt empty and sick.

At that moment, Oliver reappeared, holding a scorched earthenware pot in one hand. A wisp of smoke spilled over the sides of the pot to the ground. Oliver started to carry it to Corwyn, then stopped self-consciously as he noticed the strangers.

"Oliver," Corwyn said, "why don't you show these men what we made?" He turned to the leader of the mercenaries. "You know what alchemists do, don't you? We turn lead into gold."

The mercenary's eyes grew wide, though he frowned distrustfully. "Let me see," he ordered, his crossbow never wavering from Sebastian's chest as he looked at the pot in Oliver's hand.

Oliver inched toward the mercenary leader, reluctant to have any contact with strangers. The other mercenaries shifted closer to their captain to see for themselves whether the alchemist's claim was true.

As Oliver stopped before the leader, the man's nose twitched. He started to shy away, but the eagerness of his men vying for a look hemmed him in too closely.

"Give them a really close look," Corwyn told the broom. "Raise it up to their faces!"

The mercenary captain shifted the crossbow to his shoulder, suspecting a trap. But before he could get that far, he was struck by the terrible stench. "Aaagh!" he shrieked, dropping the weapon to clutch his face. The crossbow went off as it struck the ground. With an angry whir, the bolt ricocheted off a rock near Sebastian.

The mercenary captain stumbled back to escape the smell of Corwyn's failed experiment. The other soldiers joined their leader as the stench assaulted them as well. Together, the four men dropped over the precipice, sliding down the steep, rocky incline to the valley below.

Oliver cocked his stick head curiously, as if potential new playmates had run home for no apparent reason. Then he trotted back to Corwyn, the pot extended to the alchemist in a twiggy hand. Corwyn grasped his nose and backed away from the broom.

"No, Oliver, not to me!"

The broom stopped, bewildered. He looked at Smoke and Sebastian, but they also stepped back. Oliver shrugged and started back into the cave.

"No, no, not in there again!" Smoke shrieked.

Oliver stopped, looking exasperated. He studied his three companions as if doubting their sanity.

"Oliver," Corwyn said gently, the way one might instruct a small child who's discovered cuddling a venomous snake, "take the pot to the edge of the precipice." He pointed past the rock escarpment where the mercenaries had descended. "Throw the pot as far after those men as you can. But don't spill it!"

Oliver did as Corwyn ordered, sending the pot in a long curve over the chasm. At the top of the curve, the pot tumbled slowly and the contents oozed out, separating from the pot but following the same trajectory. Even at a distance, the contents looked vile as they fell into the depths of the gorge.

Corwyn let out his breath. "That's one way to get rid of lab-oratory wastes," he said. *"C'est bête comme chou."*

"As foolish as cabbage?" Sebastian repeated.

"Child's play," Corwyn explained. "Something that's ridiculously simple."

"I'm beginning to feel ridiculously simple," Sebastian muttered under his breath. "Or should I say, as foolish as cabbage? It's either me or this cursed French language!"

"*Comment, mon petit louche?*" Smoke asked.

Sebastian just shook his head.

"However," Corwyn went on as if he hadn't been interrupted, "getting rid of laboratory wastes so easily is only effective when one works on a mountaintop. I almost pity Hydro Phobius's men down in the valley about now."

Sebastian paced the rock surface in front of the lair, considering the implications of Hydro Phobius's message to Corwyn. "We've got to get to the Black Knight's castle right away. Once he realizes his men failed to capture you, Gwen's life may be in danger."

"I suppose you're right." Corwyn turned to regard the opening to the lair. "Smoke's cave will have to air out before we can enter again anyway."

"Corwyn," Smoke said from the edge of the precipice, "we'll have to cross that valley ourselves to get to the Black Knight's castle."

Corwyn joined the dragon and looked down, clucking to himself. "We'd better hope there's a favorable wind, or we'll never reach the castle. No armor made is effective against anything as potent as that."

"Armor," Smoke exclaimed. "That's what we need!" He darted toward the cave.

Sebastian dodged Smoke's tail as it swept the ground behind the dragon. If he'd been any slower, Sebastian realized, he would have followed the pot over the cliff.

"Smoke, wait!" Corwyn cried. "Don't go in there! It isn't safe!"

Smoke swung his head around with elaborate surprise. "I thought you said there wasn't any danger?"

Corwyn flushed. "Not much. Well, some. God's nightgown, Smoke! Stay out of there until the air clears."

Smoke grinned, displaying his enormous teeth. "This'll just take a moment. I'll hold my breath." Before Corwyn could stop him, the dragon reentered the cave.

Corwyn fumed and muttered, then turned to Oliver. "Go with him. The fool may need help."

Oliver ran eagerly after his playmate.

As he waited, Corwyn studied the valley they would have to cross to reach Hydro Phobius's castle. Here on the south side the Pyrenees were more formidable than to the north. The landscape was savage and fantastic, a haunted scene of upthrust rock and bottomless gorges. Successive ranges stood like waves of stone, frozen in their eons-old journey southward from the central chain to the high Spanish plateaus. The names given to the peaks on this side of the Pyrenees—names such as Mouth of Hell, Accursed Mountain, Lost Mountain, and Enchanted Hill—reflected the disquieting mystery of the southern side of the chain.

Corwyn grew restless with searching for a way among the jumbled rocks below and began to pace with Sebastian. Occasionally the alchemist glanced at the entrance to the cave. "It's taking too long," he said.

A slithering sound came from the cave. They heard Smoke's talons scrape against the tunnel. Moments later, Smoke's head poked out and collapsed, blocking the tunnel. His face had paled, his eyes glazed. As he fell, a load of gaudy metal plates tumbled from his grasp and clattered over the rocks.

"It's about time," Corwyn said, his angry tone revealing the extent of his concern. "What happened?"

"I almost didn't make it," Smoke moaned. "I had to breathe. The smell almost killed me."

Sebastian picked up one of the plates. "What's this?"

"Armor." Smoke looked pleased with himself. "I thought it might be useful at the Black Knight's castle."

Sebastian stacked the pieces in a pile, keeping his opinion to himself. Even to his untrained eye, this armor was obviously intended for appearances at court, not engagements on a battlefield. The metal was poor and the work incompetent. The joints and angles sported raised edges that would catch rather than deflect an opponent's sword. Decorative metalwork on several pieces, particularly the pallettes, added to the danger, apparently at the whim of the suit's designer.

Besides, battle would damage the suit's lacquered finish, its mauve gloss highlighted by swirls of aquamarine and vermilion.

Oliver squirmed past Smoke, who still blocked the entrance. On his head, the broom balanced a helmet with the most ex-

quisite enamel scrollwork Sebastian had ever seen. Too exquis-
ite, in fact, because the proper shape of the helmet had been
sacrificed to the artistry of its design. The visor extended dangerously far from the sides and face, while the slots in the visor
were too small and far apart for adequate vision. A lavender
plume trailed so far down in back that it had become tangled in
Oliver's straw feet, almost tripping him when he walked.

Adding to the broom's difficulties was the sword he dragged
along the ground behind him, a task requiring both his hands.
The hilt was so carved and bejeweled the sword could hardly be
wielded.

Sebastian realized he'd been staring at the armor with a doubt-
ful expression. Corwyn and Smoke watched him, waiting for his
reaction. "How do you get into this?" he asked Smoke, not
wishing to criticize his host's possessions. "It doesn't look like
the pieces fit you."

Smoke chuckled, making the ground tremble. "This isn't for
me, *mon petit louche*. The suit was left by a former paramour.
About your size, I think. It should fit you reasonably well."

Sebastian stared at the armor with new understanding, then
stepped back involuntarily. "Master," he whispered to Corwyn,
"I can't wear that. Please, you must explain to him."

"Hmmm," Corwyn mumbled, cupping his chin. "I understand
your reluctance, Sebastian, but Smoke has a point. It may be
necessary for at least one of us to appear to be a knight when
we approach Hydro Phobius's castle."

"But what kind of knight would wear that?" Sebastian asked,
unable to take his eyes off the armor.

Smoke pulled himself the rest of the way from the tunnel.
"Only a most inept one, I'm afraid. Guillaume possessed tre-
mendous strength and courage, but had not one whit of sense
with which to temper them. And he was far too innocent for this
world. Several other knights tricked him into confronting me,
thinking I would destroy him."

Smoke curled his tail around him and sat down, his expression
wistful. "I lived nearer to human settlements back then, so it
was easy to find me. I still remember how boldly he approached
my cave, unskilled and inadequately armed but so confident of
his abilities I couldn't help but admire him."

Sebastian swallowed hard and waited, trying to accept without
judgment what he was being told. Then, when the silence continued, he forced out his question. "Did you kill him?"

"*Dieu merci,* no!"

"Then what happened?"

Smoke shrugged, as if the answer was obvious. "He stayed. A couple of years later, his former companions returned to challenge us both. Guillaume rode out as boldly to meet them as he'd done the day he confronted me, and just as unprepared."

"They killed him?" Sebastian asked, breathless in spite of himself.

Smoke grinned, exposing a ferocity Sebastian hadn't seen in him before. "They would have, had I not flamed them first. Their bones lie upon the field to this day, still encased in the rusting slag of their armor."

Sebastian fingered one of the lacquered greaves nervously. "But what happened to your friend, Guillaume?"

Smoke's expression fell and Sebastian thought the dragon snuffled. "As I told you, I sometimes flame unintentionally, as I once did near Oliver. So it happened with Guillaume, at an awkward moment several years later."

"He . . . he's dead?"

"No. His burns have since healed. But that which was seared away in the flame can never be regrown."

A strangled sound rose from Sebastian's throat, a cry of pity mixed with horror. He stumbled away from the dragon, his hands dropping to protect his groin. "You don't mean . . . ?"

Smoke nodded. "*Oui.* I hear he's made a new life for himself at the convent of Our Lady of Contraception, where they've accepted him as if he were one of their own." He looked at Sebastian. "You know, you rather remind me of him."

Sebastian gurgled inarticulately.

Corwyn stood up, slapping his knees. "*Alors!* Enough of this chatter. We must get started." He lifted the helmet from Oliver's head and handed it to his apprentice. "Bring the armor, Sebastian," Corwyn said, walking to the precipice.

"How?" Sebastian demanded.

"Be resourceful. I'm sure you'll manage."

Sebastian let out a frustrated breath, then stooped to pick up an armload of armor. He staggered under its weight as he straightened. About half the pieces remained on the ground.

"You'll never manage alone, *mon petit louche,*" Smoke said, gathering up the rest. "Allow me to help."

"Uh, thanks," Sebastian said, regarding the dragon warily.

"Not at all." Smoke smiled, but all Sebastian could see were teeth. "I'm sure you'll find an opportunity sometime to repay the favor."

Sebastian stared, then plodded after Corwyn. He suspected he was reading more into Smoke's words than the dragon intended, but he couldn't be certain.

The descent was treacherous, yet Smoke, who led the way, moved with an agility which belied his size. Oliver hurried after the beast, while Corwyn followed with more difficulty. It was Sebastian who found the going hardest.

He could barely see around the armor he carried. His arms ached from the weight, and he couldn't use his hands to steady himself. Worst of all, the armor was dusty with disuse. With his face pressed close and the heat of the Spanish sun, Sebastian found the dust in his nose unbearable. His nostrils tickled and burned.

The band reached the final slope to the valley floor. Smoke started down cautiously, as even for him the footing was difficult. The others trailed behind. Sebastian waited till Corwyn was well ahead before stepping onto the scree. Smoke was almost to the bottom. Suddenly, Sebastian's nose revolted against the tickling dust. He sneezed, slipping on the loose stones and cascading down the mountainside. He gathered up Corwyn and Oliver like snowballs in an avalanche. Together, the three of them smashed into Smoke. The combined impact was sufficient to upend the dragon. Flying armor and bodies spilled down the slope.

When they stopped tumbling, the adventurers found themselves bruised and tangled on the valley floor. They unraveled themselves painfully. Fortunately, their injuries were minor, consisting primarily of ruffled dignities.

Corwyn brushed himself off and scowled at Sebastian. "If you wanted to lead, you had only to say so."

"I don't want to lead. It's just this armor—"

Corwyn waved him to silence. "If you're not going to lead, then stay in the rear where you belong."

Sebastian stifled a retort. Smoke picked up his share of the armor again, snorting at Sebastian, and started across the narrow valley, leaving deep footprints wherever he stepped. Oliver scampered after a grasshopper, keeping generally to the course Smoke set. Even Corwyn strayed somewhat as an herb growing in a clump of rocks caught his eye. Sebastian hastened to retrieve his portion of the armor and catch up. As he hurried over the uneven ground, one of the sollerets jostled from his grip. He bent to pick it up and the rest of his load tumbled to the dirt. Sebastian looked for the others, but they continued on their way, oblivious of his predicament. *"Tiens!* Wait for me!" he called, but they went on without hearing. Sebastian kicked the armor in frustration.

Then, in sudden inspiration, he sat down and buckled the solleret on his foot. Soon he was wearing the other pieces he'd carried. While he couldn't have hiked through the mountains fully armored, he might be able to manage wearing his half of the items. It had to be better than trying to hold them in his arms.

He stood up, wearing the one solleret on his left foot, greaves on both shins, a metal and leather girdle, a backplate, and a gauntlet over his right hand. The rest of his body was unarmored. On his left arm he slung the shield, embellished with a violet and mulberry griffin too elegant to be frightening. The solleret was adorned with a golden spur of knighthood, though Sebastian noticed the gold was merely plating over baser metal. He belted his own sword around his waist.

He started to add the jeweled sword and scabbard, then thought to check its blade first. As he'd suspected, the blade was poorly wrought metal that would bend or shatter at the first strong blow. It wouldn't even take an edge, as Sebastian discovered by running his thumb along the blade. And the jewels on the scabbard, he was certain, were nothing but colored glass. He checked to make certain none of the others were watching, then hurled the sword and scabbard into the brush. That small act of defiance left him feeling better and he lumbered to catch up with his companions.

As Sebastian drew nearer, the others quickened their pace. Smoke broke into a trot that made the ground shake. Corwyn stopped meandering through the grass to jog after the dragon. Oliver saw them hurrying and scampered across the valley, too.

At first, Sebastian thought it was a cruel trick they were playing, trying to stay ahead of him, and he ran faster. Then he encountered the real reason for their haste: the pot Oliver had thrown over the precipice had landed somewhere nearby, and a familiar, nauseating odor permeated this portion of the gorge.

Sebastian ignored the minor discomforts of heat and sweat and shortage of breath as he strove for greater speed. Soon he was gaining on the others.

They reached the opposite side of the valley in a pell-mell, hurtling mass, each struggling to be first to get free of the smell. Smoke clawed his way up the mountainside. Sebastian jumped ahead of the dragon, ignoring the talons that ripped the earth from under his feet.

Corwyn paused, sniffing the air. "It's all right," he called. "We've left it behind."

They sank to the ground to catch their breaths, all except Oliver. He'd thought the race great fun and was eager to do it again. It was a mystery to him what caused the sudden rush, or why everyone stopped. Despite his urgings, none of the group seemed inclined to continue. At last he wandered off, keeping a careful eye on them in case they should resume running without alerting him first.

Smoke averted his head from Corwyn and Sebastian as he huffed for breath. Each exhalation scorched the dirt at his side. "Corwyn, you outdid yourself this time. That is the worst alchemical concoction I've ever encountered, and I've smelled some foul ones since knowing you."

Corwyn simply stared at the ground and gasped for air, his face reddened by more than exertion.

"Is this problem common in alchemy?" Sebastian asked, wondering whether to pursue his apprenticeship if it was.

Smoke nodded, sending the tendrils of smoke from his nostrils into swirling eddies. *"Oui, mon petit louche,* it is. Having second thoughts, are you? Well, don't worry. If you decide not to complete your alchemical training under Corwyn, you're welcome to stay with me."

"Thanks, Smoke. I'll think about it." He shook his head to clear the last traces of the stench. "Phew, that's dreadful. Worse than the way the demons smell." As he spoke, Sebastian suddenly remembered a picture—a stained glass window at the duke's castle showing St. Eberhard the Unwashed casting forth demons—and what Corwyn had told him about it. "It *is* worse than the way the demons smell, isn't it, master?"

Corwyn lifted his head to glare at his apprentice. "Don't be impertinent, boy. It's bad enough Smoke won't let up. I don't have to take criticism from you as well."

"But it is worse," Sebastian persisted. "That's just it. Remember what you said about St. Eberhard the Unwashed? How some people thought it was his terrible odor that accounted for his success in exorcising demons?"

"That's just ignorant gossip."

"But what if it isn't just gossip, master? What if his smell actually contributed to his spiritual success?"

Corwyn sat up straighter. "You may be right again, Sebastian. It's just possible. But how would that help?"

"Don't you see? If we can create a smell that foul, we can use it to drive the demons out of the mines."

"Peut-être. But if we clear them from the mines, then we've simply unleashed them into the wider world that much sooner. And if we use the smell to drive them from populated areas, people and livestock will be forced from the land as well."

Sebastian opened his mouth, then stopped, crestfallen. For an exhilarating moment, he'd thought he'd found the solution to the plague.

"To succeed at this," Corwyn went on, "we must *ménageons la chèvre et le chou."*

"That's it!" Sebastian exclaimed. "That's the last straw. Or should I say the last *chou?"*

"What are you talking about, boy?" Corwyn asked.

"I finally understand that *chou* in French never means just a cabbage, it always means something else. So what does it mean this time?"

"Only that we must take care of both the goat and the cabbage," Corwyn said.

"I understand that much!" Sebastian snapped. "But what does it mean?"

"Calm down, boy," Corwyn said. "There's no call to yell at me like that. All I meant was that if we are to save Pomme de Terre, we must address each of the two opposites, the devourer and the devoured. Or in this case, the possessors and the possessed."

"And that's what you meant with this goat and cabbage business?"

Corwyn nodded.

"Do the French use this word *chou* in all their expressions?" Sebastian asked. "It seems to mean anything and everything."

"Well, you know the old saying," Corwyn said with a smirk. "If the *chou* fits . . ."

Sebastian groaned and started to get up.

Corwyn reached out and patted him on the leg. "Cheer up, boy. You still may have something. If you're right, at least this smell gives us a way of controlling the demons. Now all we need is a way to contain them, something that would hold them for a

long time and that we could use the smell to drive them into."
He grinned. "If alchemy can solve even that much of the problem, Smoke will never be able to criticize my research again."

The dragon snorted, blasting out smoke, but said nothing.

As they resumed their journey, climbing out of the valley on the opposite side, Sebastian felt happier than he had since Gwen had disappeared. He hadn't solved the whole problem, perhaps. But Corwyn had complimented him on his idea and for a moment had treated him almost as an equal. It left him with a wonderful sensation, one Sebastian hoped might be repeated.

Their route was difficult. At last, however, they crested the final ridge. Ahead, on a rise dominating the floor of a valley, sat the castle of Hydro Phobius. Pennants waved in the breeze, flapping over the curious blend of Moslem and Christian architecture. They rested for a few minutes, studying the castle for signs of life, but saw none. Then they descended to the plain below. The castle was obscured from sight during the downward climb by the clumps of woods through which they had to travel.

Eventually, the ground leveled and they came to the end of the scrub forest. A short distance away, the valley floor rose again, forming a low hill on which the castle stood. The gate was off to the right, angled toward Spain. But the gate was closed, and the feeling of desertion grew stronger.

"What do we do?" Sebastian whispered as if he might be overheard from the castle.

"We have to get inside the gates," Corwyn said. "But how?"

"That's simple," Sebastian answered. "Smoke can assault the castle. He can burn the gate and any of Hydro Phobius's men who're waiting inside."

"No," Smoke said. He gave the single word a tragic emphasis that startled Sebastian. "I'm sorry, I can't. What you do from this point will have to be on your own."

"But how can we rescue Gwen without your help?" Sebastian asked.

"I don't know. But I can't risk harming those in the castle or taking their lives with my flame."

"Why not? You did it before, for Guillaume."

"*Oui*," Smoke said. "And it's because of what I did to Guillaume afterward that I've foresworn ever harming another living creature. It is my penance. That's why I no longer eat meat."

"But . . . but . . . ." Sebastian stopped. He couldn't ask Smoke to break his oath, but he couldn't leave Gwen a captive in the

Black Knight's castle, either. He had to rescue her. But how?

"Perhaps you could just come out into the open with us and appear threatening. You wouldn't have to actually hurt anyone."

"You think I'm fool enough to get shot by an overeager archer trying to impress his favorite wench? We're within crossbow range, you know! My scales don't deflect crossbow bolts."

Sebastian glared at the dragon in disgust. "A lot of help you are."

"I brought you here, didn't I?" Smoke demanded, bristling. Then the anger faded and a pained sorrow took its place. "Besides, they wouldn't find me frightening. They'd only laugh. I know. I was seen the day I followed the Black Knight here. The guards on the wall made fun of me and threw rocks. The Black Knight's squire was the worst. He was so rude I finally slunk away." Smoke sighed, making the trees sway in the hot breeze. "I've always wanted to be a hero, a champion the troubadours could sing about. Dragons are never champions in the *chansons de geste*. We're always creatures of evil the heroes must defeat. Just once, I'd like to change that. But it won't happen, not here, not the way they react."

Sebastian patted Smoke's foreclaw hesitantly. It was the first time he'd touched the dragon, and he was surprised at the cool, dry feel of Smoke's scales. It wasn't at all what he'd expected, though he wasn't sure what he thought a dragon should feel like. "I'm sorry, Smoke. Forgive me."

Smoke lifted his shoulders in a massive shrug and smiled lopsidedly. "Now, you must get this woman of yours out of the castle." His smile broadened. "I'm afraid you're quite worthless without her. But neither I nor a tired old alchemist like Corwyn will be much help."

Corwyn stuck out his chin. "What do you mean, old and tired? I'll have you know—"

Smoke pushed his friend gently out of the way and waved him to silence. "The best thing would be to finish suiting up and challenge this Hydro Phobius to single combat," he said to Sebastian, ignoring the interruption.

"What!" Sebastian backed away. "What good would it do for me to get killed?"

"With luck and agility, you might not be killed," Smoke said. "The important thing is that while you're diverting everyone's attention, and while Hydro Phobius is outside with the gate open,

Corwyn and Oliver could slip into the castle to look for your friend."

"I don't know," Sebastian said.

"Smoke's right." Corwyn smiled. "Besides, who would suspect a tired old man and a broom of sneaking in to free a prisoner?"

"But why do I have to wear the armor?" Sebastian persisted, looking at the pieces he already wore. "I could move a lot faster without it, which would improve my chances of coming back alive."

Corwyn stared at him hard. "Because Hydro Phobius is the Black Knight, a member of the nobility to which you aspire. So you must appear to be a knight as well. Does that answer your question?"

A flush spread over Sebastian's face. *"Oui,"* he answered, realizing at once what his master meant and surprised that he'd needed to be reminded.

Fifteen minutes later, a nervous Sebastian approached the castle gate, adorned in mauve finery. He was glad armor clanked naturally; it covered the noise of his knees banging in fear. He doubted he would return from this battle alive, but if his dying would save Gwen's life, he was prepared to make the trade. Like Smoke, he was desperate to redeem himself by being a hero, the kind Gwen had initially thought him to be.

At the bottom of the rise to the castle he halted and looked up at the guard posts along the wall. He still couldn't see anything, but then the blasted visor on the helmet kept getting in the way. *"Tiens!* You in the castle," he yelled, his voice high and cracking. He forced it under control and lowered its pitch. "Is anybody there?"

"Whatever you've come here for, you've come to the wrong place," answered a voice.

Sebastian swung the helmet around and finally located the source of the voice. A broad-faced man with bulging eyes peered down from a window in one of the towers. From Smoke's description, Sebastian judged the man to be Hydro Phobius's valet and squire.

Sebastian set his feet apart in a confident stance. "I've come for Hydro Phobius," he cried.

The squire scowled. "By your appearances, I'll wager you really want that dragon who lives further up the mountain." He waved vaguely toward the northeast.

Sebastian felt his face grow hot. "I'm here to challenge your master, the Black Knight!"

The squire burst out laughing. "You? You're challenging the great Hydro Phobius? To what, pray tell—a little of this, perhaps?" He made an obscene gesture, and his laughter became uncontrollable.

Anger at the squire's insolence surged through Sebastian, mixed with humiliation over his own appearance. Yet Hydro Phobius was the Black Knight, and the code of chivalry decreed that only a knight could challenge another knight to combat. It was a vain and arrogant code, but Sebastian saw with new insight how he, like his father, had followed it as unquestioningly as any slave. It was his blind adherence to that same code of conduct that had led him to overlook Gwen's true qualities at the monastery of St. Mathurin, with the result that she was now a captive within the Black Knight's walls.

"*Tiens!*" he roared. "You, there—frog-face! Call your master to the wall!"

The squire was no longer laughing. "Who're you calling frog-face?"

"I'm calling you that, and before God that's what you are! Go lick your master's boots, squire, and tell him I've come to remove his head!"

The squire colored visibly. "What's your interest in fighting him?"

"He has a prisoner here, a woman by the name of Gwen."

There was a subtle hesitation before the squire replied. "What if he does?"

"I'm challenging Hydro Phobius on the field of combat. If I win, Gwen goes free. If I lose . . ." He shrugged, but the gesture was lost inside the armor.

The squire studied the surrounding mountain slopes, then turned back to Sebastian. "You didn't come here alone, did you? How many men do you have?"

"Enough," Sebastian said, surprised at how casual he made his voice sound.

"Enough to take this castle?" The squire spoke with disdain, but Sebastian could sense his worry.

"Enough for our purpose," Sebastian answered, hoping it wasn't a lie.

The squire pursed his thick lips and clucked to himself while he thought. "Hold on," he said at last. "I'll take your message to my master." He turned from the window and was gone.

Sebastian waited. The sun was high, and it was hot on the southern side of the mountains. He perspired inside the armor, itching in places he couldn't scratch. Worse, the heat brought out the dust, mixing it with the smell of sweat.

A fly came in through the visor grill and drove him nearly mad by buzzing around inside the helmet and alighting on his face. He contorted his facial muscles in an effort to frighten it off, but without success.

Of course, he thought hysterically, it's a French fly. I have to *chou* it away!

He started to laugh, but stopped when the sound reverberated in the helmet, blending with the insane buzzing of the fly.

Eventually the fly flew out again and landed on his breastplate. Sebastian swatted at it. His gauntlet and armored forearm clanged against the breastplate, almost unbalancing him. He staggered under the blow as the gate opened. Through the gate, Sebastian saw a column of smoke rise from the castle keep.

The squire appeared, riding a heavily-laden, braying ass which seemed to have its own notions about what direction to travel. Behind him, the squire led a knight on a magnificent charger. The knight wore black armor as richly lacquered and ostentatious as Sebastian's, but the effect was far more menacing. Contributing to that effect was the lance the knight couched in his right arm, already lowered to the ready position.

Through his helmet, Sebastian heard the muted sounds of a commotion back toward the woods. Someone was calling his name. He turned awkwardly to see, reluctant to take his eyes off his foe. Squinting through the visor, he saw Corwyn wave and shout to him. Sebastian smiled inside his helmet and returned the wave. At least he was getting a rousing send-off as he prepared to die.

He peered harder, trying to see through the clumsy helmet. Someone else was standing beside Corwyn, but he couldn't see who. He wished the alchemist would make use of this preciously purchased time by going after Gwen.

The ground shook and Sebastian turned quickly—too quickly, he discovered, as the momentum of the armor carried him on around. He caught himself and drew his sword as the Black Knight's armored charger started down the hill toward him. The steed's hooves pounded the turf, hurling grass and dirt into the air.

The yelling behind Sebastian grew more insistent, buzzing in his helmet like another fly. He appreciated his friends' support, but wished they'd stop. It was distracting. He needed all his attention for his adversary and didn't dare turn around to wave.

The Black Knight hurtled closer. His horse flew over the uneven ground, its pace quickened by the slope from the castle. Sebastian widened his stance and gripped his sword in both hands. His one hope was to lop off the lance tip as the Black Knight charged past. The knight would be forced to fight with his own sword at close quarters, where Sebastian might stand a chance. But the timing was crucial, and there'd be no second chance.

Time stretched. Sebastian grew aware of details—the way the horse's nostrils flared, the smell of fear inside his armor, and the smoke rising above the castle walls. The lance tip grew larger. For a moment, all Sebastian could see was that metal point glinting in the sun, swelling like a flower bud ready to burst into bloom.

The point was almost at his chest. He lunged to his left, the move clumsy in his armor. "For Gwen!" he cried, bringing the sword down in a short, violent arc.

The sword hit the lance behind the tip. But the blade had dulled from slicing too many bread loaves and cheeses, and it failed to cut the lance's hard wood. The point flexed downward away from the blow.

Then the lance touched the ground, the horse's momentum driving it into the turf. The horse lurched under the impact, caught itself, and strained forward. The animal's shoulder smashed into Sebastian, knocking him to the ground. Sebastian struggled to get up, or at least roll away from the hooves thudding around him. But the armor pinned him to the ground like a beetle on its back.

From there, Sebastian saw the Black Knight lifted free of the saddle by the force of the blow. He rose in a ponderous arc over the straining haunches of the horse. For a moment, the knight was a gleaming black shape suspended against the smoke that now consumed the castle. Then the knight fell beyond Sebastian's angle of vision. Armor plates tore loose from the impact and flew over the battlefield.

Relieved of its rider, the war-horse shied away. Sebastian struggled to regain his feet, afraid the other knight might already be moving in for the kill. Poor Corwyn, he thought, I haven't given you enough time for your task. Now you'll be his prisoner too. I've failed you all.

A shadow blocked the sun, and he braced for the final blow. Suddenly, hands tried to lift him up, to tear the helmet from him. He clutched at his opponent just as a face leaned over him.

It was Gwen.

"Sebastian, are you all right?" she asked.

He nodded, banging his chin on the helmet in his eagerness. "I think so." He helped her ease the helmet off. Even in the midst of his elation at seeing Gwen and his uncertainty about the Black Knight, he noticed her gown. The sun cast her silhouette against the glowing cloth, and Sebastian stared in unabashed appreciation.

Gwen studied Sebastian, her eyes concerned. Satisfied that he was unhurt, she bent to kiss him. Sebastian was as startled at the kiss as he was to find Gwen hovering over him, but he responded with enthusiasm. The kiss that began in modesty lingered, acquiring passion.

But when Sebastian remembered the Black Knight, he broke away from Gwen and looked to see where his foe had fallen. "Gwen, help me up. *Vite!* The Black Knight! I've got to fight him, got to give you and the others time to escape!"

"It's all right," Gwen said, trying to restrain him. "It's over. We're in no danger now."

"You mean I killed him?" Sebastian's stomach tightened at the thought.

"You were very brave, my hero," Gwen said, helping him sit up. "Even though you didn't know the truth about him, you went out to face the Black Knight. Corwyn says you did it to save me."

Sebastian nodded, wondering at what she'd said. "Didn't know what truth about him?" He looked for his opponent, but saw only pieces of armor scattered about the field. Corwyn and Smoke picked through the debris, talking and glancing over their shoulders at Gwen and Sebastian. Oliver played kick-the-helmet with the Black Knight's headgear. Off to one side, the war-horse munched on the sparse grass. Ahead, the castle burned unchecked. Nowhere did Sebastian see his enemy. There was no dead body in the armor, no bloody corpse littering the field.

"Where is he?"

Gwen held him closer, clutching his head to her breast. "I want you to know how proud of you I am. I always dreamed of a champion who'd fight for me, despite my lowly birth. Now you've given me that dream—"

Sebastian tried to ignore the way her breasts cushioned his face, filtering his senses through the soft warmth of her skin. "Gwen, what happened to the Black Knight?"

She cleared her throat but said nothing. Sebastian pushed away to look her in the face as Corwyn approached them. "Well done, boy. You redeemed yourself fully that time! I trust you came through the experience unscathed?"

"Master, where's Hydro Phobius?"

Corwyn looked away as if embarrassed. "Gone, I'm afraid. Escaped during the battle."

"Escaped? But how? I was fighting him."

Corwyn whistled tunelessly and refused to meet Sebastian's eyes. Gwen held Sebastian's head in her hands and turned him toward her. "Dear Sebastian, *mon chou*—"

Sebastian gritted his teeth against that word, regardless how affectionately Gwen meant it.

"What you did was brave and kind, and I'll always be thankful. But the truth is, there never was anyone inside that armor. The Black Knight was a charade to intimidate people."

"You mean there was no Hydro Phobius? But I thought—"

Corwyn put a hand on Sebastian's shoulder. "There really is a Hydro Phobius. He just isn't everything he tried to make us believe. He created an imaginary person, a powerful knight with grandiose ways and elaborate armor to gain the fear and respect he wasn't able to command by himself."

Sebastian's shoulders drooped. "So I fought an enemy who wasn't even there." He snorted. "Oh, I was brave all right. I fought an empty suit of armor." He looked at himself seated on the ground, then added with contempt, "And I almost won!"

"You *were* brave, Sebastian," Gwen insisted, trying to meet his eyes. "You didn't know the armor was empty. And the danger was real. The war-horse was well trained. If you hadn't jumped aside when you did, it would've run you through with the lance."

"Then who was Phobius?"

"The squire." Gwen's face clouded. "That vile, ugly creature! He convinced me he was only acting on his master's behalf. He even hid wires in the throne room to move the Black Knight's helmet when the armor sat on the throne, as if someone were inside. I discovered the wires while hiding behind the throne during my escape."

Sebastian shook his head. Regardless of what Gwen said, it was deflating to get knocked to the ground in a fight where he was the only participant. He looked at his armor and felt worse. Why'd Gwen have to see him like this? He started unbuckling the gaudy plates as Gwen's last statement slowly sank in.

"How did you escape so quickly? I hardly gave Corwyn time to get inside the castle."

"Sebastian, *mon petit chou,* I was already out," she said. "I escaped last night but had to remain near the castle because I couldn't climb with my ankle." She told how she twisted it during her capture.

Frustrated rage swept Sebastian. He hated Hydro Phobius for what he'd done to Gwen, but he despised himself more for his inability to avenge her. He stared with hurt, scornful eyes. *"Naturellement!* I should have known! Not only did I fight a man who wasn't there, but you'd already escaped! I couldn't even bring your tormentor to justice! Oh, some champion I am!"

Gwen put her hands on her hips and sat back. "Sebastian, don't be like that. You couldn't have known. I was hiding in the woods on the other side of the castle, wondering how to get word to you and Corwyn when I heard a strange knight challenge Hydro Phobius. By the time I found Corwyn and discovered the challenger was you, it was too late to call you back. We tried, but you only waved."

"I thought everyone was cheering me on," Sebastian said. "But why did Hydro Phobius agree to the fight at all? He had the castle and his mercenaries; he didn't need to fight me or escape."

Gwen shook her head. "He was terribly upset last night when he found I was gone. You should have seen it—the whole valley around the castle was alight with torches as Hydro Phobius and his men searched for me. I knew enough about the disposal operation and his true identity to be a threat to him.

"Then this morning, about an hour before you arrived, the mercenaries Hydro Phobius sent to Smoke's lair to capture Corwyn returned empty-handed. They had neither Corwyn nor their own weapons. They raved like madmen about a supernatural force more powerful than the demons, claiming Corwyn had summoned dread creatures to destroy them all. I heard their tale because they refused to enter the castle. They shouted to Hydro Phobius from the gate before fleeing into Spain.

"With his mercenaries gone, my escape, and Corwyn closing

in on the disposal operation at the mines, Hydro Phobius had
to abandon everything immediately. The others fled just before
you arrived. I think Hydro Phobius delayed only long enough
to set fire to the castle and destroy the evidence of what he'd
done."

Smoke ventured over and clapped a foreclaw to Sebastian's
shoulder. Then he glanced at Gwen and jerked his arm away.
"It was a good fight, *mon petit louche*," he said, his voice a
thundering stage whisper. "Regardless of the outcome, you were
magnificent!"

Sebastian tried to smile, but the effort felt unsuccessful.
Smoke, apparently sensing his discomfort, edged away.

Gwen leaned closer to Sebastian. "Why did he call you his
little basting spoon?"

"It's just a pet name," Sebastian said, hoping to evade the
question.

"I know, but shouldn't it be 'my little wolf'?"

Sebastian nodded and opened his mouth, then decided against
trying to explain. "Smoke doesn't speak the language very well,"
he said.

"I should say not." Gwen leaned back again to study the
dragon dubiously. "He speaks it like an Englishman."

Sebastian stared at her.

"Oh!" she gasped, realizing her mistake. "Oh, Sebastian, I
am sorry, *mon petit chou*." Then she smiled mischievously and
added, "Or should I say, *mon petit louche?*"

Sebastian responded with a weak grin, unable to resist her
attempt at humor. He pulled the last of Smoke's armor off and
kicked the pieces away, glad to be free of them and wishing he
could as readily free himself from his sense of failure. The voice
in his head was hounding him mercilessly.

"*Alors!* At least it's all over now," he said. " Once we get
back to Pomme de Terre with the news, he'll never dispose of
another demon inside the duchy again."

"It's not over quite yet," Corwyn said. "There are still the
demons already in the mines to be dealt with." He looked up
to see a mule train emerge from the trees on the far side of the
valley and head toward the burning castle. The small, ratty peasant guiding the train paid no attention to the flames behind the
castle walls or to the group on the field, but his heavyset companion headed toward them with a purposeful stride. Then he

stopped in confusion as he noticed the black armor littering the ground.

"And I think I've finally solved the problem of what to do about the demons," Corwyn added under his breath, hurrying over to greet the peasants.

CHAPTER 18

Miasma in the Mines

FOR OLIVER, THE NEXT SEVERAL DAYS WERE A GLORIOUS TIME. Never before had a human played with him for such extended periods or given him such undivided attention. Of course, Sebastian, the human to whose time and attention Oliver laid claim, had an entirely different interpretation of those days. But no matter. For Oliver, it was a game, and he entered into that game with a simpleminded enthusiasm that was impossible for the others to understand.

The game was one of exploring and mapping the labyrinth of dripping, flooded tunnels that made up the Goblin Mines.

"I'm to take Oliver and do what?" Sebastian had demanded when Corwyn announced the jobs to be done and who was to accomplish each. "But, master, it's suicide to go down there. The place is full of demons!" He shuddered as he remembered the condition Dr. Tox had been in when they first entered the mines and found him. When the poor physician emerged, he was nothing but a babbling idiot who'd shaken free of his rescuers and gone screaming down the mountainside into the forest.

"Of course it's full of demons!" Corwyn said. "And when we're ready to drive them into the containment vault, timing and placement of the olfactory charges will be critical. We must know where each shaft leads in order to avoid trapping any demons outside the containment system in the depths of the mines. That could thwart the entire undertaking."

"But master—"

Corwyn looked at his apprentice tiredly. Now that Hydro Phobius had escaped into Spain, eluding all efforts to find and extradite him, only the old alchemist could hope to successfully decontaminate the Goblin Mines. But the difficult, hazardous task had begun to affect his disposition. "Do it," he said.

So each morning, Oliver jostled Sebastian awake as early as he dared at their camp near (but not *too* near) the mines. Together they would set out for the mines ahead of the others. Sebastian rarely took time to eat before they left, despite the culinary treats Smoke prepared for the band. Indeed, Sebastian seldom ate at all these days. Toward the end of the game, Oliver noticed Sebastian was beginning to resemble his own emaciated figure. Naturally, the broom regarded this fact in a most complimentary fashion.

Together they would hike down the mountainside to the entrance to the mines, Oliver dashing ahead at every turn and Sebastian slogging on with stoic resignation. Each carried a supply of olfactory charges, smaller versions of the bombs which would eventually be used to herd the demons into a single location within the mines. The charges represented state-of-the-art alchemical technology, highly advanced forms of the concoction Corwyn accidentally made in Smoke's lair. As such, they were even more potent than the original and were designed for controlled release.

Sebastian was quite convinced of their greater potency—it was that which accounted for his loss of appetite. But as to the degree of control Corwyn had been able to design into the bombs, here he had some reservations.

Oliver had no opinion on either point. He was equally unaffected by the smell from the charges and by the demons those charges were intended to disperse. He simply carried the bombs through the mines, placing them and setting them off with the attention to detail one grants to the rules of a game one wants to continue playing. Throughout the day, as the supply of bombs they carried grew smaller, Sebastian would send Oliver back to the surface for more. Oliver always made sure he returned to Sebastian with the new supply before the previous stock expired. He did this to ensure that the game continue rather than through any concern for Sebastian's life. He had the impression that if Sebastian died (or became demonically possessed—it was all the same to Oliver), the game would stop. But he also timed his returns with new odor bombs to coincide with the final gasps of the last of Sebastian's previous supply. He would leave Sebastian mapping damp, slimy tunnels by the light of a candle, still well armed with olfactory charges. He would return to find the apprentice cowering like a terrorized child before a horde of demonic wraiths. For Oliver, the object of this part of the game was to always arrive just in time to save Sebastian.

Sebastian didn't understand Oliver's approach to the game. He didn't see it as a game at all. And he never could fathom why, no matter how early he sent Oliver up to the surface for more bombs, the broom always came back just as his demon-induced nightmares were about to come to their inevitable conclusion.

These visions were much like those he had experienced in previous encounters with demons, except that instead of stalking the halls of his boyhood home in search of a crying child, now he was the child, and an unseen, malevolent presence hunted him. Sebastian would hear the approaching footsteps and watch the thing's shadow as it bobbed ahead, cast forward by torches spaced along the corridor wall. He never saw who—or what—the presence was. Each time, before his pursuer could discover him, Oliver would return with fresh odor bombs and the dubious safety they afforded.

So Oliver played and Sebastian worked, and each thought the other saw it all from the same perspective. They would arrive early at the mines, set off a bomb, and hurl it through the heavy doors at the head of the mines. After the bomb had time to clear out any demons that might have wandered up so far, they would enter the mines. At this point, the long day of torment and terror began for Sebastian. He constantly had to breathe the noxious fumes from the bombs, for only within the sphere of their influence was he safe from possession. As a result, his stomach was in perpetual turmoil.

They would proceed slowly from the entrance, carrying a fuming charge, clearing out the tunnels that led to the containment vault. Here, Corwyn would spend his day, overseeing the efforts of Kwagg and Meier as the two peasants readied the vault. In return for their reluctant cooperation, Corwyn promised to overlook their role in dumping the demons in the mines to begin with. After a few days of working in the foul-smelling vault, Kwagg and Meier began to wonder if imprisonment might not have been the wiser choice.

Once the work areas were cleared for the others, Oliver and Sebastian descended into the haunted depths of the mines. They trudged through endless tunnels, always with a smoking odor bomb slung over one shoulder. Ahead of them, just out of range of the bomb, wraiths shimmered and blurred as they tried to reach Sebastian. The terror the demons generated cut through the stench to clutch at his heart, and he lived a strange kind of double existence, half in the present exploring the mines, half in some dimly remembered past full of terror and shame. Somehow, he managed to take notes on where he had been, and during periodic breaks in their explorations he added new shafts to his gradually evolving map of the mines.

At the end of the day, Sebastian and Oliver would be the last ones to leave the mines, retreating behind the safety of the omnipresent smell. Together in the dwindling light outside, they would trek back to the camp, where Sebastian would ignore the evening's meal and tumble, exhausted and sick, into bed.

Nighttime brought little relief to Sebastian, for his sleep was troubled with dreams of the presence which stalked him in the demonic encounters he experienced by day. Night after night, that presence would round the corner of his hiding place and loom before him, formidable as an angry god. Each time, Sebastian would look up, half hoping to recognize its features, but the face was usually obscured like a distant, cloud-covered mountain peak. Once, however, Sebastian dreamed he saw it fully, and his shriek of horrified recognition at encountering his own face on the presence awakened him and his companions. Gwen held him until his terror ebbed enough for him to return to sleep. Thereafter, the two of them slept in each other's arms, taking comfort from one another.

Sebastian knew little of what tasks the others pursued during the long, exhausting days, other than that Corwyn was preparing the vault and Gwen, because of her ankle, remained in camp churning out a constant supply of Corwyn's olfactory charges. Smoke handled logistics and supplies for the camp.

When Corwyn had first listed the duties to be performed, Smoke had volunteered to explore the mines in Sebastian's place. "As a cave-dweller myself, I'm uniquely suited to the task," he stated, puffing out his enormous chest.

"But Smoke, this isn't your problem," Corwyn said. "You've helped us greatly already. There's no reason for you to endanger yourself by going into the mines."

"I'm the natural choice, Corwyn, and I shall be the one to do it." But Smoke was looking at Sebastian as he spoke. Then he glanced self-consciously at Gwen. "Besides," he added quietly, "the boy has other responsibilities."

Gwen patted the dragon affectionately and whispered her thanks, to which Smoke responded with a smile. Just before the dragon entered the mines, he drew Sebastian aside. "Take good care of her," he said with a nod toward Gwen. "You seem to have your heart set on her anyway. Well, she's all right, that one. For a female."

Sebastian had been too choked up to respond and watched in silence as the huge creature squeezed through the doors of the mines.

Outside, they all listened through the heavy wooden doors to the scratching and clawing of Smoke's talons against the stone walls of the mines. But although the sounds grew more frantic as time passed, they failed to recede into the depths. Finally, Smoke opened the great doors again and thrust out his head.

"I'm too large," he said, sounding unwilling to believe such a thing. He crawled out and flung himself on the grass, making the earth tremble. "Those goblins must've been tiny. They made the shafts too narrow."

Sebastian stepped up. "That's all right, Smoke. I'll go." He shrugged, feeling awkward. "It's my responsibility."

Sebastian was surprised to notice Corwyn smiling at him approvingly.

Smoke lifted his head enough to look at Sebastian. "Just once, I'd like to do a deed worthy of a minstrel's songs. For a moment, I thought perhaps this would be that time."

Sebastian remembered his own challenge to the Black Knight, and understood Smoke's dream of being a hero. For Sebastian, the need to be worthy of his father still burned within him, unrequited and condemning. He smiled at the dragon and patted him on the shoulder. There was nothing he could say.

So Sebastian found himself mapping the mines after all, choking on the smell of the odor bombs and trembling in terror from the wraiths that hung at the edge of sight, awaiting their chance to reach him. And once started, he found he had too little time or energy to be much interested in what the others did. His only concern was to complete his portion of the job so he'd never have to enter the mines again.

Several times, Kwagg and Meier disappeared for a day or two at a time, taking leave of their duties at the mines to pursue other assignments. During these absences, Gwen would set aside her work with the bombs to help Corwyn in the vault. The first time it happened, Sebastian assumed the two peasants had run off, perhaps to rejoin Hydro Phobius in hiding. But Corwyn's hold over them must have been stronger than their desire to escape, or maybe they didn't know where their former master had gone either, for they always came back, each time with their pack mules laden. The baggage from the mules would then be hauled into the containment vault.

At first, Sebastian intended to ask what Kwagg and Meier were bringing to the site. In fact, he wondered how the containment system was intended to work; Corwyn had never bothered to explain it to him. But by the time Sebastian had the chance to talk to Corwyn about it, he was too sick from his own activities to care. He simply hoped the whole thing would be over soon, one way or another. It didn't matter to him what they did anymore, so long as he was able to get away from this place and never return. A nomadic life on the desert sands of Arabia began to sound appealing—where he'd never encounter another dripping mine shaft or band of malicious demons. Most especially, he wanted never to have to smell another of Corwyn's odor bombs again!

Eventually, the day came when Sebastian followed the last shaft to its conclusion and there were no more tunnels to be added to the map. He felt there should be some sense of relief, some elation at having finished an impossible task. But there was nothing—only a hollowness in his stomach from too many days with too little food. He crawled out of the mines and collapsed on the gravel spillway before the entrance, still gagging and letting the heat of the afternoon sun bake the clinging odors from his bones. Oliver darted around him, eager to devise some new game now that the first seemed over. Sebastian closed his eyes and ignored the broom. He listened to the sounds of the mules cropping grass and jingling their harnesses where they stood tethered nearby, until at last he fell asleep.

He awoke as Corwyn, Kwagg, and Meier left the mines, shutting the big doors with a resounding boom and barring them tight. Corwyn strolled over to Sebastian and sat down. Sebastian barely opened his eyes as Corwyn approached. "You're finished early," Sebastian said without interest.

Corwyn rubbed his hands gleefully. Sebastian noticed, however, that despite his joy the alchemist looked thin and haggard from his own work. "The vault is ready," Corwyn said. "When will the maps be complete?"

"I'm ready to add the last shaft," Sebastian said. "Oliver and I have explored them all. It's just a matter of making a few final notes."

"Bien," Corwyn said, nodding. "We can rest until tomorrow, then we'll try the system in the morning."

"Parfait!" Sebastian said, unenthusiastic. He closed his eyes again and drifted back to sleep, wishing they had caught Hydro Phobius so he could be forced to do his own cleanup work in the mines.

The next morning, the five humans, Oliver, and Smoke gathered before the entrance of the mines as Corwyn handed out olfactory bombs and gave last minute instructions. Each person was assigned certain shafts in the mine complex and was responsible for herding all the demons from those shafts up toward the entrance. Here, Corwyn and Oliver would block their retreat and force them into the containment vault. Because of his size, Smoke would wait outside the mines. As the others entered the dark interior of the earth, the dragon was already pacing nervously, anxious for their safe return.

"You must work quickly," Corwyn emphasized once they reached the containment vault. "Your candles have been notched at regular intervals so each of you can pace your work to arrive back at the main shaft at the same time as the others. If you're late, you may be cut off from escape. But you must also work carefully so as not to be overcome by demons or fumes. And you must be thorough. If any demons are left behind, they'll work their way down to the flooded portions of the mines and enter the water that eventually flows to Pomme de Terre." He looked the four humans over. "Many lives depend upon how well each of you performs here today. Are there any questions?"

"Oui," said Kwagg. "Are we on guild rates? And which notches"—he pointed a grubby finger at his candle—"are rest breaks?"

Corwyn scowled. "There'll be no rest for any of us until the work is finished. All right, let's go."

"Did you hear that?" Kwagg muttered to Meier. "No breaks!

And I'll wager we'll get no meals down here as well. Some taskmaster you've got us working under this time, Meier, that's all I've got to say."

Meier said nothing as he scurried ratlike at the rear to keep up. After all, it had been Kwagg who'd agreed they would do this job rather than face imprisonment. But even if it had been up to Meier, the outcome would have been the same. He'd discovered he rather liked working in the mines, despite the nearness of the wraiths.

Sebastian wished Kwagg hadn't brought up the subject of meals. His stomach churned, threatening outright revolt. The two peasants had been the only ones able to eat after working in the mines, and they took advantage of the others' disinterest by consuming great quantities of Smoke's culinary delights. Kwagg even put on extra weight. Just watching the two peasants gulp down food, the smell of the odor bombs still lingering about their clothes and mixing with the stench of pig farming, was enough to make Sebastian sick.

Soon Sebastian came to the fork leading to the shafts for which he was responsible. He separated willingly from the two peasants, but cast an anxious glance after Gwen. She smiled wanly at him, then hobbled on. Sebastian had argued against Gwen's participating in this part of the job. It was too dangerous, he said, especially with her injured ankle. But the argument had been decided by Corwyn, who pointed out that it would be impossible to drive all the demons up from the many shafts in a coordinated manner without her help. There were too many tunnels and too few people to cover them.

Sebastian's first tunnel was the most difficult, for it was the one leading deepest into the ground. Its end lay submerged in water which had seeped in over the years. Here, the greatest collection of demons was to be found. They would be the first to be herded toward the surface. Sebastian scuttled along, hunched over because of the low ceiling, his back already aching. The tunnel fell away steadily and soon he heard the familiar drip of water from the walls. The floor grew wet and quickly soaked his shoes. Onward he slogged, squishing now at every step.

The odor bomb Sebastian carried was set to emit only a trickle of its contents—just enough to keep the demons from reaching him. They hovered outside its sphere of influence like grotesque moths around a candle. It was not his candle flame they were after, however, but his soul. Sebastian tried to ignore them but even after so many days in the tunnels, he shuddered at their presence. Soon he could see little around him besides squirming vapor. Occasionally one would challenge the stench and roll toward him, only to rebound as the smell sent it flying back again.

The experience was like having his innermost secrets ripped from him time after time and exposed to public scrutiny. Each time, Sebastian felt himself flung into the past, where he cowered in his boyhood home. Yet each time, the spell would be broken by the strength of the odor bombs before the presence could round the corner, pursuing its own shadow in search of him.

So disoriented by this did Sebastian become that he almost missed the dip where water filled the tunnel. He brought himself up short, teetering on the edge. But it wasn't the icy water he feared so much as what the water would do to his candle and the odor bomb which protected him.

Sebastian forced himself to concentrate on the task at hand. He pulled one of the large, stationary olfactory bombs from a sack and placed it near the water. The pool wasn't wide since the shaft dipped steeply at this point. No demons would be trapped on the far side, unable to move up the shaft with the others. He lit the fuse with his candle and stood back, perversely fascinated by this device which rendered the air unsuitable for flesh or spirit. The fuse sparked and smoldered, seemed to go out, then finally reached the charge. Blue-black fog spilled out over the water, gradually filling the shaft, rising around Sebastian's feet. Where it touched, it left a clammy, numbing chill that penetrated his bones. He gripped his candle and smaller odor bomb, knowing he should keep ahead of the fog. But he couldn't resist the impulse to watch.

A wraith burst from the shadows at the far end of the pool and hurtled past Sebastian in its eagerness to escape the fog. So anxious was it to flee that it seemed oblivious to Sebastian. With ghostly wings it brushed his face, trailing an inaudible scream of demonic pain and terror. How ironic that a creature which normally caused terror in others should be so overcome by fear itself—a thought which finally roused Sebastian from his reverie. He hurried up the shaft as fumes rose around his knees. A few more minutes of standing there, and he would have been overcome by the fog before he could reach higher ground.

Demons retreated ahead of Sebastian, leading him away from the fog instead of pressing in to possess him. He had become the hunter, they the hunted. It was almost as if the crying child he became in his vision had risen up to chase his unseen pursuer back along the castle halls. Sebastian kept between the rising fog and the last of the retreating wraiths as he followed them up the slope, exhilarated at seeing them scurry away from him.

When the first olfactory bomb burned to the end of its charge, the buildup of fog slowed and stopped. Its surface lay upon the sloping floor like some turbulent, ghastly sea lapping at the beach of hell. Sebastian took another bomb from his sack and placed it on the floor near the edge of the fog. Once more he lit the fuse and started up the tunnel.

The whole time, he was still breathing the fumes of his own, much smaller odor bomb. Although less powerful, the stench of it nonetheless threatened to overwhelm him. He fought against dizziness and nausea, keeping to the schedule Corwyn had laid out for him. Demons clustered ahead until the air was viscous with terrified spirits.

Periodically, Sebastian reached the mouths of smaller side shafts. He hurried to the end of each and set off more odor bombs, always careful the rising fog in the main tunnel didn't cut off his escape before he cleared out the secondary shafts. In this manner, he herded the demons toward the containment vault near the entrance to the mines.

Sebastian finished his assigned tunnels as Kwagg emerged from an adjacent set of shafts. A little further up, Meier did the same. The three of them advanced slowly, bolstered by one another's presence. So far, everything was on schedule. The fog rose behind them, the demons hurtled away in panic. Ahead, Corwyn and Oliver would be deflecting the spirits into the vault.

But Gwen wasn't waiting at the last of her tunnels. The three men stopped to allow her to catch up, their eyes darting from their notched candle stubs to the fog lapping at their feet. Kwagg and Meier fidgeted as Sebastian forced them to wait.

Finally, Sebastian's candle burned past the last notch. "You two go ahead," he said, starting into the empty tunnel. "I'm going after Gwen."

"You'll never make it," Kwagg called, as he and Meier hurried up the main tunnel.

Sebastian plowed through a group of demons fleeing something further down. They flowed past with a touch like ice, but were too panicked to take advantage of his presence. A short distance beyond, he came to the edge of the fog from Gwen's bombs.

The blue-black mist partially covered the broken ore carts and burst shipping barrels that littered the floor. But Sebastian didn't see Gwen. She must have been overcome by the fumes.

"Gwen!" he called. Echoes assaulted him like a brittle laugh from the emptiness the demons left behind. The fog chilled his flesh, sucking at his legs with a numbing grip as he pushed into the undulating sea. He strode waist deep and felt the mist's touch penetrate his bowels. A few more steps brought its grip to his heart.

Tears streaked his face, but all he felt was irritation at the way they blurred his vision. He blinked them back and scanned the mist for some trace of Gwen. Having lost her once through his own foolishness at the monastery of St. Mathurin, he was determined never to lose her again. If she couldn't be found in time, he'd stay with her in the mines.

He wiped his eyes with his sleeve, glancing over his shoulder as he did. Suddenly, the dim outline of a shape showed on the floor where he'd passed moments earlier. The fog, weakened from a brief swirl of air stirred by his passage, thinned enough to reveal what looked like Gwen crumpled on the floor of the mine.

The swirl of air died and the fog closed back over the shape on the floor. But Sebastian had seen enough. He waded back through the deathly sea toward the form. Suddenly, his foot struck something hard and he pitched forward onto the shattered remains of an ore cart. The impact drove the breath from his chest. He gasped instinctively, drawing in a lungful of deadly fumes. He choked, his eyes unfocused, then retched. He tried to heave himself back upright, but the fumes had sapped the strength from his legs, and he sprawled on the floor. All the while, the voice in his head shrieked at him for being such a fool as to mistake the outline of a broken ore cart for Gwen.

He struggled to his hands and knees, but still couldn't get his head above the fog to breathe. He felt blindly over the floor for the rest of the cart, hoping to push off from it and raise himself higher. His hand hit something solid, but his fingers were too numbed to grip it. He was going to die, the voice assured him. That made him angry, and he dragged himself onto the upturned cart by hooking his forearms over the opposite side. The effort left him dizzy and weak with lack of air.

A pair of hands grabbed him around the chest and pulled him upright. Sebastian's eyes rolled, then steadied enough to focus on Gwen. She was like a mad woman, crying and tugging on him. Sebastian helped as best he could, and eventually they stumbled up the slope beyond the reach of the fog.

"My love," he whispered. "Why, you're crying." He reached a hand to brush away her tears, only to discover that his fingers were still too numb to feel her face.

She squeezed him to her as he coughed again, then brushed his cheek with a kiss. "I thought I heard you call," she said. "The slope was very steep and my ankle made it hard for me to climb. Then I dropped my candle and had to feel my way along the wall. I almost didn't get out before being trapped by the fog. Just as the slope leveled off a little, I saw you up ahead. But before I could answer your call, you turned and fell. Oh, Sebastian, I thought you were dead!"

"I would have been if not for you," he said. "But I had to find you."

They worked their way further up the shaft, pursued by the rising fog. Gwen limped badly, but even so she had to help keep Sebastian upright as sensation slowly returned to his legs.

More than physical distress hampered Sebastian, however. The voice in his head was berating him for having to be rescued himself when he had set out to rescue Gwen. This disgrace was merely the latest of many, the voice emphasized.

Sebastian wondered if he would ever do anything right.

Before they reached the mouth of the shaft, more fog spilled in from the main tunnel ahead, flowing along the floor to join that which harried them from behind. Sebastian couldn't see his ankles as he stepped in the mist, breaking it into swirling eddies. They reached the main shaft to find it nearly filled with fumes. The demons had fled to the higher levels as planned. All that was left was for Gwen and Sebastian to do the same.

"Hold your breath," she said, plunging into the fog blocking the main shaft. A few steps later they were above the surface of the fumes. They stopped to set a final charge, then continued up the shaft.

They arrived at the vault as Corwyn and Oliver slammed the doors shut. The massive iron bar dropped into place, locking the vault. Then Oliver smeared the cracks around the doors with pitch. Gwen grabbed a second brush and helped Oliver seal the vault.

"Nothing can get out of there now," Corwyn said, watching with satisfaction. "That will hold them for a long, long time."

Sebastian, who had slumped to the floor of the mine with his back against one wall, was listening to the voice in his head recite a litany of his failures when a chill gripped his spine. He jerked his head around to discover the biggest demon he'd yet seen rising from a puddle on the floor. Even after the abuse Sebastian's nostrils had taken from the fog and odor bombs, the wraith was formidable enough to add a burning, sulfurous stench to his agony.

Gwen stood across from Sebastian next to Corwyn and Oliver, the three of them studying the vault door. Kwagg and Meier were off to one side watching the others, content to stand back while everyone else worked.

No one but Sebastian had noticed the creature which towered between the humans and the shaft leading out of the mines, cutting off their only avenue of escape.

Behind the demon, a thin curtain of the terrible fog, which Corwyn and Oliver had set up to deflect the retreating demons into the containment vault, drifted toward them. As Sebastian watched, the demon moved away from the descending fumes and closer to him, extending a tendril in his direction.

"Gwen! Master!" Sebastian cried. "Behind you! There's one left!"

Gasps from the others told him they saw their peril. "Corwyn, what are we to do?" Gwen asked.

Corwyn sized up the demon, then glanced in the other direction, where a solid wall of fog advanced from the depths of the mines. If they didn't get out quickly, the entire group would be enveloped in its killing stench. But how could they get out with that enormous demon blocking their way?

The demon smirked and moved forward. Only Oliver withstood the creature's assault. He swished valiantly at the wraith, trying to dispel it as Sebastian had used him to do with the wraith in Corwyn's dungeon cell. But this creature was far too large to be disrupted by the efforts of the little broom.

"I don't know what to say, *ma chère,*" Corwyn told Gwen at last. "There's nothing we can do."

The demon exuded a series of tendrils, seemingly intent on possessing all five of them simultaneously. The vaporous filaments weaved a tantalizing dance of madness before their faces, inching closer.

"Hold your breaths!" Corwyn cried.

Just then, a familiar scrabbling of talons on rock sounded

behind the curtain of fog. "Corwyn?" came Smoke's voice. "Ooph! Ugh! Curse those miserable goblins for making these shafts so small! Corwyn, where are you? Are you all right?"

The demon hesitated, its attention on the veil advancing toward it from the entrance to the mines. Abruptly Smoke's head pierced the fog, straining on his sinuous neck. "Uhhh, that stuff's horrible!" He blinked watering eyes, then recognized Corwyn. "Ah, there you are. You've outdone yourself with your vile alchemical creations this time, Corwyn. What's taking so long?"

Then he saw the demon.

With a bellow of alarm, Smoke struggled to reach his friends, his talons gouging deep grooves in the rock. But the dragon was firmly wedged in the narrowing mineshaft. The demon, seeing Smoke's helplessness, returned its attention to the humans. Its tendrils resumed their dance.

"No, damn you!" Smoke cried. He fought against the walls, his claws making a hideous racket. His vestigial wings beat against the stone. The sheer membranes of his wings tore and the shaft shook with his effort. Rock and sand cascaded from the ceiling. But Smoke could gain no further ground. The humans huddled against the walls of the shaft as the demon toyed with them.

Sebastian felt the now-familiar violation of his soul and knew the demon was peering deep within him. Behind him, he heard Gwen gasp, "Mama?" Then suddenly Sebastian was a child sobbing in the corridors of his boyhood home, waiting for the awesome presence that hunted him. But this time, when that presence rounded the corner in pursuit of its shadow, its features were clear.

It was his father.

"Must you always disappoint me?" the towering vision bellowed. "Everything you do, everything you are causes me shame. You must be punished."

His father's hand, which had pointed accusingly while the image spoke, reached to grab Sebastian. Sebastian sobbed and scrabbled aside, remembering how often as a child he had felt reduced to worthlessness by his father.

Then the intensity of this particular occasion came rushing back to him, the specifics overwhelming his unwillingness to remember. He had been six years old. Three older peasant boys from the village had jumped and beaten him. His father was so ashamed of him that instead of punishing the offenders, he had dragged Sebastian before them and whipped him for having allowed himself to be dishonored.

Anger at this humiliation, so long repressed, gave Sebastian the strength to do what fear alone had not. He stood and faced his father. "I was just a boy," he croaked, advancing on the image. "I loved you. I worshiped you. All I wanted was for you to love me, too. How could you treat me that way?"

Confusion registered on his father's face, and the figure gave way hesitantly to Sebastian.

"You're dead!" Sebastian shrieked, his arms flailing now as he attacked the image. "Go back to your grave where you belong. You can't hurt me anymore. I won't let you!"

Suddenly, he stopped. Another voice joined the cacophony in his mind, and though the words it repeated were Corwyn's, Sebastian recognized the voice as his own. *Look beyond the obvious*, it said. A half smile lifted the corner of Sebastian's lip. "You're not my father," he said disdainfully. Then, with sudden insight about the voice that had lived for so long inside him, he added, "And neither am I."

It was the first time he had ever made such a statement without self-reproach. Not that it changed anything; he would still be possessed by this outer demon. Yet he stood straighter, wavering slightly on exhausted legs.

"You might possess my body," he told the monstrous wraith, "but you'll never subdue my soul. I've stood up to a demon stronger than you."

The wraith scowled, no longer wearing the visage of his father. Its tendrils extended toward its victims.

"Mama," Gwen cried again. "Oh, Mama, no!"

With a frustrated roar, Smoke hurled himself a half foot closer, peeling iridescent scales from his hide. Then he collapsed on the floor. His breath squeezed out in a single burst, igniting with rage and anguish. A wall of fire shot out, singeing the humans and making them shut their eyes. A terrible burning smell filled the shaft, momentarily overwhelming all other odors.

When the flame subsided, Sebastian opened his eyes, curious to know why the demon hadn't struck. But there was no demon to be seen. The burning smell hung wetly on the air. Further up the shaft, Smoke covered his head with his foreclaws, and moaned. Between Smoke and the huddled humans, reeking blobs steamed and quivered on the floor.

Those blobs, Sebastian realized with a start, were all that

remained of the demon. "Smoke, you did it!" he cried.

"I'm sorry," the dragon wailed. "I didn't mean to flame you."

"You didn't flame us. You destroyed the demon!"

"Huh?" Smoke opened reluctant eyes and peered about near-sightedly. "I did?"

"You saved our lives," Sebastian said, hugging and pounding on the dragon.

Smoke studied the sizzling blobs and his eyes watered again, but this time it was not from the smell alone. "Did I really? Then does this mean I'm . . . I'm . . . a hero?"

"Yes, Smoke," Gwen said, and she kissed his scaly snout. "No minstrel ever sang an act as bold as yours!"

Their congratulations were cut short by Corwyn, who pointed out that the two walls of fog were still advancing toward them. The veil from above was already moving along Smoke's long neck, obliterating his body wedged in the tunnel behind.

Ignoring Oliver's silent but emphatic protests, Corwyn used the broom to sweep the demonic blobs into a pile by the vault doors. Then, as Sebastian and Gwen opened the doors a crack, he thrust the mass inside. "Wouldn't want that one coalescing again outside the vault," he said, setting Oliver back upright. Oliver hurried off in a huff, his dignity shattered, while the humans resealed the doors.

While they were busy with this, Smoke struggled backwards out of the mines. Finally his head disappeared behind the descending curtain of fumes as the dragon pulled free. The humans could hear his choking retreat up the shaft.

After the dragon was gone, Sebastian pointed at the inky veil, still swirling from the eddies created by Smoke's passage. "How do we get past that, master?" he asked.

"It's all right. It isn't very thick." Then Corwyn added to himself, "I hope."

They let Oliver lead since he was unaffected by the mist. Oliver cheered at this prospect. The five humans spread out behind him in a chain, holding hands. Once inside the thick fog, they were thoroughly disoriented. The mist burned their eyes, and tears flowed down every cheek. Without Oliver they would have lost their direction and blundered about. But the broom soon had them through, and they stumbled out of the mines into the clear, warm light of day.

A little way away, Smoke beamed at his unaccustomed status as a hero. "And that demon wasn't even a living thing," he told

Sebastian as the humans emerged from the mines. "I didn't have to break my oath in order to save you."

Sebastian dropped to the ground, still sick from his earlier experience in the tunnel but elated over his own private act of heroism. Corwyn and Gwen sat beside him as Oliver ran off to play. Up the slope, Kwagg and Meier prepared their mule train for a hasty departure, anxious to put as much distance between themselves and the alchemist as possible.

Corwyn cleared his throat. "Something strange went on back there," he said quietly to Sebastian. "For a moment, that demon lost its grip on us. I looked up, and you were standing in front of it, saying something. What happened?"

"I was exorcizing a different demon," Sebastian said. "A personal one of my own."

Corwyn nodded. "I thought so." His gaze became distant, wistful. "Well done, bo—" He caught himself. "Well done, Sebastian. I wish I had done as well with mine."

Sebastian shifted self-consciously, pleased and surprised by Corwyn's praise. It felt good to have earned not only Corwyn's respect, but his own as well. He smiled to himself and sucked in a deep breath of clean mountain air. "So it's really over at last?"

"*Oui,* it's finally over," Corwyn agreed.

"But what about the vault? How will it keep the demons trapped?"

"It's simple," Corwyn said. "Once we closed the doors and sealed them, there's no way out. That vault is a dead-end tunnel."

"But what were the loads Kwagg and Meier brought here for you?" Sebastian asked.

"Oh, those." Corwyn looked sheepish. "I was concerned that over the years, water seepage in the mines might eventually reach the vault. If that happened, the demons would leach out of the vault into the groundwater, and from there they would again flow into the River Ale. To prevent that, I lined the vault to keep it completely dry."

Sebastian waited, but Corwyn didn't volunteer anything more. "How?" he asked at last.

"Eh, what? Oh, how'd I do it? I merely found a way to prevent moisture from accumulating inside the vault. The answer came from the alchemical text that led us to the monastery of St. Mathurin. I sent a message to François telling him I'd found a place to keep their records where the dryness would cause no ill effects on the surrounding countryside, and had Kwagg and Meier haul them back here. That solved the monastery's problem of insufficient space for the archives and, since no one ever reads the documents anyway, serves our need for creating an absolutely dry, impermeable environment. As a result, the demons cannot escape."

"That's ingenious," Sebastian said with awe. "They'll be safely trapped in there forever."

"Well, not quite forever," Corwyn corrected. "But the next best thing to it." He pulled a small abacus from inside his robes and made some hasty calculations. "Actually, I estimate that the containment system will break down sometime in the late twentieth century."

"You mean the demons will then be released into the world again?"

"*Oui,* theoretically. But by that time, I'm sure alchemical technology will have progressed sufficiently to have developed far more efficient means of dealing with such hazardous by-products of society as these demons. Anyway, that's far into the future. Nothing for us to worry about at all."

Gwen lifted her head. "Well, Corwyn, what now?"

Corwyn smiled. "Now, *ma chère,* we return to Pomme de Terre to tend to your injury. And with what you've told me about Hydro Phobius's interventions in the duchy, I think the time has come at last for us to realize Thaddeus's dream by bringing the Renaissance to Gardenia."

Gwen looked at Corwyn blankly.

"Don't ask," Sebastian whispered. "Once he gets started on this Renaissance thing of his, he can talk all day."

Corwyn's eyebrows shot up. "You mean I haven't explained to you about what lies in store? *Alors!* In the first place, *ma chère,* these new ideas from Italy everyone's been talking about are only the beginning. Why, in years ahead, all manner of new thoughts will arise. . . ."

Sebastian groaned softly as his master warmed to the subject. He settled back on the ground, preparing for a lengthy wait.

CHAPTER 19

The Renaissance at Last

THE MARKETPLACE OF POMME DE TERRE WAS PACKED WITH FES-
tive crowds, and still people streamed in from the streets and
alleys opening onto the square. Jugglers, mimes, merchants, mu-
sicians, craftsmen, prostitutes, and pickpockets from all over
Gardenia and beyond had come to Pomme de Terre to ply their
trades today. The market was a riot of delights as brocades from
Cathay, laces from Flanders, Greek olives, and Persian spices
vied with local meat pies and fruit tarts for sensory dominance.
Amid the swirl of smells and colors sounded a multitude of
voices—talking, singing, laughing, brawling, and shouting in
their efforts to be heard.

Corwyn and Sebastian pushed through the throng to the market stall where they'd agreed the night before to meet Gwen.
She was buying a Spanish fig from a merchant when they reached
her. She held it out to each of them in turn, sharing her prize
with her friends and dabbing at their chins with her sleeve as
juice ran from the fruit when they bit into it.

"I was afraid I'd be late and keep you waiting," Gwen said,
leaning close to Sebastian and Corwyn to be heard. "As I left
the tavern, Mama asked me to pick up *un chou* on the way."

Sebastian bristled and chewed more slowly, staring at her.

"What's wrong?" she asked.

"That word," he said. "It never means what I think it does, and everytime I think I've got it figured out, somebody comes up with a new use for it that makes me look like a fool. Well, what does it mean this time?"

Gwen studied him quizzically, then moved aside the cloth covering the basket she carried to expose a green, leafy vegetable.

"Just a cabbage?" Sebastian asked in disbelief. "That's all it meant this time? *Un . . . un chou?*"

"*Gesundheit!*" Corwyn said with a snicker. "Bless you."

Sebastian scowled.

"You know," Corwyn went on, trying not to laugh, "if you'd *chou* your words when you bite them off, it might not choke you so much to swallow them."

Sebastian continued to glower at the old alchemist, who chortled happily to himself. Gwen looked from one to the other as if they both were mad. She turned back to Sebastian. "Why do you make French so difficult?"

"I was raised that way, I guess," he growled. "It's a knack we English have."

"That's true," Corwyn said, wiping his eyes with his sleeve. "The English are eager to adopt French language and ways. But at the same time, any Englishmen worthy of the name would walk a mile in the rain for a chance to misuse or mispronounce a simple French phrase."

Sebastian bit his lip and said nothing.

"This is quite a celebration," Corwyn said, indicating the crowd around them. "Who'd have thought Pomme de Terre would ever hold such a fair?"

"They all seem to be enjoying themselves," Sebastian said, glad the subject had been changed. He took advantage of the crowded conditions to take Gwen's hand. Her touch was warm and firm, and he thrilled at it.

Gwen squeezed his hand and smiled, then jerked her head to indicate a group of peasants behind her. "Not everyone's pleased with the changes. Official announcement of the duchess's consent hasn't come yet, and already I've overheard complaints from the crowd."

Sebastian shifted nearer the group to listen. "Whose idea is this nonsense, anyway?" one peasant grumbled. "Things as they were have always been good enough for me." He stuck out a blocky, pox-scarred chin, challenging anyone to dispute him.

"*Oui,* you're right, Squat," commented one of the peasant's companions. "All these fancy new clothes and strange ideas— it's heresy, that's what I call it. Nothing but simple heresy that wouldn't have been allowed under the duke, God have mercy on his soul if he's still got a soul left to bless. How can an honest serf like me get on with his work when they up and change the rules every few hundred years or so? *Tiens!* A man just doesn't know what to expect these days, I tell you."

"I overheard that alchemist tell how they're going to pass an edict or such that the sun can't go around the earth anymore, that it's got to be the other way," grumbled a third man. He nodded to emphasize his words, a morose expression on his rugged face.

"No!" said the one called Squat. He spat in disgust. "Well, if that don't beat all. Bad enough they go changing things here on earth, but when they start messing with the working of the spheres, I say they've gone too far!"

"That's not all," added the third in a conspiratorial whisper. "The earth's going to be round like a peach or an egg from now on. It can't be flat anymore. And then where's an honest man to stand, I ask you? We'll all be sliding off into hell, damned and saved alike. I tell you, this foolishness is just getting started and already it's way out of hand."

Sebastian turned back to Gwen and Corwyn, leaving the peasants shaking their heads. "Master, we only gave the people what they wanted and this is the thanks we get? They seem to have forgotten the plague completely. And now that they'll be getting the change they wanted—now that our news about Hydro Phobius has helped the council of guilds bring pressure on the duchess to accept their demands—the peasants don't even care. They want to go back to the old ways before the new have even started! It makes me wonder why we bothered."

"Let it be a lesson to you, Sebastian," Corwyn said. "Always beware of giving a person what he says he wants. He may hold you responsible for the consequences. Besides, we didn't set out to bring the Renaissance to Gardenia; that's happening as a result of what we discovered in learning to stop the plague. It would have come to Gardenia eventually, whether the duke and duchess wanted to allow it or not. Even Hydro Phobius couldn't have put off the merchants in Gardenia for long. The impetus for changing outmoded social and political structures is too strong."

Sebastian smiled. "The need for change is something I've experienced from both sides now. The arguments definitely favor the side of the merchant class."

He paused for a moment, still surprised by the absence of the critical voice he had for so long identified as his father's. Not that it was completely gone, of course, but it was fainter and less strident than before, and Sebastian recognized it now as his own.

The three of them walked slowly through the crowd, allowing Gwen to set the pace. Her ankle had almost healed, but the slight limp in her step served as a reminder of what she'd endured.

"Then you no longer grieve over your family's fall from grace?" Corwyn asked with a sparkle in his eye.

Sebastian shook his head. "The title no longer means much to me. There's too much excitement over what lies ahead to mourn for lost nobility. I'm content with my apprenticeship, master, and with learning to be a good alchemist." He frowned slightly. "I just wish my mother could understand what I've learned. But unfortunately, she's locked into a way of life that was dying even before my father's day."

"Have you told her about being apprenticed?" Gwen asked, then added shyly, "and about us?"

"Us?" Corwyn interrupted. "What does that mean?"

Gwen looked at Sebastian, who blushed and stammered, "I haven't told him yet."

"Told me what?"

"Sebastian asked me to marry him," Gwen said, giving Sebastian an impish grin. "That is, he asked if I was willing to be known from now on as *Madame Cafard*."

"*Tiens!*" Corwyn said. "Not that I hadn't expected it, of course. Well, what did you tell him? You accepted, I hope. Otherwise, I'll never get a decent day's work out of him again."

Gwen nodded, blushing now as well. "*Oui*, I accepted."

Corwyn beamed and rubbed his hands, looking from one to the other as if he were personally responsible for their announcement.

"As for my mother," Sebastian said, "I sent word to her convent. I left it to the discretion of her abbess to decide how much she might understand and accept. But I don't expect to ever receive her approval." He paused, then brightened. "I also sent a letter to my brother by way of a merchant caravan headed east. I told him about us and asked about his wife. I'd like to see them someday. My brother and I have much to talk about."

A number of people from Pomme de Terre smiled as the three passed through the crowd, and some shouted greetings to the old alchemist and his companions. Sebastian listened as one man, a tanner whose shop was located near Corwyn's, thanked the alchemist for saving Pomme de Terre.

"Your neighbors seem to accept you now," Sebastian said as they strolled through the market. "How different from the way they reacted to you during the plague."

Corwyn nodded. "It's been an unexpected benefit from stopping the plague. But I don't understand how everyone knows so much about what we did."

"Ask Sebastian," Gwen said, squeezing his hand. "Perhaps he knows."

Sebastian felt his skin flush again as his master turned to him with a questioning gaze. "It's nothing. I wrote a ballad about what happened, that's all. I've sung it a time or two at the Reluctant Virgin."

"Huh," Gwen snorted. "He gets asked to sing it almost every night. And it doesn't take much asking to get him to sing."

"What sort of ballad?" Corwyn asked.

Sebastian flushed brighter. "It was for Smoke, originally. He always wanted to be immortalized in song. And after all, he did save our lives. But I soon realized any account of what happened in the Goblin Mines had to include what went on before. That brought in the brothers of St. Mathurin. And you and Gwen and Oliver had to be included, of course. And myself. Even Kwagg and Meier and Petronius." He shrugged self-consciously. "Each of us played a role in stopping the plague and overthrowing Hydro Phobius. And we all performed most nobly. Besides, the tale should be remembered lest what Hydro Phobius did ever be repeated."

"No need to get defensive," Corwyn said. "I'd like to hear this song of yours sometime. It must be very popular at the Reluctant Virgin."

"Oh, you know how the crowd at the Reluctant Virgin is," Sebastian said, obviously pleased. "They're all drunk when they ask me to sing."

"No doubt," Corwyn said. "They probably enjoy it for your unique use of French as much as for anything else. Still, I'd like to hear this ballad for myself. Just to make sure you've told the story right, of course."

They approached a green and yellow silk pavilion at the end

of the marketplace and stood where they could see the temporary wooden stage which the pavilion sheltered. The sounds of the crowd became more muted as everyone waited in anticipation for what was to follow.

"So we really can begin anew?" Gwen asked Corwyn. "Without any fear of unfinished endeavors returning to plague us?"

Corwyn winced. "Poor choice of words, *ma chère*. But essentially you're right. The council of guilds has requested that I monitor the waters below the Goblin Mines for any evidence of demons leaking from the containment vault. The commission from that work alone has allowed me to restore my shop and will keep Sebastian busy for years to come while I pursue new avenues of research."

Sebastian groaned. "You've already had me running so many breath of demons tests I can hardly keep up with the work." He held out his hands. "I'm elbow deep in water so much of the time, it's a wonder my skin hasn't shriveled up."

"None of your complaining, now," Corwyn said. "After all, the breath of demons test showed us what was happening to the duchy's water supply and helped us find the source of the demons. And now it'll help keep the duchy safe in case the containment vault ever leaks." He shuddered. "Which it had better never do."

"I know, I know," Sebastian grumbled. "We probably owe our lives to your test. But what about the Inquisition's demons? What will become of them now that we've stopped Hydro Phobius?"

"The Inquisition in Spain denies any wrongdoing, of course. They maintain those weren't even their demons to begin with. But the Inquisition continues to grow and become increasingly secular in Spain. They shall have to find other ways to dispose of their wastes, perhaps by dumping them far out at sea. There have been rumors the Spanish monarchy is preparing to send ships on voyages west across the great ocean to find a suitable disposal site. But whatever they do, they dare not trouble us with their demons again."

"But what about Hydro Phobius?" Sebastian persisted. "We never found him after his escape. Do you think we'll ever encounter him again?" He clenched his fists unconsciously.

"Undoubtedly," Corwyn said. "We didn't catch him this time, but we'll almost certainly have a chance to try again."

"Oh, no," Gwen moaned. "Corwyn, we barely survived one

encounter with that dreadful man. You don't seriously think we might have to face him again, do you?"

Corwyn sighed. "I'm afraid so, *ma chère*. The man is a confirmed profiteer, a parasite who benefits from the natural sloth and indifference of others. My guess is that he's out there somewhere even now, devising new schemes which will someday draw us inevitably into his web."

Gwen chewed her lip as she considered this. Sebastian slipped an arm around her waist and hugged her. "Don't worry," he whispered. "At least next time, we'll have each other. Together, we'll destroy him." He grinned. "After all, what can a man like Hydro Phobius do when confronted with two poor but loving common folk like us?"

She smiled and snuggled against his side.

A stir passed through the crowd as members of the council of guilds filed onto the stage under the pavilion. Soon a heavyset merchant dressed in expensive leather and silk attire newly imported from Italy strode onto the stage waving a sheaf of parchment. Cheers arose from the crowd at the sight of the man and everything his parchment sheets signified.

"The duchess has conceded to our demands," he shouted above the roar of the crowd. He unrolled the sheets and displayed them, pointing to a signature at the document's end. "Here is her seal upon a covenant allowing the council of guilds a greater voice in the affairs of Gardenia. No longer shall we be bound by the whims of the nobility. The new order shall belong to all."

The yelling and whistling increased as the crowd went wild. The merchant motioned for silence, and when the crowd quieted sufficiently, he gave the pronouncement they had come to hear.

"And now," he bellowed, his voice echoing from the buildings around the market as if rebounding from the mountains themselves, "from this day forward, in Pomme de Terre and throughout Gardenia—

"Let an era of change begin!"

Afterword:
The Breath of Demons Test

(A Modern Arcane Technology)

THE BREATH OF DEMONS TEST WHICH APPEARS THROUGHOUT THIS book is more than a fictitious alchemical procedure, for it's modeled after a fundamental test in water pollution control. In its unaltered form, the real test (called biochemical oxygen demand, or BOD), bears an astonishing resemblance to alchemy.

As with alchemy, the BOD represents an arcane rite performed and interpreted by adepts who preserve its secrets through the use of strange jargon, obscure symbols and mysterious apparatus. It has a history of acceptance amounting to blind faith among its adherents, while its detractors oppose it vehemently. It demands tedious effort and exacting skill in an attempt to duplicate the required technique, with little chance of doing so correctly. Its political importance (based primarily on misconceptions) far outweighs its technical significance. And finally, it offers an approach to knowledge which, although deficient from a practical standpoint, is nevertheless rich philosophically.

The BOD may be an analyst's nightmare, but it's a poet's delight. Within each bottle there exists an entire ecosystem, a world constantly evolving as it struggles between the forces of life and death during the five days of the test. The BOD is thus a microcosm of the larger world we inhabit, and if we understand or measure that microcosm with only limited success, perhaps that's just a further reflection of our incomplete understanding of the world outside. In the face of this, is it really so important that the test isn't scientifically defensible?

Although several aspects of this novel are drawn from real technology, it's the breath of demons test, the alchemical analog to the BOD, which runs as a theme throughout the novel. It seemed fitting that this test should form the basis of medieval and Renaissance pollution control, much the way its real counterpart remains the bulwark of water pollution technology in our own world today. After all, they have so much in common.

DOUGLAS W. CLARK spent much of his childhood playing at and around the small sewage treatment plant in southern New Mexico where his father worked as a civil engineer—an experience that was to influence him for the rest of his life. He writes, "Water takes on a mystic quality in any desert culture, and so it did for me. Yet in the world I was introduced to at the treatment plant, water was also irrevocably associated with mechanical systems and analytical thinking, with logic and reason and conscious application of the human mind. So it has come to symbolize both aspects for me, maintaining them in an uneasy state of dynamic tension, a constant struggle that somehow straddles the unbridgeable gulf between logic and illogic, between reason and intuition, science and art." Later he traveled to Europe with his parents, visiting the usual tourist attractions—and exploring the history of Western civilization as revealed by its legacy of water and sewage works, from ancient Roman aqueducts to modern treatment plants.

Mr. Clark earned his B.S. in biology at the University of New Mexico, but after a brief foray into graduate school, found himself back in the "family business" as a laboratory technician at the local sewage treatment plant. Eventually he began publishing technical articles on the subject and founded a newsletter, *The Bench Sheet*, for laboratory analysts involved with water and sewage. It was on the pages of that newsletter that Corwyn, the world's only aquatic alchemist, was born. Though he has since sold the newsletter, Mr. Clark has continued to write about Corwyn's adventures, in short stories and his first published novel, *Alchemy Unlimited*, which you are holding.

In a time of medieval magicks and slovenly personal habits,
bumbling young Sebastian yearns to regain his rightful place among the nobility
and win the hand of a gorgeous maiden. Instead, he'll have to
settle for being apprenticed to Corwyn, the world's only aquatic alchemist.

Expert in the ways of water and its enemies, ancient Corwyn faces
his second biggest challenge (his first being how to control his impossibly
inept new assistant). Now he must embark on a perilous adventure
through the Valley of Despair to the gates of the Black Knight himself — to
free his beleaguered town of Pomme de Terre from a terrifying
epidemic of demonic possession.

ISBN 0-380-75726-5